Dragonrook

~

The Treasure of Askelon

Daren Hatfield

Praise for
The Treasure of Askelon

"The plot delivers a rollicking adventure...The Treasure of Askelon: Dragonrook, Book 1 was a great read, and I enjoyed the stellar storytelling, the characters, and the suspense built around the artifact. This narrative features superb storytelling, captivating settings, and a conflict that drives the plot."
- Ruffina Oserio for Readers' Favorite

"A Swashbuckling Triumph!"
- 5-Star Amazon Review

Praise for Daren Hatfield's
Nothing Ever Happens on Main Street

"Hatfield's compact but well-developed historical fantasy tale seems perfectly calibrated for a YA readership...A fun time-travel caper that has more of the quaint ambiance of a cozy mystery than an epic SF adventure. Our Verdict: Get it!"
- Kirkus Reviews

"...this story made me feel like a kid again, where every new discovery could open a door to a grand adventure...it's constantly displaying the inherent positive nature of the human spirit. It's a very hopeful tale with messages that are meant to build up, not tear down. It felt good every time I sat down for another chapter."
- The Tome Tavern

"Hatfield's prose is both accessible and profound, capturing the essence of life's subtleties with disarming simplicity...Its ability to transport readers, evoke emotion, and spark introspection is a testament to Hatfield's storytelling prowess...For anyone seeking a tale that weaves magic into the mundane and celebrates the quiet heroism of the every day, this novel is an absolute must-read."
- Literary Titan

Books by Daren Hatfield

The Treasure of Askelon

Nothing Ever Happens on Main Street

DRAGONROOK

The
TREASURE
of
ASKELON

DAREN HATFIELD

This is a work of fiction. Characters, places, and events portrayed in this work are the products of the author's imagination. Any resemblance to actual events, locales, organizations, or persons, living or dead, is entirely coincidental.

Author website: www.darenhatfield.com

Dedicated to
my incredible daughter,
Sierra

who thinks dragons are pretty neat.
Pirates, not so much.
(but I added them, anyway.)

contents

Appointment at Fangshard

Captain Riga stood tall in the stern of the small row-boat, one foot upon the curious locked chest nestled within the floor of the craft. His first mate, Arbo, a pudgy yet competent hand, labored as he forced the boat through the choppy waters toward the island. Arbo's lungs were working as hard as his arms. He was, after all, a bit past his prime...nature's cruel reward for surviving. Despite the bobbing and jerking of the craft, Riga seemed unfazed and was smiling—to Arbo's mind—like the proverbial cat that swallowed the canary. I hope he chokes on it, thought Arbo, as he pulled the oars through the obstinate tide.

After several strenuous minutes, the boat finally scraped upon the sandy shore of Fangshard. Arbo dreaded this place, and even though he had left it safely on previous occasions, the fear that his next visit would be his last never left him.

Riga, on the other hand, hopped from the rowboat with glee. "Bring the chest, Arbo!" he ordered. "We have an appointment with avarice!"

"Aye, Cap'n," Arbo grunted, more in exasperation than exhaustion as he hauled the craft onto the beach. Riga was unquestionably a handsome man, but there was a slimy smugness about him, particularly when he barked commands so jovially, that really nettled Arbo. But orders were orders, so Arbo clumsily worked the small chest from the boat and lugged it after the captain who was already proceeding into the tropical foliage, looking for all the world like a man on a midday stroll.

Captain Riga knew the trail well—the two had taken it several times to the base of the mountain cliff—but this time his pace was a bit quicker, fueled by anticipation. Arbo huffed to keep up under the surprising weight of the small, locked box.

"You can almost taste the riches, can't you, Arbo?" Riga encouraged as he marched through the tall grass.

"Aye, Cap'n," muttered Arbo.

"You do realize, don't you, that this shall be our final visit to this wretched place, with its nasty bogs and slime pits and relentless insects, to say nothing of its vile inhabitants?" Riga had an odd way of keeping that smug grin on his face even when talking about unpleasant subjects. It was as if they were someone else's problems.

"Aye, Cap'n." Arbo was surprised that this news didn't bring him more cheer. Perhaps it was because it didn't quite ring true. If everything went according to plan, then this would indeed be the last time they set foot on Fangshard Island. But, Arbo mused, how often do things go according to plan?

Soon, they reached the treacherous footbridge that spanned a ravine to the cliff. Built of decaying wood and desiccated rope by someone with questionable skill, it was a miracle that it was still standing. The rickety construct would have been classified as Arbo's least favorite part of the journey...if he didn't know who was waiting for them on the other side.

Riga marched across the bridge without pause, its boards resounding with hollow thumps under his boots. As always, Arbo waited for Captain Riga to make it completely across before he ventured his first step onto the wobbling bridge. Arbo was not a light man by any stretch of the imagination. The extra burden of the locked chest didn't help. He fully expected to drop through the wooden scraps like an anchor into the sea. To his relief, the boards held.

"Don't dawdle, Arbo!" the captain shouted from the other side.

"Aye, Cap'n," Arbo mumbled as he shuffled across the uneven planks. "Aye." Despite Riga's command, Arbo still paused to peer over the edge. He immediately clenched his eyes shut at the sight of the precipitous drop below. "Oh, mercy! Why do I always look down?"

"Buck up, Arbo! We've crossed this bridge a hundred times. It's completely safe!"

As if in spite, the plank beneath Arbo's foot splintered with a shocking crack. He felt the sickening drop as his leg plunged through the bridge. Falling sideways, Arbo's belly smacked against the edge of the footbridge. The locked chest, still clutched tight in his hands, dangled over the ravine.

Riga's eyes bulged. "Don't drop it!" He dashed to the fallen seaman. "Don't drop it! I've got it!"

Laying alongside Arbo, who was now frozen in fright, Riga carefully pried the chest from the floundering crewman's hands and lifted it to safety. With a sigh of relief, he clutched the small lockbox in his arms. "I've got it!"

"What about me, sir?" whimpered Arbo.

"You're fine! Just pull yourself out of that hole."

"Aye, Cap'n."

Riga coddled the box like a precious child as he crossed the remainder of the bridge. Arbo, meanwhile, nervously extracted himself from the clutches of the splintered planks.

Safely on the other end, Riga called back. "Onward!"

It was a needless order since Arbo clearly had no intention of staying on the bridge. He hastened across, brushing the splinters from his trousers. Riga planted the chest at his feet. "Very good. Shall we continue?"

Arbo sighed. Hefting the box from the dirt, he trudged after the departing captain.

The massive stone doors built into the mountainside were only a few yards further down the path. Easily standing over twelve feet high, the doors were engraved with strange and intricate carvings. At first glance, the markings would have been mistaken for random scratches and cuts that crisscrossed in a jumble of patterns. At closer inspection, however, the intersecting patterns were clearly purposeful and deliberate. Arbo didn't know what they meant, but it wasn't difficult for him to imagine that they were intended to be a warning. He had yet to determine, though, if they were a warning to keep people out...or a warning to keep the inhabitants in.

Riga straightened his coat and brushed any evidence of jungle from his sleeves. A hint of nervousness showed through his usual smug countenance. He motioned to the door.

"What, sir?" Arbo asked.

Riga motioned again. "Go ahead, man. Knock."

"Why me, sir?"

"Because you always knock. It's tradition."

4

Arbo was unconvinced of the captain's reasoning but obediently stepped toward the stone portal. It had already been established that a rap on the door with bare knuckles was both unproductive and painful, so Arbo hefted a nearby rock and pounded it against the monolithic entrance.

Almost immediately, a melon-sized hole appeared near the top of the door with the raspy grumble of stone on stone. Arbo stepped back to see the customary giant red eye peering at them from behind. The diamond-shaped iris flicked back and forth between Riga and Arbo. That monstrous eye was all they had ever seen of the mysterious gatekeeper, and Arbo was perfectly content to never see more.

Captain Riga discreetly stifled a gulp and attempted to project an air of command. "We've come to see Arcrellis!"

The big red eye flicked back and forth again before responding. "Why?" The voice was guttural and harsh, like iron on granite.

Riga lifted his head proudly. "We've brought him what he seeks. We've brought him the treasure of St. George!"

Silently, the eye continued to dart back and forth between Riga and Arbo. Then it noticed the chest resting at their feet. For a moment, the eye simply stared silently at the box. With a thud, the hole sealed itself, and the massive door rumbled open.

No sign was visible of the doorkeeper and his big red eye. Only darkness greeted them beyond the entrance. Uncertain what to do, Riga motioned to Arbo to bring the box. The first mate lifted the chest and the two hesitantly proceeded into the blackness. They had only taken a few steps before the grinding voice of the gatekeeper spoke. "No further! Put the chest down."

The men obeyed immediately. Neither dared to risk the wrath of their unseen host.

"Wait. And do not move," the voice growled.

An uncomfortable and seemingly interminable amount of time passed, in which Arbo chose to imagine himself being in more enjoyable places. Maybe a dungeon or a rat-infested coffin. Yes, those would be nice, he thought.

And then the wait ended. Although they could not see into the shrouded passage, the two men felt the floor tremble under the footfalls of a new arrival.

Arcrellis.

The mysterious host stopped short of the weak light that fell through the open portal. "Captain Riga." His growling voice rolled from depths of the cavern like an unwelcome fog. "You have returned."

"Y-yes," Riga stammered. "And I have brought what you asked."

"Let me see."

Hastily, Riga produced a key from his topcoat and knelt to unlatch the waiting chest. With a flourish, he swung the lid open to reveal a stunning cornucopia of treasure... rubies, sapphires, emeralds, and gold coins flashed brilliantly despite the darkness. Riga gestured proudly. "The lost treasure of St. George! Magnificent, is it not?"

Unexpectedly, a large, clawed hand reached from the shadows. It had the likeness of a bird of prey's talons, except for the black, leathery skin that stretched around its bones. Riga and Arbo stepped back in trepidation and watched the gruesome claw grasp the open trove of jewels and drag it into the darkness.

The tinkling sound of coins and jewels chimed from the blackness. The two men could sense the clawed talon

sifting through the chest of treasure. A loud snort erupted into the air, breathy and sonorous like the sound of a
blacksmith's bellows.

"Where did you find this?" Arcrellis asked.

Riga smiled. "Just where the map said. It led us straight
to it. The chest was buried beneath the ruins of an old
cathedral, long forgotten in the countryside."

Arcrellis did not respond. The only sound was the soft
tinkling of claws through jewels.

"It was very deep. It took us days to dig it up," Riga added.

Still, Arcrellis said nothing.

Riga's confidence began to crumble. In different
circumstances, Arbo would have enjoyed seeing the beads
of sweat on the man's lip. However, since Arbo happened
to be standing right next to him, he felt it wasn't a good
time to jeer.

The silence persisted. Riga was growing increasingly
pale. "So," Riga continued with a quivering voice, "I have
kept my end of the arrangement. I have brought you the
treasure. Now I believe you owe me something. Tell me
the location of Dragonrook."

The sound of sifting jewels stopped. Riga and Arbo waited for a response.

And then it came.

The chest of jewels shot out of the darkness like a
cannonball, spewing a trail of gems and coins in its wake.
The box with its glistening contents exploded against the
cavern wall as the two men ducked in surprise.

The rumbling voice of Arcrellis simmered with anger. "I
am not amused by your lies!"

Riga's eyes widened with fear. Before he could utter a
defense, the vicious talon stretched from the cave and

yanked the powerless captain into the shadows. Riga didn't even have the chance to let out a panicked scream.

Arbo fell backwards in shock and horror. The earth beneath him rumbled at the creature's approach. Trembling, the first mate raised his hands in pointless defense.

"Your captain has failed me!" Arcrellis hissed.

"Please! Please!" begged Arbo. "I didn't know. He claimed he had the map! I knew nothing!"

"Do you still have the coin?"

"Yes! Yes, I have it!" cried Arbo.

"Then find another to bring me the treasure!" Arcrellis ordered. "Or else your bones will lie with Riga's."

Arbo didn't waste a single second. He sprinted from the cavern while discarded rubies and diamonds scattered beneath his scurrying feet. As he dashed back to the beach in terror, he realized the captain had been correct...this was indeed the last time Riga would ever visit Fangshard.

The Unusual Widow of Shorty Buckets

A few months had passed since the disappearance of the nefarious pirate Esteban Riga. As a general rule, pirates are typically not missed in their absence. And since the King's Navy could not openly take credit for any lack of Riga upon the high seas, very little attention was given to this matter.

On the other hand, the Admiralty was very pleased at the recent capture of the mostly-unremarkable pirate Shorty Buckets. Buckets, however, was not captured during the conflagration and bombast of broadsides and cannon fire that accompanies a mighty sea battle. Instead, the pirate Shorty Buckets was captured while upon land—in the small sea village of Peahaven, to be precise—where the short, bald brigand unwittingly walked into the local constabulary office looking for directions. This alone would not have been a dead giveaway were it not for the fact that Shorty Buckets also carelessly mentioned his name. After making several braggadocious claims that he had just returned to shore after months of robbing on the open seas, the sleepy constables of Peahaven began to suspect that this was indeed the pirate Shorty Buckets.

As mentioned, Shorty Buckets was not an impressive pirate. His shortness in physical stature, which did not make him a very imposing marauder, was equally matched with a lack of zeal and cunning. Shorty Buckets had cobbled together a modest living as a brigand raiding small fishing villages throughout the Caribbean. The upshot of his strategy was that his tiny vessel never received a single blow to its hull from these undefended targets. The disadvantage was that his prizes consisted mainly of freshly-caught fish...except on the occasional poorly-timed raids when the fishermen had not yet returned from their nets, leaving Buckets and his crew to suffice themselves with meager bounties of day-old fish.

Due to the unremarkable career of Shorty Buckets, or perhaps due to his unexpected and underwhelming capture, only three citizens were present for the public execution of the pirate. The Admiralty, eager to conduct a hanging in the interest of morale and public image, had hurriedly dispatched two representatives to conduct the ceremony.

Behind the local jail of Peahaven stood a dilapidated gallows that had long been without purpose in the quiet village. No one really remembered for whom it was originally built, but it remained because parents felt it served as a good warning to errant children known for pulling hair and being mean to wandering puppies. For this day's sudden ceremonies, though, it was discovered that the decaying rope was no longer serviceable, so Constable Bernard Trowell (the arresting officer) requisitioned the rope from the town's church bell, promising the minister that it would be returned promptly once it was removed from the finished corpse.

Bound at the wrist, the diminutive prisoner was marched up the wooden steps to the gallows. In front of the gallows was the King's Navy representatives First Lieutenant

Nigel Yardley and his aide Ensign Endicott. Constable Trowell followed behind, beaming with pride as he marched the grim pirate to his doom. And why shouldn't he be proud? After all, it was Constable Trowell's quick-thinking that allowed him to deduce that the short, briny man who had strolled up to his desk and said he was the Pirate Shorty Buckets was, in fact, the Pirate Shorty Buckets.

When Buckets had reached the top of the gallows where the hooded executioner (who was also the town baker) stood patiently holding the noose, the constable spun the pirate around to face the waiting Lieutenant Yardley and Ensign Endicott. The lieutenant, seated at a small wooden table and impromptu desk, pompously cleared his throat.

"Good people of Peahaven," he began. In this case, the three 'good people of Peahaven' consisted of an elderly woman enshrouded in a heavy hooded cloak, a tall slender man with a black coat and broad-brimmed hat that obscured his features, and an unkempt drunkard, who was sleeping against the stone wall of the constabulary and who had apparently been there since before the whole affair had started. "We are gathered here to witness," Yardley continued, "the execution of the pirate Shorty Buckets, who, by his own admission, is guilty of the crimes of piracy against His Majesty's citizens and colonies."

At this, the diminutive Buckets let out a loud, unintelligible scoff.

"Mr. Buckets, I remind you that your sentence of execution may be commuted should you be willing to lead us to the capture of your villainous cohorts."

"Bah!" retorted Shorty Buckets.

Despite Mr. Bucket's clever response, Yardley continued. "Did you not serve under the infamous pirate Archibald Royal, charged with immeasurable counts of theft and carnage against King and Country?"

"Bah!" was Bucket's reply.

"I have the authority, Mr. Buckets, to lessen your sentence from Death by Hanging to Life Imprisonment, but only if you tell us the whereabouts of Archibald Royal."

Shorty's lips tightened in a grim lock of silence.

"Very well," Yardley sighed. "Let it be noted that before these witnesses—" he motioned to the tall man, old woman, and unconscious drunk "—that Mr. Shorty Buckets has waived his opportunity for leniency. Proceed with the execution."

The hooded executioner stepped forward to place the noose around the prisoner's neck and realized he had a problem. Tugging on the rope, the loosened noose only reached down to Shorty's nose.

"He's too short!" came the executioner's muffled announcement.

Shorty stared up at the dangling rope in disgust. "Bah!"

Yardley looked around in consternation. He whispered to Ensign Endicott. "Have we got a box or something he can stand on?"

Constable Trowell quickly blurted a response. "I've got it, sir!" He dashed down the gallows steps and into the jailhouse. A few awkward moments passed while Buckets stood waiting on the gallows and Yardley, Endicott, and the non-slumbering witnesses looked on.

Soon, Trowell returned with a small empty keg. "Here you go, sir." He ran up the steps and placed the up-ended keg on the trapdoor of the gallows. Giving it a quick brush with his hands, he assisted the bound Mr. Buckets onto it.

The hooded executioner fitted the noose around Shorty's neck. "It works now!" the executioner needlessly announced.

"Very good." Yardley stood up from his seat and addressed the glowering pirate. "Do you have any final words, Mr. Buckets?"

For a moment, Shorty Buckets was silent. Then a sneer worked itself across his pinched face. "Archie Royal is the least of your problems! Do you hear me?" he shouted. "Royal's the least of your problems!"

With that, Yardley gave a simple nod. The executioner pulled the lever, the trap door opened, and Shorty Buckets, keg and all, dropped to the ground beneath.

+ + +

The pirate's body was ingloriously dumped into the waiting pine box and the lid was fastened with the fewest number of rusty nails possible.

"Isn't that the way of things?" growled the executioner (perhaps 'baker' is now more appropriate as the hanging was completed). He was holding Shorty's left boot against the bottom of his foot for approximate measurement. "One bloomin' execution in this town in years, and it has to be someone with smaller feet than my own! These boots aren't likely to even fit a child!"

Constable Trowell examined the boots. "What a pity! And such fine boots, too!"

The constable's admiration of the victim's footwear was interrupted when Lieutenant Yardley marched towards the two men. "What the blazes is going on here?" he inquired indignantly.

The baker *nez* executioner looked sheepish. "Well, sir, it seemed a might silly to bury such a pair of well-crafted boots. It's not as if he'll be doing a lot of walking any time soon." At this, the baker and constable broke into roars of laughter.

"Enough of that!" The two men quickly stiffened under Yardley's anger. "I don't care about those silly boots!" he continued. "I want to know what you're doing with this brigand's corpse!"

The baker and constable swapped puzzled looks. Trowell shrugged. "We're cartin' him off to the cemetery."

"Yeah," chimed in the baker. "Dead bodies tend to stink a bit if you leave 'em lying about, sir."

"This man is a condemned pirate!" countered the lieutenant. "His body should be hung in a public place to be made an example of!"

"That's a mite disgusting, sir," replied Trowell.

"Aye," echoed the baker. "And, besides, bodies tend to stink."

"With all due respect, Lieutenant," the constable continued, "I don't think the local townsfolk would appreciate... er...airing such dirty laundry in public, so to speak."

Yardley's face reddened. "This man's body should be hanging at the nearest crossroads, to serve as a warning to other lawless rapscallions!"

"Rapscallions, sir? We don't have many of those here. Better that this man be given a proper burial, Lieutenant. A dangling corpse isn't quite the thing Peahaven goes for. People will talk, it will attract lots of flies, and kids will be constantly poking it with sticks. That's not the proper way to raise children, is it, Lieutenant Yardley?"

14

"Um," stammered Yardley, "I suppose not."

"There you have it, Lieutenant," Trowell continued. "Think of the children."

"And the stink!" contributed the baker.

Before Yardley could argue further, the small, hooded woman who was present for the execution ambled toward the group of men. "I beg your pardon, kind sirs..."

"What is it?" the navy lieutenant barked.

The hooded woman shrank back. "Oh, pity, sir! Pity! Could you not spare but a few patient words for a grieving widow?"

Yardley gave a puzzled look to the constable and baker. "What is she talking about?"

The two men could only shrug in response.

"I beg your kindness, sir, but it's so hard to have lost a loving husband and then to have his body bandied about in argument before his everlasting soul has barely had a chance to depart!"

Yardley frowned. "Are you trying to tell us that you're the widow of this rascal?"

"Oh," the woman cried. "The callousness!"

Constable Trowell gave the lieutenant a vicious look. "Have some decency, man! Can't you see the poor woman is in mourning!"

Yardley's agitation grew. "I very much doubt that! This woman is no more this pirate's widow than I'm his scullery maid!"

"Pity, sir!" wailed the woman. "Oh, the mercy! The kind Virgil Buckets has been my doting husband since we was rosy-cheeked sweethearts! And all I ask is that you give my grieving heart one last chance to express its love by allowing me to honor his final wish."

"And what final wish is that?" Yardley asked suspiciously.

"Why, it was his lifelong wish ever since he was a babe to be buried at sea."

"As a baby he wanted to be buried at sea? I've never heard such preposterous lies!"

At this rebuke, the hooded woman let out another wail. "Oh, the depravity!"

Constable Trowell gave Yardley a quick cuff on the arm. "That's enough of you, sir! I would have expected an officer of the King's Navy to behave more like a gentleman!" He turned to the crying widow. "Don't you worry about a thing, Missus Buckets! We'll be more than happy to see to your husband's dying wish."

"Oh, thank you!" rejoiced the woman. "I have my cart right over here!" She scurried around the corner of the jailhouse and out of sight.

Yardley straightened in indignation. "Constable Trowell, I must protest this charade!"

"Your protest is noted. Now, if you'll excuse us, we must assist the Widow Buckets with her dearly departed! Kindly send our gratitude to His Majesty for your aid in rendering justice. Good day!" With that, the two men hefted the coffin and waddled after the widow.

Yardley snorted in disgust. "This is madness. Let's get out of here, Endicott," he said to the waiting ensign.

As Yardley marched off, Ensign Endicott was observing the empty boots that had been discarded on the grass. "Excuse me!" he called to the baker and constable. "May I have these?"

The baker grunted an affirmative as they lugged the coffin to the waiting cart.

"Why in the world do you want those smelly things?"

grumbled Yardley as Endicott plucked the boots from the grass. "They won't fit your plank feet!"

"My brother-in-law runs an orphanage. He might have a need for them, sir. Do you mind if we deliver them?"

Yardley rolled his eyes at the thought of escorting the foul boots across the countryside. "Why do I feel life would have been simpler had this idiot pirate never been captured?"

+ + +

The widow's cart ambled up the hill and away from the small village of Peahaven. Once the hamlet was well out of earshot, the lone, hooded widow began whistling a rather jaunty sea chanty. Were it not for the jostling pine coffin in the back, no one would have mistaken her for a mourning widow. And one striking detail betrayed the fact that she was not headed for a burial at sea.

"The sea is in the other direction."

The widowed pulled the reins taut at the sight of the sudden stranger alongside the road.

The coffin slid forward roughly as the cart jerked to a stop. The hooded woman peered at the black-coated stranger and his broad-brimmed hat. "What kind servant is this," she said, "that would aid a poor widow in her hour of grief?"

The stranger sauntered toward the waiting cart. "Not much aid, really." He motioned to the wide view of the ocean behind them. "Just mentioning the obvious."

The hooded widow studied the stranger's features. He was a tall man, with a sharp and weather-lined face. Beneath the large brim of the hat, an eye patch could be seen covering one of his eyes. "Why, of course," the woman stated. "You're the man who also witnessed the hanging of my poor dear husband."

"Aye, that's correct. But you," he answered, "are no widow!" Like a flag snapping in a gale, the stranger's arm lashed out, pulling back the widow's hood to reveal the stubbled face of a man.

Just as rapidly, the pretending widow suddenly flourished a pistol from the depths of his cloak. The stubble-faced man grinned. "Right you are." He pointed the flintlock at the stranger's one good eye. "And who are you supposed to be?"

"A fellow mourner, perhaps?" the one-eyed stranger answered.

"I'm not sure anyone who mourns the death of Shorty Buckets is a trustworthy sort."

"I could say the same about anyone interested in claiming his corpse—especially when he says he's going to bury him at sea and hauls him inland instead. What's your scheme?"

"I guess you'll never find out!" The man squeezed the trigger, but the one-eyed stranger was too fast. With a shove of his arm, he pushed the pistol's barrel away and it fired harmlessly over his head.

Harmless or not, the unexpecting horse attached to the cart bolted in alarm under the sound of the booming shot. The wagon rattled past in a spray of mud and gun smoke.

"Blast!" the one-eyed stranger muttered. Without a moment's hesitation, his gloved hand grabbed the passing sideboard of the careening cart. He clambered into the back of the wagon with the sure-footedness of one who had spent years upon the twisting decks of a sea vessel.

The unfortunate coffin of Shorty Buckets bounced helplessly as the maddened horse tore down the rough trail. The stubble-faced driver tugged on the reins but the horse refused to heed. "Stop, you brainless nag!" he shouted uselessly. He tossed the flintlock at his feet and redoubled his efforts on the reins.

As the crudely-fastened nails of Shorty's coffin began to bounce from their holes, the one-eyed stranger steadied his stance on the shuddering cart. From beneath his flapping coat, he pulled a long, curved sword with a graceful arc. "Avast, you fiend!" He sliced downward at the driver. The blow was intended to force the man off the cart, but it had an unexpected result. Instead, the driver dropped the reins and drew a broad dented sword of his own from beneath his cloak. With a deft parry, he blocked the strike.

"So!" the one-eyed man laughed, "it's broadswords and cutlasses, is it? Come and face me properly!"

The stubble-faced man climbed to his feet, brandishing his worn blade with fury. The crazed horse continued to flee wildly down the road, oblivious to the duel behind it. The wheels of the cart crashed violently through the ruts and rills beneath.

"I don't know what you're up to, old man!" shouted the driver, "but you picked the wrong wagon to waylay!" He punctuated the threat with a wild jab of his sword.

The one-eyed man's cutlass swept the blade away with practiced ease. "It's your cargo I'll have! The wagon is yours to keep."

"You're not takin' nothing!" With another savage lunge, the driver stabbed with his broad blade. The steel found only empty air as the one-eyed man adroitly leapt aside. With firm confidence, his feet landed on the bouncing coffin. A downward parry and twist of his cutlass wrenched the broadsword from the driver's grip. "You'd have better luck with a butter knife, widow!"

Raising his right boot, he delivered a solid kick to the man's stomach. The driver doubled over before tumbling backward onto the wagon seat.

The timing was fortuitous. As the stubble-faced driver crumpled, the one-eyed man spied the sharp turn in the dirt path ahead. "Look alive! This ride's about to capsize!"

With split-second judgment, the stranger spotted a soft clearing and jumped from the cart. The driver, bug-eyed, could only watch as the galloping horse jack-knifed to the right. Unable to keep up with the fleeing horse, the wagon flipped helplessly on its side, spilling both driver and coffin into the brambles and brush. The hitch snapped into splinters. The horse, freed from its load, galloped away without remorse, leaving the wrecked carriage in a cloud of drifting dust.

The one-eyed man lifted himself to his feet and sheathed the large cutlass. He examined the teetering wreckage of the cart.

Beside the wreck, the driver coughed and sputtered in the settling dust. At the sight of the approaching stranger, he lunged for his pistol now lying in the grass and leveled it at the one-eyed man.

The stranger paid him no heed, however. Instead, he was leaning over and examining the bootless body of Shorty Buckets. The coffin and lid had parted ways during the crash, and Shorty's corpse had rolled unceremoniously from the wooden box and onto the ground.

"Get away from that body!" shouted the driver, as he pulled back the flintlock's cock.

The one-eyed man looked nonchalantly at the stubble-faced widow. "Oh, for heaven's sake! You're not wasting your time with that silly thing, are you? You've already fired it."

"You're not taking anything!"

The one-eyed man looked down at the bare feet of Shorty Buckets once more. "You're absolutely right. I'm not." With a look of chagrin, he turned away and strolled down the road from whence they came, leaving the perplexed driver alone in the mud behind him.

Dempster House

At the end of Twofarthing Lane, on the outskirts of the city, stood a rather large manse that had every appearance of being very old. It was, in truth, constructed only a few decades previous, but the fact that it was home to roughly a dozen young orphans might have contributed to its aged condition. The mansion was Dempster House and it was a privately-run wayward home for children. Founded by Virgil Dempster, who himself was an orphan once, and funded by a modest but dwindling fortune he created in the shipping business, the home was now under the supervision of his grandson Duncan Dempster.

Despite its worn and lived-in atmosphere, the many children at Dempster House loved it very much (except for one who will be discussed later). The grounds were expansive and reasonably green, and served as an acceptable arena for the children's outdoor activities. As for the home's keeper, Mr. Duncan Dempster, one would be hard-pressed to find a kindlier, more protective soul. His concern for his many wards was evident in his friendly yet disciplined expectations in their daily lives. And together, the occupants of Dempster House operated as a well-oiled family, performing the many duties naturally incumbent within a household, such as doing the washing, preparing the meals, and helping one another with schoolwork.

On this particular day, however, the children of Dempster House were not washing or cleaning or doing sums, but instead were gathered with much excitement and consternation around a hole in the plaster of the parlor wall.

"I say!" exclaimed Mr. Dempster, as he came down the stairs. "What the deuce is going on?"

Elliot, one of the older boys, promptly answered. "Chronos is trapped in the wall! He's been cornered by a cat!"

"A cat? How the dickens did a cat come to be here?" replied Dempster. He leaned his long face forward, peering into the depths of the hole with curiosity. "What are we to do?"

"Someone will need to go in there!" cried Elliot.

"Yes!" pleaded Lizzie (one of the more sensitive of the girls). "We have to save Chronos!"

"It's an awfully tight breach," answered Dempster, studying the small space. "I'm not sure anyone can fit."

One boy spoke up. "I can do it!"

The boy was Arthur Cross. Arthur was indeed a slight boy for the age of nine, but dauntless when it came to big tasks.

"Yes, I do believe you can, Arthur. Do you think you can give it a go?"

The boy nodded, and with a cheer, the children pushed him forward to the tight hole.

"Be careful, Arthur!" cried Nora. "It's dreadfully dark in there!" Nora Primm was always protective of Arthur, not only because he was a bit on the small side, but also because Arthur was, in Nora's opinion, a very nice boy who deserved protecting.

Urged on by the crowding children, Arthur hunkered down on his hands and knees and awkwardly slid himself into the small opening. Soon only his small feet were left protruding from the hole. The space was indeed tight and dark, and it took some tedious maneuvering for Arthur to squeeze his body within. Anyone who has spent a respectable amount of time inside a wall knows most walls have beams within them for support, which can make moving about very difficult. The walls of Dempster House were no exception. Many of the beams, however, were old and dry and nibbled away by insects. Within the dark confines, only slightly illuminated by the hole behind him, Arthur could hear the terrible growling and hissing of a cat. Beyond, he could hear the squeaks of the terrified Chronos, desperately cornered somewhere nearby.

Chronos the mouse was something of a mascot for Dempster House, and was noted for his keen sense of smell and hearing. Whenever meals were being prepared in the kitchen, he would leap from his cozy nest, jump from the rafters, bounce off the dinner bell and bound down the rope in anticipation of a morsel of food. The ringing bell would alert everyone of what was transpiring in the kitchen and thus would always be followed by a crush of hungry children stampeding to the washroom to clean up for mealtime. It wasn't long before Chronos had become Dempster House's official resident dinner bell and, as he was furry and cute and didn't eat too much, was widely accepted into their home. Every day since his arrival, Chronos had been punctual and consistent, and known for never missing a meal.

But this day, the poor mouse's residence at Dempster House was in danger of being cut short. Behind a cracked beam, of which Arthur was simply too large to work past, he spied a mangy orange cat hunkered in the shadows. The scruffy feline was feverishly stretching its ragged paw into a crevasse beyond, fishing and clawing for the frightened mouse huddling within.

Arthur wiggled himself as close as he could and tried to snake his hand past the feline. After a couple of failed attempts, Arthur did something he normally would not do and grasped the beast's twitching tail. The cat let out a nasty yowl and sputtering hiss. It slashed its claws into Arthur's skin (which is exactly the reason he normally would not do such a thing) and he quickly pulled his arm back.

"Ouch! You filthy thing!" Re-doubling his efforts, he reached once again past the worm-eaten beam and grasped a handful of skin on the cat's back end. With a yank, he tried to extract the animal. The cat anchored itself to every available surface like a hairy orange grappling hook. With more ferocious spitting and tearing, it began ripping into Arthur's already bloodied arm once more.

Despite the pain, Arthur continued tugging at the flailing ball of claws and fur. "Leave Chronos alone! Come out of there!" His efforts were futile, though. Arthur dropped the cat.

"What's going on in there, Arthur?" Dempster's voice shouted from the hole behind.

Arthur called back. "Chronos is trapped! I can't reach him. And I can't get a hold of this cat!

"Try yanking his tail!" shouted one of the boys helpfully.

"I tried that!" Arthur replied. "Just give me a minute to think." For a moment, Arthur sat crunched in the wall considering his predicament while the boys and Mr. Dempster waited in silence.

And then Arthur spoke up. "I've got an idea! Bring me a pipe!"

One of the boys scratched his head. "A pipe?"

Dempster brightened. "Yes! That's it! Good show, Arthur!" he turned to Elliot. "Go fetch a length of pipe!"

"Where do I get a pipe?"

Dempster ushered him on. "Any pipe will do! Try the gutterage on the wall outside." Without a second thought, Elliot and a handful of other boys dashed out the front door.

Within moments, they returned with a long rusty and bent rain gutter pipe in their hands, brackets and screws still dangling upon it from where they tore it from the wall.

"Excellent!" smiled Mr. Dempster. "Sit tight, Arthur! We're sending in a pipe!"

With a great deal of clumsy effort, the crew shoved one end of the drainage pipe into the hole. Arthur grasped it as it slid toward him and worked it through the splintered beam.

The cat, with much consternation, scrabbled as the strange metal intruder shoved its way past and butted up against the hiding place of the terrified mouse.

"Run, Chronos! Run!"

Chronos needed no such urging. Arthur could hear the pitter patter of its tiny feet as it bolted through the drain-pipe. With a confident leap, the mouse flew out of the other end of the pipe and into the coat pocket of Duncan Dempster, accompanied by the victorious cheers of the children.

Elliot and Jeremy grabbed Arthur's poking feet and dragged him, dusty and disheveled, from the crumbly wall.

"You did it, Arthur!" cried Nora.

"The cat's still in there!" Arthur grasped the other end of the pipe. Drawing a deep breath and cupping his hands, he blew into the iron drain. Like some ghastly instrument, the rain gutter amplified the boy's hearty bellow throughout the depths of the house. Plaster dropped from the reverberating walls and a cloud of abandoned dust spewed from the hole. With a terrified screech, the mangy cat shot out of the wall's breach like an orange shell from a cannon and skittered through the open front door.

With cheers and clapping, the boys lifted Arthur onto their shoulders. "Hooray for Arthur! Hooray!" In a flash, the children were parading Arthur around the house and outside upon the grounds, singing impromptu odes and cheers to the valiant rescue of Chronos the mouse. While the odes were not necessarily in rhyme, and the songs a bit off key, their hearts were in perfect step as they lauded their hero of the day.

+   +   +

At lunchtime, as if to punctuate that all was once again in proper form, the bell rang as Chronos scurried to the kitchen. Awaiting him was an extra piece of cheese that Mr. Dempster had set out in recognition of the mouse's return to duty. Oftentimes, whenever something horrid comes close to happening, one discovers an appreciation for the many non-horrid things which happen every day. In this case, Duncan Dempster had realized that it was a much better situation to have one less morsel of cheese than to be without Chronos.

Like clockwork, the ringing of the mealtime bell was followed by the scurrying of small feet toward the washrooms as the children prepared for lunch. Although everyone was hungry and eager, it was not necessarily the food they were rushing for, but were in fact all keenly aware that this was a very particular luncheon. The day was Friday, and at Dempster House, lunchtime on Friday was "The Exceptionally Special and Meritorious Awards" meal. Each week, Duncan Dempster rewarded one child with a special prize in recognition of a week well-lived. Good deeds, polite behavior, exemplary obedience, and acts of heroism were all the ways in which to be honored with The Dempster Exceptionally Special and Meritorious Award for the week. The nature of the prize varied and was entirely dependent on whatever fate and means decreed that week. Sometimes it would be a piece of candy, a second helping of dessert, a tuppence, or maybe a book, or a day free from chores. It was never the same prize twice, and some days the prize was wholly unique—like it was on this day.

The children took their usual seats along the long tables in the dining room. Bowls and spoons were in their places as well. Everyone waited quietly as Mr. Dempster brought a large vat of delicious-smelling beef stew and set it on the serving table. He was about to speak but paused to give young Miles Budger a reproving look. Miles quickly took his elbows off the table and folded his hands in his lap like the other children. Mr. Dempster resumed. "Residents of Dempster House," he greeted, "welcome to the Exceptionally Special and Meritorious Awards Meal!"

The children cheered in anticipation, and Duncan Dempster continued. "Today, as is the Dempster House tradition, we honor one who has provided us with a superlative example of behavior, dignity, decorum, and decency.

While no two people are identical, and no two weeks unfold themselves in quite the same way, each Friday we laud the same thing: an individual that has made the week an exceptional one! And this week, the prize goes to... Arthur Cross!"

The children hurrahed (except for one who will be discussed later) for they all cared a great deal for Arthur and were still a bit giddy from the morning's adventure. Dempster raised his hand and waited patiently for the exuberance to lull. "I want it to be known," he said, "that while Arthur's bravery and sharp thinking were certainly demonstrated this morning, it is not the sole reason he is being given today's award. This past week, Arthur has been prompt to class, executed his lessons expertly, made his bed every morning without being reminded, and was caught in the brave act of washing behind his ears."

"What's so brave about washing behind your ears?" asked Carlton Fish.

Dempster arched an eyebrow. "Have you looked behind your ears lately? There are some places that even angels fear to tread!"

At this, Carlton's face turned several shades of red.

"But," Dempster continued, "there's still no ignoring Arthur's feat of bravery in his rescue of our good friend Chronos the mouse. And it's fortuitous that today I have a very unique prize that befits a very unique act of heroism! Please come forward, Arthur."

Arthur Cross rose from his seat and walked to the end of the table. While he tried to remain appropriately stoic, everyone could see his attempts to suppress a slight grin of pleasure.

Dempster put his hand on Arthur's shoulder. "Arthur

Cross, in recognition of your fine spirit and for your achievement of a week well-lived, I bestow to you to-day's Exceptionally Special and Meritorious Award!" He reached down behind the table and produced a worn yet handsome pair of leather boots. "These boots were given to me by my brother-in-law just this morning."

Arthur's eyes grew wide with excitement. They truly were a well-crafted pair of boots, and unlike anything any of the other children had ever seen.

"I know they smell a bit strange," said Dempster, "but with all the excitement this morning, I didn't have an opportunity to clean them properly. They look to be just about your size, too!"

The children again cheered magnificently and show-ered Arthur with applause and congratulations. It must be noted that there's always someone who has a hard time being happy for someone else, as was the case with one of the children (who will be discussed in a moment), but otherwise everyone was very excited about Arthur's fabu-lous award. After all, they knew that if the situation were reversed, they would certainly want everyone to be happy for them when the time came.

In amazed delight, Arthur took the boots in his hands and admired their expert craftsmanship. Duncan bent down and whispered in Arthur's ear. "My brother-in-law tells me that they belonged to a pirate! But I suspect that's probably just a fanciful story. You know how brothers-in-law are!"

Arthur really had no clue how brothers-in-law were, but pirates or no, the boots were magnificent. He polite-ly thanked Mr. Dempster for the gift, and then dashed back to his seat, boots in hand, amidst the applause of the others.

"Very good! Let us say Blessing for our meal and then we can start serving some of this scrumptious beef stew. Arthur, kindly do not put the boots on the dinner table."

Arthur hurriedly grabbed the boots from next to his bowl and set them on the floor.

After Blessing, Nora Primm assisted Mr. Dumpster in serving everyone a generous helping of beef stew and one biscuit made of cornmeal. Not until everyone was served and Nora had returned to her seat alongside Arthur, did they begin to enjoy their luncheon.

Each table sat six children. Arthur, along with Nora, always sat at the same table with four other boys: Elliot Powers, Miles Budger, Phillip Queazy, and Percy Lawrence. As the five boys made short work of their stew, they congratulated Arthur personally on his accomplishment.

"Good show on the boots, old bean!" complimented Elliot.

"Yes," agreed Nora, "very well done." She shot a disapproving glance at Elliot. "Don't talk with your mouth full."

"Boy!" gurgled Miles, as stew dripped from his mouth, oblivious to Nora's demands for etiquette. "I thought Chronos was a goner! Where did that nasty old cat come from anyway?"

Arthur sat silently in thought. A distant look was on his face as he stared into his bowl of stew.

Elliot put his spoon down. "I know that look, Arthur. What are you thinking? You always get that look on your face when you're thinking, like your eyes are looking inside your skull instead of out."

Arthur scratched his chin. "I think it was Warty."

"Warty?" Nora asked. She stole a secretive glance at

Arthur's suspect, who was devouring his stew across the room. The other children were sitting as far away from Warty as possible, due partly to the number of warts he had on his hands and face, but also to avoid the extensive spray he was causing as he consumed his lunch. "Why would he want to get rid of Chronos?"

"I don't know...yet," Arthur replied.

Percy chimed in. "It might have been him. We really don't know anything about him. He's only been here for a couple of weeks. We don't even know if he has a last name!"

Elliot shrugged. "Well, I'm not about to start thinking the worst of someone just because I don't know anything about him." He slurped a spoonful of stew noisily, as Nora rolled her eyes in exasperation. "Still," he continued. "We best keep a close watch on him."

The conversation gradually turned to other things, such as books they had read, or what games they might play that afternoon. When the bowls of stew were empty, a rare treat of chocolate pudding was served for dessert. As Arthur delved into his pudding with delight, his enjoyment was lessened when he caught Warty watching him with beady, dagger-like eyes.

Visitors Both Welcome and Unwelcome

After clearing the tables and washing the dishes, the children of Dempster House scattered to their various Friday afternoon activities. This usually consisted of the boys going outside to run rampant on the Dempster House grounds, while the girls preferred sitting inside to read or converse, giving the boys disapproving looks, and shaking their heads in disgust as they dashed noisily past the windows.

Duncan Dempster strolled past the rampaging children and down the path in front of the orphanage grounds. On his way to dump the dishwater into the gutter, he halted suddenly at the site of a shrouded man examining the house through the gate's iron bars.

He was a sinister looking man, and there were only a few details that Dempster could pick out underneath the broad-brimmed hat, one of which was that the stranger wore a black patch over one eye.

Duncan Dempster straightened with indignation. "You there! What do you think you're doing?"

The one-eyed stranger looked at Dempster through the bars as if seeing him for the first time. "Who are you?" the stranger asked.

Duncan set the sloshing bucket of water onto the ground.

"I might very well ask you that same question. What do you want?"

The stranger peered curiously over Dempster's shoulder at the boys running back and forth. "What is this place?" he asked.

Dempster huffed in consternation. He was not accustomed to the bald rudeness of having his questions ignored and then be handed questions in return instead. "This is an orphanage! Who do you think you are? You've no right to come snooping around here. Leave, or you'll force me to call a constable."

The threat of a constable snapped the stranger's attention back to Dempster. "There's no need for that. I've come in search of a pair of boots."

"Boots? There's a perfectly acceptable cobbler two streets over. I'm sure he would be happy to help you with whatever you need."

"No. I'm searching for a particular pair of boots. I was told they were brought here. I'll pay money for them. Good money. From the looks of this place, that seems like an equitable arrangement."

For a moment, Duncan Dempster studied the one-eyed stranger on the other side of the wrought-iron gate. Then, his face twisted into a stern glare. "You have the smell of the sea about you. And I won't have your kind lurking around and insulting our home. Off with you. If I catch you creeping about again, I'll not waste a moment calling the authorities!" Dempster hefted the brimming bucket and with an angry toss flung the water through the bars, narrowly missing the one-eyed stranger. Without giving the man another glance, he marched back into the manor.

+ + +

At four o'clock sharp, a lanky young man carrying a covered basket arrived at the front door of Dempster House and politely rapped the knocker. Only a few moments passed before the door swung silently open. A very tiny, curly-haired girl peeked from the entrance with big brown eyes.

"Hello, Marjorie," the young man greeted. "It's me. Clay."

The girl remained silent, not from any sense of rudeness, but simply because that was who she was. Marjorie McFlinty was probably the shyest girl anyone would ever meet, even with people like Clay whom she knew for many years.

"Is Mr. Dempster in?" It was a rhetorical question. Duncan Dempster was always in, unless Clay was there to watch over the children.

Quietly, and like always, Marjorie swung the front door fully open, shuffling backward and staying as hidden as possible behind the large door.

Clay stepped in just as Duncan Dempster was strolling down the stairs. "Hello, Clay!" he smiled.

"Hello, Mr. Dempster! How are you today?"

"Just fine! I trust you're doing equally well?"

"Yes, sir. Mr. Garfox sent some loaves for you." Clay handed him the covered basket full of bread.

Dempster accepted the gift graciously. "The good Mr. Garfox! Bless his heart!" Glancing over Clay's shoulder through the open door, Dempster quickly changed topics. "Did you happen to have any problems letting yourself through the front gate?"

Clay was understandably a bit confused. "No problem at all. The key worked fine, anyway, if that's what you're asking. Is something wrong with the lock?"

"Nothing to do with the lock," he replied, as he continued peering outside. "There was an unusual scoundrel milling about. I suspect he's probably gone by now. No matter!" Dempster shut the door, was a bit startled to see Marjorie McFlinty still quietly hiding behind it, and then ushered Clay into the drawing room. "Come inside. I suspect you'd like to see Arthur."

Bending down to the quiet young girl, Dempster whispered, "Marjorie, kindly locate Arthur and tell him his brother is here." Marjorie scurried off without a word.

"I see the drainpipe outside is missing," Clay remarked as the two strolled through the house. "Do you need me to repair it?"

"Huh? Oh, not at all. We had a bit of an escapade this morning. I'm sure Arthur will tell you all about it."

"He hasn't been any trouble, has he?"

"Quite the opposite!" answered Dempster. "He's always a helpful young man. A real joy to have around." Dempster stopped suddenly. "You're not here to—"

Clay finished his thought. "Take him away? No, sir. Not yet. Perhaps in a few more months, when I've saved a bit more money. Things have been slow at the Owl and Hearth. Frankly, I'm surprised that Mr. Garfox continues to keep me on."

"Not to worry, Clay. Your brother is welcome to stay as long as is necessary. And there will always be a room for you, should you ever need it."

Clay shook his head. "I appreciate your generosity, Mr. Dempster. You raised Arthur and I our whole lives, but

I'm old enough now that I should be making my own way. Besides, I think you have enough mouths to feed."

Dempster nodded in agreement. "I can't argue with that. With every day that passes, my grandfather's trust depletes a bit more."

The news caused Clay's brow to furrow in concern. "You're not in any danger of losing the property, are you?"

"It hasn't come to that yet. Fortunately, we've been shrewd enough to keep things running. By forego-ing a few repairs and upkeep here and there, we've had adequate food on the tables and coal in the cellar. I try not to sound like an alarmist, but I must face the reality that it's only a matter of time before I'll be forced to consider alternatives."

"I won't let it come to that, Mr. Dempster. You know that."

Dempster smiled ruefully. "Your attitude is uplifting, but I'm afraid it will take something a bit beyond either of our powers. Something truly extraordinary. Ah! Here's Arthur!"

"Clay!" Arthur dashed into the drawing room joyfully, his footsteps made louder by the new pair of boots on his feet.

"Arthur, you little nose-drip!" Clay teased as he gave him a brotherly hug. "What have you been up to?"

"Look at my boots!"

Dempster smiled. "You two have a lot to talk about, and I have a dinner to prepare. Please give Mr. Garfox my gratitude for the loaves of bread." With that, he left the two brothers alone to chat.

Clay admired the boots on Arthur's feet. "Where in the world did you get those?"

"They were this week's prize. I won them for saving Chronos!"

"Saving Chronos? From what?"

"A nasty old cat. I think Warty let him! And I—"

"Hold on!" interrupted Clay. "You're going too fast. Who's Warty?"

Arthur pointed out the drawing room window which afforded an unobstructed view of the yard all the way up to the front gate. "That's Warty. He showed up here a couple of weeks ago. No one knows anything about him other than the fact that he's terribly rude."

Clay squinted through the window to see a rotund boy. He was standing at the front gate and appeared to be engaged in conversation with a large man on the other side. "Who is that he's talking to?" Clay asked.

Arthur took a hard look and shrugged. "I don't know. I've never seen him before."

"Curious," murmured Clay, recalling his earlier conversation with Mr. Dempster. "Very curious."

Pushing the thoughts aside, Clay settled down on the parlor settee and let his brother regale him with the rescue of Chronos the mouse and other interesting tidbits that had occurred since they last spoke. The two laughed as Clay recounted an incident at the Owl and Hearth when a drunken guest had mounted his horse backwards and accused everyone who walked by of stealing his horse's head. Arthur told him about when Nessie Longwater screamed at the sight of a cricket, which in turn leapt in panic and landed promptly in her open mouth. For at least an hour, they swapped stories of their days at Dempster House, and what a future would look like elsewhere. And with each joke chuckled over, each recollection revisited, and each dream expounded on, the thought of the stranger at the gate grew more and more unimportant to Clay and Arthur Cross.

✦   ✦   ✦

The strides of the one-eyed stranger were fueled with purpose as he made his way down the cobbled street. The evening had closed in, bringing with it a sudden cold rain that made the gray buildings more dreary than usual. With the broad-brimmed hat slouched low over his head, more to hide his features than to shelter them from the elements, the stranger paused to examine the sign that swung above him. In the yellow light of the building's window, he could read the words 'Owl and Hearth' painted on the dripping shingle. Pulling the hat brim down further over his face, the one-eyed man slipped through the waiting door.

The Owl and Hearth was nothing particularly special as far as inns were concerned. It was primarily a tavern, but with the letting of two small rooms upstairs, it had been granted the rank as a modest inn. The interior was dim. Only a few bilious lanterns burned so customers could navigate the wooden tables scattered about the room. A few groups of patrons were laughing and cajoling, while a handful of solo individuals contemplated their meals in silence. In the corner, a beggarly musician squeezed discordant notes from an accordion, weakly attempting to infuse some cheer into the musty air.

The one-eyed stranger found a corner table with a comfortable volume of shadow and settled his back to the wall. From the dim vantage point, he watched as the young man bustled from patron to patron, picking up empty mugs of mead and demolished plates of food. The stranger had timed his arrival to coincide with the Owl and Hearth's closing. One by one, individuals slid from their stools as the young server gathered up the empty dishes at their seats. Soon, the inn was vacant save for the young man and the one-eyed stranger.

"Boy!" called the stranger. "How about something warm to help an old man fend off the evening's chill?"

Clay (for it was indeed he who was cleaning up the tables) jumped at the sound of the man's voice. "I beg your pardon, sir! I didn't see you sitting in the dark. I'm afraid we're closing for the evening. You'll have to leave...unless you intend to pay for a night's room."

"I might," answered the stranger, in that rather vague manner that said he really wasn't considering it at all. "I've come more for the conversation."

Clay shook his head. "I'm sorry, sir, but you'll have to go. I hate to turn you out on a rainy night but I can't stay and chat with you."

"Even," the stranger responded, "if I were to tell you about Dempster House? And the peril that awaits all who live there?"

As if on cue, the storm broke forth with a thunderous crack of lightning. Clay stared in shock at the stranger's grave words and menacing eye-patch. "Who are you?" he asked.

"Perhaps you have heard of me," the stranger replied. "My name is Archibald Royal."

Clay simply stared in amazement. "Did you say Archibald Royal? The Pirate Archibald Royal?"

The one-eyed man nodded grimly. "Aye. The very same."

Skepticism filled Clay's face. "And why, pray tell, would an infamous pirate who has been missing for over twelve years come in here and tell me that Dempster House is in peril?"

The stranger pushed an empty chair from the table with his boot, inviting Clay to sit down. "I see you are a young man with questions. I have answers. Bring me a mug of warm cider, and perhaps we can barter."

Clay hesitated but decided that any threats against Dempster House were too serious to disregard. He bolted the inn door and stepped behind the counter to pour a drink. "So if you are indeed the dangerous Pirate Royal," Clay asked, while he filled the mug, "where have you been all these years? When I was a boy there was news of you from the Caribbean every week in the broadsheets. The Admiralty had put quite a bounty on your head, and no more has ever been heard of you since." Clay placed the full tankard in front of the one-eyed man.

"True," Royal answered. "The reward for my capture, either dead or alive, was so high that it enticed even my own crew. There wasn't a man-jack among them that didn't begin to entertain the idea of betraying me for the sake of reward. Not to mention gaining the King's pardon for my capture and then taking my years of hard-earned spoil for their own."

"They mutinied?" Clay asked.

Royal took a sip from the mug, took a moment to consider the taste of it, then wiped his lip. "They tried. Avarice is a double-edged sword, though. Not only did each want the reward for themselves, they also didn't relish the thought of having to share it with each other. I was the prisoner of about five different men, including my own first mate, before I had enough of that nonsense and escaped."

"Escaped? How did you manage that?"

Royal leaned back in his chair and sat in silent contemplation. "A respectable pirate does not share all his secrets," he answered eventually.

Clay snorted. "Is there such a thing as a respectable pirate? It seems to me you've made a living off of ill-gotten means." He gave Royal a long, hard stare. "As far as I know, the bounty for your capture still stands. What's stopping me from turning you over to the authorities and claiming the reward for myself?"

The pirate took another swallow from his tankard. "Two things come to mind. First is the length of steel blade beneath my cloak. I'm not a bloodthirsty man, but I will defend myself if need be. The second is that if you betray my confidence, you'll be in no position to help your friends at Dempster House."

Clay stiffened. "That's the second time you mentioned the orphanage. What game are you playing at?"

"No game. I've been watching the house all day. I saw you come and go and followed you here after you left. What's your connection to that place?"

"Connection? It's an orphanage. I grew up there. Look," Clay retorted, "you mentioned that they were in peril. What possible peril could they be in? And what business do you have spying on innocent children?"

"Innocent?" Royal lifted an eyebrow. "I gather at least one of them is not. And I need your help if we're to have any chance of keeping the rest of them out of danger."

+ + +

The rain beat steadily on the orphanage windows. Despite the sporadic boom of thunder, the ceaseless patter of the downpour eventually lulled the wards of Dempster House to sleep. The boys slept in the west bedrooms of the third floor, while the girls' rooms were on the east end of the second floor. Duncan Dempster abode on the third floor in a room closely situated near the staircase, to discourage any sudden midnight escapades on behalf of the boys. Fortunately, the girls were always well-behaved. But just in case, Nora Primm still kept a watchful eye out on behalf of Mr. Dempster, a fact for which he was exceedingly grateful.

All the boys seemed to be fast asleep. Except for one. Trying his best to imitate stealth, Warty tottered down the hallway on his tiptoes. But he wasn't very good at it. Despite the noisy plodding of his hurried footfalls, however, none of the boys awoke from their slumber.

Warty reached the door where Arthur shared a room with Carlton Fish and Jeremy Ibble. Softly pushing the door open, he peeked inside. A flash of lightning momentarily illuminated the room and Warty could see the still, sleeping form of Arthur Cross.

"Curse the brat!" Warty muttered to himself. The brief flash from the storm revealed that Arthur was sleeping with his new boots still on his feet. "What kind of person goes to bed with boots on?"

Warty slipped into the bedroom and closed the door quietly behind him. He wasn't sure what he was going to do. He had indeed come for the boots, but he wasn't certain he was a clever enough thief to steal a sleeping person's boots from off his feet. For a full minute he stood and studied the slumbering Arthur. After several seconds of painful mental calculations, Warty eventually decided he would start with the right boot. Tentatively, he reached for Arthur's ankle.

But before he even laid hands on the boot, Arthur leapt from the covers. "Aha!" he shouted.

The sudden exclamation caused both the sleeping Carlton and Jeremy to jump from their beds in confusion. "Whazzat?" sputtered Carlton.

Warty froze in panic. Being surrounded by three conscious people had not been part of his scheme. Even an amateur thief like Warty knew that this was not a very confident position.

Using his blanket like a net, Arthur bound onto Warty and tackled the surprised intruder. Without thinking, Carlton and Jeremy quickly jumped on the squirming bundle alongside Arthur. "We've got you now!" cried Jeremy. He turned to Arthur. "Who do we have?"

"It's Warty!" Arthur replied. "He's come to steal my boots!"

"Ha!" laughed Carlton. "This will teach you, Warty! No

one steals Arthur's boots except for Arthur." He didn't spare the time to consider the logic of that statement.

Arthur expertly tied the ends of the bundled blanket in a knot. "Go wake the others, Jeremy. It's time for a Secret Council. Do it quietly!"

Jeremy hurried from the room to tell the others. It had been sometime since the wards of Dempster House had covertly called for a Secret Council. Little did Duncan Dempster know how often trouble was averted by these clandestine gatherings. Whenever one of the residents of Dempster House was causing trouble, such as not doing his or her fair share of the work or simply making life generally disagreeable for everyone, the culprit was brought before the others without Mr. Dempster's knowledge. Together, the group discussed the problem and determined any appropriate method of punishment should the troublemaker refuse to comply with the Dempster House code of conduct. Sometimes the proposed remedies included putting sand in his or her meals, being excluded from any of the children's games, or (and this was Nigel Quimby's favorite) everyone taking turns waking the guilty individual every fifteen minutes in the night.

No one liked being the subject of a Secret Council, and for the most part, the children remained on their best behavior to avoid it. Life was simply better when everyone followed the agreed-upon rules. As a result, a midnight gathering had not been needed for quite some time. But Warty had not been at Dempster House long enough to know about the Secret Council and was wholly unaware of what kind of punishments were about to be brought down on him.

Silently, Carlton and Arthur pulled on the squirming bundle of Warty and carefully dragged him down the hall.

Sneaking past Mr. Dempster's bedroom door, Carlton felt around the lumpy blanket to locate Warty's mouth, clamping his hand over it to muffle his protests. Other boys soon stealthily filled the hall, awakened by the urgent prodding of Jeremy Ibble. One of the boys dashed down to the second floor to give Nora Primm the news about the Secret Council and instructions to wake the other girls.

Once in the parlor, Arthur and Carlton rolled the blanket-bound Warty onto the floor. Elliot revealed Warty's head but left the rest of him tangled in the blanket. Holding his candle high, Elliot turned to Arthur. "What's this all about?" Being the oldest and usually the one least involved with any trouble, he was always put in charge of the council meetings.

Bleary-eyed girls filtered into the parlor. Young Lizzie Marchcombe dragged her worn teddy bear behind her. Arthur waited for everyone to take a seat around the circle of candlelight before he answered. "Warty was caught trying to steal my boots!"

The girls gasped, and the boys simply shook their heads in brotherly disdain. "You should be ashamed of yourself, Warty." Nora scolded. "Stealing boots! From an orphan, no less!"

"It's a lie!" defended Warty. This was Warty's usual defense when someone accused him of something. It was typically not followed by any other explanation.

"It's not a lie," defended Jeremy. "Carlton and I both caught him in our room. For no good reason!"

Arthur folded his arms across his chest. "Not only did you try to steal my boots, Warty. But I know it was you behind the attempted murder of Chronos!"

At this terrible revelation, everyone's jaws dropped. "Attempted murder?" cried Carlton.

"That's not true!" Warty countered. But his face paled considerably in the candlelight.

With arms still folded and the boots still on his feet, Arthur marched in a slow circle around the accused. "I wondered what you were up to all of those afternoons chasing that stray cat around the grounds. At first I thought you were just being your usual wretched self and simply tormenting the poor beast. It wasn't until I found this—" Arthur held up a string of shoelaces knotted together in the form of a snare, "—that I suspected what you were doing. Using your very own shoelaces to capture it. You left your snare in the bushes where it sleeps."

"Now we know why you've been tromping around without your shoes on!" deduced Nora.

"Why would I want to catch some mangy cat?" defended Warty.

Arthur gave Warty a shrewd look. "Because you needed to get rid of Chronos. You knew that if you tried to break into the larder, Chronos would think it was mealtime and ring the bell!"

"I never broke into the larder!" Warty retorted.

Arthur reached behind the parlor sofa and produced a small bag. He dumped the contents onto the rug. "Then how do you explain this dirty bowl and spoon I found under your bed this afternoon?"

Elliot examined the bowl. "Pudding! That's what we had at lunch. You stole some pudding from the kitchen while we were busy trying to save Chronos!"

"After all those nasty looks you gave me at lunchtime, I suspected you were behind the whole thing. So I went looking for clues!"

Warty had grown considerably fidgety and pale as

Arthur laid out his case, which is never convincing behavior for someone who wants everyone to think he's innocent.

Arthur continued his explanation. "I was already expecting to call a Secret Council tonight and let everyone know what I found. That's why I had my boots on, the dishes hidden, and your shoelaces in my pocket. What I wasn't expecting was for you to come into my room to steal my boots!"

"I wasn't stealing your boots!"

Carlton scoffed. "You're still clinging to that old lie? What were you doing in our room, then?"

Warty screwed his face into a look of spiteful reproach. "Maybe I was trying to get my shoelaces back!" he countered, not realizing that he had just admitted that they were indeed his shoelaces.

Elliot grabbed hold of the blanket and gave Warty a firm shake. "Why were you trying to steal Arthur's boots?" he asked. As he shook the bundled Warty, something shiny dropped from the folds of the blanket and it hit the rug with a solid thud.

"What's this?" Nora asked, picking it up from the floor.

Elliot pulled his attention away from Warty and looked in Nora's open hand. With a soft whistle, he raised it up and watched it glitter in the candlelight.

"It's a Spanish doubloon!"

+ + +

At the same moment that Elliot was whistling over the golden doubloon, grappling hooks were flying through the rain and snagging the rooftop of Dempster House. With skill and experience, the sodden, burly men scrambled up the taut lines to the third story windows just as if they were boarding an enemy vessel. The sporadic flashes of lightning betrayed their swarthy, growling faces. Some had straight, razor-sharp knives clenched in their jagged teeth, while one had a long, sheathed sword dangling from his leather belt.

There was no denying from their clothes and appearance that these men were pirates. They were, in fact, the very same men from whom Warty had received the golden doubloon. In return, Warty was to perform the simple task of stealing Arthur's new pair of boots from underneath his bed and deliver them to the brigands. But when Warty failed to show up at the gate, they were convinced that they had been swindled and decided to take matters into their own hands. The bandits, however, were not exactly certain which third-floor room Warty was in and decided that they'd simply invade them all.

The rain-soaked pirates crashed through the bedroom windows, swords and knives at the ready. But they were taken aback when they realized all the beds were empty.

+   +   +

Lizzie Marchcombe was the first to jump out of her seat at the sound of breaking glass. "What was that?" she cried.

All the children in the parlor had heard it and any thoughts of Warty's impending punishment fled from their minds. Elliot peered into the foyer. "Sounds like trouble! Come on, guys!" Immediately, he and the other boys dashed up the staircase. The gang of boys, being what they were, didn't take the time to consider what manner of danger might be waiting for them on the third floor.

After all, there comes a unique kind of confidence when a person is in his own home and surrounded by good friends. With the clamor of shattering windows and the thunderous rampage of several boys on the staircase, it was no wonder that Duncan Dempster had been awoken from his sleep.

Just as they reached the landing of the third floor, Mr. Dempster had yanked open his bedroom door to be greeted by their stunned faces. It was a confusing moment for everybody, and several questions raced through the minds of the children. What was the cause of the shattering glass? What was going to happen now that Mr. Dempster had caught them out of bed in the middle of the night? Where did Mr. Dempster get that unusual night cap on his head?

"What the devil is going on?" demanded Mr. Dempster irritably. "What's all this racket?"

"We're not sure, sir," answered Elliot. "It came from our rooms!"

As if to add to the disorientation, the doors of the boy's bedrooms flung open and five dripping and horrid pirates filled the corridor. The sight sent Nigel Quimby and a few of the other boys running back down the stairs in terror. Duncan Dempster and the others simply stood dumbfounded on the landing.

The largest of the invaders was a barrel of a man. A stiff, jagged beard jutted from his weather-scarred visage like bristles on a horse-brush. His eyes were shielded by thick dark brows that were connected over a bulbous nose. And most disturbing of all was the gnarled wooden stump that the man used for a left leg. The brutish scoundrel approached Dempster and the boys with a menacing skill that belied the fact that he had only one proper foot.

"Avast, there! Where's them boots?" he shouted. Just as the fearsome pirate spoke the words, his eyes landed on Arthur at the top of the stairs. "There they be! Get him, men!"

"Snakes and garters!" shouted Dempster. "Run, lads!"

Dempster and the boys dashed down the steps with unprecedented speed. The band of pirates scrambled over each other, brandishing their blades and clubs. The young boys had a distinct advantage--they had sprinted down the stairs countless times before. For an adult, Duncan Dempster did an impressive job of keeping up. The pirates were not quite as fast, especially as they crowded around their one-legged captain.

When they reached the bottom, Arthur pointed to the floor. "The rug, guys!" Elliot and Carlton understood immediately. The two boys grabbed the carpet that ran down the length of the staircase. With a mighty yank, the rug pulled taut and slid from beneath the feet of the descending marauders.

What followed was an avalanche of tumbling bandits whose yells of terror became howls of surprise, each trying to prevent themselves from being sandwiched between the wooden steps and their sodden comrades.

Everyone at the bottom of the stairs scattered as the invaders spilled from the steps. Elliot dashed to the parlor where the girls were still gathered. "Run, everybody! Quickly!"

Duncan Dempster had reached the front door, but as he grasped for the knob, the door flew open.

Another figure burst in from the pounding rain, a dripping cutlass in his hand.

In the doorway stood the pirate Archie Royal. Behind

him, Clay Cross pocketed the key to the front gate. "Well, well!" remarked Royal as he spied the heap of men at the base of the stairs. "If it isn't my old first mate, Thaddeus Schark, and that old worm-infested log you use for a leg. How have you been?"

The burly bearded pirate picked himself awkwardly from off the floor. His band of men clumsily attempted to assist him, but Schark shoved them away. "Royal! It was only a matter of time before you showed your face again. I have to say the eye patch is a distinct improvement. At least that's one piece of your sorry visage we no longer have to look at."

Royal sheathed his dripping cutlass and unbuttoned his long coat. Hanging neatly within were four flintlocks. "I don't expect you and your men to get any clever ideas—it's never happened before—but just in case, you should know that the powder in these pistols is quite dry." He handed two of the weapons to Clay and Duncan. "Keep these guns leveled at our guests and be ready to shoot." At the sight of the loaded flintlocks, Schark's crewmen paled visibly.

"I remember you!" Duncan replied. "You're the stranger from earlier today! How is it you know these intruders?"

"This isn't the time to be trading tales," Royal answered. He leveled his own pistol at Schark. "Alright, Thaddeus. We're taking the boy. Boots and all. And I don't want to see so much as your misshapen shadow behind us or it will mean the worst for you. Understood?"

"You're not going anywhere," Thaddeus growled. "If you run out of here, you'll be leaving every soul in this rotten booger factory at my mercy! Who knows what will happen to all these helpless little children after you're gone?"

Duncan looked nervously at Royal. "He's right! It's too dangerous for the boys and girls!"

Thaddeus smirked at Dempster's anxiety and licked his lips in victory. "That's right. But if you hand over the boots, me and my men will leave, never to return. How's that for an arrangement?"

Royal responded by pulling back the cocks of the pistols. "No deal, Thaddeus. The children are leaving with me. And you and your men will stay right here. Boy," he looked at Arthur, "gather everyone together and we'll take our leave of this place."

"The girls are in the parlor," informed Arthur as he dashed away.

Thaddeus Schark's eyes turned pitch black in anger. "You'll never get away, Royal! You're still outnumbered, even with a brace of pistols in your paws. It's gonna take a lot more than a few lead balls to stop us!" He looked at the uncertain Dempster and young Clay Cross, who both seemed a little too unfamiliar with the guns in their grips. "And I'll wager your comrades here couldn't hit a broadside at five yards."

Royal glanced over his shoulder as Arthur returned from the parlor, the girls following him with wide eyes. Royal turned his watchful gaze back to Schark and smiled. "You know, Thaddeus, you're right. I guess I'll simply have to even the odds!"

Suddenly Royal squeezed the trigger of his right pistol. The lead ball ripped into Schark's wooden stump of a leg and it erupted in a shower of splinters. Schark's hefty frame toppled helplessly to the ground and the pirates jumped for cover. The girls screamed in unison and the foyer erupted into chaos.

"Run!" Archie Royal shouted.

The children didn't hesitate. They bolted out the front

door and into the pouring rain, with Clay, Duncan, and the pirate following behind.

As the brigade of shouting children fled the orphanage, Thaddeus Schark's men clumsily stumbled over each other to help him to his feet. "Leave me be, you lousy oafs! Bring me those boots!" he bellowed. The four pirates dropped their heavy captain and scurried for the door.

In only a few ticks of the clock, Dempster House was vacant and silent. Thaddeus Schark awkwardly tried to climb to his good knee but slipped under his weight. "Blast!" he growled as he studied the broken and splintered remains of his stump. He glanced around the large empty foyer. A wriggling form in the parlor caught his attention. There rolled the chubby form of Warty, still bound in blanket and bedclothes, unable to free himself. For a moment, the two stared at each other in silence. "Double blast!" Schark muttered.

+ + +

The rain continued to drench the band of children fleeing down the streets. Archie Royal grabbed Arthur's arm and turned to the others. "We'll have to split up. It's the best chance we have!"

Dempster with his soaked nightcap and dripping flintlock stared in befuddlement. "Where on earth are we to go?"

"Take the children and head to the Owl and Hearth," Clay answered. "Mr. Garfox will let you in. You'll be safe there!"

"But where are you going?" Dempster asked.

The yells of pursuing pirates halted any answers. "No need to concern yourself with that!" replied Royal. "Now, run!"

And so, the groups parted ways. So frenzied was that moment in the relentless downpour and so disconcerting were the oaths of their angry pursuers that Arthur didn't have the wits to think things through. If it had occurred to him that he may never see dear Mr. Dempster again or play once more with his friends upon the grounds of the orphanage, he might have said goodbye, or daresay, even cried a little. But there was neither time nor choice. In the bleak, damp darkness, Arthur and Clay dashed after the pirate Archie Royal, and the good Mr. Dempster bustled the gang of frightened children down the winding streets of town.

6
The Ivory Typhoon

As Arthur followed Clay and Royal through the dank alleys, it slowly occurred to him that he had never been in the city at night, nor did he recall ever being down these particular streets. His lungs were burning from their desperate pace, but he knew that if he didn't keep up, he would be utterly lost. The soaking rain dripped through his hair and into his eyes, and he continually wiped the blinding drops from his face. His feet stumbled on the wet cobblestones, and on one occasion, he tripped and landed so hard into a puddle that he was certain his kneecap was bleeding.

But there was nothing to done about it. Clay grabbed him by the hand and picked him up rather forcefully. "Come on, Arthur! I know you're tired, but we can't stop!"

"Where are we going? Who are those people?" Arthur asked.

"Quiet!" barked Royal. "No noise until we're safe!"

The mysterious pirate slipped into the shadows of a dark alleyway and when Arthur followed, the sharp, salty air of the sea filled his nostrils. "We're near the docks!" he exclaimed.

"Shush!" scolded the pirate. "Of course we are. Can you think of a better place to moor a ship?"

Royal reached the end of the narrow alley and peered around the corner. Between the walls, Arthur discerned the stretching yardarms of a vessel, draped with furled sails and rigging. After one more searching gaze up and down the street—and one more behind them—Royal beckoned. "The coast is clear. Follow me!" He dashed from the alley and into the open rain. Clay and Arthur followed without any argument. Soon, the three reached the foot of a gangplank that stretched above the water and onto a three-masted ship. It was a handsome vessel, well-kept, and neat. But Arthur noticed her lines were a little unusual. The hull had an odd shape in some places, and much of the ship's rigging consisted of strange, square-ish chain instead of rope.

"Alright," Royal said, as he pocketed the spent pistol in his grip, "this is where we part ways. Give me the boots, boy."

Arthur was stunned. Clay spoke up first. "What do you mean? You're going to rob us and leave us here in the rain? With those brigands after us, no less?"

"You've got nothing to fear from them. It's Shorty's boots they're after. As long as I have them, it'll be me they'll pursue. If you know what's best for ye, you'll hand 'em over!"

"What's this all about?" demanded Arthur.

"This isn't a time for explanations. Schark's numb-skulls may not have all their oars in the water, but they have enough brains to look for the *Typhoon* at the docks. They'll be here in no time! Now, off with the boots!"

"I have no more intention of giving my boots to you as I was to those bandits!" countered Arthur.

Royal whisked his cutlass from beneath the folds of his coat with one sudden sweep. "And what makes ye think

I'll take no for an answer? What's keeping me from taking those boots, with or without your little feet still in them? I could settle this quickly and silently with one blow."

Arthur's eyes narrowed. "You had a loaded pistol pointed at your enemy, and you didn't kill him. Why do you think I'd be convinced that you'd kill a simple boy?"

At this, Royal stood frozen and grim, raindrops bouncing off the silver blade of his cutlass. His one good eye studied the boy for what seemed an eternity.

"Enough of this!" interjected Clay. "Those brigands are on their way. We don't have time to play games!" He grabbed his brother around the waist and started running up the gangplank.

"Avast there!" shouted Royal, as he chased after them.

"You said you'd take his boots with or without his feet in them," Clay called back as he ran onto the ship. "Well, now you have them! Feet and all!"

"Broadsides and conflagration!" muttered Royal angrily. He bolted up the gangplank after them. "Get aboard and stay out of the way while I disembark!"

Clay dropped Arthur onto the wooden deck. Wiping the rain from their faces, they looked about them in amazement. The two had not been on a ship before, but they knew enough about them to recognize that this craft was truly unusual. Like other sea vessels, this one had a wheel aft for turning the rudder (although this one seemed unusually large), and a capstan forward for weighing the anchor. Rigging reached upward into the top sails, and hatches could be seen going below decks. But amidst all of these, several levers and brass handles with white bone grips protruded from the deck. Many were clustered around the captain's wheel. Others dotted the rails. Here and there, the odd chains with square links hung from the yard arms connected to immense gears that protruded from slots in the ship's wooden deck. In other places, the chains were connected to ornate cranks.

Clay looked around him and noticed another strange detail. "Where's your crew?"

Royal climbed behind the ship's wheel. "The *Ivory Typhoon* needs no crew but me. Stand back, and don't get too close to anything." The pirate gripped one of the bone-handled levers and gave it a yank.

Immediately, the ratcheting sound of turning chains ripped the air. Arthur felt the ship vibrate beneath him as something massive groaned within the depths of the lower decks. The sound of sloshing water signaled that a dripping anchor had lifted from the sea.

With another deft pull of a lever, the metal chains whirred overhead. Sails unfurled and Arthur and Clay felt the ship list under the harnessed force of wind. Soon, the entire vessel was turning out to sea and slipping away from the dim lights of the docks.

And not a moment too soon. "Look!" Arthur pointed to the quay where two of their pursuers emerged from the black streets. One of them tugged a rusty pistol from his trousers and leveled it at Royal's head. Luck was against him, though. The hammer of the pistol fell with a disappointed thud.

"Ha!" laughed Royal. "You won't accomplish much with wet powder in them pea shooters!" he shouted at them.

The other pirate pulled his own flintlock from beneath his cloak. This rascal was a bit more careful with his arsenal. The pistol belched with an explosive cloud of smoke and the ball whistled vengefully through the air.

Royal dropped to the deck in surprise. The lead ball buried itself into the wooden mizzen mast inches above Arthur's head.

In his brief span of life, Arthur had never been shot at so it was no discredit to him when he yelped in fright and dove to the deck. In his haste, he smashed against one of the many levers and it fell backward with a determined clank.

Another heavy thud jolted the floor beneath and a small cannon rose up from the aft deck. Without hesitation, the cannon bellowed to life. A screaming cannonball burst mercilessly into the cobblestones beneath the feet of the two bandits. With cries of surprise, the two men were sent reeling into the air in a cloud of stone and mortar.

Royal lifted his head from the deck, his amazement quickly turning to mirth. "Haha! That's what we call 'parting words', you rascals! Give my regards to that one-legged bilge pump you call a captain!"

He made a small adjustment to the ship's massive wheel and the vessel set itself toward the open sea. Then the pirate strolled toward Arthur. He pulled the boy from the deck with a quick yank. "I told you not to touch anything!"

"It was an accident," Arthur replied.

"What kind of ship is this?" Clay asked.

"A sunk one if the King's Navy investigates who it be that's firing cannons in their port," Royal answered. "Let's get below and dry off. The *Typhoon* isn't built for guests, but I'm sure I can find you a billet."

+ + +

The sunbeam that fell through the porthole wandered back and forth with the listing of the *Ivory Typhoon* and played across Arthur's sleeping face. His eyes blinked open and shut as his memories slowly gathered themselves. He was on a ship, and he could hear the sloshing of the waves slapping the hull on the other side. Immediately, the events of last night sprang into his consciousness.

Arthur bolted upright before realizing he was in a swaying hammock. He tumbled onto the wooden floor with a thud. He looked about him and spied his boots standing neatly near the door. The events of last night were something of a blur, and he must have pulled them off before falling asleep. He snatched them up and began examining them carefully. These boots, and their mysterious past, were the center of all the evening's escapades, and it was clear to him that they must be hiding something of value.

Arthur's fingers poured over the left boot. As far as he could see, the boot had nothing particularly curious about it other than the smell. The inside leg held a slim pocket, though, which he surmised (to his delight) was for sheathing a small dagger. The most useful place to hide something in a boot, Arthur figured, was in its heel. The heel seemed firmly fastened, though, and Arthur saw no physical way to remove it.

He turned his attention to the right boot and was excited to see that this boot's heel was slightly different. A small, barely visible seam could only mean that it was meant to detach. With great effort, Arthur began twisting at it furiously. Despite his persistence, the stubborn wooden heel wouldn't budge.

"Perhaps a bit of coaxing," Arthur figured.

He hammered the boot onto the hard floor with all his

might. His brother, snoring in the next hammock, awoke with a start. "What's that?" he blurted.

Arthur paid him no attention but instead kept banging the obstinate boot against the deck.

"What are you doing, Arthur?" growled Clay groggily. "I'm trying to sleep."

"There's something hidden in this boot. That must be why the pirates wanted it so badly. But I can't get it open."

Clay laid back in his hammock. "Well, it's not going to open with you beating it on the floor. If that were the trick, it would have opened every time you ran up and down the stairs at Dempster House."

Arthur stopped and stared at the boot. "I hadn't thought of that. There must be a catch inside." He peered within the stinky interior. Sure enough, a small indentation lay at the bottom. Arthur fished his finger into the hole and with a click, the heel of the boot easily slid open. "It worked!"

Clay was suddenly revived with curious energy. He slid out of the hammock. "What's in there?"

Arthur peered into the opened heel. His face fell. "It's empty!"

Clay sighed as he climbed back into the hammock. "Isn't that always the way with pirate stories! The treasure is long gone by the time you reach it."

Arthur's face twisted in indignation. "Royal!" Jumping to his feet, he threw open the door and ran out of the cabin.

Clay slid back out of his hammock again. "Arthur! Where are you going?"

When Arthur had finally found his way to the *Ivory Typhoon's* topside, he halted as his squinting eyes adjusted to the bright sunlight. The pirate Royal was standing benignly behind the over-sized wheel of the ship. He stared casually at the bedraggled, fuming boy. "So, you finally decided to wake up!" he greeted gruffly. "Perhaps the sun doesn't rise until noon for you landlubbers."

Arthur threw the boot onto the deck and pointed. "You stole it!"

Royal's one eye filled with an odd mixture of offense and bemusement. "What is it you accuse me of stealing, lad?"

Clay emerged from the decks below. "What are you doing, Arthur?"

Arthur pointed again at the boot and then at Royal. "He stole...he stole the...he stole whatever was in my boot!"

Royal laughed. "The boy calls me a thief, and he doesn't even know what I'm said to have thieved!"

Arthur thrust an angry finger at him. "I may be a boy, but I'm not stupid. You went through a lot of trouble to keep these boots from those ruffians at Dempster House—boots with a secret compartment that holds nothing."

Clay intervened. "I'm sorry, sir. My brother is a bit impetuous."

Royal interrupted Clay with an upheld hand. "No apologies. Your brother is right about my wanting the boots. But I take offense at being called a thief."

"You slipped into the cabin while we were sleeping and stole whatever was in this boot, didn't you?" insisted Arthur.

"Well," Royal said shiftily. "The word I would use would be more along the lines of 'borrowed.'"

"You stole!" refuted Arthur.

"Borrowed," Royal repeated. He reached into his jacket and pulled out a small round object. "And to prove it to you, I'm giving it back." He tossed it to the boy. It was a small coin, both sides of which were terribly scratched and scarred.

"This is gold!" Arthur exclaimed excitedly.

"Let me see that!" His brother grabbed the coin and examined it closely. "This must be worth...worth...well, I don't know how much. It must be a lot."

"Aye," shrugged Royal. "As far as gold goes, it would fetch a fair price. If money's all you want, that is."

Arthur's eyes narrowed. "Why are you giving it back?"

"I told you. I only borrowed it." Royal turned his attention back to the ship's wheel and the distant horizon. "You're welcome to it. Provided you don't mind blackards like Thaddeus Schark hounding you all your days."

Clay crossed his arms. "It may be worth a lot, but not enough to send a band of thugs into an orphanage for. I'd think pirates like Schark—or you, for that matter—would be after bigger prizes than this. There's something you're not telling us."

"You're right. It's not worth my time. That's why I'm giving it back."

Arthur shook his head in mock surrender. "I guess if those pirates back there want it, we should just hand it over to them. Shouldn't we, Clay? I mean, it's not worth having them hold a sword over our heads."

"What?" asked Clay in surprise. "Hand it over? Are you mad? It's still gold."

Arthur elbowed him in the side...a quick brotherly reminder to play along. Clay caught on to Arthur's ploy.

"Oh, yes!" Clay somehow nodded and shook his head at the same time. "It's not worth our lives, Arthur."

"And then," Arthur continued, "Thaddeus Schark will have it. And will know everything Royal knows."

Archie Royal stopped turning the wheel of the *Ivory Typhoon* and gave Arthur a hard stare. "What is it you're getting at, lad?"

The boy merely shrugged as he took the coin nonchalantly from Clay's hand "It seems obvious that this coin is important enough to chase after, but not important enough to keep. That means you were only interested in something else. Perhaps this curious inscription around the edge."

Abruptly, Royal lunged for the coin, but Arthur deftly ducked behind Clay. "What are you talking about? What inscription?" the pirate asked.

"Didn't you see it? Is that why you were so ready to throw it out?" goaded Arthur.

"Give me that, boy!" Royal growled.

Clay stood firmly in front of his younger brother. "Not until you tell us what this is about!" he demanded, shielding Arthur from the scowling pirate.

"And give us some breakfast," added Arthur.

The pirate Archie Royal uttered a single 'Blast!" and trudged to the galley below.

✦ ✦ ✦

The two boys delved into their plates of salted bacon and biscuits. It was meager fare, but after their exciting night and late rising, it was utterly delicious to Clay and Arthur. While the two were devouring their breakfast between gulps of cold cocoa, Archie Royal was squinting at the edge of the coin with his one good eye. "Blast and conflagration!" he muttered. "Whoever engraved this must have been the size of boll weevil's button. I can barely make it out!"

"What does it say?" asked Clay while he munched on a biscuit.

"Didn't your mother ever teach you not to talk with your mouth full?" Royal replied.

Arthur gave Royal a look of contempt. "Does the word 'orphan' mean anything to you?"

"Hmmph!" Royal returned his attention to the coin.

"What is it?" Clay asked, after swallowing the rest of his biscuit. "Is it some sort of treasure map?"

Royal continued his examination of the piece of gold. "Of a sort. Yes. This here coin is rumored to be the lost Coin of Cordura. It's been missing for several hundred years."

"The Coin of Cordura? Where's Cordura?"

"Not where. Cordura is a who. A Spaniard who made a map that, along with this coin, led to El Khudir, an old kingdom that holds a very special treasure. The map was found, but the coin had always been missing."

"So it is a map!" Arthur exclaimed.

"For years," Royal said, as he studied the inscription closely, "I searched for this coin. It finally surfaced in the hands of the insufferable Captain Riga, who has since vanished mysteriously. His disappearance would normally have delighted me, but I feared that the coin had vanished with him. Fortunately, that's no longer the case. The Coin of Cordura eventually found its way into the hands of my old shipmate Shorty Buckets and then into your little orphanage. And so here the three of us sit, sailing through the Straits of Gibraltar."

"If you had been searching so long for this coin," Clay asked, "why were you so willing to let us keep it?"

Royal tipped back in his chair, rubbing the gold coin between his fingers. "The faces of the coin have been so badly scratched, it seemed whatever clue that had been there was gone forever. Without the clue from the coin, I figured the location of El Khudir would remain lost for all time. That all changed when young Master Cross spied this tiny inscription."

Arthur beamed proudly. Clay leaned forward for a closer look at the coin. "Can you read it?"

Royal turned the coin in his hands. "It says *Where the two that shall never meet come face to face S75°E, N12°E.*" Puzzled, he tore his gaze from the coin and stared into the dark corner of the galley.

"It sounds like coordinates for a map," Arthur said.

Royal remained in contemplative silence.

"So what does it mean?" Clay asked. "Where's S75°E, N12° E?"

"It's nowhere," muttered Royal. "Those aren't map co-ordinates. They're compass bearings. But they don't mean anything without a starting point. And even if you knew where to start, you still know nothing about how far to go and when to stop. Blast!" Without warning, Royal threw the coin hard against the *Typhoon's* bulkhead, leaving it spinning on the galley floor. He jumped from his seat and marched irritably up the steps to the deck.

Clay called after him. "So what are we going to do now?"

Royal stopped. "We? We aren't doing anything. You are going to decide whether you want to be put to shore in Spain or Italy."

It was Arthur's turn to jump from his seat. "You mean you're going to maroon us?"

Royal gave him a dirty look. "It's not marooning if it's in a city."

"It makes no difference," Clay argued. "We don't speak Italian or Spanish! It might as well be a desert island!"

"And I'd be happy to oblige you, if there was a convenient desert island nearby! I've taken you boys further than I intended, so it's time we parted ways."

"Is that the kind of man you are?" Clay retorted. "You got what you wanted and now you're going to cast two orphans overboard when you have no need for us?"

Archie Royal waved a stern finger at Clay. "It was you who insisted on coming aboard. All I wanted was the boots!"

"Then why don't you take us back to Dempster House in England instead of abandoning us on some strange coast?"

"That would be utter madness. I'd be lucky to have a day's lead on Thaddeus and his crew. I won't be doubling back with him chasing me. To say nothing of the King's Navy prowling about. I'm a wanted man, after all."

"What about Thaddeus Schark?" asked Arthur. He picked the discarded coin from off the floor. "What's stopping us from handing the coin over to him and his gang? Then he would have the clue to the lost city."

"And fat good it would do him, too!" Royal shot back. "That clue is as worthless as a barnacle on a bench seat, especially to an oaf like him."

"Wait!" Clay exclaimed. "What if we were to figure the clue out? Would that be helpful to you?"

"Yes!" joined in Arthur. "If we can discover its meaning, can we stay aboard?"

Royal cast his good eye up and down the two boys while he contemplated their proposal. "You're not just pulling my leg, are you? Are you telling me you can decipher that bit of gibberish?"

"It's perfectly reasonable to think that this Spaniard wouldn't leave a clue if he didn't intend someone to discover what it means," Clay answered. "And if you need a clever head to figure it out, you're not going to find anyone better than Arthur." Clay put an arm around his little brother. "He has a knack for these kinds of things."

Royal scratched a gray sideburn in thought. "You want to stay aboard that badly, do you?"

"We've no place to go," Arthur pleaded.

Royal pondered the situation silently. With Schark pursuing not far behind, putting to shore would only cost valuable time. And there was still the possibility that the boy could unravel the mysterious riddle on the coin. If that were so, then it certainly wouldn't do to leave them to be captured by Schark and his brigands. On the other hand, the boys couldn't possibly comprehend the peril in which they were placing themselves.

The pirate continued to balance these thoughts in his brain. Clay and Arthur Cross waited in rapt silence.

"Alright, boys," Royal finally answered. "You can stay aboard. But," he warned, "you had better have an answer to that silly riddle in a few days' time."

"What happens in a few days?" asked Clay.

"We land near Malta," Royal answered. "And if you don't have it figured out by then, I cast off without you. And you," he continued, pointing a finger at Clay, "are going to help me sail this vessel, cook the meals, and help keep a watch for that scoundrel Schark on our stern while your brother tries to make sense of that lousy doubloon."

"Yes, sir!" Clay and Arthur heartily replied.

+ + +

The following days were like none Clay had ever experienced. He had never dreamed about being a sailor, although the idea had crossed his mind on occasion. As long as Arthur still resided at Dempster House, it would have been impossible for Clay to even consider a life at sea. He was surprised at how it seemed almost second nature to him. He adapted easily to the rolling of the *Ivory Typhoon* under his feet and he never once felt any seasickness. Arthur, on the other hand, spent the next two days in misery as his stomach adjusted to the constant motion.

Aside from the expected pitching and rolling, Clay found that the *Ivory Typhoon* was a ship like no other. It was not a huge vessel. There were three decks, not counting the top deck. The lower decks consisted of a hold at the very bottom and the upper deck seemed innocuous enough with cabins and galley. The tween deck, though, was the most peculiar thing. Stuffed with all manner of mechanisms and contraptions, it was the heart of the vessel. Intricate pulleys and gears allowed operation of everything from the sails to the cannons with just the simple pull of a lever. Like a giant pocket watch upon the sea, the mechanics needed constant winding, and Clay was tasked with checking these hourly. A clever wheel-like device at the stern protruded into the sea, which was turned constantly by the force of the rushing water. This motion was then transferred to some of the workings of the tween deck, keeping the many levers primed for action.

After a few days of working with the odd devices, his curiosity got the better of him and he worked up the courage to ask Archie Royal about it.

"Where did this ship come from?"

Royal stood at the wheel, his attention focused on the expanse of sea before him. At first, he seemed reluctant to answer but then replied. "It was built by a friend of mine.

He's a genius when it comes to mechanical things. As he was building it, I told him it would never sail. Or even stay afloat, for that matter."

"I guess you were wrong," Clay said.

The look in Royal's eye was not one of appreciation.

"Sorry!" Clay quickly corrected. "I didn't mean to insult you. I just meant that it sails very well. I mean, not that I would know better than an expert seaman like yourself."

Royal softened a bit. "Well, you're right. She does sail mighty fine. A better ship I've never known."

"I have a hard time thinking you do much pirating in it, though. How do you ever manage without any crew?"

"I told you," Royal replied. "I'm not a pirate any longer. I gave that up many years ago."

"The King's Navy isn't convinced," pointed out Clay. "I still read about their bounty on your head and about them searching for you."

"Well, it takes an unimaginative sort to be in the King's Navy. Once a pirate, always a pirate in their eyes. Don't get me wrong, boy. The things I did weren't particularly nice, no matter which way you cut 'em. Let's just agree that the Navy thinks those things I did shouldn't be forgotten, while I, on the other hand, think they're not worth remembering at all."

Clay settled onto a nearby cask. "If you're not a pirate anymore, what do you do? Why are you out here, sailing to Malta, being pursued by a band of buccaneers, looking for some secret treasure? Sounds a lot like a pirate to me."

"I guess you can say that I carry a very peculiar letter of marque."

"A letter of marque? From whom?" asked Clay.

Royal jerked his attention from the horizon and frowned

at Clay. "Don't you have something better to do than to nettle me with questions?"

Clay shook his head. "No. Your ship virtually runs itself."

"Good. That gives you plenty of time to start cooking supper, then. Beef and gravy, buttered biscuits with jam, boiled peas, and fresh lemonade."

"Lemonade?" Clay's brow wrinkled with confusion.

"Fresh lemonade, with lots of sugar." Royal retorted. "When you hear the bell chime, I'll be down in five minutes to eat."

"When does the bell chime?" Clay asked.

"When I'm hungry."

Clay considered this for only a moment before realizing it was a dismissal. Hopping from the cask, he wandered below deck. *Might as well see how Arthur is doing,* he thought to himself.

Arthur, as was his routine, was buried in their makeshift bunk. Deciphering the inscription or discerning the marred surfaces on the coin had been unpleasantly and consistently interrupted with waves of seasickness. But the past day, the churning in his stomach had lessened, and the clouds of discomfort began to clear.

"You're looking a bit less green around the gills," Clay greeted.

Arthur sat in the corner, studying the mysterious gold coin closely. He looked up and grinned sheepishly at Clay. "Yeah, I'm feeling a lot better. I guess I'm not cut out to be a pirate."

"That's not such a bad thing, I suppose. How's it coming with our little puzzle?"

Arthur shook his head. "I can't figure it out. '*Where the two that shall never meet come face to face*' doesn't make any sense. Who is that referring to?"

"Maybe it's not people, but something else. Landmarks, maybe?" suggested Clay.

"I considered that. I wish I could see the map that Royal mentioned. It might have some helpful clues."

Clay shook his head. "We won't see that map until we reach our destination somewhere near Malta. By then, it might be too late. I'm not certain we can string Royal along once we get there. He'll want answers or we're stranded."

"How much time do we have?"

"Royal's expecting to reach the island in a few days. With this wind at our back, we might get there even sooner."

Arthur's spirits sank. "I'll keep at it, I guess."

"I'll do what I can to help you, but it's really beyond me." Clay decided to change the subject. "I'm off to the galley to make some dinner. Do you feel up to beef and gravy?"

Arthur's face turned a distinct shade of green at the mention of food. He clasped his hand to his mouth. "No thanks!" he muffled.

+ + +

Clay bustled feverishly in the galley, preparing the evening supper for Captain Royal. Over the past few days at sea, Royal never demanded anything more complicated than baked beans and tea, and Clay simply assumed that this was the extent of his diet. Now, he was forced to strain the limits of the *Ivory Typhoon's* larder. Fortunately, his job at the Owl and Hearth had given him sufficient skills at preparing food. Despite his valiant efforts, however, he was unable to hide the overpowering taste of salt in the beef. The biscuits were as hard as bricks, and no amount of butter could soften them. Next, Clay turned his attention to the lemonade. He found a crate of lemons, but they appeared to have been picked before the invention of the wheel. Their peels were shriveled and as dry as stone, and the pulp was not much better. Each pathetic lemon offered up only a few drips of juice, and Clay realized he had exhausted the entire crate with only half a pitcher to show for his labor. He had just finished doctoring the jug with water and sugar when he heard the warning chime of the bell.

Quickly, Clay set the table with the food, plates, and silverware. The sound of Royal's boots marched toward the galley at a merciless pace. Clay masterfully filled an empty tankard with lemonade without spilling a single drop—another skill gained from his service at the tavern—just as the captain entered the galley.

"Your dinner is served, Captain," Clay greeted.

Royal stopped abruptly. His good eye narrowed with suspicion. "That smells like awfully fine grub. Where did you get it?"

"From your stores, of course." Clay slid a chair from the table and beckoned the pirate to sit. As Royal accepted the seat, Clay expertly draped a napkin about his dinner guest's neck.

Royal peered into his tankard. "What is this?"

"Lemonade."

"Freshly squeezed lemonade? How on earth...?"

"Freshly strangled would be more accurate," responded Clay.

Royal took a cautious sip from the tankard. The glint in his eye changed from suspicion to pleasant surprise and he smacked his lips in delight. "Well, saddle me a seahorse! Lemonade hasn't touched this tongue of mine in years!"

Rapturously, he took a long draught before setting it down and wiping his lip with his sleeve.

Clay began heaping beef onto Royal's plate. The delighted captain watched the young man keenly as he served. "I'll tell you this, Mr. Clay...you've got the makings of a gentleman."

The sudden compliment took Clay by surprise that he almost ladled gravy into the mug of lemonade. "Thank you, Captain, but I would think the expectations for a gentleman do not include serving dinner."

"Nay. Being a gentleman is not what you do, but how you do it. It's been quite some time since I've been in the company of people. It's not hard for even me to realize that my manners are a bit...gruff." Clay was about to politely protest, but Royal prevented him with a raised hand. "I've tried to take your property, pilfered from under your noses while you slept, and threatened to maroon you in a foreign land. In all, I've been far from cordial. Yet, despite all that, you're still gracious enough to make me a fine meal. I've met noblemen who can't hold a candle to such behavior."

The somewhat embarrassed Clay wasn't sure how to respond. "I appreciate the compliment, Captain Royal, but I guess I don't quite feel the same way. As I see it, you saved both my brother and me from Thaddeus Schark and his men. To say nothing about saving Mr. Dempster and our friends at Dempster House." Royal made a slight harrumph as if clearing his throat. Clay surmised this was his way of hiding his own embarrassment. "And," Clay continued, "you've been gracious enough to provide us a with a berth, even though we invited ourselves aboard."

"Small things," Royal countered. "Not worth mentioning."

"Well, I suppose I'm not fit to be in the King's Navy, then. I prefer to remember the decent things people do, and not the horrible ones. I've found it's a helpful attitude to have when one is an orphan like Arthur and myself."

"I would never have guessed it," Royal laughed, "but it seems we have something in common. We're both orphans, of sorts. No real place—or people—to call our own."

Clay seated himself across the table. "If it wasn't for Duncan Dempster taking me and Arthur in, I don't know what would have become of us. He's not family, but he certainly feels like it."

"Aye," Royal nodded. "I know the feeling. Years ago, my own crew, led by Thaddeus Schark himself, mutinied against me. I barely escaped with my head on my shoulders. I never felt more alone than when I was adrift with nothing but a barrel in the midst of the ocean."

"How did you survive?" Clay asked.

Royal was silent for a moment. His eye was staring right through his dinner plate at some distant memory. "Cog, sailing this very vessel, found me bobbing in the sea. A kind soul, he is. He took me in, much like your Mr. Dempster. Even though they had every reason to hate me, Cog and the others treated me as one of their own."

"Every reason to hate you? I take it they didn't care for pirates, then?"

"Pirates?" Royal seemed to wake from his memories. "Well, I guess you could say that." He picked up his fork and began tearing into his slab of gravy-covered beef. He chewed silently while Clay watched, waiting for the captain to continue his tale. Royal stopped eating and returned Clay's stare. "What are ye gawking at?" he asked.

"I'd like to hear more about Cog," Clay asked.

"Nay. Enough of that. I suggest you call your brother in here and eat up. We're going to have a fair day's exercise when we get to shore tomorrow."

Clay shrugged and began helping himself to a slice of beef, and then suddenly bolted upright. "Tomorrow?" he exclaimed. "We reach land tomorrow?"

Royal nodded as he smeared butter on a piece of biscuit. "Aye, the wind's been good. We should arrive at Ozo sometime in the night, but we'll stay aboard until daylight."

It was doubtful that Clay heard the last sentence. He had already leapt from his chair and was tearing down the deck to warn Arthur.

+   +   +

"Arthur!" Clay shouted, as he flew into the cabin. It took a few searching glances, but Clay soon spotted Arthur propped upside down in a different corner, feet in the air, contemplating the mysterious coin inches from his face. "Arthur," Clay repeated, "we make landfall tomorrow morning!"

Arthur didn't respond at first. He simply stared at the coin dejectedly. "Tomorrow. Today, Next year," he sighed. "I guess it doesn't make any difference. I'll be just as close to figuring this out as I'll ever be."

Clay understood what Arthur was feeling. Ever since Arthur was able to walk, Clay remembered his brother as someone who had a desire to be useful. If it meant fetching your shoes, or doing a chore no one wanted to do, Arthur was always eager to please. And now, when it really seemed to matter, he was useless. The grim shadow of failure clouded his face. Clay slid onto the cabin floor next to him and shook him by the shoulder. "Don't be so hard on yourself, Arthur. It's not important."

"Not important?" Arthur exclaimed. "Thanks to me, we're going to be left on some island, where we don't know anybody, we don't speak the same language, and no clue on how to get back home! We'll probably be eaten by cannibals are something!"

Clay stifled a chuckle. "Well, I don't think it's that kind of island. I'm sure we'll think of something. Besides, I wouldn't be surprised if Captain Royal changes his mind about abandoning us on shore."

"What makes you think that?"

Clay shrugged. "Not sure, really. I just suspect that he's not the scoundrel he leads us to believe. Besides, the coin is still ours, and if he doesn't want it to fall into the hands of his adversary Schark, then he'd do well to keep us around. The longer we have the coin instead of Schark simply means more time for us to figure it out without having to race Schark to the answer."

Arthur fingered the mysterious doubloon. "But how do we figure it out? What does it mean? '*Where the two that shall never meet come face to face*'? I still think we need the map. It must be talking about some landmarks or roads that meet. Cliff faces, maybe? They don't move but could be facing each other. If the map and coin are supposed to be used together, then there must be something on the map that it's directing us to."

Clay shook his head. He plucked the coin from Arthur's hands and examined it himself. "I'm not so sure, Arthur. Royal himself said these aren't coordinates."

"Yeah, I know. So what do you think they are?"

"I honestly can't make heads or tails of it, Arthur. He

said they were compass bearings, so maybe the map has a point of origin—"

Arthur suddenly righted himself and lifted his head from the floor. "What did you just say?"

"I said maybe the map has a point of origin."

"No, not that!" Arthur snatched the coin from Clay's hands. "I think you might be on to something! I need some paper. And a piece of charcoal! Quick!"

Clay climbed to his feet in confusion. "Okay. I'll find something. By the way, dinner is served in the galley if you want anything to eat."

But Arthur was oblivious. His eyes were glued feverishly to the small golden riddle in his fingers.

7

Marco Mishmal Mossarian

Just as Captain Archibald Royal had predicted, the *Ivory Typhoon* arrived at the small island of Ozo under the light of the full moon. The sea was placid, giving the appearance of a polished marble floor underneath the blue night. The island jutted from the flat line of the ocean and the bright moonlight did not veil its harsh and barren nature. It offered no flora or vegetation that Clay could see. Only rough boulders and craggy cliff faces. There was no sign of life at all. Not even the glimmering hope of a lit window or campfire.

"How many people live on this island?" Clay asked.

Royal grunted as he minutely adjusted the ship's wheel. "Only one that I know of...which is too many for a scrap of rock like that. But of course, that's the way Marco prefers it."

"Who's Marco?"

"Marco is one of the most annoyingly intelligent men I've ever had the displeasure of meeting. I'd say more about him, but I'm sure he would tell you that everything I said was wrong, right down to the color of his eyes." Royal motioned toward the front of the ship. "Go forward and prepare to drop anchor. There's a small cove ahead. That's where we'll spend the night."

Clay looked up at the moon. "Why don't we go ashore tonight? There's plenty of light." The honest truth behind Clay's question was that he found the sight of land—even land as uninviting as the small island of Ozo—refreshing and it stirred his desire to be on solid earth again.

"I don't care how bright the moon is. I don't have an appetite for scaling sharp cliffs in the night. What I do like is getting a decent night's rest before having to scramble ashore like a mountain goat. In the morning, you'll be thanking me."

Clay gave the island a closer look. As the *Ivory Typhoon* slipped quietly closer, he realized just how forbidding the cliffside was. Its face towered above the highest mast of the *Typhoon*, and at the base, even the calm swells of the sea angrily churned against the rocks. As much as the dry land beckoned to him, Clay decided it would be more enjoyable without two broken legs. "I'll go drop the anchor."

+ + +

When the sun rose, Clay stumbled sleepily from his cabin. Despite the early hour, the heat was stifling. He found Arthur leaning on the ship's railing and staring at the jagged face of white rock. Clay wasn't certain if Arthur was feeling the same longing for landfall that he was, or if he was simply dumbfounded by the looming task of climbing ashore.

Arthur turned from the railing with a big smile. "Good morning, Clay!"

"You're certainly in a good mood."

"Can't you smell it?" he replied. He took a long, deep breath. "I can smell dirt!"

Clay sniffed the air. "I guess so. It seemed like you were on to something last night with the coin. Did you solve the riddle?"

Arthur kept his face pointed to the island, trying to hide a small grin of satisfaction. "We'll find out!"

Captain Royal's plan to go ashore at dawn proved to be a wise one. Scaling the heights of the craggy cliff face was treacherous enough in the daylight, to say nothing of the challenge of securing their dinghy from crashing against the rocks at the base. Royal's demand for haste added another layer of stress to the climb. He was growing irked at Clay and Arthur's lagging pace. "Have you got ballast in your britches? We'll be lucky if we even have a few hours before Schark and his crew arrive. Trust me when I say we don't want to be here when they do."

"Surely if someone lives on this island," gasped Clay as he scrambled for another handhold, "then there must be any easier way to come ashore."

"Aye. There's a cozy bay on the leeward side, but we don't want Schark to know we're here. If he spies no ship, he may think we've come and gone. Besides, it might be better for us if Marco doesn't know we're coming, either."

This last part caught Arthur's ear. "Is this Marco dangerous?"

Royal paused his climb to give the question some thought. "I wouldn't say he was dangerous, but he has no fondness for me, that's for sure. But maybe that particular gale has blown over since then."

After what seemed to be hours (when in fact it had only taken a little less than one), the three pulled themselves onto the top of the cliff. Looking down on the crystal blue ocean, they could see the decks of the *Ivory Typhoon* gleaming in the mid-morning sun. Arthur was fascinated to see the shadow of the ship upon the floor of the shallow sea beneath it. Clay, however, was considering the unavoidable fact that they would eventually need to find a way back down.

After a few moments of catching their breath, Royal stood to his feet. "Let's go, lads."

Arthur and Clay deemed the trek as something of a disappointment. Having never been on such an island before, they had no idea what to expect. But they both felt, however, that even one tree would not have been too much to ask for. Ozo was indeed a perfect specimen of a desert island and Royal's proclamation that not even one person could live here was understandable. The island was nothing more than a very white chunk of rock. And not a very smooth one, for Arthur was continually tripping over the rough cracks and boulders.

"Who is this Marco, anyway?" Clay finally felt brave enough to ask. "And what is his connection with this treasure?"

"Marco Mishmal Mossarian is his full name. He's a mapmaker. And a librarian of sorts. He has detailed maps for every corner of the globe...many of them drawn by his very own hand. To hear him talk, you'd think he circled the globe more than the moon itself. He keeps a vast collection of maps, scrolls, and tomes and guards them like it was a horde of gold. It may not look like it, but in a real sense, this little scrap of land is like a secret Alexandria with its great library."

"And he has the Map of Cordura?"

"He should," answered Royal. "If he hasn't destroyed it."

"Destroy it?" interjected Arthur. "Why would someone

destroy a treasure map? And what is this special treasure, anyway?"

Archie Royal halted and leveled his stern eye at him. "I don't fault you for having questions, but they best be kept unasked. And unanswered."

Clay quickly defended Arthur. "Listen here, Captain. We must agree that we're in this together, whether we like it or not. Arthur holds the clue that will help you find what you're looking for. I think it only fair that as long as we're sharing the risk in helping you, then we also should share in a portion of the treasure."

Royal focused his eye on Clay. "So that's how the land lays, eh? Riches? Is that what you think this is about?"

Clay didn't budge. "You said it was a treasure map."

"Aye," Royal agreed, "but not the type of treasure you're thinking of."

"What other kind of treasure is there?" Arthur prodded.

Royal looked at him and then to Clay, and then back to the boy. "It's like swimming with tiger sharks with you two. Listen here. I won't deny that you boys are in grave danger, and that fact alone earns you some answers. But I didn't ask you two to come along, either. You want answers? I'll give some to you. Only some, mind you. And only if Marco has the map. Which will be as good as worthless if you haven't unraveled that riddle on your little coin." This last comment was directed at Arthur. "Have you?"

Arthur hesitated. "Yes. Maybe. I need the map to be sure."

"And there you have it. You have no answers for me, and I have none for you." He pointed into the distance where the ocean merged with the sky. "You see out there? Over that line is civilization and safety. If we get the answers we're looking for, then I take you there and you live to a ripe old age picking pasta from your teeth. If we don't get any answers, then we'll all be lucky to get out of this alive. Either way, the best sort of treasure anyone gets out of this little quest is their life. And the less you know, and the less you stick around, the better chances you have. So what is it you want? A life of relaxation? Or days full of danger and peril on the high seas?"

As Royal concluded his speech, the two boys stood in silence, simply staring at the one-eyed captain.

"What's the matter with ye?" Royal asked. "Why are you just standing there?"

"We're thinking about it," Clay answered.

"Thinking about it?" Royal exclaimed. "What's there to think about? You're supposed to want to stay alive!"

"A life of danger as a pirate sound's pretty fun, though," commented Arthur.

Royal rolled his eye toward the empty sky in exasperation. "Mercy! Enough of this tongue-wagging. We need to get that map and sail off this rock. Just over this hill is Marco's home. Don't touch anything and let me do the talking. Oh, and be prepared to dodge a musket ball or two."

Soon, the trio crested a small rocky knoll. A short distance away stood a dwelling...although Arthur and Clay would have categorized it as merely a hovel. The house was made of rough-hewn stone, presumably quarried from somewhere on the island. It offered precious few windows, and the ones that were visible would be more aptly described as arrow slits. A small chimney protruded from the wooden roof, but since it was a very warm and clear day, there was no reason for it to show any signs of use.

In contrast to the dwelling, the view was spectacular. Perched upon a high cliff of its own, the house overlooked the glittering blue Mediterranean. A winding pathway led down a slope where Arthur could see a modest but pleasant bay. A small sailing craft was moored to a tiny dock. Arthur assumed the boat belonged to Marco since it was far too small to crew a band of pirates like Thaddeus Schark's. Royal must have thought the same because he didn't appear concerned at the sight of it.

The captain cautiously surveyed the perimeter, assuring himself that there were no other surprise guests and then strolled to the crooked front door. He rapped on the sturdy wooden panels.

After a few moments, Royal tried again. "Marco, it's Archie Royal!"

Before Royal had even closed his mouth, a panel on the door slid open and a large face appeared. The nose was fleshy and the mouth was wide, which gave its current frown an impressive level of gravitas. Two small, dark eyes pointed at Royal unblinkingly.

Royal smiled. "Felicitations, my friend!"

The wide mouth and dark eyes remained still, framed in its little window.

The smile on Royal's face began to falter. "Good to see you!" he greeted again. To Arthur, it sounded more like a question.

Finally, the face of Marco spoke with a deep, heavily accented rumble. "What happened to your eye?"

"Yes, of course, you must not have recognized me! We have a lot of catching up to do, Marco. Why not open the door and let us in?"

Without giving a reply, the face disappeared. The panel slid shut and the house settled once more into silence. Despite Royal's request, the door didn't budge.

"I assure you I wouldn't be here without good reason, Marco," Royal called loudly. "We must talk!"

Again, Royal's requests went unanswered.

"We've come for Cordura's map! Do you have it?"

More silence.

"I don't think he was expecting company," Clay suggested.

"Not from the likes of me, anyway. He hasn't seen me in almost ten years. Blast! I've had it with this!" He began pounding fiercely at the wooden panel. "Marco! Don't make me tear this door off its pathetic hinges! We need that map!"

Royal's threats still prompted no response.

Finally, Arthur chimed in. "We have the coin! The Coin of Cordura!"

As if by magic, the door swung open with such forceful speed that the three visitors stepped back in surprise. The large stocky frame of Marco Mishmal Mossarian stood in the doorway but this time his tiny dark eyes darted between Arthur and Clay. "What are you two? Pirates-in-training?"

Arthur gulped at the large, swarthy man. He was scruffily dressed, and for the first time Arthur and Clay could see his bald, shiny head and the dark stubble that dotted his olive-colored chin.

Royal interceded. "No need to concern yourself with them. We need the map. Do you have it?"

Marco gave Royal a suspicious stare. "You have the coin?"

"Yes."

"Let me see it."

Royal nodded to Arthur and he fished it from his pocket.

Marco wasted no time in snatching it from his hand and holding it closely to one squinting eye. "This would very much appear to be the lost Coin of Cordura. Why is it all scratched up? Did you drop it?"

"Rubbish! We found it that way," Royal answered.

"Then someone with better sense than you did everything they could to erase the clue." He tossed the coin back to Arthur. "Your little coin is worthless. The map will do you no good. You may leave now." With that hurried conclusion, he began to shut the door.

"Wait!" Royal roughly braced the closing door with his boot. "If the map is worthless, then you have no reason to keep it."

"If the map is worthless, you have no reason to take it," Marco challenged.

"If I don't take it, Thaddeus Schark will."

Just when Arthur thought Marco's eyes could show no expression other than disdain, they went completely round. Stark white surrounded the little brown irises. "Schark? Schark is coming here?" Without warning, Marco grabbed Royal and pulled him through the doorway.

Clay and Arthur hurried in also as the door swung shut behind them. As their vision adjusted to the dim light, they could spy honeycombs of cubbies piled with an abundance of scrolls, papers, and rolled parchments.

"Why do you bring that monster to my doorstep?" demanded Marco. "What have I done to deserve your existence, Royal? You have been a blight on every day I draw breath!"

"Hold fast there!" Royal bit back. "I stayed away from you for over ten years!"

"Yes, but in one day, you curse my home with the shadow of Thaddeus Schark! Therefore, you can take no credit for any of those years! I was doomed from the very day I set foot upon your vessel!"

"You have nothing to fear from Schark," calmed Royal. "Give me the map and I'll go. When Schark arrives, simply tell him that I have it and he'll waste no time in plotting course after me."

"Schark is no fool! He'll torture me! He'll want to know details about the map, what I told you, in which direction you set sail, and what the coin revealed."

"If the map is worthless, then you've got nothing to tell him."

Marco grabbed the lapels of Royal's coat and shook him furiously. "He won't believe me! He'll flay me alive and use my skin as a jib! Are you satisfied with the misery you have inflicted upon me, Royal, or is there perhaps some other way my demise can bring you pleasure?"

"Why don't you just leave with us?" suggested Arthur.

Marco and Royal both looked at the boy in bewilderment.

"You can escape the island with us," Arthur repeated. "Schark will have no clue at all where we're headed."

Clay agreed. "That's a great idea! Get the map and we'll go!"

"Belay that!" shouted Royal. "I don't need any more passengers on my vessel."

Marco, however, was not listening to Royal. Instead, he was nodding in agreement. "Yes! I will get you the map, but I will not sail with you. I already bear the clinging stench of death on my body from sailing with Archibald Royal years ago! I will leave in my own boat." With that, Marco dashed from the room into a darkened hall.

While he was gone, Clay looked at Royal in puzzlement. "He's a bit excitable, isn't he?"

Royal ignored the indictment. Instead, he turned to Arthur, who was taking Marco's absence as an opportunity to admire the sea from the narrow window. "I told you to keep your mouths clamped! Instead, you decide to invite him aboard the *Typhoon* as if we were going on a pleasure cruise."

"I was just trying to be helpful."

"At least he's getting the map for us," admitted Royal. "Good work there, I suppose. The sooner we're off this rock, I'll feel safer."

Clay cocked his head to one side. "Say, what's that noise? Sounds like a brook."

Royal and Arthur paused to listen. "That's water, alright," agreed the captain. "But where's it coming from?"

Arthur placed his ear against the cold, stone floor. "It's in the ground."

Clay lowered himself to the flagstones to listen also. "You're right. There must be some type of spring under this house. I wonder if Marco knows about it."

"Of course I know about it!" stated Marco in irritation. He had returned with a rolled parchment in his hand, and also a hastily packed bag which Arthur assumed contained clothes and other belongings for his impromptu travel. "Why do you think I built this house on this dreary rock? There's a natural aquifer that runs fresh water from the earth and out to the sea. The water flowing under here gives me plenty to drink, grow squash, and down there," he pointed down the dark hallway, "I draw my bath. I have a very comfortable tub."

"I'm very happy for you," sighed Royal. He stretched his hand out to Marco. "May we see the map?"

"Oh, of course! The map is yours."

Royal immediately unrolled it and his eye glowed with satisfaction. "The Map of Cordura! We're finally one step closer to putting this mess behind us!"

Arthur peered over Royal's arm. The map was about the size of a platter and scrawled about with Spanish words he didn't understand. Before he could get a closer look, though, Royal rolled it back up.

"Very good!" waved Marco, as he headed towards the door. "Enjoy your now worthless map. I must now take my leave before Thaddeus Schark arrives to use my skull for a paperweight!"

Marco swung open the door to depart, but stopped and let out a wail that sounded like a cow falling out of a barn. Standing in the doorway, with a primed flintlock at the ready, was none other than the awful pirate Thaddeus Schark.

"And what a fine paperweight it would make," he grinned.

8

Escape from Ozo

Thaddeus Schark's silhouette in the bright doorway could not hide the hideous sneer of triumph on his bearded face. The dark pistol in his grip was aimed squarely at the heart of Archibald Royal. "And now," he gloated, "the shoe is on the other foot!" Carefully he hobbled into the room, and Arthur noticed some unfamiliarity with the newly carved wooden stump that had replaced the one Royal had blown to splinters. Behind him, two crewmen entered with cutlasses clasped in their weathered fists.

"Here's how our little pageant is going to go, Captain Royal," he continued. "First, you're going to keep your hands where I can see them and then you will carefully pass me that precious map." He stretched out his open hand to Royal, while the other hand kept a steady aim at him with the menacing gun.

"And then you leave?" Royal replied.

"Ach! Not before I bury a ball in your chest, Royal. You've been a thorn in my craw for far too long. There was a time when I relished collecting the bounty on your pretty little head, but that time is past! Things have changed and I've got bigger fish to put in my pot. Any reward they offer for you is nothing compared with what that piece of map can get me!"

Royal let out a short chuckle. "You think this map leads

to riches? You've been told a lie." He gestured to a pasty, round man who had entered behind Schark. "Did Arbo here tell you that?"

"Arbo told me enough! He told me that our old friend Riga was offered unimaginable wealth to find the map to St. George! It could lead to the queen's bloomers for all I care. As long as there's a handsome reward, I aim to have it." With that, he raised the pistol and, looking through one squinty eye, he pulled the cock back with his thumb.

"Yes!" cried Marco. "This is good, Royal. Give him the map and let him kill you. Then we can all return to our lives as they were before."

Royal scowled at Marco. Reluctantly, he held out the rolled map. Schark wasted no time in snatching it from his hand.

"You have the map," said Royal. "Now go and leave the others alone. They have nothing to do with this."

Schark shook his head. "Not on your life! The last thing I need are more nosy troublemakers who are in on the secret." His finger slowly squeezed upon the trigger.

"Wait!" The sudden cry echoed through the room as Clay Cross jumped boldly in front of Royal. The pirate halted his aim in surprise. "If you want to shoot Captain Royal, you'll have to go through me!" Clay threatened. "You have only one shot in that pistol. You won't stand a chance if you waste it on me."

Schark leered at the young man. "You don't know Ol' Jezebel...she's loaded with a double ram of black powder. At this close range, that's enough to pass a ball clean through the both of you." He grinned evilly and took aim once again. "All you've done is saved me a bit of trouble by letting me kill you both at the same time."

"You're forgetting one thing."

This time it was Arthur who spoke. He stood defiantly with his arm stretched out the narrow window overlooking the steep, rocky cliff. In his hand, he clutched the small gold Coin of Cordura. "Let them go, or I drop the coin into the sea!"

Schark froze while his brain reassessed the situation.

Royal took advantage of the hesitation. "Do you understand, Schark, or do I have to peel the banana for you? That map is useless without the coin. You fire your single shot, the coin is lost forever, and you'll still have to deal with the rest of us. Or you can leave with the map and neither of us will have to soil Marco's pretty rug here with our blood."

"I like this rug very much. It's Persian," Marco noted.

Schark chewed on the bargain. His eyes flitted back and forth between Royal and Arthur.

"Why don't you step outside and think it over?" Royal suggested.

A sly grin slowly stretched across Schark's face. With his pistol still trained on Royal, he carefully stepped backwards out the door. "That sounds like a good idea. Back off, men!" he barked over his shoulder. "These fools aren't going anywhere. We'll just enjoy some sunshine while they fester in here."

Together, the three brigands slowly retreated from the house. Once they were a reasonable distance away, Clay quickly slammed and bolted the front door. "Whew!" he breathed. "I thought we were done for! Good thinking, Arthur!"

"Don't bust your buttons yet," replied Royal as he peered through the door's small opening. He could see Arbo bustling down the rocky path to the bay while Schark and the other brigand stood watch. "He's sending for reinforcements. Schark was never very good in a fair fight. Not with that leg of his. But once he knows he's got numbers on his side, they'll swarm this hut like jackals on a bone."

"I hate you," Marco said. "Before we die, I thought you should know."

"Enough of that," Royal said. "Is there another way out of this house?"

Marco shook his head. "It's not a house any longer. Now it's a mausoleum, thanks to you. A very fine mausoleum with a Persian rug. And like any mausoleum, it doesn't come with a back door."

"How are we going to get that map back?" Arthur asked. It was frustrating to have had it for only a few fleeting minutes.

"We'll wrestle with that later," Royal answered. "First, we need to save ourselves. I'm guessing you don't have any weapons about?" he asked Marco.

"I have a steak knife and a corkscrew."

Royal grimaced as he looked through the small opening again. "Our only choice is to rush them through the front door. There's only two of them at the moment. We'll have to do it now, before the rest of his crew show up. With surprise on our side, Schark's shot may go wild and there's at least a small chance we'll make it."

Clay, Arthur, and Marco were about to express their skepticism in Royal's plan but a booming sound outside the narrow window interrupted their protests. Then the entire house shuddered around them.

"Cannon fire!" exclaimed Royal. He peered through the door slot again. Schark and his crewmember were scurrying down the path to a safe distance.

Arthur looked out the window to see a ship—presumably Schark's vessel—anchored in the cove below. A puff of gray smoke drifted from one of its open ports. "They're firing on us!"

Before anyone could react, Arthur saw another flash from the cannon. This time, the whistling sound of the round shot could be heard as it plummeted through the air. The second shot struck closer to the small house atop the cliff. The walls trembled violently and clouds of plaster and dust dropped from the ceiling. Everyone flinched under the falling debris.

"Schark is smarter than I thought," Royal grumbled. "He intends to force us out and shoot us as we leave. Or simply wait to sift through the rubble for our bodies."

"I wished he had taken the deal where you bled on my rug," Marco snapped.

"Shut up!" Royal yelled.

"No! You shut up!" Marco retorted. "You've barged into my home and invaded it with pirates who are now going to sink it like a rowboat!"

The two men began yelling back and forth, hurling every manner of epithet they could think of while another cannonball rocked the house. One wall began to crumble and lean inward. The floor shifted and a large crack tore under their feet as the structure's entire foundation split in two.

The quake knocked Arthur to the ground. As he brushed more falling plaster from his eyes, he noticed something odd. "Hey! Look at this!"

Royal and Marco ceased their arguing as Arthur pried at one of the flagstones on the floor. The giant crack had revealed a narrow opening gurgling with the sound of water.

"This must open to the aquifer that runs under the

house," Clay said. He helped Arthur heave the flagstone aside. The gap revealed a small river of running water that had worn the surrounding stone to a smooth polish.

"You said this empties to the sea!" Arthur yelled. "Maybe we can escape through here!"

"That's madness!" the mapmaker exclaimed. "We have no idea what's down there!"

"There's nothing for it," replied Royal. "I'll take my chances. That water has to go somewhere, and right now any place is better than here." Arthur was already lowering himself into the hole. Royal placed his booted foot on his back and with a solid shove, sent the boy shooting down the wash of water.

Another distant boom outside the window was soon followed by the screeching cry of an approaching cannonball. The ever-loudening whistle heralded a well-aimed shot and Clay, Royal, and Marco dove into the flume.

+ + +

Sprays of water shot up Arthur's nose as he slid rapidly down the dark chute. He felt the slick, water-worn stone beneath him angle sharply downward and he plummeted even faster. He tried to clear the splashing water from his eyes, but there was little point—the narrow tube of rock was pitch black as he zoomed along. The water twisted him left and right as he spiraled like a bug in a drain. At one point, Arthur thought he glimpsed a sudden flash of blue sky above him as the watery fissure broke the island's surface. It soon rushed past, and once again, he barreled into the dark.

Suddenly, the water and stone around him vanished. Arthur broke into sunlight, and for a moment he was greeted with the bright sky and the clear view of sparkling ocean that happened to be dozens of feet below him.

"Oh no!" Arthur cried. He hung in the air for the shortest of moments before he dropped to the blue bay beneath. With a splash, he sunk into the salty water. Fortunately, Arthur was a capable swimmer. On several occasions, Mr. Dempster had taken the boys and girls on excursions to the seashore. This was the first time, however, that Arthur had ever attempted to swim with boots on and he found it much more difficult as he kicked for the surface. In a matter of seconds, his head broke through and he gasped for breath.

The air above him was immediately filled with cries of surprise. He looked up to see Clay, Royal, and Marco squirt out of the opening in the cliff and come tumbling into the sea. They smacked into the surface in three tremendous splashes.

Royal's head was the first to pop up from the waves. "Bless my rudder!" he spat. "I think I got fishes in my britches!"

Clay and Marco burst to the surface, coughing and spitting. "Are we alive?" Marco cried.

"Arthur!" Clay called. "Are you okay?"

"I'm fine! We made it!"

"Aye!" Royal laughed. "And it looks like this gutter deposited us right where we needed!" He pointed to the welcoming view of the *Ivory Typhoon*, floating smartly in the bay before them.

With renewed vigor, they struck through the water to clamber aboard the waiting vessel. Arthur wasted no time in dumping the seawater from his boots while Royal quickly assumed his position behind the *Typhoon's* large wheel. With a throw of a lever, the anchor lifted from the seabed and the sails unfurled and swelled with wind. As the *Ivory Typhoon* spun its bow to the open ocean, they could hear the continuing boom of Schark's cannons bombarding the far side of the island.

"You owe me a house," Marco grumbled.

"You'll find a new place. At least you still have a head to put in it when you do," Royal retorted.

"Where are we going?" Clay asked.

"As far and as fast as we can at the moment," the captain answered. "We've been given a nice advantage...once Schark is satisfied with demolishing Marco's little abode, he'll spend a good day picking through the rubble for our bodies and the coin." Royal afforded himself a pleased chuckle. "I wish I could be there to see the question marks on his ugly face trying to solve the mystery of our vanishing corpses!"

"We're going to have to face him sooner or later," Arthur said. "He still has the Map of Cordura."

"But we've got the coin," Royal replied. "We don't need the map."

Clay was visibly perplexed. "What do you mean we don't need the map? That was the whole point of coming here."

Archie Royal pointed to his one eye. "But I saw it before he got his grubby mitts on it. The map clearly was a chart of the coast of the Levant and smack dab in the middle of it was Acre. So, to Acre, we go!"

"But we need the map!" Arthur argued. "If my solution to the coin's riddle is correct, we need the map and coin together."

Royal's confidence dissipated. "Are you certain?"

"Yes! We have to go back and get the map from Schark."

"No!" Marco and Royal yelled. Both of them seemed shocked that they were in agreement.

"Yes!" Clay and Arthur countered.

The captain attempted to reason. "I know Schark's ship, the *Sea Scar*. It has us outgunned three-to-one. To say nothing of his willingness and enthusiasm to kill us all. I'm sure that between what I saw on the map and with Marco's own familiarity with it, we should know enough to get what we need."

"No!" This time it was Arthur and Marco agreeing. Arthur gave the mapmaker a puzzled look. The boy continued. "You don't understand. The coin is part of the map! We have no choice."

Marco bristled. "You are both wrong!" he shouted. "Listening to you is like listening to two lobsters arguing about the best way to climb into a pot of boiling water. You," he pointed at Arthur, "are wrong. We don't need to get the map back from Schark—and be riddled with musket balls for our efforts, I might add. And you," he pointed to Royal, "are wrong that it points to Acre."

"Away with ye!" Royal shot back. "I know those coasts like my own knuckles. And I know what I saw."

"You saw what you saw, but you didn't see the map."

Royal froze. "What are you saying?"

Marco looked sheepish. "What you saw wasn't the Map of Cordura. It was a fake."

In a flash, Royal sprang from behind the ship's wheel and grabbed Marco by his shirt lapels. "Are you telling me you tried to swindle us!"

"No! Not at all!" Marco defended. "It was for Schark."

"You gave that map to me before Schark and his lousy

crew even showed up! You were more than happy to let us go our merry way, knowing we had the wrong map! I ought to throw you overboard like the piece of flotsam you are!"

And it looked like he was about to do it, too, but Marco shoved Royal's hands away. "Yes, you are right. I gave you the wrong map. But for some reason, fortune shines upon your rotten existence, as it always does! Schark got the wrong map instead. But don't be so quick to toss me aside, otherwise the real map goes with me."

From his dripping pouch of belongings, he produced the sodden Map of Cordura.

9

The Trek to El Khudir

The four of them unfurled the map over the wooden table in the galley. The parchment was old but thick and seemed unperturbed by the dunking in the bay. Upon it was scrawled several phrases in Spanish and it appeared to depict a coastline and parts of an unknown village. Details within the map were sparse and a middle portion was completely blank.

"If the writing on this chart is to be believed," Royal said, "then this is indeed the Map of Cordura. By my reckoning, this is a coast on Northern Africa."

Marco nodded. "While I don't need your uninformed opinion to tell me what I already know, I will agree that this is Cordura's map. I have seen many poor forgeries and nefarious hoaxes, and I know beyond a doubt this particular map is genuine."

"As maps go," Clay remarked as he studied it closely, "it's not very impressive. Other than a coastline and a few random scribbles, it doesn't say much. If Captain Royal says it's Africa, I have neither reason to doubt nor believe him."

Marco agreed. "The map is vague, just as Cordura intended. The tale is that the map cannot be read without the Coin of Cordura. The coin which you possess—assuming it is not a fake."

Arthur fished into his pocket and produced the large, gold coin. As he placed it on the table, Royal grumbled. "The coin gives only compass bearings. I had hoped the map would provide a starting point but," he said, gesturing to the somewhat blank parchment, "it's as worthless as the coin."

"There is no such thing as a worthless map!" Marco countered in offense. "Maps are like mirrors. If you stare at them blankly, then that is what they give back to you." He leaned over the unfurled chart and peered intently at the markings. "But if you study them with purpose, and seek out their details, you will see depth and breadth and height. It will return your efforts with direction and understanding for the world in it."

"I believe the coin holds more than just compass bearings," Arthur added. "It also mentions a clue...'*Where the two that shall never meet come face to face.*' At first, I thought it must be referring to two fixed landmarks on the map. But then I realized there are two other things that never come face to face. The two sides of a coin." He reached into his pocket again and produced a small scrap of paper. "To test my idea, I did several rubbings of both sides of the coin on the same piece of parchment. Together, the scratches on the coin seemed to form a map of its own."

Arthur flattened the small piece of paper over the map. The rough smear of charcoal on the parchment contained several broken lines that formed crude, curious letters.

Royal's and Marco's eyes widened. Intrigued, the pirate brought a lantern to the table. "Well, break my bones and call 'em ballast! This little rubbing fits like a glove in the blank space of the map."

"Look at this," Marco pointed. "These markings on Arthur's rubbing line up with those on the map to form words. *Silene* and *Sepulcro*. The drawing appears to be of a graveyard in a village."

"Silene was a city in the Maghreb of Northern Africa. Possibly Cyrene," the captain said, "but this coastline looks to be a completely different place. It must be a different Silene. A graveyard, you say?"

Marco nodded. "*Sepulcro* means grave. You are looking for a grave in a place called Silene."

Clay's face shone with excitement. "There must be buried treasure there!"

"Not quite," Royal said as picked up the coin and examined its edge. "There are still the compass bearings to follow. *S75°E, N12°E*. I suspect this *sepulcro* is just the start of our journey."

Clay's enthusiasm vanished. "Oh, right. You said this pointed the way to a place called El Khudir."

Marco's face darkened. "You are fools to seek after El Khudir's secret. In my zeal to finally unravel Cordura's riddle, you distracted me from your true endeavor. With El Khudir ahead and Schark behind, you may as well chain us to the anchor and throw us overboard. It would be a much more peaceful way to die!"

"What's so bad about treasure?" Clay shrugged.

"Treasure?" Marco scowled. "Is that the lie he told you?"

"I told them there wasn't any treasure!" retorted Royal. "I'm going topside to set course." He snatched the map from off the table and marched from the galley.

Arthur and Clay looked at Marco with confusion. "If it's not treasure, then what is it?"

"Doom," Marco muttered and he, too, left.

+ + +

Royal calculated that they would reach the coast by morning. The wind was fair and only a few puffs of cloud dotted the sky. Arthur was given the task of scanning the horizon for any appearance of the pursuing Thaddeus Schark and his vessel, the *Sea Scar*. After a prolonged period of squinting at the distant skyline, he thought he was beginning to imagine everything from masts to mountains in the distance. He was relieved when Clay wandered over to break the monotony.

"How are you holding up?" Clay asked.

Arthur rubbed his eyes. "The problem with the sea is that it's constantly moving while standing still all at the same time. I don't think I'll ever get used to it."

"Give it time," Clay encouraged. The two of them shared a moment of silence as they gazed at the open water.

Arthur finally spoke. "I miss Dempster House. Standing here watching the waves, I realize with every minute, Mr. Dempster, Jeremy, Nora, and all the others are drifting further and further away. Do you think we'll ever see them again?"

Clay's mouth twisted into a slight frown. "I don't see why not. We'll get back. Somehow. Once Captain Royal finds what he's after, then maybe he'll agree to take us home."

"But what about the things Marco said? It sounds like Royal is taking us into danger. How do we know we'll even survive?"

"You can't think like that, Arthur. We'll be okay. And so will everyone back home." Clay laughed. "And, boy, won't we have some stories to tell them when we get back!"

Arthur chuckled in agreement. "I'll say!" His heart lightened. Adventures were nice to have, he thought, but they were only worthwhile when you could share them with others. He cast his eyes back across the water. Something caught his attention. He gave his eyes another rub.

The surface of the blue water was spotted with dark patches. Sometimes they were shadows from the clouds, and sometimes they were simply patches of sea weeds on the ocean floor. But they were always motionless. This time, though, one of them was moving.

"Clay, what is that?" he pointed.

His brother shielded his eyes from the sun. Sure enough, one of the dark patches appeared to be moving, seemingly keeping pace with the stern of the *Ivory Typhoon*. "I don't know," he said. "Maybe a school of fish? Or a whale?"

Together, they continued to watch the mysterious shadow beneath the water. It remained distant and soon it began to blur with the rest of the formless shapes beneath the waves. And then it was gone completely.

Clay shrugged. "Well, I need to get back to my job of checking the machinery below. Don't go cross-eyed!" And with that, he returned below deck.

Arthur searched again for the nebulous dark patch but it was nowhere to be found. Abandoning the fruitless task, he renewed his vigil for any sign of the *Sea Scar*.

+ + +

By morning, they had reached the coast. What was before merely a meandering line on Cordura's map had now become a vista of warm, golden rock that rimmed the blue and white waves of the sea. Several small huts and buildings dotted the land, all the same color as the dirt and sand, making them almost invisible to the eye. If it wasn't for the deep shadows of doors and windows, and the occasional wandering villager herding goats, Arthur would have doubted that it was indeed a town.

The *Ivory Typhoon* dropped anchor and they rowed the small dinghy to the flat beach. "Shouldn't be too difficult to find the cemetery in this heap they call a village," Royal said.

Finding the cemetery was simple enough, just as Royal surmised. The local inhabitants pointed helpfully along a worn dirt trail, showing little interest in the crew's purpose. Together, the four of them strolled up the dusty path, but their shoulders slumped when they reached the graveyard. The cemetery was filled with countless marked graves that stretched in every direction. The headstones were all hewed from the same type of orange stone, but that's where any similarity ended. Every stone varied in size and shape. "This town's been doing a lot of dying," Royal remarked. "It's going to be a chore looking at every single headstone."

"What are we looking for, exactly?" Clay asked.

"I haven't the foggiest," Royal replied. "I guess we'll know it when we see it."

"Why do we even have to look?" asked Arthur. "We have the bearings from the coin. If this is the starting point, then we can head out from here."

Marco, being very familiar with maps, jumped at the opportunity to share his knowledge. "We have a starting point, but no stopping point. There is nothing on either the map or coin to indicate how far we are to travel. Cordura must have left a clue here. I, for one, do not relish the idea of walking for all eternity into the desert."

Royal grumbled. "No one invited you. You're free to part ways with us at any time."

The mapmaker bristled at the sea captain's words. "You owe me for the house. And for having disturbed my appetite for the past several years. And for haunting my future with the shadow of Thaddeus Schark. I'm sticking around for my portion of the treasure."

"You said there was no treasure!" Arthur argued.

Marco looked sheepish. "Well, there's a little treasure," he admitted.

"Stop your jawin' and start checking these headstones," barked Royal. "If we're lucky, we can get out of this bone barn before it's dark."

The four of them spread out, examining each marker carefully. They quickly discovered that each was chiseled with rough Arabic script. "These make no sense to me," Clay called.

"Cordura was a Spaniard," Marco answered, as he leaned over to study one of the headstones. "If he left a clue, it would likely be in Spanish."

There search continued for at least two hours. Royal was becoming visibly irritated, and part of him was wondering if they were wasting their time. Suddenly, Marco excitedly waved his hand from behind a small headstone. "Come! Come! This must be it!"

Royal, Clay, and Arthur hastened to reach Marco's side.

"Look!" he pointed to the rough orange stone. Crudely carved were the words 'VIII LEUCA' and beneath it was a chiseled cross ornament.

"That's it?" Clay wondered. "How can you be sure?"

"This is the cross of St. George. And there is no date. Only a distance."

"What has St. George have to do with Cordura?" Arthur asked.

Marco shot Royal a confused look. "Didn't you tell them anything? Didn't you tell them who El Khudir was?"

"I told them all they needed to know," Royal muttered.

"You said El Khudir was a kingdom," Clay replied.

"Bah!" Royal grunted before changing the subject. "What does *leuca* mean?"

"It's the old Roman measurement," Marco answered. "We would use the word *league*. This, along with the Roman numeral indicates we need to travel eight leagues from here using the first bearings Cordura gave us on the coin...southeast, seventy-five degrees!"

"For about twenty-five miles," Royal calculated. "I guess this means I'll have to barter for some camels."

+ + +

Camels were not hard to find in the little village of Silene. Convincing their owners to part with them was another matter entirely. Royal proffered a small bag of gold currency, but it was of little interest to the trader. Food and merchandise seemed to be the preferred coin of the realm. Among the four of them, they had little to barter with. Rummaging through Marco's pouch, however, Royal found a bottle of wine and a small handheld mirror which delighted the camel owner. "These are all the possessions I have left from my house!" Marco argued.

"Which I'm sure adds to their rare value," Royal shot back as he took the reins of the three camels.

"You drain the joy from my life like a vampire. That's what you are...a joy vampire!" Marco growled.

Some of Marco's departed joy returned within only a few minutes into their desert ride as he witnessed Royal's discomfort atop his camel.

"What kind of confounded beast is this?" he bellowed as the camel loped over the hill. "It feels like my spine is being barraged by cannon fire. This is worse than keelhauling!"

Marco laughed as his camel strode behind. "These are magnificent creatures. The locals refer to them as *the ships of the desert!*"

"I've never been aboard a ship that yaws like this! One leg heads to sea while the other is tethered to the shore. It's unbearable!" He then reached into a pouch and tossed a small stone to the ground. When the four of them had mounted their rides, Arthur had spied the captain gathering a good number of pebbles and counting them twice before filling the pouch.

"What are those for?" Arthur asked. He and Clay were both riding together on their third camel, which obediently trailed behind.

"Makeshift knots," Royal replied, "to track our progress."

Marco rolled his eyes at the captain's crude methodology. If Royal noticed, he didn't let it show.

"So," Arthur began, "is anyone going to finally tell us what this treasure—or non-treasure—is that we are headed for?"

"I told you," Royal answered. "The map leads to the kingdom of El Khudir."

Arthur heard Marco snort.

"And is that where St. George lived?" Clay asked. "Is that why the headstone had his cross on it?"

"More or less," was Royal's only reply.

Again, Marco snorted.

Royal shot a hard scowl at Marco over his shoulder. "What are you all drawn and quartered about?"

"Why do you lie to these children?" Marco retorted. "What kind of monster are you? If you are going to captain this caravan of martyrdom, you should at least tell them the truth."

"If you know so much, why don't you tell them?" spat Royal and returned his stare to the desert ahead.

"I would be happy to," Marco brightened. "First, Royal is wrong—" he said those words with unconcealed glee "—in that El Khudir is not a kingdom. It is a person. And that person is none other than the famed St. George."

"As in St. George and the dragon?" Arthur asked.

"The very same. We all know the glorious tale of St. George and how he saved a small kingdom from a terrible dragon. The king was so grateful for the saving of his people and precious daughter that he showered their hero with riches and the entire kingdom converted to Christianity."

"Why is he called El Khudir?" Clay inquired.

"It means 'The Green One' in the local dialect. No one is really certain why he was given that title," shrugged Marco. "Perhaps it has something to do with the stories that he could make dead wood come alive with his touch. But that is just a myth."

"So, if we are not going to a kingdom," Arthur pressed, "then where are we headed?"

"Again, Royal was wrong!" Marco gave unnecessary emphasis to the word. He stretched out the word so that he almost sounded exactly like his grunting camel. "What we are looking for is not a kingdom, but a tomb. The secret tomb of St. George."

Royal simply fished into his pouch and tossed another pebble onto the ground before checking his compass.

Marco seemed miffed that his words failed to perturb Royal, so he resumed his lecture. "It is widely believed that the body of St. George lies at rest in the city of Lydda, in the heart of the Levant, entombed after being martyred by a Roman emperor. But a Spaniard named Cordura uncovered another chapter regarding St. George...a secret chapter that eludes historians to this day. Except for me, of course, otherwise I wouldn't be able to tell you this.

"Cordura believed that St. George avoided being beheaded by summoning a fire-breathing dragon that consumed his evil judge, Dacian. In fear for his life, the Roman emperor secretly released St. George and executed an imposter in his stead. St. George once again returned triumphantly to the small kingdom that he had saved from the dragon, and the people celebrated the return of their hero by showering him with wealth and gratitude until he passed away peacefully at a ripe old age and with his head still firmly joined to his neck. His body was reverently laid to rest in an elaborate tomb filled with a tribute of riches from his loving mourners. A tomb which has remained lost to this day."

"So, there is treasure!" Arthur exclaimed. "Do you hear that, Clay?"

Clay however was not impressed. "That's a fine little piece of story, Marco, but there's one problem. Since dragons don't exist, St. George would never have become a dragon-slaying hero and therefore would never be showered with treasure. This whole story is a myth. Just like the ability to bring dead trees to life. It sounds like we're marching into the desert for no good reason."

Marco scoffed. "Fine. I'm sure in your many years of existence, you have amassed so much knowledge that it eclipses the sun and affects the tides! But answer this question for me...if there was no tomb and no treasure, why would the Spaniard Cordura go to so much trouble to leave a trail to find it?"

"Well," Clay countered, "if there was a treasure, then why would Cordura even bother marking a trail instead of just taking the booty for himself?"

Marco was silent. Clay took this as a winning point and grinned.

"The truth remains," Marco replied, "that Cordura did, in fact, leave a trail. As is evidenced by the fact that I am in the middle of the sweltering desert with a one-eyed sailing jackal and two snot-nosed kids."

Royal's camel came to a stop and he twisted around in his saddle to look at the two bickering individuals.

Clay continued his argument. "But since there are no dragons, and therefore no treasure, maybe someone is playing a big trick on us. You said it yourself that there were plenty of fake maps! Swindlers probably sold a dozen copies of Cordura's map. There's no practical reason for Cordura to know the location of a treasure and not claim it for himself, much less make a trail for others to find it!"

"Maybe there are some treasures people wouldn't want to take, and Cordura was smart enough to know that!" With that, he gave Royal a dark look.

"Shut your traps, the both of you," Royal barked.

But Clay persisted. "That makes absolutely no sense! A treasure a person doesn't want? What kind of treasure is that?"

"I said to knock it off!" repeated Royal loudly. Clay and Marco turned their attention from one another to stare at the captain. Royal pointed to a large mass of stone rising from the desert floor.

"We've arrived at our bearing."

The giant rock was a dark monolith that stood in incredible contrast to the yellow desert around them, towering over the sands by about twenty feet. Arthur wasted no time finding a seat within the cool shade of the rock face.

"What now?" Clay asked.

"We look around," Royal answered, "just like in the graveyard."

The four of them marched around the chunk of rock, peering into every crevasse and crack, but nothing seemed out of the ordinary.

"Maybe there's something up top." Royal's words echoed the same conclusion everyone else had come to. Together, they searched for an easy way to ascend the rock. One side of the monolithic stone had crumbled, and the fallen chunks created steep yet accessible footholds. They clambered to the top.

"Wow!" exclaimed Arthur as he took in the scene. The top of the massif gave them an impressive view of the desert in all directions. There was no sign of the sea from which they had come, and Arthur realized just how far inland they had ridden.

The top of the monolith was bare accept for one large, flat stone of the same dark color. Marco and Royal marched straight to it. "Well, look at that!" Royal said.

Carved upon the flat rock was the same marking they saw in the graveyard.

"The cross of St. George," Clay remarked.

"All of ye, help me move this thing," Royal said. He hunkered down and pushed against the stone.

Marco, Clay, and Arthur all joined in, heaving against the flat piece of rock. Grudgingly, it began to move aside with a hollow groan. With persistence, the four of them were able to slide it aside to reveal a shallow depression within the rock. They stepped back and looked within the hole. Arthur's jaw dropped and Clay's face froze in shock.

Inside the depression was the largest skull Arthur and Clay had ever seen. In front of its dark empty eye sockets stretched a long white snout. Bursting from the jaw beneath was row upon row of crooked fangs, as long as fingers, that greeted them with a silent, hideous grin.

Royal turned to Clay with a bemused smile. "What was it you said about there being no such thing as dragons?"

10

Within the Tomb of St. George

"Is that—" Arthur stammered, "—is that real?"

"It has no reason not to be," Royal answered.

"Surely that can't be the skull of a dragon," Clay said. "It must have belonged to a crocodile or something."

"I don't care if it belonged to my granny's pet poodle," replied Royal, as he knelt to take a closer look. "All I care about is that scrimshaw work on it." He pointed to something engraved in the skull's forehead. "Looks like it reads 'III LEUCA' to me. It's awfully small."

Arthur poked his nose closer to the whitened skull. "That's a Roman three, for sure. We're getting closer!"

Royal drew his compass from his pocket. Meanwhile, Marco gave Clay a smug look. "Do you still believe there's no treasure to be found in that tomb?"

Clay pondered the giant skull in bewilderment. "I'm not sure what to believe anymore."

"I've got our second heading. North and twelve degrees east," said Royal, snapping the compass shut. "Let's cover up our helpful monster's noggin and get on our way. We should be able to reach our destination before sunset."

Together, they heaved the giant flagstone back into place, letting the skull resume its secret repose.

As they journeyed from the massif, the hard desert

ground succumbed to drifts of sand which then gave way to dunes that stretched around them in golden waves. The empty horizon shimmered in the afternoon heat as their camels traced their winding course.

"Do you think those were the bones of the dragon that St. George killed?" Arthur asked.

"If so, then maybe Marco is right," Clay answered, "and there is loot waiting for us at the end of this map after all."

"Maybe I'm right?" Marco challenged. "I'll assume your insult is not intentional."

Royal simply remained silent as he tossed another pebble onto the ground from his pouch.

"Assuming no one has beat us to it," Clay added.

Marco shook his head. "I find the idea of someone discovering the tomb without the map, bearings, and markers hard to believe. Besides," he added, "most people—learned people—know to stay away from the treasure of St. George."

"That's the second time you said there was danger. What's there to be afraid of?" questioned Arthur.

Marco was silent as the camels loped forward.

Royal finally spoke up. "Well, Learned One, aren't you going to enlighten them?"

Clay and Arthur pivoted their attention to the pirate. "Do you know what he's talking about?"

"Aye," Royal answered. "And there's no point in hiding the truth since we're this close to the end." He shifted in his perch upon the camel, attempting to find some figment of comfort. "You see, most people are never asking the right questions. They want to hear about St. George and his valiant act of slaying the dragon. They want to hear about how he was lauded with riches. They want to know where he was buried and how much fortune did he take to his grave. But they never consider the more curious question."

"Which is?" the boys asked in unison.

"How did St. George kill the dragon?"

Seeing that neither Clay nor Arthur had any response, Royal elaborated. "Slaying a dragon is no simple feat, so what was Georgie Boy's little secret?"

Clay and Arthur looked at each other, mystified. "So, what was it?"

"Askelon," Royal answer simply.

"What's Askelon?" Arthur pressed.

"That's the name given to St. George's lance. The weapon he used to slay the dragon. It is said that whoever holds Askelon holds incredible power. The wielder of Askelon rules all dragonkind and can command them to do his very bidding. And so, St. George was able to hold sway over any manner of dragon that he chose. He used Askelon to save a kingdom. And used it to send death upon his potential executioners. He who finds Askelon, finds unrivaled might. That's what they say, anyway."

"And this lance, Askelon, is buried in St. George's tomb?" asked Clay. "That sounds like quite a treasure, were it true! Even if just a story, the lance of St. George would be a real prize! I don't see what's so dangerous about that."

"Of course you wouldn't," Marco argued as he rolled his eyes. "Never mind that you've been threatened at sword point and showered with cannonballs since looking for it. I would expect that kind of blindness from a cyclops pirate like Royal, but not from somebody who has two working eyeballs in his head. For centuries, Askelon's location has remained a secret, but if you remove Askelon from its resting place, you summon all manner of destruction upon yourself. Men will kill for it," Marco warned. "And it's not just men that will kill you for it," he added forebodingly.

"If it's so dangerous, then why are you sticking around?" grumbled Royal.

"I just want to get my treasure and go," Marco defended. "Is that too much to ask?"

Again, Royal scoffed and tossed another pebble from his leather pouch.

Marco couldn't suppress his annoyance any longer. "Will you stop pitching those silly little pebbles? It's the most useless thing I've ever seen anyone do."

"I'm measuring distance," barked Royal. He counted the remaining stones in his pouch. "By my calculations, we have about four miles remaining. I've measured our rate of speed and dropped a pebble every fifteen minutes."

"Save me from pirate mathematics!" Marco pleaded toward the sky. "Even if the sand you use for a brain was encased in an hourglass, I still wouldn't trust it to be accurate. I'm a mapmaker and can tell you that our destination is just over the next dune."

"Balderdash!" argued Royal. "I know how to reckon longitude whether it be on sea or land."

"It's a miracle we ever made to the coast," Marco shot back. "In a moment, you'll see I am correct."

As they crested the next dune, it appeared that Marco had spoken too soon. Royal was on the verge of gloating but stopped to reach for his spyglass instead. He gazed through it for a silent moment before speaking. "Well, butter my boots and call 'em biscuits! There's something there!"

Arthur and Clay squinted into the sandscape. The sun

was at their backs, causing their shadows to stretch before them. The bright, reflecting sand made it difficult for their eyes to navigate the glow of the dunes and the dark depths of the shadows. Barely discernable was a sand-pelted dome of bricks that protruded from among the desert dunes.

Royal prodded his camel forward and the three followed. Soon, they reached the odd construction and slowly circled the brick mound. "This must be it," he answered.

"Seems awfully small," Arthur commented.

"This is just the tip of the iceberg," Royal answered. "The desert must have swallowed the entrance. We'll have to dig."

"We have no shovels," Marco noted unhelpfully.

"You got flippers, ain't ya?" With that, he dropped and began scooping sand with his hands.

The others joined in. Not knowing where to start, they all took different sides of the dome to dig. Slowly, the large mound of bricks emerged from its prison of sand. It wasn't long before Clay uncovered the beginnings of an opening. "I think I found the way in!"

Royal, Arthur, and Marco hurried over and assisted with Clay's excavations. What Clay had discovered, though, was not any type of door, but appeared to be a breach in the stonework.

"Looks like someone's been here already," suggested Royal. He continued clearing sand away from the hole. "Woah!" he blurted abruptly. The remaining stone suddenly collapsed beneath him and he spilled forward into the opening under a cascade of sand.

"Royal!" Clay shouted. The three gawked into the darkness of the breach. All they could see or hear was the hissing of the soft sand as it spilled into the abyss. "Royal, are you okay?"

The captain's voice rose from the darkness. "I'm fine. I took a tumble down a stairway. Looks like this tomb goes deeper than we thought."

"Can you see any treasure?" Marco asked.

"All I see is your three slack-jawed gobs staring down at me. Get in here and we'll see where this leads."

Carefully, they entered the small opening. Royal was right. Narrow steps descended into the depths of the desert. Royal produced a scrap of cloth from his tinder box and struck a flint onto it. The small flame glowed around them but barely penetrated the darkness.

"Ah!" smiled Royal. "That's what we need." He gestured to two small metal torches resting in sconces, and flanking a dark passage. He ignited one of the torch's tallow-soaked wicks. The passageway filled with yellow light. "No telling how deep this passage runs or how long this flame will burn. We best move fast." Removing the flickering torch from the sconce, he held it forward to push back the darkness.

"Look at the walls!" Arthur whispered in amazement. The corridor was painted with detailed scenes, each depicting an armored knight in various acts of valor. One of them showed the brave hero, astride a rearing steed and thrusting a lance into a cowering dragon. "This must be it," the boy said. "This must be the tomb of St. George!"

Marco rolled his eyes. "Oh, thank goodness," he muttered sarcastically. "For a moment, I was worried we might have wandered into the wrong crypt in the middle of nowhere."

Arthur gave Marco a reproachful glare, but Royal simply agreed. "Aye. We're only a few paces away from our quest's end!"

They followed the dark corridor to where it emerged into a broad, domed chamber. Clay and Arthur stared in awe as, dumbstruck by the scene. Royal's single eye sparked with delight. Marco gazed about the chamber and licked his dry lips in anticipation.

The tomb was elaborately decorated and ornate. The first thing that commanded their attention was a huge half-sphere that rose grandly from a round dais in the center of the room. The dome was covered with an intricate relief of stars, sailing vessels, and detailed depictions of warriors in battle. Surrounding the circular room were four imposing statues upon pedestals. Each stood rigidly in differing poses, their bows drawn stoically and aimed downward toward the sphere in the center. The detailed sculptures were so finely crafted that Arthur imagined they could spring to life at any moment.

"Incredible!" exclaimed Marco. "It's beautiful!"

"Aye," Royal replied in simple agreement. He held the torch higher as he took in the tomb's lush architecture. For a quiet moment, the four of them stood mesmerized by the wonder of the burial chamber.

Royal's torch sputtered, nudging him from his reverie. He glanced around and spied braziers nestled between each of the stone archers. Plunging the torch into each one, the tomb of St. George immediately glowed with magnificent light. Now, unhindered by darkness, the four of them could admire the polished black stone and golden reliefs upon the huge sphere beneath the cobalt blue dome of the chamber. The dancing shadows from the firelight made the scultped forms of the archers and their readied bows seem even more alive and ominous.

Suddenly, Arthur yelped in fright. The fresh illumination revealed a terrible sight. Collapsed upon one side of the dark sphere was the decaying form of a skeleton.

"Who is that?" Clay asked, eyes wide.

"Must be the gentleman who busted through the stonework for us," Royal surmised. He scrutinized the corpse closely with his good eye. The skeleton was garbed in a leather tunic and breeches. A round, metal helmet rested atop its skull. "Looks to be some medieval explorer. A *knight errant*, maybe." Royal spied two lengths of arrow that protruded from the back of the leather jerkin. "He was shot in the back."

"There must have been two of them," Marco suggested. "He was double-crossed by his partner who shot him in the back and left with the treasure."

Royal peered closer. "I don't think so," he replied. "At close quarters like these, a bow would be an unlikely choice for an attack. And two shots in the back? Even a skilled archer would have a hard time loosing two arrows in succession like this."

"What's this?" asked Arthur. He pointed to the skeleton's gloved hand resting upon a metal shaft protruding from the base of the large, black sphere. Before Royal could protest, Arthur tugged on the metal rod. It slid from the sphere with ease and the disturbed skeleton clattered to the ground.

"Don't be touching things!" growled Royal.

"It's some sort of iron bolt or arrow," Arthur said as he examined it closely.

"It's definitely not any sort of treasure," Marco bristled. "If this unlucky soul was not marauded by another, then where is the treasure? Or Askelon? Or St. George, for that matter?"

Royal ran his hands over the decorated surface of the black dome. "This must be St. George's sarcophagus. But it's not like any coffin I've ever seen." He shoved at it firmly, but it didn't budge. "It's closed tighter than a drum."

"You think St. George—or what's left of him—is in there?" Clay asked.

"Aye, and all his worldly goods, too, I reckon. But how does it open?" He marched around the sphere, his hands running across the countless raised images, seeking any indication of an opening. He noticed that the circumference of the dome contained several slots like the one from which Arthur had pulled the bolt.

Arthur continued to turn the curious item in his hands. "This is odd. There are notches and grooves in this arrow." He was about to slide it back into the hole from which it came, but Royal leapt forward and snatched it from his grasp.

"Avast there!" The pirate gave the mysterious bolt a wary look. "This is no arrow. It's a key."

"It must be the key to unlocking the sarcophagus!" added Marco. "Our problems are solved!"

"Hmph," the captain responded. He pointed to the collapsed remains of the skeleton. "I'm sure that's exactly what Sir Pincushion thought."

Royal's eye glanced around, tracing invisible lines in the air. He looked past the statues of frozen archers and then studied the dark blue ceiling. Virtually indistinguishable in the firelight, he saw that the dome above was dotted with several small dark openings. "It's a trap," he groaned.

Marco froze with dread. "A trap? Where?"

"Over our melons," Royal gestured upward. "It's a booby trap. And if we don't play things right, we'll be stuck with arrows like this sorry sod. Nobody touches anything.

I didn't come all this way to have an arrowhead making a nest in my ribcage."

"What do we do?" asked Marco. "This is your little quest of doom, Royal. Did you lead is in here only to die or leave empty-handed?"

"We've got a key and a plethora of keyholes. I ain't inclined to try and unlock this sarcophagus if it means getting an arrow in my scalp. There must be some type of clue. Was there anything written on Cordura's map?"

Marco shook his head. "The map said nothing about booby traps. Or the need for a key. Where did this key come from?"

"I think it came from here," Clay said. He had been carefully examining the chamber for anything that could enlighten them. He pointed to one of the statues. The stone archer with its cold eyeless gaze stood with arrow nocked and bow drawn. Resting against its leg was a stone quiver, but it was empty. "All of these statues have a quiver, but this is the only one that has no arrow in it."

Royal approached and dropped the odd metal arrow into the empty quiver. It landed with a heavy *clang*. He strolled to the next statue. The pose was different. The archer was kneeling, arrow at ready, and a quiver hung from his shoulder. Royal slid the single arrow from its quiver. Like the one in the skeleton's grip, it had assorted notches on it. "Looks similar to the other one, but not quite the same." He grimaced as he looked at the four statues, each with its own odd arrow. "Now we have four keys instead of one. Our chances of unlocking this thing went from slim to fat chance."

"Maybe we need to use all four," Clay suggested, "and that's why it didn't work for our unfortunate friend."

"There's must be two dozen keyholes in that thing," Royal said as he gestured to the sarcophagus. "We're missing something."

"Does anyone know what that says?" Arthur asked, pointing above them. Encircling the wall around the dome was chiseled writing, but it wasn't in any language Arthur knew (he only knew one, actually.)

Royal squinted. "It's Latin, by my guess." He swiveled in a circle as he read the inscription aloud.

SAGITTA UNA DESUPER
UNUM VIA DUO VENTI
ASKELON EST UBI SAGITTA QUIESCIT

"What does it mean?" asked Clay.

"Burned if I know," Royal replied. "I'm no Latin scholar."

They all turned and looked at Marco.

Marco returned their gaze with a blank expression. "What? You're expecting me to translate it?"

"Do you understand it?" Royal asked.

"Yes. But why should I help you? You're chasing Askelon. I came here for treasure only. You are asking me to give you the power of St. George and I am not sure I want to do that."

"Don't test me, Marco," Royal growled. "If all you want is treasure, then you can have it. But what you want and what I want both rest inside this sarcophagus. You can give up your silly fears about Askelon or you can leave this tomb a poor man. Just remember when you're poor and desolate that the only thing that kept you from your precious treasure was yourself."

Clay and Arthur watched the two men glower at each

other. The weight of their stand-off filled the tomb. Marco finally spoke. "We will split the treasure. But Askelon remains here."

"No deals, Marco," Royal said. "You want your booty, then you'll have to tell us what the inscription says. The only thing you have to bargain with is your fate. You can leave rich, or poor, or not at all. Which is it going to be?"

Marco's jaw clenched, and Clay and Arthur could see that Royal held the upper hand. The mapmaker's greed was on the captain's side. Finally, Marco succumbed. "Fine! I will help you. But whatever treasure is in this sarcophagus belongs to me!"

"Hey!" Arthur cried. "What about us? I was the one who figured out the coin!"

Marco scowled. "You chose the wrong friends. Your lousy pirate of a captain just gave me your share."

Clay and Arthur looked angrily at Royal.

"Enough of this," barked the captain. "I'll square with the both of you, but nothing is happening until we solve this last riddle. Tell us what the inscription says."

Staring at the chiseled Latin far above them, Marco began to translate. "Well...the writing goes in a circle, so I'm not sure where it starts. But roughly it says: One arrow from above. One path. Two winds. Askelon rests where the arrow lands."

"Well, that's not helpful at all," Royal grumbled.

"I didn't write it, so don't take your frustration out on me."

Arthur was already noodling on the words as he looked at the four archers with bows aimed down at them. "That answers our first question, I think. Since it says 'One arrow from above' then we must only need one of the arrows, and not all four."

Clay chimed in. "The last part seems straightforward, too. 'Askelon rests where the arrow lands' must be referring to inside the sarcophagus. We're halfway there!"

"That's just fine," Royal replied. "Why do I feel we're no closer to the answer, then?"

The four of them lapsed into thought. Arthur clasped his hands behind his back and began trudging in a circle around the chamber, his head hung in concentration.

"Perhaps the 'path' refers to the holes on the sphere. One key and one keyhole?" Marco suggested.

"That makes sense," Clay responded.

"Bah," Royal exclaimed. "So now we have four keys and twenty-four keyholes and somehow there's only one correct combination. How many possibilities is that?"

"Ninety-six," Arthur answered promptly, still circumnavigating the tomb in contemplation.

Marco nodded, a hint of impressed surprise on his face. "He is correct."

"That gives us a one-in-ninety-six chance of choosing the right combination or else we get showered by an arrow from one of those holes in the ceiling," Royal replied. "I don't like those odds."

"One-in-ninety-five chance, actually," Clay said. "Our dead corpse here already eliminated one of the wrong answers for us."

"I stand corrected," Royal muttered. "Are you sure there's nothing else in the writing, Marco? Are you holding out on us?"

"Why would I do that?" Marco fumed. "I want to leave here as much as you do, preferably laden with gold."

"I'm not so sure," countered Royal. "How do I know you're not playing us for fools? Now that you know the location of St. George, you probably think you can come back at some other time to collect your rewards, long after we've all given up and sailed into the sunset! After all, that's what you did to us eight years ago aboard the *Sea Scar*!"

"The *Sea Scar*? Isn't that Schark's ship?" Clay asked.

"Aye! We were all one fat and happy crew—Marco included—until he claimed ignorance about a certain island and a heap of rubies. Only to find that he slipped away in the night to try and salvage the treasure for himself! I found him, though. And saved his rotten, trapped, neck while I was at it!"

"Lies!" Marco yelled back and then halted. "Well, not lies, exactly, but still a wildly vague representation of what actually occurred!"

"Regardless," Royal continued, "I know what kind of snake you are. And not to be completely trusted."

"I have regretted my actions ever since that day, and you know it! And you know that's exactly the reason I don't want Askelon to leave this tomb!"

Clay was thoroughly confused. But before he could ask any questions, Arthur interjected. "Look! It's something we missed!" Arthur dropped to the ground and was brushing away bits of wayward sand. "There's a cross on the floor."

"St. George's cross," Royal answered. "I noticed the pattern when we entered." The dark red arms of the cross extended from four sides of the dais holding the sphere. They stretched from the center of the chamber to end at each of the four stone archers. "What of it?"

"There's a name on each."

Immediately, they scrabbled to see what Arthur was

129

looking at. "See?" he said. "This one is *Favonius*. That one says *Septentrio*. That one is *Auster*. And over there is *Subsolanus*. Are those the names of the archers?"

Marco's eyes began to glow. "This is it!" he exclaimed.

"That is what?" Royal asked with irritation.

"These are the names of the directions on the Roman map. *Septentrio* is North, *Auster* is South, *Subsolanus* is East, and *Favonius* is West."

"I don't see how that gets us any closer to an answer," remarked Clay.

"Of course you wouldn't," said Marco, resuming his arrogant demeanor. "Why should you know that the original names given to the Greek and Roman compass were based on the names of winds?"

"Winds?" Royal looked up at the stone archers. "The inscription mentions two winds."

"*Unum via. Duo venti*," Marco nodded. "One path. Two winds."

"Confound it!" Royal snapped. "That makes even less sense. How can we possibly put one key into two keyholes?"

"And even if we could, we still don't know which key," Clay added. "Or which keyholes."

Their momentary elation subsided as they were once again faced with a mystery. Arthur simply leaned against the wall and fiddled with his chin. "One path. Two winds. One key. Two keyholes," he whispered. "One path. Two winds. The arrow is the key. The wind is a direction. One arrow. Two directions."

"It's gibberish," Royal muttered bitterly. "I think we're on the wrong tack."

"One arrow. Two directions," Arthur repeated.

"I hate to admit it," Marco said, "but I think Royal is correct. We are as lost as we were before."

"One arrow. Two directions," Arthur said again. "That must be the answer."

"That makes no sense, Arthur," his brother replied. "How can you send one arrow in two directions? The inscription says Askelon is where the arrow lands. It can't be in two places."

If Arthur heard his brother, it didn't show. He simply stared at the large half of the sphere upon the dais. He slowly strolled around it, trying to reveal its secret. "One arrow. Two directions."

Then he stopped.

"One arrow! Two directions!" he exclaimed.

"Saying it louder doesn't help," Marco said.

"I think I understand!" Arthur replied. The excitement in his voice was palpable.

"What are you thinking?" Clay asked.

Arthur's ebullience bubbled over. "What happens," he said, "if you fire an arrow to the east?"

Clay, Royal, and Marco looked at each other and shrugged. "It hits an eastern squirrel," Clay replied.

"Well, yes, I suppose. But its headed east, right?" said Arthur. "And what happens if you fire it west?"

"Is Royal standing to the west?" Marco commented.

"It goes to the west," Clay answered. "I'm not following you, Arthur."

"Suppose you could fire an arrow that never falls. Or hits anything. Which direction does it fly? East or west?"

"It depends on which direction you fired it."

"And what happens if I shoot an arrow to the north. Which direction does it go?"

Clay shrugged. "It goes north."

Royal, however, straightened. "No, not necessarily," he said. "If it never falls, it flies north. Until it passes over the pole."

"In which case," Marco joined in, "it would then be flying south."

"One path. Two winds," Arthur summarized.

"Poseidon's Pants!" exclaimed Royal. "I think he's figured it out!"

"Hold on a moment," Marco interjected. "There are still two possibilities. You can choose the path to the north or you can choose the path to the south. Which is it?"

"The clue says 'one arrow from above.' Maybe it's telling us we fire the arrow from the north?" Arthur suggested. "Which would be the northern archer. Which one was that?"

"*Septentrio*," Marco answered.

Arthur strolled to the statue and pulled the metal arrow from its quiver.

"That seems reasonable," Clay opined. "But are we certain which hole it goes into? If this sphere is a globe, there would be a keyhole at the top but they're all on the sides."

"There's no reason to assume this is a globe," said Royal. "There are no land masses or names on it to give any bearings." He pulled his compass fom his pocket. "It must be referring to true north on the map." He watched the needle wobble within the compass. As it steadied, Royal pointed to the northernmost hole in the globe. "It goes here."

They all simply stood and stared at each other.

"Who's going to do the honors?" Clay asked.

No one was eager to risk being skewered by an arrow that could come from virtually any direction.

"I should do it," Arthur said.

"Absolutely not!" objected Clay.

"But I'm the smallest," Arthur answered, "and less of a target."

"Clay is right," Royal said to Arthur. "This isn't for you. I should be the one who does it. Everyone stand back."

Arthur, Clay, and Marco stepped away as Royal leveled the strangely-notched arrow at the hole. He was about to shove it into the opening when Marco suddenly rushed forward and grabbed his hand. "Wait!" he shouted.

"What's wrong?"

"This cannot be correct," Marco said.

"Why not?"

Beads of sweat beaded on Marco's forehead. "At the time St. George was entombed, they did not have magnetic compasses. At least, not in the Occident. They would not consider this the northernmost keyhole."

Royal's good eye narrowed. "If not this hole, then which one?"

Marco looked around. "Perhaps," he answered, "the cross of St. George on the floor is meant to be a crude compass rose. In that case," he pointed to the *Septentrio* archer, "that would be the north indicator and we should use the keyhole facing it."

"That keyhole is four notches off-course," the pirate answered. Royal studied Marco for what seemed like an eternity as he ruminated on the situation. Which was the path he should follow? The north on his compass or the north on the floor? Marco was right. Saint George, or the people who interned him, would not have had a compass to tell which was true north. Royal's gripped tightened around the metal key as it wavered in front of the keyhole. If he made the wrong choice, it would likely be the last decision he'd ever make.

And with that, he plunged the arrow into the keyhole.

As the arrow slid into the slot, a sonorous clap reverberated from the depths of the sphere, followed by anxious silence. The four of them held their breath as they waited for something to happen. No deadly bolts flew from the darkness. After another quiet moment of trepidation, Royal carefully twisted the unusual key and another deep knock resounded within.

After a weighty pause, they simultaneously came to the same conclusion. "It worked!" cried Arthur.

"How did you know?" asked the perplexed Marco.

"Hmmph," Royal grunted. "Sailors don't need a compass to know true north. They have the North Star." His one eye gave Marco a wary look. "I'd have thought a decent mapmaker would have known that."

"Whether I was right or wrong is inconsequential," Marco replied. "The tomb is still shut."

"All we did was unlock it," Arthur answered. "Now we need to open it. The clue says Askelon rests where the arrow lands. We have to move the arrow so that it flies north, then south."

Without another word, Royal used the arrow as a handle and lifted upward. With surprisingly little effort, the giant sphere began to revolve. The raised images of the dark sphere rolled upwards, and from the depths of the dais, more images began to reveal themselves. The intricate designs of knights and castles gave way to snake-like, writhing forms of serpents and dragons. Some were large with broadened wings, while others sported spines and fins as they dove into the waters. One appeared to be breathing fire while another clawed at a crumbling turret with long, curving talons.

Royal continued to push the handle over the sphere's pole. Abruptly, the arrow handle escaped his hand as the counter-balanced dome began to open of its own accord. As the dome retreated into the dais, it revealed a large hollow interior...and within, a breathtaking display.

"Wow!" Arthur whispered in awe.

"Incredible!" echoed Clay.

Inside the hollow sphere was a round slab, upon which two decaying bodies lay in quiet repose. One figure was bedecked in chain mail and leather. The other was adorned in an elegant silk dress. Resting upon the faces of both were shining gold masks, richly mimicking the regal features of the departed man and woman.

But what really captured the attention of the onlookers was the stunning array of rubies, sapphires, emeralds and pearls that surrounded the two figures. The gems, both large and small, were intricately arranged upon the bier, creating a perfectly smooth and ornate mosaic of a summer landscape. Verdant emeralds formed winding vinework that danced around the couple. Shimmering sapphires displayed a waving sea, frothing with shining pearls. Rubies glittered about them in the shape of budding roses.

Also lying in repose, ensconced amongst the jewels

were various artifacts. Around the woman was a golden hair comb and a delicate vial of oil. Around the man were several weapons...a rather simple-looking mace, a small buckler, and a short knife. And between the two of them rested a long shaft that stretched about a meter and a half before terminating in a vicious, four-flanged point of iron.

"Askelon," breathed Royal.

"The treasure of St. George!" exclaimed Marco. "We found it!" Immediately, his hand swept into the display of gems, leaving a large smear in the intricate mosaic. His plump hand grasped as many of the precious jewels as it could.

Royal reached forward and delicately lifted the long lance from its bed. The weight was surprisingly light in his hands. Clearly a weapon designed to be as easy to wield as possible.

Marco halted and gave Royal a wary stare. "You finally have your precious lance," he said. "What are you going to do with it?"

"I'm going to return it to its rightful owner."

If Marco had any further questions, they were quickly forgotten when he spotted Arthur's hand reaching over the bier. He immediately swatted it away. "Off with you! This treasure belongs to me. That was the deal!"

Arthur gave him an angry glare. "You can keep your jewels. I wanted to look at the knife." Arthur plucked the small weapon from the slab. Mollified, Marco returned to sweeping as many of the gems as he could into his satchel while Arthur examined the solid blade and hilt.

Clay turned to Royal. "What do you mean you're going to return the lance to its owner? Even if St. George stole it from someone, that person must be long since dead."

Royal pretended not to hear. Instead, his attention was directed to the golden face mask of the man lying in the tomb. Curiously, he lifted the covering. Beneath, resting in grim repose, was the whitened skull of St. George. The skull was unassuming in every way except for a fraying eyepatch that covered one of its sockets. "Huh," Royal muttered in mild surprise.

Clay was about to press Royal for an answer to his question but halted. The entire crypt began to quake. An ominous pounding rumbled from the walls.

"What is that?" yelped Arthur. "Another booby trap?"

Dust vibrated from the ceiling as Royal glanced around. "I don't know. I think it best that we depart, though."

Marco hurriedly began plunging more jewels into his bag as Royal, Clay, and Arthur dashed to the passageway. Suddenly, the stones within the corridor collapsed in an explosive cloud of dust.

In the dim light of the torches, a gigantic row of jutting fangs emerged from the dusty air, stretching from wall to wall. Behind the thrust of sharp teeth glared two snake-like green eyes. A furious roar rumbled from the depths of the stretching maw. Its resonating force shuddered the stone floor and rattled the very bones of the four trapped men.

Arthur immediately did what any reasonable person would do and screamed at the top of his lungs. Marco joined in.

"Back!" Royal yelled as he ushered them all into the safety of the tomb.

The giant snout of teeth protruded further from the opening, snapping ferociously through the breach of stone while the four scrambled for safety behind the open sarcophagus.

"It's—it's a—" stammered Arthur.

"It's a dragon!" Clay finished the sentence for him.

"Not just any dragon!" yelled Marco. "It's a *browgie*!"

Clay and Arthur gave him a puzzled look.

"Aye!" Royal exclaimed. "A *browgie*. A big dragon. All muscle. With rocks for brains. Literally."

As if to punctuate the pirate's sentence, the enormous beast rammed its head against the small entrance, attempting to breach deeper into the tomb. Again, the crooked fangs snatched at the air. A falling brick of stone tumbled into the monstrous maw. With a mighty snap, the fangs clamped down and pulverized it into dust.

"He's too big to get in here," Royal noted.

"We're trapped!" cried Arthur.

"Royal," Marco yelled, "you have the lance! Use it! It's the only way to escape!"

The captain stiffened as he gripped the shaft of the long weapon. Cautiously, he crept from around the sarcophagus, lance at the ready. The hideous jaws of the dragon continued to snap frustratingly through the narrow opening. Royal then noticed the long, winding scar that twisted from one of the flaring nostrils to its grimacing maw. "Well, well," he remarked. "If it isn't my old friend, Balfour. Looks like I'm getting a second crack at you!" He raised the lance over his head, preparing to drive it into the growling snout.

Before he could land his blow, the green eyes of the monster instantly narrowed and the giant nose vanished into the darkness of the corridor. The tip of Royal's lance clanged harmlessly against the stone floor where the dragon's snout had been.

Royal staggered to regain his footing when a tremendous, clawed hand shot through the breach, flinging the captain and his weapon across the room. The leathery talons thrust about the stone floor blindly, grasping for any possible victim.

"Royal!" Clay called into the darkness. "Are you okay?"

The captain rolled across the hard stones, stunned by the blow. "I think so," he groaned as he regained his senses.

The giant claw retreated back into the hole. For a moment, the tomb filled with eerie silence.

"Did it leave?" wondered Arthur, hopefully. "Maybe the lance scared it away."

Arthur's hopes were quickly dashed as a sudden pounding shook the dome. Cracks splintered the stone above. "No such luck," Royal muttered. "Find cover!"

The four of them scurried behind the different archer statues—the only place that provided any type of shelter from the crumbling dome.

After another severe pummel, the ceiling of the tomb burst inward. Stone and plaster collapsed to the floor. Desert sand poured through the breach and they could see the night sky through the widening crack. They had been in the tomb for hours, Arthur realized, and the sun had long since set. The dark shape of the giant dragon eclipsed the stars as it peered through the breach.

The crooked fangs, surprisingly bright in the dim light, bared themselves again as the beast let out a bone-shaking roar. Immediately, it began pounding the compromised dome with its head.

Royal grasped the shaft of the fallen lance but to his dismay, it was now lodged beneath a pile of fallen stone. "Hide yourselves while I try to free this lousy thing!"

To everyone's relief, the ceiling held strong under the

assault of the fierce *browgie*. In frustration, the persistent dragon bellowed again and reached through with its scaly claws, fishing for its four trapped victims. Royal wrestled with the stuck lance.

Arthur was in the worst spot, in a clear line of sight from the dome's gap. He fervently tried to wedge himself behind the pedestal of the statue as much as he could. The beast stretched its arm to its limit and the curved talons scrabbled at the boy's pathetic hiding place.

Arthur realized he was still clutching the small knife he lifted from the sarcophagus. It was a tiny weapon compared to the huge, bony claw reaching for him, but it was all he had. Swiftly, he calculated the most vulnerable part of the beast and, with fear and desperation, jammed the short blade where the dragon's hard claw protruded from its leathery skin.

The screech of pain that ripped through the air shocked everyone. Instantly, the grotesque claw whisked back from the dome and vanished completely.

Once more, foreboding silence filled the tomb.

The four of them peered upward through the ceiling's breach, seeing only the quiet stars above.

"That startled him, for sure!" Royal exclaimed. With one more tremendous yank, he pulled the lance free from the pile of stones. "Quickly! We can get out this way." Using the collapsed stone and pile of sand as a crude ramp, he ascended to the crumbling breach of the domed ceiling. He poked his head into the night air and surveyed the surroundings. "Looks clear. For now. Good show, Arthur. *Browgies* are tough, but when you hit 'em in the right spot, they're big babies. Go for their eyes and nostrils and they get pretty shy. Looks like you found another soft spot!"

"Are you sure it's safe?" Marco asked.

"Would you rather huddle in this sandpit until he returns?" Royal growled. "Stay here with your treasure if you wish, but I'm weighing anchor!" He scrambled from the tomb. The others quickly agreed with his reasoning and clambered up behind him.

"Blast!" Royal growled as he looked about the barren landscape. "Looks like Balfour spooked the camels and they ran off. You can see their tracks. No telling how far they went." Having little alternative, the four of them followed after the sandy trail of camel prints.

They finally found the frightened animals, huddled together several dunes to the west. Marco wasted no time mounting his ride and bolting over the next dune. No one chastised him. They climbed up on their camels without a word and chased after him. Clay and Arthur nervously watched the sky above. "I feel like a sitting duck out here on the open desert," Clay shouted to Royal as they urged the camels forward.

"If we keep a good pace, we'll be back to the *Typhoon* by early morning." Royal called back. "We don't have to zig zag across the desert looking for clues. We've got the cover of darkness on our side. And we have Askelon."

"Askelon is the whole reason Balfour is hunting us!" argued Marco. "I told you that if you removed that stupid lance from its hiding place, you'd be courting a terrible death!"

"Who is Balfour?" Clay asked. "How do you know this thing by name?"

"Balfour's nothing," Royal snapped back. "He's chasing after Askelon because his leader told him to. But he's wary of us now. He'll keep his distance because he knows we have the means to slay him. He won't sacrifice himself for it. If we get Askelon to our destination, we've nothing to fear."

Marco erupted in a hearty belly laugh. "Ha! I find your optimism as adorable as your stupidity! Once a *browgie* senses its prey, it won't let up."

"All the more reason to quicken our pace, then," answered Royal. "You, on the other hand, are more than welcome to go your merry way. You have your precious loot. You've nothing to gain by following us."

"It so happens that my merry way coincides with yours since you captain the only sea vessel within a hundred miles. You deposited me on this miserable coast and as long as a *browgie* is flying about, I fully expect you to give me passage to civilization and safety." With that, he goaded his camel onward.

Clay and Arthur followed his example and urged their own mount to gallop faster. The sprint back to the coast was riddled with anxiety and false alarms. Arthur spent the ride jumping at shadows, imagining movement behind every dark dune. Royal kept a watchful eye on the skies, seeking any sign of the giant dragon's horrible silhouette. But their ride through the night remained uneventful. With each mile behind them, they began to grow more at ease.

The sky in the east lightened and Arthur welcomed the sense of comfort that came with being able to discern the desertscape around them. Despite their rise in optimism, though, no one dared express it. They merely continued their press forward.

Soon, the crisp scent of the ocean tinged the air. The morning sun broke the darkness, and they could see the welcoming stretch of the sea ahead. Gently bobbing in the ocean, just as they had left it, was the *Ivory Typhoon*, the golden morning rays bouncing off its masts.

"We made it!" Arthur shouted.

"I've never seen a finer sight!" said Clay.

"Aye, but it's no time to celebrate!" Royal replied. "Get to the dinghy!" Their small boat still rested where they had dragged it ashore. It was hard for Arthur to believe that it was only yesterday morning that they had set foot upon the coast.

No one wasted a moment jumping from their camel. Royal tossed the lance into the bottom of the craft and Marco did the same with his bag of gems. Together, all four of them put their shoulders to the boat and shoved it into the lapping waves. Marco and Clay wrestled a bit over the oars, both eager to reach the ship as quickly as possible. Soon, they were plying the waves steadily with rapid strokes. In only a matter of minutes, the crew had scrabbled aboard the sturdy deck of the *Typhoon* and hoisting the dinghy into its davits.

Royal pulled a lever. The familiar, clanking chain in the hawsehole vibrated the hull as it lifted the anchor from the seabed. "With the wind at our back, we can make good speed and hightail it away from here before the beast catches our scent again." With the yank of another handle, sails unfurled from the yardarms and the vessel sliced rapidly into the sea.

"And good riddance!" breathed Clay as he watched the golden beach retreat into the distance.

Exhausted, Arthur settled down against a lashed barrel. Immediately, he felt the prick of the small knife that he had tucked into his belt. He pulled it out and examined the dark blade. The heft was simple but expertly crafted. With a little polish, it would be a handsome knife, thought Arthur. To his delight, it fit easily into the secret sheath inside his boot. More and more, he was beginning to feel like a pirate. He settled back, grateful to finally get some sleep. An animated discussion between Royal and Marco, however, interrupted his rest.

"We're not going north!" argued Royal. "My course is west into the ocean."

"You owe me safe passage off of this floating coffin!" countered Marco. "I know of a place in the Greek isles that we can reach in only a day or two."

"This ain't no charter," Royal spat. "If you don't like where I'm headed, you should never have climbed aboard. These two, however—" he pointed to Clay and Arthur "—I'll drop somewhere on the Iberian Peninsula. If you want, you can go ashore with them."

"Iberia?" Clay interjected. "Our home is in England."

"And so is a fleet of naval warships who want my hide," the captain answered. "I was lucky to escape once. I'm not willing to risk it again. Don't worry. I'll give you enough gold so that you can find passage the rest of the way. And you—" Royal turned to Marco "—can use your haul from the tomb to take a pleasure cruise from there to wherever you want. I'm not wasting any time meandering around the sea. Not while we know Balfour is on the hunt."

"Hmmph!" Marco huffed. He hefted his rattling bag of gems and found a secluded spot to sit and count his jewels.

Clay turned to Royal. "You said this Balfour was hunting Askelon for someone else? Who?"

Royal kept his one eye focused on the ocean as he pointed the *Ivory Typhoon* westward. "That's of little importance to you. I wouldn't worry your little head about it. Once I plant the two of you ashore, you'll never see Balfour again."

"Unless it catches up to us before then."

"The ocean is a mighty big place. Each minute that passes, it'll be harder and harder for him to find us. But keep your eyes peeled for anything odd in the sky."

Arthur and Clay both surveyed the air above them with worry. "I still can't believe there really are such things as dragons!" Clay exclaimed.

"I guess it never occurred to you that something can exist whether you choose to believe in it or not," Royal replied. "Dragons? They're out there. They're elusive. Secretive. After centuries of being hunted and attacked, they've found themselves new places to hide, fleeing to the fringes of the places we know."

At this, Marco paused from assessing his treasure to chime in. "People called me silly whenever I would note on my maps 'here there be dragons!' Despite my very accurate warnings, they would chide me for being fanciful or poetic. Ha! As if I don't know what I was talking about. Fools!" he shouted to no one in particular and then returned to his gem-counting.

Royal shrugged at Marco's commentary and continued. "There was a time when people folk and dragons actually co-existed without any problems. Many dragons are very intelligent and capable. But when the nasty kind come along...well, they tend to ruin things for everyone."

"So the dragon that attacked us is one of the nasty ones?" Clay asked.

"Balfour? I suppose you could say that. *Browgies* like him don't have too much going on in their crow's nest—"

Royal pointed to the side of his head to illustrate the point "—so they just take orders from whomever they give their allegiance to. Balfour's master is the nastiest dragon of all, so I guess that makes Balfour a nasty sort, too."

"And who is his master?"

Royal was silent. After a moment's thought, he answered. "It don't matter. It looks like we lost Balfour so once we get this lance to where it belongs, his boss will stay in his little hidey-hole."

"And where exactly does this lance belong? Where are you taking it?"

Again, Royal's reticence simmered, but something triggered his words. "I'm taking Askelon to Dragonrook, where it will be kept safe from the clutches of those who would misuse it. But I go alone. No one other than myself knows the location of Dragonrook and it's my charge that it remains that way. And that's why I must drop you ashore."

Marco shuddered at the mention of the name Dragonrook. "A vile place."

"Don't listen to him," Royal said. "He and dragons don't get along very well."

Clay was about to press for more answers, but Arthur interrupted. The boy's attention was stolen by a massive shadowy patch in the water that was growing larger. And closer. "What is that?" he pointed.

Before anyone could answer, the ocean exploded in a flash of foam and spray. The dark form of Balfour burst from the water and its bone-crumbling roar rattled the entire vessel.

12

Shipwrecked!

"Blast!" shouted Royal, as the massive torrent of water pummeled the deck. He cranked the *Ivory Typhoon's* wheel furiously to give the sails every breath of possible wind. "Curse my thick skull! I should have seen him coming!"

"How did he find us?" Clay cried.

"We were so busy watching the skies, that it never crossed my mind he'd be swimming beneath us! Get below, all of ye!"

Marco, Clay, and Arthur dove down the hatch to safety. Gawking from the steps, they called for Royal to join them. "What are you doing, you one-eyed fool?" called Marco. Royal wasn't listening, he pulled the ancient Askelon from over his shoulder as he watched Balfour's bulky form circle high above them in the sky.

"I've bested this boy once!" Royal answered. "I can do it again. Once he descends, he'll get his final come-uppance."

But Balfour never bothered to approach the deck. To Royal's surprise, the gigantic beast descended only low enough to allow his large talons to clutch the top of the main mast. Rope and rigging snapped under the razor-sharp claws and Royal ducked as the severed lines and blocks crashed to the deck around him.

"What's it doing?" Arthur asked.

Royal lowered Askelon and could only watch in disbelief.

With a beat of his enormous wings, Balfour pulled upward. Arthur felt the *Ivory Typhoon* heave and sway below his hands and feet. The timbers groaned around him and the showering sound of falling water rushed beneath. The steady horizon of the open sea tilted at an odd, dizzying angle.

"He's picking us up!" Clay exclaimed. "He's taking the entire ship!"

Royal spun around and watched the ocean drop away from the rail. In frustration, he shook his clenched fist at Balfour. "Come at me, you coward! You're afraid to face me as long as I have this lance, aren't ye?"

Marco turned visibly green, but Arthur couldn't tell if it was from the swaying vessel, the ever-increasing height, or the threat of the monstrous dragon. The boy gawked at the scene above him. He watched the rippling muscles of the giant claws as they clutched the mast in an iron grip. The harsh sunlight shone through the thin membranes of the beast's wings and Arthur could feel the pulse of air underneath them with every giant flap. The dragon's blocky head arched around and observed the helpless passengers tauntingly.

A sharp explosion cracked the air. Arthur saw Royal brandishing his smoking flintlock. "Bah!" he growled, tossing the spent gun onto the deck. "This thing is only tickling him."

"Use the lance!" Marco yelled. "That's what it's for!"

Royal studied the sharp weapon in his hand and then gazed upward at the flapping dragon. "I ain't no harpooner! I'm not gonna risk missing and watching my prize fall into the sea! Besides," he added, as he peered over the railing, "I'm not sure I'm fond of the idea of his letting go at the moment." Indeed, the surface of the sea had quickly dropped further and further away. "I think he's got us right where he wants us."

Balfour let out a mocking snort. His crooked fangs snarled in contempt as he turned his head forward, plowing the air with his massive wings. One wing paused, and the entire vessel swung sideways as the dragon navigated a lengthy southward turn.

"Where's he taking us?" Clay asked with alarm.

Royal surveyed the circle of blue ocean beneath them. "My guess is we're bound for Fangshard."

At that, Marco groaned. "We're doomed! We might as well throw ourselves overboard now."

Clay was confused. "What's Fangshard?"

"It's not as bad as that!" Royal replied, ignoring Clay's question. "We still have Askelon. Once we're at Fangshard, there's still nothing Balfour—or his master—can do to us." But even as he said the words, he didn't sound perfectly convinced of it himself.

"I thought Askelon was able to control the dragons," Arthur said. "Why isn't it working like it did with St. George?"

Royal slung the long lance back over his shoulder as he took in the giant gliding form of Balfour above. "There's a lot of distance between the stories of the past and the reality of today. Either the legends of Askelon aren't true or I'm not wielding it properly. But one thing's for certain...Balfour's keeping us at arm's length. He's got more brains than I gave him credit for. His job is to deliver the lance and that's exactly what he's going to do. One way or the other."

"We need to kill him!" shouted Marco. With that, he flung himself at Royal, grasping for the lance behind his back.

Royal shoved him back. "You'll kill us all, you fool!"

"Me?!" Marco argued. "I told you to not chase after

Askelon! I told you to leave it in the tomb! I told you that you would lead us all to the grave! But you," he pointed, "wouldn't listen! You never listened! You always chase after the things you want or what you think is best! That's why you failed as a captain! And that's why you are the one solely responsible for all our misery!"

"I've had it with you!" Royal angrily shoved Marco again. The mapmaker stumbled backward. Losing his balance, he sprawled onto the swaying deck. "I'm tired of you heaping blame upon me for all of your problems! Do you think you can constantly trick and deceive people and cause mayhem, all while pretending you're innocent? Do you think it escaped me that you almost got me killed back in the tomb? You knew I had the key in the right slot in the sarcophagus, didn't you? You figured you could gull me into trying the wrong lock and leave me with an arrow in my back! Don't try to tell me that ain't the truth!"

Marco's only response was a guttural roar of rage. Leaping to his feet, he barreled into the pirate and pinned him to the deck. In a flailing ball of hatred, they rolled upon the planks, trading blows and hammering each other with hardened fists. "You pirate piece of filth!" Marco shouted. "I'll kill you! And then I'll take Askelon and kill all of your precious dragons!"

"I'll use your head as a cannonball before that happens!" growled Royal, wrapping his hands around Marco's throat.

"Knock it off, you two!" Clay sprung between the two men and attempted to wrestle them apart. Finally, he was able to force his shoulder into Marco's paunch and thrust him away. As he fell backward, the mapmaker swung his fist and landed a clean blow on Royal's nose before landing against the railing, out of breath.

Royal propped himself up from the deck and gingerly dabbed at the dripping blood from his nose.

"What's the matter with the both of you?" yelled Clay heatedly. "We're trapped on this ship and all you can do is bicker with each other! You're not helping anything or anybody!"

Royal wiped his bloody fingers on his pantleg and sighed. "Aye." He clambered to his feet. His shoulders were slumped in remorse. "Aye. We've lost our footing, that's all."

He stepped over to the winded mapmaker resting against the railing. "Marco's right. I ain't fit to be a captain. I never wanted to be a captain. There's a reason I pilot a vessel that needs no crew. I never intended to lead anyone into this mess. I'm sorry."

Marco lowered his eyes, uncomfortably avoiding Royal's gaze. "I was told it was a sign of weakness for a captain to say he's sorry."

Royal scoffed. "And I say it's a sign of stupidity if he doesn't. A good captain knows when to correct course." Royal studied Marco silently. When no more words were offered, he turned to Clay. "What we need is a plan."

Before Clay could respond, Arthur cried out. "I see land!"

The three of them hurried to where Arthur was pointing over the *Typhoon's* railing. Their eyes followed his out-stretched finger. Far in the distance, they could discern an unmistakable mound of green.

"Is that Fangshard?" asked Marco.

Royal immediately snapped his spyglass from his belt and raised it to his good eye. "No. Fangshard is further from here. I don't know this isle. You're the cartographer. You tell us."

Marco grabbed the spyglass and studied the small spec of land carefully. "I don't know it, either," he concluded.

"One thing I can say for certain," said Royal, "is that it's a better place to be than Fangshard. We just need to find a way off this flying tub."

"There must be something we can do to force Balfour lower," Clay said.

Royal studied the hardened, thorny hide of the dragon above them. "My flintlocks and muskets don't do a thing to him."

"What about your cannons?" Arthur asked.

The pirate scratched his chin. "Aye. They might do the trick. If we were able to land a volley, that is. But all my guns are pointed out the sides."

"Who says we can't point them upward?"

Royal grinned. "Nobody. Between the four of us, I'm sure we can pull one into position!"

"Wait a moment!" argued Marco. "I thought it was already decided that we don't want that beast dropping us."

"If we wing him," Royal said, "he might be inclined to land. If we wait until we're over the island, we stand a chance. Hop to it!"

The four of them scrambled below to the gun deck. The *Ivory Typhoon* was not a large vessel and sported only eight guns in total—four each along the port and starboard sides— to defend itself in battle. There was room for more but, as Royal explained, with only a one-man crew, the *Typhoon* was never intended to be an attack ship. All the cannons were connected to a confusing array of ingenious clockwork that allowed the fuses to be sparked with the pull of a single lever.

"Quick!" Royal pointed to one of the carriages. "Free the cannon from its track. Arthur, bring some rope so we can muscle this topside!"

Arthur scurried off while Clay and Royal hammered at the cannon's trunnion. With concerted effort, the bulky iron weapon slid from the carriage with a deep, hollow groan. It dropped to the deck with a sonorous peal like some deadly church bell. Arthur returned with a coil of rope and Royal looped it about the barrel.

"Heave!"

Together, they dragged the hefty cannon to the steps leading to the top deck. Royal peered upward. The hatch afforded a perfectly framed view of the flapping Balfour above them. "That's a peach of a shot! Quick! We'll need to land a blow before the island passes! Brace the bottom!"

With grinding teeth, they swiveled the barrel of the cannon toward the sky. Its muzzle poked menacingly from the open hatch. As best he could, Royal gauged the path of the cannonball. "Hold her there while I lash it in place." He gave the rope several passes around the black cannon and then looped the other end around a nearby beam. "There's already powder and roundshot in the bore, but we'll need to ram it again. Clay, fetch the rammer and a fuse." He pointed to a cabinet against the bulkhead.

As they jammed the long rod into the bore, Royal checked the aim once more. "I think that will do it." He gave the group a somber look. "We only got one shot at this. Once I light this fuse, there's no saying what will happen. Any last words from anyone?"

Marco opened his mouth to speak, but Royal interrupted. "Very well! Stand back!" He struck a flint against the oil-soaked fuse.

Everyone scattered. The cannon roared. The entire vessel vibrated violently as the bottom of the cannon cracked the timbers beneath it. The deck filled with sparks and smoke and they could hear a horrendous shriek break the air outside the ship. The black smoke quickly whisked away and they gawked upward from within the crooked hatch.

Balfour still clutched the mast above tenaciously, but now one of his wings was crumpled with a horrific slash. The burnt, tattered wing fluttered helplessly and smoldered with whiffs of flame. The dragon let loose with an ear-piercing howl that rattled the sky. Arthur saw him turn an angry gaze at the huddled crew as it tried to maintain its flight with only one remaining wing.

"We're going down!" Clay called. The surface of the water approached as Balfour tried desperately to lift the ship despite his injury.

Arthur pointed. "We're heading for the island!" The mysterious mound of land grew closer. They could see a single mountaintop, crowned with lush green foliage. But the *Ivory Typhoon* was still too high. "We're going to skim over it!"

Royal clambered over the smoking cannon that was now embedded in the wreckage of stairs. "Time to weigh anchor!" He pulled himself onto the open deck and sprinted to the helm. The others followed. The deck of the *Ivory Typhoon* was listing dangerously to one side under the crippled grasp of the *browgie*. It was all they could do to keep from sliding to the railing. Royal's hand clutched the ivory-handled lever next to the wheel. "Brace yourselves!" he called back. With a firm yank, he pulled.

The heavy chain rattled chaotically beneath them as the iron anchor fell from the *Ivory Typhoon*. The vessel shuddered. Arthur lost his footing on the slanted deck and slid against the rail with painful force. Catching his breath, he watched wide-eyed as the anchor plowed through the island tree-tops beneath them, tearing a ragged wake of snapping tree limbs and exploding leaves behind it. Occasionally, the jagged anchor would snag a branch and the taut chain would force the whole ship to lurch violently.

"He's not letting go!" Clay pointed upward to Balfour's relentless grip on the mast. Royal, still clutching the ivory handle, grimaced at the unyielding, beating wing of the furious dragon.

The anchor found another purchase within a thick tree and the movement of the *Ivory Typhoon* halted abruptly. The heavy chain stretched tight and the poor, abused ship became suspended in the air, caught in a deadly tug-of-war between the steadfast anchor and Balfour's mighty talons. The timbers and beams of the vessel creaked and groaned in agonized protest.

"I don't like this at all!" cried Marco.

Balfour tugged mercilessly, trying to free the snarled vessel. Each forceful yank sent its helpless crew tumbling and scrambling for a firm hold on anything they could find. Royal eyed the smoldering cannon, helplessly trapped in the splintered stairs. "Marco!" he called. "Help me load this cannon again!"

"What are you doing?" Marco replied. "That thing is stuck for good. There's no way we can hit Balfour with that."

"Just do as I say!"

Grumbling, the mapmaker clumsily found his way below deck where he salvaged a rolling cannonball. Royal rummaged for wadding and powder and stuffed into the breech.

"How is that going to help us?" Clay cried. "This cannon is lodged tight. We'll never be able to aim it at that dragon!"

"I'm not aiming for him," he answered as Marco rolled

the ball down the bore of the cannon. Royal thrust the rammer inside and packed the ball tight.

Clay traced the aim of the cannon's muzzle and gulped when he saw where it was pointed. "You're shooting your own ship!" Clay shouted.

"I sure am!" Royal answered back. "Everyone, hold on to something!" And with that, he struck another flint.

An explosion of smoke, fire, and shattered wood slammed the air and the cannonball burst cleanly through the thick beam of the mast. The splintering mast ripped from the vessel. Loosed from its heavy prize, the surprised Balfour shot upward.

Arthur, Clay, and Marco screamed in unison as the ravaged *Ivory Typhoon* plummeted toward the foliage. With a cacophony of snapping wood and crying timbers, the ship plunged into the trees. Arthur felt the hull crack open as it came into violent impact with the ground. The deck pitched forward and together, the crew tumbled toward the twisted bow as the collapsing ship began sliding down the mountainside.

The *Ivory Typhoon* vibrated apart as it tore down the slanted ground, shredding the trees before it. Beams, rope, chain, and ivory handles burst from the cracking deck as the demolished vessel spilled down the mountain. The bouncing and jolting chaos of flying debris surrounded Arthur and the last thing he remembered was the sight of Balfour dropping the broken piece of mast from its talons and what appeared to be an even larger dragon chasing after him.

Then, with one final, thunderous crash, everything went black.

13

"Penny" Gayle

The first thing Arthur noticed when he awoke was the stillness. The constant motion aboard the *Ivory Typhoon* was gone and he felt the cold, solid earth beneath his back. Instead of the unceasing wash of the waves, he heard the quiet staccato of chirping crickets. He opened his eyes wider. Above him, the circle of a white moon shone within the night sky, broken only by the stark silhouette of the bars of a cage.

A cage?

Arthur sat up and immediately regretted it. His head pounded with a terrible throbbing pain.

"Arthur!" The voice was Clay's. His brother appeared at his side. "You're awake! You got a pretty bad bump on your head. How are you feeling?"

"Not as good as when I was sleeping." Arthur rubbed his forehead tenderly. "What happened?"

"I'm not exactly sure." Clay studied the large cage around them. It was crudely but sturdily crafted with thick logs, bound with rope. The openings were small enough to prevent anyone inside from getting out but large enough to let any manner of snake, rat, or sharp stick in. "We must have all been knocked cold in the wreck. I woke up just a few minutes ago and saw you were hurt. Royal and Marco are over there." He pointed to the two unconscious forms on one side of the cage.

"Where are we? How did we get in here?" Arthur asked.

"I don't have a clue," Clay answered.

To Clay and Arthur's surprise, a voice answered from a shadowy corner.

"You're in a cage. A trap. On an unknown clump of a dirt in a forgotten expanse of sea."

The voice was distinctly female, but Clay and Arthur could not discern any form or face to go with it. "You were brought in here by the miserable crew of the marauder ship *The Feral*—or rather what's left of the crew."

"Who are you?" Clay asked.

"Me? I'm nobody."

"My name's Clay Cross. This is my brother, Arthur."

"I didn't ask," the voice replied.

A coughing fit erupted in the cage as Marco stirred to consciousness. "Blech! It tastes like I swallowed a roach!" he spat.

"You probably did," the mystery voice responded. "You've been drooling in that muck since you were thrown in here."

Marco looked stunned as he sat up. "Who are you? What is this place?"

"That's what we're trying to find out," Clay answered.

Marco began to furiously kick the unconscious form of Archie Royal. "Wake up!"

The groggy pirate stirred. "Get your muddy boots off me! You're interrupting the first decent night's sleep I've had in a week." He looked about the cage with his one eye. "Where are we?"

"According to our cellmate we are in a cage on an island in the sea," Clay replied.

"That's a start, I suppose," Royal groaned.

"First we're taken hostage by a *browgie* and now we are prisoners to some new unknown menace!" Marco lamented. "Yet another horrid mess the great Captain Archibald Royal has delivered us into."

A gasp broke from the dark corner. "Did you say Archibald Royal?" the woman's voice whispered. "The Pirate Archibald Royal?"

"I'm no pirate," Royal answered. "Not anymore. And who be ye?"

Royal's question was answered with silence.

Marco suddenly exploded in a fury of oaths as he felt around the dank dirt in the cage. "My satchel! My jewels! They're gone!"

In alarm, Royal immediately reached over his shoulder. "And so is the lance! And my cutlass!"

"What did you do with my treasure?" Marco bellowed. The furious mapmaker reached into the darkness and yanked the owner of the mysterious voice into the moonlight.

Clay and Arthur gasped when they saw the face of the stranger in Marco's clutches. "You're just a girl!" Clay exclaimed.

The delicate, yet muddied, features under the billow of wavy black hair were pinched with anger. "I'm not a girl! I'm older than you by at least a year!" she spat. "I've put musket balls into men twice your age for making that mistake!"

Royal grinned. "She's right. She's not just a girl. I'd know that mane of raven hair anywhere. You're the infamous marauding Captain Gayle of the dreaded ship *The Feral*."

Marco bawled with laughter. "Ha! Captain 'Penny' Gayle, the terrible marauder!" The mirth on his face quicky vanished and was replaced with a scowl. "Where is my bag of jewels!"

The girl wrenched free from Marco's grasp. "I didn't take your lousy jewels. And don't call me Penny!"

Marco took immense joy in finding a sore spot. "You don't like to be called Penny, Penny? Why is that, Penny? Haha!"

"Stop it!" she shouted.

"What's wrong with the name Penny?" Clay asked. "Is it short for Penelope?"

"Haha!" Marco continued to laugh. "She wishes!"

"It's not my name!" she snapped back. "My name is Constance. Constance Gayle. Captain Constance Gayle!"

"Then why do they call you Penny?" Arthur asked. He shrank back in fear when he saw the girl's face swell with irritation.

"My. Name. Is. Constance!"

"Aye," Royal said. "Penny is just a nickname. Short for Penniless."

Marco laughed even louder. "Yes! Penniless Constance Gayle. The poorest marauder on the Seven Seas! Haha—OW!"

Gayle had delivered a tiny fist straight to his nose. "The next person who laughs at me will be spitting teeth!"

"Wait a minute!" exclaimed Arthur. "You said the crew of *The Feral* are the ones who threw us in here. But how can that be if you're their captain?"

"Because they're all lousy MUTINEERS!" she shouted at the top of her lungs, making sure anyone else on the island could hear her. "All except John Dunney here." She pointed to a lanky form no one had bothered to notice sleeping peacefully in the corner. "He's as loyal as they come."

"You're telling us that they locked you in here?" continued Royal.

"Yes. They're the ones that took all your weapons. And loot."

"But why?" asked Clay.

"Because when we landed upon this stupid rock, they all got uppity and decided they could run things better than me! They sailed away with all three of my ships...*The Lock*, *The Stock*, and *The Feral*, leaving me with nothing but a few of my crew. Who then mutinied again and locked us up in here. DOUBLE MUTINEERS!"

"Technically, I think they each only mutinied once," noted Marco.

"It doesn't matter. There were four of us in this rotten trap, but slowly they've been feeding us to the Beast to save their own wretched hides!"

"A beast?" Marco paled.

Arthur remembered the second creature he saw when they crashed. "Do you mean a dragon?"

"Beast. Dragon. Bugaboo. I don't care what you call it. But every few nights, they come in here and march one of us away. Tonight, it was going to be either myself or Dunney. But it looks like there's a new menu now."

Arthur turned to Royal. "Could there be dragons here like Balfour?"

Royal shrugged. "Could be. We're in uncharted waters now and not too far from Fangshard."

Gayle's eyes narrowed. "What are you jabbering about? Do you know about this creature?"

"It doesn't matter," Royal replied as he examined the cage around them. "I don't intend to sit around and become anybody's board of fare. We need to get out of this cage and sail off this rock."

The young girl filled with hope. "Do you have a ship?" she asked excitedly.

Marco laughed. "Not anymore. The great Archie Royal! The only captain to crash his vessel into a mountaintop!"

Gayle looked confused. "What does that mean?"

Before Marco could delve into their adventure with Balfour, a jumble of voices emerged from outside the cage. Torchlights dotted the jungle, accompanied by the muffled, sinister plotting of conspiratorial conversation. Four men emerged from the brush. A tall, bald man with long, braided mustaches and a poorly executed tattoo around his right eye stepped to the front and leered menacingly. "Hello, mates!"

"Get lost, Skinner!" Gayle snapped in reply.

"We can't do that, Penny!" he answered mockingly. "It's feedin' time!" The smile dropped from his face and he surveyed his prisoners. "On your feet! All of you!" He motioned to the sleeping man in the corner. "And that includes Dunney!"

Gayle gave the slumbering form a swift kick. Without arguing, the figure rose to his feet with the awkward grace of a marionette on strings. John Dunney was a tall, beanpole of a man. So tall that he needed to hunch in order to make room for his long head and curly, mussy hair. His eyes remained shut and his mouth hung slack in sleepy surrender. He gave no indication that he even knew why he was standing—or that he was standing at all.

The man named Skinner perused the cage's muddy occupants. "It was my plan to serve Dunney up as the main course tonight, but he's more suited to a be a toothpick." His threatening eyes fell on Clay. "You, however, are a much better choice. A strapping lad like yourself should be prime eatin' for our master. Step forward!"

Arthur immediately protested. "No! You can't take him!"

From out of nowhere, four loaded flintlocks thrust in unison through the wooden bars.

"Stand back, all of you!" Skinner growled. "I didn't hike up here to shoot fish in a barrel. You'll do as I say or die wishin' you had."

"What's this about?" Royal asked. "We haven't crossed you in any way. If it's treasure you want, we can make a deal."

"A deal?" laughed the bald man. "And what would you have to deal with? We found you in that heap of a shipwreck in the jungle. A ship that had no cargo nor stores. Nothing but four unconscious passengers. You got no loot. No ship. And no reason to be runnin' your mouth. Step back! You—" he pointed to Clay "—come here!" Skinner pulled a heavy key from his belt and unlatched the even heavier lock hanging on the cage's door. He reached in, grabbed Clay, and sent him sprawling toward the other ruffians. Quickly shutting the small door, he fastened the lock and tucked the key back into his trousers.

"Tie him up," Skinner ordered his crew.

"I'll get you, you treasonous maggot!" Gayle spat.

Skinner simply gave her a big smile and wink. "You're next, Captain." He let the threat linger and then the four men shoved the bound Clay into the tropical brush to vanish into the night.

14

Flight from Rogue's Island

The captors abandoned Clay at the top of a cliff. The bright moonlight was enough to obscure the stars above but not enough to penetrate the black canyon that gaped at his feet. With his wrists still bound, he reached down to the heavy shackle and chain that the laughing marauders had clamped on his ankle. With a tug, he discovered that it was fastened to an abandoned ship's anchor that had become joined with the earth at some point in the past long ago.

Clay let the chain drop back onto the hard earth. He was not fully ready to accept the truth that he was helplessly trapped. His eyes searched about in the dim light for any means of escape. Odd, shadowy shapes littered the clearing and he craned his neck to discern what they were. He quickly turned his head in horror when he realized what they were. Rotting, severed feet.

Clay was suddenly grateful for the darkness.

So, this is it, he thought to himself. There was nothing he could do but wait for whatever this beast was to wrest him from the chain around his ankle. Odd, he mused, that it didn't frighten him more. In his chest, he felt a wave of resignation, tinged with an odd weightlessness of freedom. Everyone has an end, after all, and he knew that he was no different.

But then he thought of his brother, and the sadness welled up within him. "I'm sorry I'm leaving you, Arthur," he said aloud. "I hope someone will take care of you."

He didn't dare let himself consider the idea that his poor little brother would soon be stuck in the very same shackle, possibly staring at Clay's own severed foot in the darkness.

+ + +

"Where are they taking him?!" cried Arthur after Skinner and his men had departed. His eyes were wet with tears but he didn't care. "We have to save him!"

"I told you," Gayle answered. "Their taking him to the beast." Her face was cold and unaffected by Arthur's desperation.

Royal pulled the small boy to him with one arm. He didn't put his arm around him in an embrace, but Arthur didn't care. The boy clung to the pirate's muddy cloak and sobbed. Royal frowned at the young woman. "What do you know about this so-called beast? Can you describe it?"

"I only saw it once," she grimaced. "And I was running at the time. Large. Gray. Giant fangs. It flew and had horns or spikes on it."

"Where were the spikes? On the top of its head?"

The lady marauder shook her head. "No. They stuck out of its jaw. Like a beard."

Royal looked at Marco. "Sounds like a *duskar*."

Marco was ashen. "*Duskar* or *browgie*. It doesn't matter. It's a dragon."

Royal examined the cage once more. "Well, we're not much good trapped in here. We need to find a way out."

Reaching through the crude door, he fumbled with the heavy, rusted lock. "Maybe I can pick this contraption." He scrabbled around the dirt, looking for anything of value, but all he could find was a broken stick. He scraped it a few times to sharpen it and then forced it into the keyhole. With a few twists, it found a grip within the lock. Royal pressed harder, but the piece of wood simply broke in two with a pathetic snap. "Blast!"

Arthur's eyes widened. "Hold on a second!" He reached into his boot. It was there!

Arthur drew the small knife from its secret sheath. "Will this help?"

Royal snatched the blade from Arthur's hand and examined it curiously. "Where did you get this?"

"I swiped it from the tomb. It was in my boot. I guess they never thought to look there when they took your weapons."

Archie Royal grinned. "Good lad!" He stuck the small point into the lock and began twisting away.

Gayle rushed forward to watch. For the first time in days, she was experiencing the glimmering hope of escape. Even the sleepy John Dunney's eyes began to open and observe with interest.

With a few deft turns of Royal's wrist, the lock fell open.

Arthur rushed to escape the cage. "We have to save Clay!"

Royal stopped him. "Hold on! We need a plan."

Gayle tried to shove her way past. "Let's kill Skinner."

Royal grabbed her, too. "We ain't killing anyone!"

Marco also tried to squeeze through the open cage door. "They have my treasure!"

Royal pressed his boot into Marco's belly and pushed him back. "Knock it off, the lot of you! Our first job is to save the boy's brother, but to do that we'll need our weapons." He turned to Gayle. "Where is this crew of yours hiding out?"

"It's not far," she said. "That's my plan! We kill Skinner and his men and take all their weapons. Then we can kill the beast and save the boy. It's a good plan!"

"And exactly how are you planning to take them before you have any weapons?" Royal argued. "I said we ain't killing anybody. I don't aim to start any tussle. There's four of them with pistols and all we have between us is one small knife. I'm not liking those odds." With that, he handed the blade back to Arthur. The boy slid it into its hiding spot in his boot. "Listen to me. Time is not on our side. We slip into their camp, get our stuff, and reach Clay before this beast does. No dilly-dallying or wasting time trying to get revenge." His single eye glared directly at the girl. "Understood?"

"We need to go save Clay now!" Arthur argued.

"I know you're anxious, lad, but if this beast is what I think it is, the best chance of rescuing your brother is to get Askelon back."

"What's Askelon?" Gayle asked.

"Never mind that. Just lead the way."

Silently, the five of them crept into the jungle. Gayle's information that the camp was not far proved to be correct. After following a narrow path down an incline and over a meandering trail through the brush, they spotted the tell-tale sign of a fire. Arthur peered through the leaves and could see a make-shift camp constructed of various pieces of flotsam, jetsam, and ship materials. Barrels and crates served as makeshift chairs and tables, hammocks were strung between tree trunks, and part of a large canvas sail was stretched wide for shelter. Beneath it, two men were occupying themselves with some manner of dice game. Arthur didn't know what the game was, but after every roll, one of the men would reach over and slap the loser across the face.

"Ouch!" cried one. "You don't have to hit that hard!"

"If you don't like it, then you should roll better."

Royal carefully studied the camp until his eye glimpsed its target. "There it is!" he whispered. The lance was laying unceremoniously in a small rowboat alongside a single oar and a coil of rope. He turned to Dunney. "You and I are going to drop that sail on them. Then you two—" he said to Gayle and Marco "—are going to bind them up with that rope there. Arthur is going to nab Askelon. Got it?" Everyone nodded.

Silently, Royal and Dunney crept behind the makeshift tent. The two men, engrossed in their odd dice game, failed to notice the two lurking shapes encroaching upon their shelter. The canvas was secured with simple bowlines and, at Royal's signal, they easily unhitched the knots.

The heavy sail dropped like a stone. The two unsuspecting sailors didn't even have a moment to realize their predicament before Marco and Gayle sprung upon them from the shadows. Gayle was wielding the oar from the boat. With a firm swing, she smacked one of the flailing, shouting lumps under the canvas. "Take that, you traitor! Tell me where Dozer took my ships!"

"I said to tie them up!" shouted Royal.

Marco was no help. He was kicking the other trapped man beneath the tent. "Where are my jewels?"

Royal grabbed the coil of rope and shoved past the two angry assailants. "Enough of that! Stop thinking about yourselves for once and bind them tight so we can get out of here! And fast, before Clay becomes a midnight snack!"

With only slight looks of guilt, the two quickly wrapped the rope around the struggling forms, sail and all. Once tightly bundled, Royal admired their work. "Looks like a trussed-up, lumpy Christmas ham. Now, which way did they take the boy?"

"Up there." Gayle pointed to a path that meandered up the side of the mountain. "The other two mutinous pieces of garbage must still be on the trail."

"I have the lance!" Arthur exclaimed.

"And here's my cutlass," said Royal, picking it up from the bottom of the rowboat. As he did so, he saw the lady marauder tucking two purloined flintlocks into her belt.

"Did anyone see my satchel?" Marco asked.

"There's no time for that! Follow me!"

Royal hurried up the jungle path, not noticing Penny Gayle giving the bound lump of sailors one last swat with the oar before following.

✢   ✢   ✢

Skinner and his crewmate, a rather dour deckhand name Ollie, lumbered down the trail at a brisk pace. It was uncertain if Ollie's dourness was caused by hunger, weariness, or that fact that he didn't feel his leader was walking quite fast enough.

"The sooner we get off this island, the better," he said. "I can't sleep at night knowing that monster is lurking around."

"Stop your blubberin'," Skinner answered, twirling the large key for the shackle on his finger. "As long as we keep the beastie's belly full, it'll leave us alone. And now that we got ourselves a few extra prisoners, it buys us more time until Cap'n Dozer returns to pick us up."

"I've been thinking about that," Ollie answered, "and I'm starting to think he's not coming back."

"Codswallop!" replied Skinner. "He said he'd be back once we took care of the annoying Miss Gayle and her little band of followers. That was the plan."

Ollie scratched his head. "But why didn't he just maroon her here and we all leave together? That seems like a better plan. You don't think he was lyin' to us, do you?"

Ollie couldn't see it, but Skinner's face fell a bit in the dark. The deckhand's sensible reasoning was now festering in his head. He quickly shook the idea from his mind. "Nah! That's ludicrous! See what happens when you think too much? We ain't paid to think. We just follow orders!"

"But Cap'n Dozer isn't here to give us orders," Ollie reasoned, "so what else are we supposed to do?"

Skinner stopped and angrily thrust a finger into Ollie's chest. "Cap'n Dozer is coming back! When has he ever let us down?"

The confronted deckhand looked surprised. "Well, leaving us on an island with a man-eating monster isn't a real pick-me-up."

Before he could begin to counter Ollie's logic, the abrupt report of pistol split the quiet night. A scream of pain shot from Skinner's lips as a musket ball ripped into his thigh. "AAAGHH!" He clutched his leg and fell to the dirt.

Penny Gayle stepped from the shadows with her smoking flintlock. The second flintlock was aimed squarely at Ollie's chest. "So," she growled, "you're all in cahoots! Tell me where Dozer took my ships! A lead ball to whichever of you answers last."

"Stinky Cove!" Skinner and Ollie sang in unison. "They sailed to Stinky Cove!"

Royal, Arthur, Marco, and Dunney came sprinting up the dark trail. Royal immediately snatched the unfired pistol from Gayle's hand. "Would you stop trying to kill people! What kind of girl are you?"

"These lousy mutineers have it coming!"

"If this is the way you treat them, then maybe they have the right idea!"

Gayle's mouth opened in anger, but any words she was about to utter were cut short by the tremendous rumbling that rolled through the air. Everyone searched the dark sky warily. Penny's eyes filled with dread.

"The beast is coming," she whispered.

+ + +

Clay felt the ground shudder under his feet. The quake forced a chatter from the links of chain at his ankle. With an odd mix of trepidation and curiosity, he peered into the darkness of the canyon beneath him.

The powerful rumble coursed through the ground again and the groaning of the earth reverberated ominously against the canyon walls. And then, the air moved under the force of immense flapping wings. Enormous, bat-like appendages rose and fell from the harsh shadow and into the moonlight. Two massive pale eyes appeared in the darkness. A huge, gnarled head emerged from the canyon depths. Fresh earth poured from the scaly, crevassed hide as the behemoth continued its rise from the canyon.

Clay simply stared, rigid with shock and horror.

Each mighty downstroke of the dragon's wings buffeted Clay's body with wind. The gray eyes flicked back and forth. Monstrous, cracked nostrils flared as they probed the night air. Rows of cracked and jagged fangs leered over a horny jaw.

The wheezing nostrils caught a scent and the gaping maw of the dragon opened. From it bellowed a deep and sonorous cry that shook trees and rocks and sent the blood in Clay's veins rushing to his feet.

Still frozen in terror, Clay could only watch as the giant jaws with its army of ragged teeth descended toward him. To his surprise, he didn't scream. He only clenched his eyes shut and waited.

And waited.

Nothing happened.

There was silence, interspersed only by the sound and thrust of the steady, beating wings.

"Clay! Clay!"

It was Arthur's voice! Clay opened his eyes to look behind him. Royal and Arthur were sprinting from the jungle. Royal raised the long lance from St. George's tomb over his head. They both skidded to a stop and gazed in awe at the sight of the gargantuan beast hanging in the air.

A rumbling growl permeated the night.

"Askelon." The word had emanated from the depths of the dragon's gravelly throat. "Askelon," it repeated. The gray eyes of the beast searched about, seemingly oblivious to the arrival of Arthur and Royal.

Together, they watched as the dragon cast its snout back and forth, sniffing the air.

"It's blind," whispered Clay.

"These ancient bones," groaned the dragon, "sense Askelon."

Royal stepped forward. Mustering an extra breath after his sprint up the trail, he called. "Askelon is here!"

The dragon stiffened. "Have you come to slay me?"

Clay and Arthur gave Royal a questioning look.

But their attention was distracted when more figures emerged from the bushes. Marco, Gayle, and Dunney all slid to a standstill at the scene of the monstrous dragon hovering over the cliff. A cry of terror began to peal from Marco's lips, but Gayle quickly slammed her hand over his mouth. "Quiet before he eats us all!"

Royal lowered the lance and examined the huge gray creature. Its bulky claws and torso hung heavily in the air under the powerful, straining wings. "How are you called?" Royal asked.

The dragon paused, as if trying to remember. "I am called Hogarth. Have you come to slay me?" it asked again.

"How are you doing this?" Gayle whispered to Royal.

Royal beckoned her to be quiet. He returned his attention to the dragon. "No," he answered.

"Why is Askelon here?" Hogarth breathed.

"We are here to command you," Royal answered. "Not to slay you."

"What," growled the dragon, "is your command?"

Royal took a deep breath. "We seek flight to Dragonrook."

At this, the beast released a ferocious roar into the night sky. The sudden, terrible din caused them all to crouch in dread.

"Dragonrook!" roared Hogarth. "This command is impossible. These bones are *rogueskein*. I cannot venture to Dragonrook."

"It is my command," Royal continued. "Take us. Or be slain."

The dragon called Hogarth pulled its head back and un-

leashed another hideous roar. The cry seemed interminable. It grew louder. Arthur clapped his hands over his
ears. The cliffside quaked and rocks tumbled from their
purchase into the darkness below. Clay felt as if his bones
would rattle to pieces.

Finally, the unyielding roar began to fade. Hogarth's
head hung in exhaustion. Silently, the hovering beast
struggled with its thoughts.

"Flight to Dragonrook is my command," Royal repeated.

After another stretch of silence, Hogarth spoke. "As you
command."

Slowly, the gray dragon grew closer and with effortless
strength alighted on the ground.

Arthur was the first to break from his stunned disbelief. He rushed to Clay and wrapped his arms around his
brother in relief.

Marco stood, mouth agape, gawking at the resting beast.
"I can't believe it! It worked! Askelon worked!"

Royal shook him from his reverie and handed him
Penny Gayle's absconded flintlock. "Fetch some rope!
Dunney, go with him. There must be some more at the camp."

"How did you do this?" Gayle asked.

"There's no time to explain. Free Clay."

Gayle looked down at the iron key in her hand that she had
taken from Skinner. She dashed to the shackled young man.

Cautiously, Royal approached the waiting dragon, lance
at the ready. "Hogarth," he said, "you will carry the six of
us to Dragonrook. Once we are there, you have my protec-
tion. You will be free to return here. Do you believe me?"

The gray Hogarth didn't answer. He simply crouched
and waited stoically.

Marco and Dunney came huffing back up the cliff.

"The crew of *The Feral* are all gone," Marco reported, gasping for breath as he handed over a bundled of rope. "I can't find my jewels, either."

Royal sighed. "Oh, let it go, Marco." He reached over the waiting Hogarth's back and began coiling the rope around the dragon's shoulders. He hitched it tight.

"Alright, everyone. Climb aboard." Carefully, he clambered atop and straddled Hogarth's neck, keeping a firm grip on the rope. Arthur and Clay wasted no time on finding a seat behind him.

"I'm not climbing onto that thing!" Marco argued.

"Suit yourself. For now, this is the only way off this island. You're welcome to stay and cozy up to those *Feral* crewmates, wherever they are...assuming they forgive you for kicking them in the head over your stolen jewels."

Penny Gayle and Dunney crawled up onto the back of Hogarth. "You don't have to tell me twice!" she said.

Marco was still reluctant. "I hate dragons. And I don't want to go to Dragonrook. Fly me to Greece."

"No dice, Marco. I've had enough gallivanting after this lance. It's straight to Dragonrook for us."

The mapmaker sighed with resignation and Arthur thought he was about to cry as he reached for the rope. He grimaced as his hands came in contact with Hogarth's dusty, armor-like scales but he managed to haul himself to the top.

"Stop your blubbering! Think of it like riding a camel," Royal said. He turned around and studied the line-up of passengers along Hogarth's spine. "What a motley crew we make. Everyone got a grip? Then let's bid farewell to this place!"

With one giant stroke of its wings, the massive Hogarth lifted from the ground and peeled into the night sky.

15

Here There Be Dragons

"I have so many questions right now," Penny Gayle said.

Hogarth's massive wings sliced the air as he and his six passengers soared far above the dark water. The sky to the east grew pink and the undulating waves beneath them slowly became visible in the burgeoning light. As the dawn revealed the harrowing height of their flight, the riders upon the dragon's back tightened their grips on the rope. Penny relieved her anxiety by saying just about anything that came to mind. Without waiting for a response, she continued.

"What is Dragonrook?" she asked Royal. "How far is it? What's going to happen when we get there? And how are you able to make this thing carry us there? How is that even possible?"

"He's controlling it with Askelon!" Arthur replied happily. Of all the group, the boy appeared to be the least concerned that they were only slightly tethered to a flying dragon high above the sea. On the contrary, he seemed to be enjoying it. "It's the lance that St. George used to slay the dragon!"

Royal stiffened. "Mind your tongue, lad."

"Really?" Arthur asked. "Are you still trying to keep it a secret even though we're obviously flying hundreds of feet in the air on the back of a dragon? What difference does it make if you tell her?"

The pirate sighed. "Well, I suppose the cat is out of the proverbial sack...there's no sense in denying it. What the boy says is true."

Penny's eyes widened. "You can control dragons with a lance? Where did you get it? Where can I get one?"

"As far as I know, it's the only one that exists. The lance of St. George is something that's been lost for centuries. I'm not the one to explain exactly how it works. For some reason, Hogarth reacts to it more than Balfour. All I know is now that it's been found, it can finally be put in a safe place."

"How did you find it?"

Royal proceeded to share with her the legend of St. George, the deciphering of the map, their adventure in the tomb, and how their encounter with Balfour the *browgie* had caused them to be deposited on the same island with her. This time, however, Marco didn't interrupt or bother to correct any of Royal's possible errors. Indeed, the poor mapmaker looked quite ill and uncomfortable. Whether it was from the dizzying altitude or from being in such close contact with a dragon, no one was certain. He feverishly clutched the rope with white knuckles and clenched his eyes shut, oblivious even to Gayle's long black hair flapping in his ashen face.

"And so," Royal continued, "when we come to land in Dragonrook, Askelon will be returned to its rightful home."

"But what's Dragonrook?" Clay asked.

"Normally, I wouldn't say," the pirate replied. "It's supposed to be a secret, but since we'll all be there shortly, I guess you might as well know. Dragonrook is the last bastion of dragonkind."

"More dragons?" Arthur asked. "How many dragons?"

"Scores, I would say. I guess I never counted. After being hunted, slain, and driven from the land, they all fled for refuge to a single, solitary place where they could live in peace, free from threat or danger."

"Threat or danger?" Clay exclaimed incredulously. "What could possibly threaten a dragon?"

"Aye, seems strange, doesn't it?" Royal answered. "But dragons are more vulnerable than you'd think. Look at Hogarth, for instance." He motioned to the gliding beast beneath them. "Who'd have imagined that we'd be riding the same creature that was about to feast on you like a mincemeat pie?"

The bright bands of sunlight broke the dim sky and Arthur and Clay could see the giant form of Hogarth more clearly. The large, hardened scales were gray and gritty. In some places they were cracked and broken and a few were missing completely. They shifted and rippled with each mighty stroke of the wings. The stout neck tapered toward a broad, low-slung head, riddled with small horns and points that had been worn dull over time. Most intriguing to Arthur were the pale, large eyes that had whitened from age. The dragon must not have been completely blind because its eyes darted back and forth as they searched the sky. To the boy's surprise, the two lifeless eyes moved independently from one another, allowing one to peer forward while the other would gaze in a completely different direction.

A thought occurred to Arthur. "If Dragonrook is supposed to be a refuge, then why did Hogarth say he couldn't go there?"

Royal silently surveyed the circle of sea around them.

"Things aren't all calm and cozy amongst dragonkind. There's a rift. To be honest, one could call it an outright rebellion. Most dragons are simple, good, and obedient to their kind. Loyalty is in their blood and lungs. But there are some, though, who bristle and gnash against that very nature, and thus, against their own kind. They call them the *rogueskein*. They're considered a threat and too dangerous to co-exist with others. Therefore, they've been banished from Dragonrook forever. Hogarth here carries a rogue's blood. For him to return to Dragonrook is to court doom. It will be up to me to protect him."

"How do you know so much about dragons?" Gayle asked.

"Dragonrook has been my home for many years now. The dragons there have done me a great kindness, and now, with the return of Askelon, I can at least partly repay them for their hospitality."

Both Clay and Arthur wanted to hear how Royal had come to find himself living with dragons but before either could press for details, a new sight appeared on the horizon. Jutting from the sea was a chunk of island. It was encompassed by tranquil, sandy beaches that disappeared into the shade of verdant tropical forests. But its most striking feature was the dramatic mountain that thrust above the canopy of trees. The mountain was unmistakably the weathered remnants of an ancient volcano. An expansive ring of rock created precipitous cliffs that were dotted with smaller caves and crevasses. The giant ring angled toward the water where one side had given away to the forces of sea and time and now formed a deep blue bay. Within the high cliffs, Arthur could make out numerous dark openings. Caves and passages that disappeared into the island's interior.

"We've reached Dragonrook," Royal announced.

The riders felt a shudder vibrate through Hogarth. The wind that had been rushing past their faces for the past hours softened as the ancient, gray dragon paused in flight. Any budding sense of victory and completion that Royal was feeling dimmed when five dark shapes rose into the sky from the depths of the island.

"Looks like they're sending a welcome wagon," Clay noted.

"Aye," muttered Royal with a hint of concern. The five forms grew closer and the riders could see the sleek, black shapes of the darting creatures split formation as they approached the hovering Hogarth. "They've sent a phalanx of *flamespires* at us."

"What are *flamespires*?" Arthur asked. His question needed no answer, for the jaws of the flying dragons began spewing columns of fire. Four of the shadowy dragons created a spinning circle around them, surrounding them with bellowing flame and smoke. Arthur winced at the sudden bite of heat on his face.

The fifth dark dragon held its flight above the entrapped riders. "Announce yourself! Who approaches?" it roared. But before anyone could respond, the flapping dragon tilted its head in recognition. "Royal? You have returned to Dragonrook!"

Relief washed over the pirate. "Indeed, I have, Grindash," he called. "And I have returned with Askelon."

The dragon seemed to hear the words before they were spoken. "Askelon! Yes! I sense it!" the hovering dragon replied. The creature's red eyes examined the crew of riders. "But you also bring intruders. This is distressing. And forbidden. You cannot proceed."

"These are my companions and are under my command—"

Gayle erupted. "Since when? I'm not under anyone's command!"

"Quiet!" Royal snapped. "Or do you prefer to be roasted alive?"

The girl's jaw clenched in frustration, but she obeyed the warning.

The hovering Grindash examined the giant gray Hogarth. "*Rogueskein*." His lips curled in a snarl and his nostrils sparked with a flash of heat.

"Hogarth is also under my command. He is no threat to you."

"*Rogueskein* has no place here."

"Let us go to ground," Royal suggested, "and together we can find terms to bring Askelon to Neera."

Grindash once more cast his red eyes across the team of explorers while he contemplated the proposal. "Very well," he finally breathed. "You may come to land on the shore, but no further. Should you try to go inland, my *flamespires* will rend you to char and scrap." The last words were leveled directly at Hogarth.

The four circling dragons ceased their blasts of fire and in perfect unison peeled away toward the sandy shore of the island.

Arthur felt the tension leave Royal as he patted the dragon beneath him. "To land, Hogarth. Keep to the shore and you'll be safe. You have my word."

Ever so slowly, Hogarth descended toward the soft waves upon the beach. The gray talons cautiously dipped into the sloshing water and sought purchase in the moving sand. The salty waves coursed around his scales as the bulk of his massive torso lowered into the surf.

Royal wasted no time. He dropped from Hogarth's back into the waist-high water. He checked to make sure the lance was secure on his back and began sloshing toward the beach where Grindash and the other black dragons waited.

"Really, beastie?" Gayle muttered. "You couldn't drop us off a little closer?"

Royal called back to Penny. "He doesn't dare touch the dry land of Dragonrook. We'll have to wade the rest of the way."

Clay and Arthur slid from Hogarth's back and into the waves. Marco, in haste, spilled from the dragon's back, splashing into the water on hands and knees. Immediately, he began retching and vomiting. Grimacing, Penny Gayle and John Dunney carefully avoided the ill mapmaker as they climbed down, leaving him kneeling in the shallow sea.

Grindash eyed Royal marching toward him across the sand. "Explain yourself, Royal," the dragon growled quietly.

"There's nothing to explain," he answered. "I was asked to find Askelon and I did. It wasn't easy, but you can tell Neera that her quest is finished."

"And what of the *rogueskein*? To bring such an abomination here—a *duskar*, no less," the dragon's lips curled in disgust, "—is an affront to our peace. Your league with him is league with our enemies. For me to even allow it this close can earn my own banishment. His presence casts suspicion on your purpose."

"Hogarth is no threat. He brought us here and will depart at my command. As for my purpose," he said as he hefted the lance from this back, "it remains the same. I've come to fulfill my oath and restore Askelon to

Dragonrook. Take us to Neera and I'll give her Askelon. Unless—" he offered the lance to Grindash "—you would like to present it to her yourself."

The black dragon shook his dart-shaped head. "None but the High Dragon dares to wield Askelon. We will escort you and your crew to Neera. For now, tell the rogueskein to leave and we will be on our way."

Royal looked back at the gray form of Hogarth hunkered in the crashing waves. The top of the dragon's head peered from the water, his white eyes casting back and forth as he watched in apprehension.

"Look sharp," Royal said to the sodden passengers waiting on the sand. "We'll be marching inland." He waded into the water and helped Marco to his feet. "Dragons never agreed with you, Marco, but you'd do well to get over that quickly. Here there be more dragons than you've ever set eyes on. We'll do our business, then after that, you'll depart from this island and go back to Greece or Malta or wherever you wish."

Marco seemed too ill to argue. Ashen-faced, he stumbled to the shore to join the others.

Royal examined the half-sunken head of Hogarth. "You are free to depart, Hogarth. My thanks for bringing us here."

The dragon rose its head from the water. "Why do they not slay me? I am *rogueskein*."

"Yes. But they are not. However, that doesn't mean they won't change their mind. For now, you're allowed to return to your home." With that, Royal waded back to the shore.

Hogarth merely watched, his head unmoving, seawater dripping from his thorny jaw.

"Why does he not leave?" Grindash growled.

Royal looked back at the gray Hogarth lying motionless in the waves. "Beats me. You dragons are a strange lot."

Grindash turned to his four waiting flamespires. "Stand watch over this *duskar*. Do not let him ashore. I will take the humans to Neera."

The large black dragon marched into the trees. Hefting the lance onto his back, Royal stepped behind and his five companions followed.

+ + +

"Where are we going?" Penny asked.

After a lengthy walk, it became apparent that the dark Grindash was not stopping anytime soon, and the six followers had to keep a brisk pace to match the dragon's larger strides. "He's escorting us to the High Seat," Royal answered. "We probably have a few more miles before we get to the mountain."

"Isn't there some way you can ask your stinky friend to fly us there?" Penny asked.

"She's right. He does stink!" Marco agreed, waving the air in front of his face. He found the the march on solid ground to be restorative and he was quickly returning to his irascible self. "It smells like someone fired a day-old tuna out of a cannon. Burnt fish and gunpowder."

Marco's mouth immediately clapped shut as the giant Grindash spun around with a snarl. "I would sooner die than bear your pudding-skin carcasses on my back. Even if it were possible. But," he continued, "I am not fool enough to fly into the High Seat of Dragonrook with Askelon and six strangers strapped to me. Fire and fang would rein down on us and we'd all be torn into a thousand flaming pieces before your little bite-sized heads knew what happened."

"I'd like to say that I'm quite enjoying the walk," Clay quickly commented. He gave Penny a stern look, silently warning her to keep any further comments to herself.

Mollified, the black dragon continued forward. For the next hour or so, Arthur and Clay examined the tall jungle above them as they hiked. Birds called among the branches in strange, unusual sounds that were new to the orphans. Occasionally, something would skitter in the brush. At one point, Arthur spied the monstrous silhouettes of winged shapes streak above them. "What was that?"

Grindash examined the air. "My sentries, doing as they are told. They are no doubt reporting on our approach to the west gate."

As he said this, the foliage gave way to a clearing against the base of a cliff. The travelers craned their necks at the dizzying tower of rock. "This must be the crater ridge we saw from above," remarked Clay.

Carved into the rockface was an ornate round stone, which Arthur guessed served as a door. The stone was intricately sculpted with patterns of sea, fire, and all manner of dragons in flight. Descending vertically down the round door were indecipherable characters whose meaning Arthur could only imagine.

Without a word being uttered, the heavy door rumbled open, revealing a long, sloping corridor beyond. Together, they followed Grindash within. A large green dragon stood aside as they entered and then, using its massive arms, it rolled the stone door shut behind them.

Arthur was expecting to see the rocky interior of a cave,

but to his surprise, the floors and walls were polished to smooth, glassy perfection. The arched corridor was finely sculpted with delicate filigree and detailed patterns, all shaped from the living stone of the mountain interior. The length of the passage was regularly illuminated by burning braziers adorning the hall. Two dragons strolled past them and gave the small band a curious look. They both locked their eyes on Arthur and observed him intently as they proceeded down the corridor. Grindash warned them with a brusque snort and the inquisitive dragons quickly hastened on their way.

"Wow!" whispered Arthur. "This is like a palace!"

Grindash merely huffed and continued leading them up the gradually sloping passage. Along the way, the crew encountered more dragons, who all leveled peculiar stares at them. Arthur marveled at their many different sizes and appearances. Some were large and brawny, like the monstrous Balfour. Others were green, with fins and spines that ruffled around their jaws. To Arthur's surprise, he saw several small ones, no larger than a dog, rapidly flit through the air above him.

"It's incredible!" Arthur whispered to Clay.

Clay could only nod in agreement as he took in the world around them. From the tales of his youth, he had imagined dragons as being mythical and vicious creatures that lurked in holes, but now he was coming to the realization that everything he envisioned was far from the truth. "It's an entire city of their own!" he replied.

Marco was not as impressed. In fact, he seemed increasingly edgy. "I'm sure many a chicken was amazed at the grandeur of a scullery. Mark my words. We are about to be served on a platter to one of these awful beasts! I'm sure after so many centuries, they regard the taste of human meat as something of a delicacy."

A look of discomfort was also growing on Penny Gayle's face. Even the usual sleepy-eyed John Dunney seemed a bit more alert.

"Indeed," Grindash growled. "It has been some time since the inhabitants of Dragonrook feasted on your kind." A grim leer stretched across his snout and Marco and Penny both blanched. The dragon changed the subject and motioned toward another large door.

"This," he said, "is the entrance to the High Seat chamber." His red eyes bore into Captain Royal. "Follow me, and do not say a word. Already, I risk my neck bringing your crew here. If I'm to be executed, my dying request will be to snap each of your heads off personally."

"He means it," Royal said gravely to the group. "This ain't no highfalutin, fancy-schmancy peacockery going on in there. We don't belong here and the last thing we want is to give them a reason to remember that. Keep your traps shut and your hands to yourselves." He turned to Grindash and nodded. They were ready.

The giant doors swung open.

Everyone but Royal gasped in amazement. The chamber was immense. The high domed ceiling that floated above them was dotted with open skylights that arrayed the room with golden beams of sunlight. The floor was of polished stone that reflected the falling light like a mirror. Columns—massive columns the width of houses—reached upward to the ceiling far above them. But what really stole their breath was the parade of dragons that filled the hall. The creatures stood in rigid alignment, in rows that fanned out across the chamber, radiating from one central point.

"The High Seat." Grindash motioned toward the end of the chamber where, atop a rough, raw slab of unpolished stone that contrasted with the finished appearance of everything else, sat a single dragon. The creature was of a smaller size—about the size of a horse, Arthur estimated—and glistened like silver. The dragon shifted slightly and the scales glimmered with an iridescence that rippled and flowed along its back like a cascade of water. "And that is Neera, the High Dragon. Scion of Lockswift. Holder of the High-Thrall. Keeper of Dragonrook."

Some manner of council was taking place within the chamber. One dragon stepped toward the large stone slab and bowed respectfully. "High Dragon," it said, "at this very moment, the new corridors are being burrowed beneath the north wall, but there are delays. The *browgies* have encountered stubborn granite that has posed difficulty and exhausted their strength. At your command, we will increase our efforts to make up for the lost time."

The silver dragon shook her head gracefully. "Time is not the enemy, but rather the stone is. My command is that the *browgies* shorten their day's work. Give them extra portions of meat. They must have time to rest and renew. The secret of a stone's strength is that it does nothing while letting others break upon it. We conquer the stone by protecting our strength, and not by letting the stone consume it."

"As you command." The dragon lowered its head in deference and stepped back into the crowd.

Grindash nodded to Royal, and the small group stepped quietly into the chamber.

Even though Arthur thought they were being exceptionally quiet, something triggered a wave of gasps and whispers. The head of every dragon swiveled at their entrance. The perfectly arranged row of creatures faltered as many stepped back in alarm. The sleek, silver dragon perched upon the slab of stone straightened her slender neck and gazed at the new arrivals.

A large, greenish dragon with a ridge of horns across his brow, lurched forward and stood between them and the stone slab. "Grindash!" he growled. "Proceed no further!"

"With my respects, Arch-Dragon Quill." Grindash gestured toward Royal. "I announce the arrival of Captain Archibald Royal. And his crew." Grindash added the last sentence reluctantly.

At this, the green dragon softened. "Royal, you have returned!"

"Aye!" Royal smiled. "And I bring a gift for the High Dragon Neera." He pulled the lance from behind his back. "I give you Askelon."

At the mention of its name, another wave of murmurs and gasps washed through the crowd.

The silver dragon upon the slab of stone spoke.

"So, it is true. We felt the presence of Askelon when it came upon our shores. The pulse of the High-Thrall is strong within it. Bring it closer."

Royal stepped across the polished floor toward the rough stone. "You spoke the truth that Arcrellis sought it also," he said. "It was he who had given the Coin of Cordura to Captain Riga, which found its way to another brigand named Buckets. And now, Arcrellis has enlisted the aid of my own nemesis, Thaddeus Schark. It appears that our enemies are in league with one another." Royal paused when he reached the stone perch of the dragon. He examined the lance in his hand one last time. "To our good fortune, we deciphered the riddle leading to the tomb of St. George before they did. And now we bring it to you."

With those words said, he carefully laid the long lance onto the cold surface of the High Seat. He contemplated the weapon for a moment as it rested there. Was that it? he thought to himself. Did months of searching and hunting culminate with the simple act of setting a lifeless weapon on the hard rock? The lance lay motionless, without regard to the many sword points and flintlocks that had been aimed at his belly to bring it this far. And for a moment, Royal was conscious of his empty hand, and he wondered what purpose now remained for him.

Neera studied Royal silently. Her gaze was cold. "This is not all you bring," she said.

Royal shook himself from his wandering thoughts. "What do you mean?"

"You were entreated to find Askelon for us, yet now you return bringing strangers into our High Seat and *rogueskein* onto our coast. An explanation is required."

"These are my companions," Royal answered. "Without them, I would not have been able to restore Askelon to you. As for Hogarth, he has been released to return to his home."

"The *rogueskein* remains."

"Still?" Royal was perplexed. "He was instructed to depart."

Neera's golden eyes narrowed. A scowl simmered on her lips. "And yet he does not. You are not being forthcoming with me, Captain Royal. I advise you to hold nothing back, or else I will have no choice but to construe your actions as treachery."

Royal raised an eyebrow. Beneath it, his good eye burned with offense. "I assure you, High Dragon Neera.

There's no treachery here. The truth is that I've retrieved Askelon, a nearly impossible task that even your own could not accomplish. And at great peril and risk to myself and my friends, I will add. The circumstances of our arrival may not be what you would have preferred, but rarely is life so accommodating. Sometimes, we must accept the prize with the pestiferous. Let's take the victory we are given, and then I will turn my hand to addressing these new challenges."

The High Dragon bristled. "As you say. But we will address these challenges on our terms. Call your companions forward."

The confusion was evident on Royal's face. He motioned to the others. The six bedraggled followers approached uneasily. Neera scrutinized each one. Her golden eyes lingered on Arthur.

Finally, she spoke. "Surrender your weapons."

At this, Royal's consternation let loose. "What's the meaning of all this?"

The black dragon, Grindash, interjected. "Do as the High Dragon commands!" A hint of black smoke curled from his flaring nostrils.

Penny Gayle wasted no time in pulling her flintlocks from her belt and throwing them on the ground.

Royal hesitated.

Marco was sweating nervously. "What are you doing, Royal? Do as it says!"

Reluctantly, the pirate unbuckled the cutlass that hung at his hip. It was his only weapon. His pistols had long been lost in the wreckage of the Ivory Typhoon.

Arthur began to reach for the small hidden knife in his boot, but a subtle glance from Royal stopped him.

Royal dropped the sheathed cutlass onto the polished floor atop Penny's surrendered flintlocks. "You have our weapons, High Dragon. In exchange, I request an explanation."

"The explanation is simple, Captain Royal," she answered. "You and your companions are our prisoners."

16

Prison Stew

Arthur would not have construed their chambers as a prison if he had not been told otherwise. The six of them were escorted along a sloping corridor, passing a few large portals as they ascended higher into the mountain. When they were finally instructed to enter one of the side chambers, no door or stone was shut behind them. Instead, a dark scaly dragon much like Grindash hunkered down in place, completely blocking any escape.

The room was fairly spacious. The first thing they noticed was a large hexagonal opening from which the clear sky admitted a fresh, brisk breeze. Braziers burned in opposite sides of the chamber, warding off any uncomfortable bite from the incoming mountain air. Water bubbled from a spout to be caught in a small basin beneath. The chamber had no corners to speak of. Everything was rounded and smooth, even where the floor met the walls, as if it were a giant stone burrow.

Royal eyed the thick bulk of the dragon's hide that filled the entry way. He felt the rising impulse to serve the guard a strong kick. The blow would probably make him feel better but would have had next to no impact on the dragon other than irritating it, so Royal stifled the urge.

"From one prison to another," grunted Marco. "Life under Captain Royal has not changed."

"He's not my captain!" countered Penny. "I'm getting really irked by people saying that!"

"Oh no!" mocked Marco. "Penniless Gayle is irked. And I thought the day was going so well." Marco plopped himself on the smooth floor.

Penny shot Marco an angry scowl and then decided to find herself her own spot to sit and fume. John Dunney rolled himself into a ball and quickly fell asleep.

Clay took in the astounding view through the large opening. Their prison cell was situated high within the cliff where birds and the occasional dragon soared above the waving forest. Beyond, the blue sea sparkled tantalizingly beneath the sun. "There's no escaping through this way," he said.

Royal gazed at the distant seascape. "Not unless we had wings," he added. "This is a rookery meant for dragon-folk. We might as well make ourselves comfortable. No telling how long we'll be here." He perched himself on the ledge and let his boots dangle over the cliffside as he watched the motion of the distant waves.

"And who's fault is that?" barked Marco. "Maybe if you kept the lance instead of relinquishing our only bargaining chip, we'd be sailing off into the sunset. But that never crossed your mind, did it? Leave it to Royal to do whatever he wants instead of thinking of his crew!"

"I'm not a part of his crew!" Penny snapped.

Royal didn't respond. Instead, he kept his silence and continued to gaze at the sea.

Marco, irritated that his insult failed to ruffle Royal's feathers, fell back against the wall and attempted to sleep.

Clay decided that sleep was a good idea so he, too, found a place to stretch out. Soon he, Marco, Penny, and the already slumbering John Dunney filled the large space with the snores and whispered breaths of their slumber.

Arthur, however, didn't sleep. He climbed onto the ledge and joined the pondering Royal. The two of them watched the vista quietly. Arthur could sense frustration in the hunched captain. Finally, the boy broke the silence. "If it helps, Captain, I appreciate what you've been doing for us. Without you, who knows where we would have ended up. Marco is wrong. You do think of your crew."

"Bah!" muttered Royal. "We're no crew. It takes more than dumping people in the same boat to make 'em a crew. If they ain't pulling together on the same line, or if they're just along for the ride, then they're not crew. They're just..." His thought trailed off and he eyed the sleeping forms on the floor.

"They're just what?" Arthur asked.

"Cargo, I guess." The captain turned his gaze back to the open sea.

Arthur shrugged. "Is cargo such a bad thing? It's just stuff that happens to be in between two places. The trick is getting it to where it belongs so it can be what it's supposed to be."

Royal's good eye scrutinized the boy. "And where is it you're supposed to be, Arthur Cross?"

As Arthur studied the far away world beyond the window, memories of Dempster House flooded his mind. Was that where he belonged? It was just an orphanage. Does anyone really belong in an orphanage, he asked himself. It was only a matter of time before he would have to move on, like his brother Clay did. He thought about Nora, Jeremy,

Marjorie, and all the others, and tried hard not to think of them as simply cargo that needed to be sent someplace else. He now had a deeper appreciation for Mr. Dempster and how he was able to make every one of the children feel like they belonged, despite being trapped between two places. "I guess I don't know where I'm supposed to be," he concluded.

"I guess that goes double for me," Royal mused. "I never felt comfortable with any crew. And now it looks like I'm not wanted here, either. But you can put bubbles in my boots and use me as a buoy before I turn into a skeleton in someone's jail cell. I need to find us a way out of here."

Mustering resolve, Royal climbed out of the window and strolled to the entry that was still barricaded by the dragon's bumpy hide. He raised his foot in the air and was about to pummel the creature with the heel of his boot when the dragon stirred and slid from the doorway.

When the massive bulk moved, it revealed another dragon holding a large iron pot within its jaws. Lowering its head, it placed the pot on the floor and, with a shove of its snout, sent it sliding into the chamber. The heavy pot slammed into Clay's dozing head and he jolted awake. The pot held a selection of fish and vegetables that looked like leeks and potatoes.

"What's this?" Royal asked.

"Feeding time," the dragon grinned. It turned to depart.

"Hold on!"

The dragon halted and gave the captain a look of annoyance.

"Tell Quill I want to see him," Royal said. "Tell him I want to make a deal."

The dragon snorted and Royal saw him march off before the guard once again blocked the doorway.

"Well, at least we won't starve," Clay said as he examined the pot's contents. "I think I can make something out of this. It'd be nice if I had something to clean the fish with, though."

Arthur produced the small knife from his boot. "Try this!" he said, excited at the prospect of eating a full meal.

"Thanks, Arthur!" Clay got to work, busily chopping the vegetables and preparing the fish. Soon, he had a pot of broth boiling over one of the burning braziers. Marco, Penny and Dunney stirred at the aroma of cooking food. In only a matter of minutes, they were all gathered around the steaming pot, mouths watering.

"Stew!" Penny exclaimed. "I don't think I've had a hot meal in a month!"

Clay handed the knife back to Arthur. He pulled the pot from the brazier and set it on the floor for everyone to reach. Using a pointy bone from the fish, he speared a chunk of potato and popped it in his mouth. "It could use some salt," he commented.

"I don't care about that!" Penny exclaimed, as she did the same.

Marco reached into his pocket and produced a spoon. With it, he helped himself to a full bite.

Everyone stared at him in surprise. "What?" he asked innocently. "It's not my fault I'm the only one who always carries a spoon."

The others simply shrugged and returned their focus to the hot, delicious food. The pot quickly emptied, leaving only one last remaining bit of boiled fish. Penny was about to reach for it when Royal stopped her. "That piece belongs to the chef," he said. He motioned to Clay.

Clay grinned as he plucked it from the pot with his make-shift fork. He watched Penny's face fall in disappointment.

"Tell you what," he said. "I'll auction this last piece of prison stew to the highest bidder."

Everyone looked at him, befuddled. "None of us have any money," Arthur replied.

Clay shook his head. "Not for money. Anyone who wants this last bite of fish has to tell me something about themselves. The most interesting fact is the winning bid."

Dunney scratched his chin in thought.

Marco immediately piped up. "I lost my left pinky toe in a card game with a very unusual woman!"

Clay seemed impressed. He looked at Penny. "How about you?"

She hunkered down in bitterness and defeat. "There's nothing to tell."

"There must be something," Clay prodded. "How about telling me why everyone calls you Penniless?"

Penny's face tightened into a simmering scowl of rage. "Not on your life!"

"Ha!" laughed Marco. "I'll tell him, then! Penniless Gayle refuses to pirate for gold or money. She raids ships and packets loaded with cargo instead of treasure. She's rich with rice, tea, cloth, and parasols, but she hasn't got two farthings to rub together!"

Penny fumed. "Careful or you'll be tasting both ends of that spoon!"

Marco moved his utensil away from Penny's reach. "Anyway, she sails around the seas with her poor, destitute crew, begging for alms at every port!"

"Did it ever occur to miserable sorts like you and the crew of the *Sea Scar*," Penny countered, "that the people you constantly pirate are getting rich from selling their cargo at port?"

"Did it ever occur to you," Marco shot back, "that pirates do pirating because they don't want to be traders? It's no wonder your crew mutinied! You have no business being a captain!"

Marco's insult was the final straw. Penny jumped to her feet and clawed at the mapmaker's throat. "I wasn't joking!" she shouted. "Give me that spoon!"

Clay and Arthur scrambled to pull the enraged girl from off the cowering mapmaker. "Knock it off, you two!" Arthur shouted.

Somewhat mollified at the sight of the huddled Marco, but still scowling, Penny resumed her seat on the floor. "I can be just as good and rich as any of them," she muttered. "I don't need their money. I just want their opportunity."

Clay's face lifted into an appreciative smile and he offered her the last piece of speared fish.

"Hey!" Marco argued. "That should be mine. She didn't even tell you anything. I did!"

"On the contrary."

Penny seemed shocked as she took the proffered morsel. "Really?" she said.

"I consider it a very fair trade," he replied.

Penny's face lit up with victorious satisfaction as she popped the fish into her mouth.

"Thank you for the meal, Clay," Arthur said.

"You're welcome."

"Let's just hope it's not our last one," grumbled Marco. "These beasts are probably fattening us for the slaughter."

"I think we're about to find out," Royal said as the giant bulk of the dragon guard moved away from the opening again. From the corridor, the large familiar form of Quill regally entered the chamber. He leveled his yellow eyes at Royal. "Captain," he said in simple acknowledgement.

Royal rose to his feet. "I see you got my message and have come to bargain."

Quill shook his spiny head. "There is no bargaining to be done. I have come to extend an offer," he said. "And a very gracious one, I should add."

"And what is this magnanimous offer you bring us?"

The dragon's nostrils flared. "Take heed, Royal. Sarcasm rarely curries favor. We are not bound by any terms or code to spare the life of you or your friends. You would be wise to remember that." The flare of irritation behind Quill's eyes subsided, however, and was replaced with a demeanor of calm before he continued. "Despite the breach of trust you have displayed by bringing strangers— and *rogueskein*—to our island, Neera and I have agreed to let you live. And what's more, you may leave here in peace. We do this as a gesture of gratitude for bringing us Askelon. And, be assured, you will not leave empty-handed. Our coffers will be opened to you and each may draw whatever treasure you wish from our stores. We hope that this will compensate you for any loss or inconvenience you have suffered during your quest."

"As much treasure as we like?" Marco's spirits seemed to lift significantly.

Royal held his hand up, halting Marco's question. "This is indeed a kind offer, Quill. I know that dragons do not easily agree to part with treasure. But there's a hook at the end of this line, no doubt. What is it you want from us?"

Quill's large yellow eyes narrowed. "You may leave us. But there are three conditions. Failure to agree to any of these terms would be to forsake our offer completely. First," he growled. "You may never return to Dragonrook—"

"Agreed!" Marco interrupted.

Royal shoved the mapmaker backward in frustration.

"Second," Quill continued, politely disregarding Marco's outburst, "the location of Dragonrook must remain a secret that you all shall carry to your graves."

"That's understandable," Royal mused, "even if it is a bit nebulous. What token could we possibly give you as assurance that your secret is being kept?"

The large dragon cast his ominous gaze upon each of the attentive prisoners. "This brings me to the third and final condition," he continued. "All of you may depart, except for one." Quill's eyes fastened onto the young Arthur Cross. "The small boy," he said, "must remain. And never to leave."

17

Luggers, Troves, and Murder

Stunned silence filled the chamber. Then the stillness was ripped apart with cries of confusion and consternation from both Clay and Arthur. "What do you mean he can never depart?" hollered Clay.

Archie Royal attempted to calm the young man. "Ease off, lad." He turned his single eye to Quill. "I'm not quite understanding your request. Arthur doesn't belong here. He's under my care and I have every intention of seeing him and his brother are returned to their home. If it's a hostage ye want, then I'll take his place."

Quill snorted. "The boy must stay."

Clay bristled with frustration. "He'll not be staying here with the likes of you, you filthy beast! I'll never let that happen!"

"I said ease off! I'll handle this," Royal snapped. He took a deep breath before addressing the looming dragon. "Take me as your hostage, and let the rest go. In return, we will eschew the reward. We don't need any treasure. Just let the boy leave with the others."

Marco immediately protested. "He means his portion of the treasure. Not mine!"

The scales around Quill's jaws quivered and his brow lowered over the deep, lidded eyes. A sharp, quick roar belted from this throat. "Enough! I said there would be no bargains! The little one stays. Or you all stay."

"But why?" Clay asked.

Again, Quill snorted another roar of impatience. "Yours is not to question. Only choose."

Once more, outbursts, protests, and refusals erupted amidst the prisoners. Marco demanded his treasure, Penny called for her freedom, and Clay ardently defended Arthur. Finally, Royal barked above the din of arguments. "Quiet, all of you!" he snapped.

The din of contention diminished. Once Royal had their attention, he gave Arthur a sober stare. "This clearly has to be Arthur's choice. And I'll throttle anyone who tries to make up his mind for him!"

Arthur's face fell in dismay at the anguishing dilemma placed before him. No matter what he chose, he was destined to remain on this strange island. Was it better to spend it alone, away from Clay and the others, with no chance of ever seeing anyone again? Or should he make them stay and live an embittered life trapped for his own sake? His heart and mind were locked in indecision. "I – I can't—I don't know," he stammered.

A soft rumble emanated from Quill's throat. "I understand that this is not an easy path to choose, and I will not demand an answer at once." He eyed Arthur curiously, a glint of respect and empathy burning behind his yellow eyes. "I cannot alter the options but," he continued, "perhaps I can give your mind some peace...for both you and for your companions."

Quill turned and his lithe tail swung behind him. "Come," be called. "All of you. Follow me, and I will show you what your futures may hold."

He lumbered through the chamber opening, and the six curious prisoners cautiously tread behind.

Quill led the group through the spiraling passages of Dragonrook. As before, several passing dragons studied them curiously before proceeding on their way. Soon, the group emerged into daylight. Arthur studied the slanting sunlight that sliced over a high canyon ridge. Only a narrow ribbon of blue sky could be seen. Quill had brought them to a round, smooth platform at the bottom of a tight canyon. The walls were dotted with several of the same hexagonal windows like the one in their impromptu prison cell. Between the many dark openings, dragons of all sizes and shapes were flitting across the open air of the gorge.

The crew were transfixed by the unusual view except for Royal who seemed very familiar with it. Arthur and Clay watched the busy scenes unfold above but shook their attention away as Quill continued across the open platform and disappeared through another dark opening. The two brothers hurried to rejoin the departing group.

Unlike the previous smoothly polished and ornate passages and corridors, this tunnel was rough in every detail. In the light of the few flickering torches and braziers, the dark, brooding forms of dragons lurked in the shadows. Pinpoints of firelight reflected in their wary eyes as they silently watched Quill and his human followers venture down the passage.

The dark corridor ended in an unassuming round entrance. Above it, the wall was etched with a simple diamond shape surrounded by three small circles. The group entered and found themselves within a pitch-black chamber. Even though Arthur could not see above him, the thick silence that encompassed them hinted at a spacious and cavernous room.

Quill spoke. "Tindlass."

A brief scraping sound whispered nearby. A spout of flame tore the blackness as fire burst from a waiting dragon. The yellow flame sparked within a gutter and a spreading line of light whisked along the stone wall in a flickering circle around the chamber. Collectively, Arthur, Clay, Marco, Penny, and even the usually quiet John Dunney gasped in amazement.

The chamber glittered to life with firelight that bounced upon piles and piles of glimmering gold coins, shimmering jewels, sparkling gilded urns, and glistening plates of silver. Chests and coffers spilled with gems of every size and color. It was a treasure trove greater than any could ever have imagined. The piles reached above their heads and stretched into the deep recesses of the chamber.

Marco's eyes glowed brighter than all the treasure combined. "I've died and gone to heaven!" he exclaimed.

"It's unbelievable!" whispered Penny.

"Aye," Royal remarked. "The trove of Dragonrook. The treasure of the ages. The dream of every avaricious soul upon the oceans."

"Where did all of this come from?" Clay breathed in awe.

"There was a time," Quill said, "when we dragons were the vassals of man, and tasked to be guardians over their fortunes and spoils from across the map. Merciless time has consumed the men, but their treasures—and our oath—continue. Eventually, their lost and forgotten wealth was brought here, and we continue our eternal sentry over it. Should Arthur choose to let you depart, you may take whatever you wish with you."

Marco whooped with delight. "Whatever we wish? And as much as we wish?"

"Yes," Quill answered. "Provided you can carry it."

Marco laughed and dashed toward the trove of riches and began plunging coins into every pocket. "Haha! The greatest treasure of all time!" he cried. "And it's all ours!"

Penny's face brightened as the realization anchored in her mind. She, too, hurried to the piles of gems and scooped handfuls of rubies and sapphires into her hand. A rainbow of colors reflected in her beaming eyes. "They're beautiful!"

Marco suddenly froze. "Hold on a moment." His eyes narrowed in suspicion. "This treasure isn't cursed, is it? Dragon treasure is always cursed."

Quill shook his head dismissively. "There is nothing special about this trove. These are just bits of stone and metal that have been pulled from the earth and hammered and cut to man's pleasing."

"Ha!" Marco laughed again and dived into another mountain of coins.

"Of course, the arrangement remains," Quill reminded. "You must leave here, never to return. And should you ever tell another of the location of Dragonrook, it will not end well for you. That is a promise and an oath."

"And Arthur must stay behind," Royal reminded.

Marco thrust a finger at Arthur. "That boy is welcome to stay. And he has my solemn promise that he will never see me again!"

The glow in Penny's countenance quickly dimmed, though. She slowly let the gleaming jewels trickle from her hand.

Arthur hung his head. Clay looked up at the watching

dragon and put an arm around his brother. "What about me? Could I choose to stay, also?"

Quill stiffened. "There is no altering the agreement. One human on Dragonrook is more than enough. There were many who were uncomfortable with Captain Royal's presence and heralded it as a dangerous beginning. I will not stoke those fears with facts."

Penny was crestfallen. "It don't seem right, abandoning a boy on an island of beasties while we sail away with a bunch of riches. Why does it have to be him?"

The dragon gave no answer, simply remaining silent and stoic.

Royal spoke up. "Tell me something, Quill. Your offer of booty is quite generous, but you seemed to have forgotten that we don't have any vessel to haul ourselves away from this place. How do you plan to solve that little problem?"

"I suggest you see your friend, Cog. He has been busy in your absence. Meanwhile, the boy Arthur will come with me."

"Where are we going?" Arthur asked.

"You and I will meet with the High Dragon." Without another word, he swung his massive tail and stomped from the treasure-laden chamber.

Arthur gave the others an uncertain glance.

With a nod of his head, Royal encouraged Arthur to follow. "You've got nothing to worry about. Everything will be alright. Go on."

Slumping, Arthur trudged after the departing dragon and out of sight. Clay immediately spun toward Royal. "What are you going to do about this?" he snapped. "We can't leave Arthur here!"

"Relax! I have no intention of letting them keep the

boy." Royal answered. "I don't know what they want him for. We'll talk with Cog. Maybe he has some answers that will help us come up with a plan."

Marco interjected. "You're trifling with dragons, Royal! We have a chance to get off of this island with a fortune in loot. I suggest that whatever it is you are planning involves me being far away from here when it happens."

"Who is Cog?" Clay asked.

"He might be our only true ally in this place. Come with me and I'll introduce you."

"But what about the treasure?" Marco asked.

"None of it's going anywhere unless you play along."

Marco gave the trove a rueful stare, reluctant to part with the piles and gold and jewels, but followed as Royal led them from the vast chamber.

Royal took them up from the dark cavern and together they emerged once more into the open platform at the base of the canyon. The long stretch of rock walls now permitted even less sunlight as the day slipped further away. Marching across the platform, Royal gave every indication that he knew where he was headed. His brisk pace took them to a hexagonal passage on the other side that was rough and unhewn, much like the corridor to the hidden trove of treasure. This one, however, appeared to reach much further in and barely descended at any considerable depth.

Soon, Clay and the others could smell the musty bite of salty seawater, and a sloshing sound bounced from the passage walls. The shimmering dance of reflected water played upon the high ceiling at the end of the corridor. At the end of the passage, Clay saw an inlet of ocean water and a darkened cave that presumably wound its way to the sea. Waiting in the midst of the water was a large sea vessel, sails furled and bobbing placidly.

"A secret cove!" Clay exclaimed.

At the sound of his voice, a throaty rumbling sound rattled nearby. What Clay had mistaken to be a large boulder rolled around, revealing a squat, reddish head of a dragon. It peered at them with curious yellow eyes. One of those inquisitive eyes squinted through a round, magnifying monocle strapped to its head. "Royal!" the dragon roared, when it spied the captain. "The half-sighted vagrant returns!"

"Much to everyone's chagrin, you land-lubbing lizard!" Royal jeered in response.

"Wish not that the dull axe is never visited by the whetting stone," the creature answered oddly. "Your arrival has upended the aimless lull that blankets our island." The stony dragon gave Royal a firm embrace and nearly knocked him to the ground as he clapped his back with a monstrous paw. Then the dragon studied the gang of followers through his eyepiece. "The coming of strangers wafts the inhale of anticipation and the unavoidable exhale of change."

"Cog," gestured Royal, "these are my comrades...Clay, Marco, Penny, and John. Everyone, allow me to introduce you to Cog, the craftiest mind on Dragonrook."

The squat dragon dipped his head in a slight bow. "My mind but takes the scraps that others discard."

"Cog is a creator. An inventor," Royal explained. "He's the one who built the *Ivory Typhoon*."

"And how fares our machine of the seas?" Cog asked.

Royal's mouth twisted into an awkward frown. "About that..."

"He dropped it on a mountain," Marco blurted.

If this statement perturbed the dragon, he showed no sign. "A curious end befitting a curious vessel. From the earth, its parts were ripped. And by the earth, they were ripped."

"I see that you have been busy on another craft. Looks like a lugger." Royal pointed to the vessel that rocked softly in the pool of water.

"Yes!" Cog lumbered to the edge of a wooden dock. "Sharp in sail. Narrow in keel. New ventures to reveal. Faster than its predecessor by far. I have christened her the *Ivory Zephyr*."

"Why would a dragon build a boat?" Penny asked. Which was a very reasonable question, Clay thought.

Royal shot a reprimanding glare at her, but Cog responded, nonetheless. "No *artica*, am I. Nor a bird to climb the sky. But my thoughts extend farther than the gaze in my eye. A vessel that is built is much better than the vessel that is not, wouldn't you agree?"

"This dragon is mad," Marco whispered, and Penny nodded imperceptibly in agreement.

Royal murmured to them quietly so that Cog could not hear. "Cog was not born like other dragons. He has no wings. It's bad enough that the others look down on him. Don't do the same."

Cog reached out over the water and clutched the ship's rail with his monstrous claw. He rocked it back and forth like a toy. "She is yours, if you wish. I can use the space to build another. Or something new entirely. A crew of one is all she needs."

"I'm afraid I must take you up on that offer," Royal answered. "Quill and the High Dragon have commanded that the five of us leave."

The dragon nodded. "The vessel is ready for the sea. But is the sea ready for the vessel?"

"I suppose we'll find out. I'll need rations aboard. And guns. Can you arrange to have cannon, shot, and powder pulled from my armory?"

"Very well."

Royal was silent for a moment. Then he said, almost reluctantly, "I won't be coming back."

Cog's gaze locked on the captain. Unwittingly, his breathing had stopped, but then he finally exhaled with resignation. "Neera's wish, is it? The leaf on the tree does not see the root in the ground. Yet each need t'other."

"Perhaps in time she will change her mind," Royal shrugged. "Until then, all I can do to protect Dragonrook is to help keep its location a secret."

With a snort, Cog wagged his head, pushing the unwelcome news from his mind. He beckoned them further into the cavern where an odd assortment of tables and workbenches crowded the rocky walls. "Before you leave, then, I will show you some of my other endeavors. Things that only humans seem to appreciate."

Royal was about to follow the creature when Clay held him back by his sleeve. "This our chance, Captain!" he whispered. "We have the ship. Once it's provisioned, we can sneak Arthur aboard and escape in the night."

"Slow down, lad. We're not even sure where they took the boy. Besides," Royal said, as he plucked Clay's hand from his coat, "disobeying the High Dragon will have this entire island snapping at our heels and breathing fire down our blouses."

Penny piped up. "Maybe you can steal Askelon back from these critters. Once you have that, they wouldn't dare attack, right?"

"What about my treasure?" interjected Marco. "We need to have that brought aboard also!"

Royal was fuming. "Leave off! Absconding Arthur? Stealing Askelon? Loading treasure? With everything you three are planning, we'll never make it off this island in one piece. We need to do some more fact-findin' before we can even begin to plot our next move. But don't worry. I've got some ideas. And for the sake of all our lives, don't none of you go off on your own crusade!"

With that, Royal broke from the group and returned to the waiting Cog.

Arthur cautiously stayed behind Quill as the two stepped within the spacious throne room. He had persistently received peculiar stares from every dragon they passed, and he found some small measure of security by keeping Quill's bulk between him and any lingering gazes.

Unlike yesterday, the palatial chamber was not populated with an army of attending dragons. The iridescent and graceful form of Neera reposed calmly on the flat, coarse stone. To Arthur's surprise, the long lance still lay upon the stony dais, exactly where Royal had left it...abandoned and untouched.

At first, the High Dragon paid them no notice. Her gaze seemed directed inward, as if lost in a distant memory. At the approach of Quill and Arthur, however, her reverie dissipated, and she swiveled her stare toward them.

"You are the boy they call Arthur," she said directly.

Arthur, unsure of what to do, simply bowed his head. "Yes, ma'am." He nervously put his hands in his pockets, but then, thinking better of it, clasped them behind his back.

"Do you know why you have been brought here?"

Arthur replied awkwardly, keeping his eyes averted. "No, ma'am." He hoped an explanation would be forthcoming, but that appeared to not be the case. Instead, the High Dragon's eyes gave Quill a questioning look.

Quill cleared his long throat, which Arthur realized was a much more involved process for a dragon than a person. "The arrangement has been presented to the band of humans. At this time, there has not been a formal acceptance of our terms. They are reluctant to leave the boy behind."

Neera nodded. "That is understandable. But I see no other way."

"Please, your Highness," Arthur pleaded. "I would very much like to return to Dempster House. I'm sorry that we've caused any trouble and I promise to not tell anyone about your island." With his finger, he drew a large "X" across his chest in the shared oath amongst the boys at the orphanage. "Cross my heart and hope to die. Feed my toes to vermin and my teeth to flies."

The words puzzled Neera and a brow above her silver eye lifted in failed understanding. She simply chose to disregard the promise. "Dragonrook is now your home. I have instructed Quill to acquaint you with the island."

"But I don't understand," moaned Arthur. "Why must I stay?"

"Perhaps in time understanding will come." Neera's answered seemed cold on the surface, but beneath the words the boy sensed a quiet sorrow...and something else. A slight, warm hope? Perhaps a tinge of desire that Arthur truly would come to understand? She nodded to Quill.

"Come with me," Quill said, striding to the large chamber doors.

"Where are we going now?" asked Arthur.

Quill gave the boy a rare smile. "Do you like to fly?"

+   +   +

Two small dragons, no larger than mastiffs, flitted about Quill as they girded him with a golden braided rope that buckled around his shoulders. Additionally, a red cushion was fastened to his hardened back. Once the adornments were fitted, the two small dragons settled to the floor and watched patiently as Quill stretched and shifted under the new accoutrements. Assured of comfort, he knelt and motioned to Arthur. "Climb up," he said, "and hold tight."

Obediently, Arthur mounted onto Quill's shoulders, firmly gripping the golden rope, He found the red cushion much more comfortable than his experience atop the ancient Hogarth.

"All set?" Quill asked. "Then we shall go!"

With a mighty beat of his graceful wings, Quill rose effortlessly into the air and together they wheeled into the open sky.

Arthur's hair whipped backwards. He was amazed at how flying upon Quill's back differed from his journey upon Hogarth. The cushion helped a lot. But what surprised him the most was Quill's grace. While the beating of Hogarth's wings was strong, they always seemed to be fighting the air and racking his entire body with punishment at each stroke. In contrast, Quill rode the air as if the winds belonged to him. He was a master of the sky, and he slipped through the air as smoothly as a fish in the sea. And as quiet as a fish, too. All Arthur could hear was the breeze whistling in his ears, rather than Hogarth's labored breathing and Penny Gayle's constant questions. Closing his eyes, Arthur savored the sensation of the cool brush of wind and the play of sunlight on his face as Quill soared in a lazy circle over the island below.

"Behold!" Quill said. "This is Dragonrook. The last bastion of dragonkind."

Arthur opened his eyes and once again saw the ring of sandy beaches and green forests, capped with the rocky, peaking crater dotted with its hexagonal passages. Amongst the rocks, Arthur spied the long rift on one side of the crater...the long canyon floor that he had been crossing only a short time ago. Descending above the lush canopy of trees, Arthur could spy the teeming life of dragons amidst the foliage. Quickly, the rush of green turned to sand and surf. They glided over the coast and over the glistening water, and for the first time Arthur saw shadowy, wisping forms beneath the surface.

"Look!" he pointed.

Quill was unsurprised. "Yes," he answered. "A fleet of *articas*."

"*Articas*?" Arthur asked in confusion.

"Dragons of the sea," explained Quill. "Dragonrook is home to dragons of all sorts. You have seen one *artica* already."

"I have?"

Quill nodded. "The High Dragon Neera is an *artica*."

"Oh. What kind of dragon are you?"

"I am *hyrex*," Quill answered.

This answer was less helpful to Arthur than he realized. Quill sensed his confusion.

"There are many types of dragons. *Articas*, *hyrexes*, *browgies*, *lockets*, and *flamespires*, for example. Each has a special gift and calling. *Articas*, for instance, are graceful and playful. They live in the two worlds of land and sea. They bring the precious gift of beauty and feeling to our kind. They encourage us with song and color. The many carvings that grace the halls of Dragonrook were fashioned by the skilled hands of the *articas*. They see beneath the surface to find the life within that is common to all of us."

"Is that why they are your leader?" Arthur asked.

Quill seemed confused. "Do you mean Neera? She is not the High Dragon because she is *artica*. The High Dragon is decreed by fate, not by kind. When the time comes, Neera will pass her rule to the next scion, but only time will tell what ilk of dragon that will be."

"And what do—" Arthur tried to remember the name "—*hyrexes* do?"

"*Hyrex* like myself provide order. We give safety through discernment. It is my duty as the Arch-Dragon to be sure that all within Dragonrook live peacefully for the good of the others. Surely, there are similar kind in your lands."

"You mean like policemen?" Arthur said. "I guess so."

"It is more than keeping law," Quill said. "It is seeking solutions. Finding answers that are beneficial to those around us. We seek the ideas that bridge others to one another. Sometimes we are administrators. Sometimes we are arbitrators. We find contentment in resolution."

Arthur felt Quill angle beneath him as the dragon wheeled

back toward the land. He marveled at the pristine waves of the ocean whisking by as they returned to the island.

"I have told you something of myself, young Arthur," Quill mused. "Perhaps you can share with me your tale. Where do you come from? How did you come to sail with Captain Royal? I desire to hear everything."

"Gee," Arthur thought about where to begin. "It's hard to say where I came from. I'm an orphan."

"An orphan?" Quill asked in befuddlement.

"I have no mother or father that I know of. I've been raised by others."

"Ah!" Quill nodded. "A foundling."

Arthur told Quill all about Dempster House and his friends. He shared how Royal burst into the orphanage and saved them from Thaddeus Schark, and how they traveled across the sea and desert and deciphered the riddles of the lost tomb of St. George.

"Hmmm," mused Quill. "You are a puzzle solver. You achieve progress through resolving obstacles. If you were a dragon, you would be a *hyrex* like myself."

"Really?" Arthur scratched his chin as he considered this. "What kind of dragon do you think Clay would be?"

"Your brother?" Quill asked. With another beat of his wings, they gained altitude. "I do not know him. I could not say."

Arthur thought further. "How about Captain Royal? You know him, don't you?"

He felt the dragon stiffen beneath him. "Royal is head-strong and independent. He is akin to a *duskar*. He is neither a leader nor a follower. *Duskars* are dangerous. They disrupt order with chaos. By doing so, they pose the threat of harm on those around them for no purpose."

These words dismayed Arthur. He didn't see Captain Royal in that way at all. "Surely, they must have something good about them. Otherwise, why would they exist?"

"Existence alone does not define purpose. *Duskars* reach beyond the borders of safety. They toy with the rebellion of *rogueskein*." Suddenly, Quill peeled to the left, circling back to the northern part of the island. "This reminds me," the dragon said, "that I must check on the one that lies in our waters."

He must be referring to Hogarth, Arthur thought. He felt the sleek dragon's outspread wings twist slightly and the two descended toward the sandy shore. From the air, Arthur saw the gray bulk of the ancient Hogarth still crouched in the shallow water. The four dark dragons stood on the beach, vigilantly watching over the still form. Effortlessly, Quill fluttered his long leathery wings and descended lightly to the sand. Arthur used the moment to slide from the cushion on Quill's back and stretch his legs.

"The *rogueskein* remains," growled Quill. The dragon contemplated the scene silently.

"Why?"

Quill bristled. "Who can understand what takes place in the mind of a *duskar*? Their reasoning defies logic. As *rogueskein*, he courts death staying here. He is making the others uneasy. If he does not depart, he may force us to do the irrevocable for the sake of peace."

"What exactly is *rogueskein*?" Arthur asked.

"*Rogueskein* are those who defy the High-Thrall."

Arthur nodded. "Oh." Then he shook his head. "I still don't understand."

Quill studied the small boy, seeking a way to explain further. After a few moments of thought, he gestured to his scaly chest. "Place your hand here," he said.

Puzzled, Arthur hesitated then, slowly, he placed his small palm against Quill's heaving body. The scales were smooth and softer than his sturdy back. "Do you feel that?" the dragon asked.

"It feels like your heart beating," Arthur answered. "But it's different. It feels like it's beating three times."

"The thrice-beat of a dragon's heart speaks of three things. One beat gives us life, another gives us our passion, and the third pulses for the High-Thrall...the allegiance to the High Dragon, the leader of dragonkind. It is said that the heart of *rogueskein* only beats twice, leaving them no choice but to chase after their own lusts and desires."

Arthur studied the stoic form of Hogarth in the waves. "It looks like Hogarth's desire is to just sleep in the water."

"Hmmph," snorted Quill. "*Rogueskein* are never so placid. They despise the authority that their hearts should beat for. They dangerously seek to calm their savage yearning by destroying the one that is over them. They desire the death of any High Dragon. Thus, they are not welcome here. We must not be deceived by Hogarth's slumbering appearance. Come," he said. "We must return. I will report my findings to Neera."

Arthur hoisted himself once more onto the back of Quill. As they lifted into the sky, he considered all that the dragon had told him. "If Hogarth were to kill Neera—not that I think he could, by the way. He's seemingly as blind as a bat—would that make you the High Dragon?"

Quill shook his head. "No. I am only a consort chosen by Neera as her mate. When it is time for Neera's leadership to end, she will return to the place of her birth and the new keeper of the High Thrall will be hatched."

"So, your leaders are born, then. Like a king or queen."

"Being born does not make one a leader. The scion only happens to possess the High-Thrall." Quill turned his head and gave Arthur an inquisitive look as they breezed over the island. "Tell me, young Arthur, what do you think one must have in order to be a leader?"

The boy pursed his lips in thought. "A leader must be brave, I suppose. They would have to be to fight enemies like the *rogueskein*."

Quill heaved with what Arthur guessed was a dragon's version of a shrug. "Bravery is special, yes. But often the simplest warrior who charges into the fray has greater bravery than their commanders who stand afar off. And yet they are not the leaders. No. Bravery does not make a leader. Perhaps there is something else?"

Arthur thought some more. "Wisdom, then," he replied. "A leader must know what to do and how to do it."

At this, Quill let out a throaty chuckle that almost sounded like a cough. "If a leader held all the answers there would be no need for advisors such as myself. Wisdom comes to all if they earnestly seek it. You yourself are an example of this. You find solutions and answers to locked mysteries, yet none lead you to it. Again, no. Wisdom is not what makes a leader."

"So, what is it, then?" asked Arthur.

Quill smiled. "The answer is simpler than you realize. Think upon it some more. Perhaps we can explore this subject again tomorrow. The sun is setting, and we must prepare for the night."

Together, the two dived steeply into the canyon rift to

land upon the polished courtyard at its floor. The gorge was now deep in shadow. Dark, fire-breathing dragons marched around the perimeter, bringing torches and braziers alive with flame as they blew upon them.

Quill led Arthur to a new chamber, much like the one they were kept in earlier. This one, however, was much more ornate. Within, a soft mattress covered a small, raised platform. Beside it, a blazing brazier filled the chamber with light and warmth. "Your quarters are ready, young Arthur," Quill said. "This is where you will stay. A dragon's den was not intended for men, but instructions were given to make it as comfortable as possible for you. I will see you in the morning."

Arthur was distraught at suddenly being left alone. "Where are you going?"

"I must report to Neera and attend to my other duties. You will be safe here."

"But when will I get to see my brother? What about the others?"

Quill's jaw tightened, as if holding back a grim secret. "I will return in the morning," was his only answer as he marched out of the chamber entrance. In his place, two menacing dragons – fire-breathing *flamespires* like Arthur had seen previously – assumed rigid stances outside the entryway.

Arthur glanced about the lonely chamber. Despite the heat of the blazing brazier, the room still echoed with the coldness of solitude. He huddled onto the center of the bed and shuddered. In all the years that he could remember, he realized he had never been alone...whether he was spending the day with Clay, eating with Mr. Dempster, or sleeping in the boy's room with Jeremy or Elliot or

Carlton. The loneliness crept upon him like shadows that defied the firelight.

But why?

He still had no answers as to what these dragons wanted from him. Quill had talked quite a bit, but nothing he said seemed relevant to Arthur. Clutching his arms around his legs, he drew his knees in tighter and buried his head in his chest. Tears swelled in his eyes and he forced them back. One never wasted time blubbering at Dempster House. But then, he remembered, that Dempster House was far away.

So very, very far away.

The dam of tears burst. And for the first time in his life, Arthur Cross cried himself to sleep.

+ + +

Arthur was not certain how long he had slept. Nor was he entirely sure what had awoken him from his slumber. The dying brazier next to the bed glowed with embers, providing warmth but very little light. Sounds of alarm and urgency echoed from the passageway. Roars and inundecipherable orders were shouted back and forth. In the dim light, Arthur saw the two guarding dragons part and Quill stomped into the chamber.

"Come with me!" he shouted hurriedly. There was a sinister tinge of rage that burned in his voice. "Come!" he snapped again when it seemed Arthur wasn't moving fast enough to his liking.

"Where are we going? What time is it?" Arthur asked.

Quill ignored the questions. He beckoned to each of the sentries. "Stay with me," he commanded them. "And guard the boy."

Arthur chased after the marching Quill, trying his best to keep up with the dragon's urgent pace and also avoiding being inadvertently stepped on by the crowding pair of guards. He had little bearings as to where they were, but soon he recognized the large doors of the High Chamber. A crowd of dragons stood nervously outside the entrance.

When Quill and Arthur stepped into the bustling chamber, silence immediately swallowed the many voices that were shouting back and forth. Dragons of all sorts were present. They all froze when they saw Quill. Slowly, they parted to reveal the cause of confusion.

Upon the stony High Seat, Neera's body sprawled lifelessly. Her graceful neck draped over the edge of the flat boulder, eyes closed. The iridescent luster of her scales was gone and dark blood oozed from a horrific wound within her chest.

The abandoned lance that Royal had laid upon the stone was missing.

18

Askelon Revealed

Quill's violent roar of rage and despair shattered the air. Arthur clasped his hands over his ears, his bones rattling under the onslaught of sound. It was as if the earth and columns themselves threatened to crumble under its terrible peal.

Then, spent of breath, the roar subsided and the dragon haltingly approached the still form of his companion. "Neera!" he uttered in shock and disbelief. The ridge of spines above his eyes furrowed in grief and then lowered in simmering wrath. "How is this possible?" He spun toward the usually stoic Grindash but who was now visibly uneasy. "The *duskar*! Where is Hogarth?"

"The *rogueskein* still remains on the shore, Arch-Dragon. Even now, my guards watch over him. They reported that he has been there the whole time."

Quill's lips curled, baring his glistening row of razor fangs. "The humans, then," he growled. "Bring me Royal and his crew! I will shred them all to scraps!"

Grindash nodded. "Guards are bringing them as we speak, however..." The *flamespire* hesitated before he shared the last bit of information. "However," he continued, "there are only four of them. One is missing."

Quill's rage-filled eyes narrowed. "Which one?"

"That I do not yet know. My dragons are scouring the island for the fifth."

Arthur's heart sank. Who could do this? Someone had slipped into the High Chamber in the cover of darkness and plunged the deadly lance into the chest of the sleeping Neera. But why? His mind immediately went to Quill's words of how dangerous and unpredictable Royal was. Did the captain feel betrayed by his treatment after recovering Askelon for them? And then his heart sank when he thought of Clay. In his heart, Arthur knew that Clay would fight tooth and nail for him. There was absolutely no way that Clay would abandon Arthur on Dragonrook. Did this truth drive Clay to commit such an appalling act?

A commotion broke out at the entry, and the crowd of dragons parted to make room for a parade of fire-breathers. "The prisoners are here," Grindash announced. "Except for the fugitive," he added.

Arthur was almost afraid to look. If Clay was not among them, then that would mean his brother had certainly fled with the murder weapon. The guard leading the captives stepped aside and Arthur could see the four faces.

Relief immediately washed over him. His brother was at the front of the parade of prisoners. "Clay!" he cried with excitement.

Clay's face lit up with joy. "Arthur!"

The two brothers began to dash towards each other. But another bone-cracking roar stopped them immediately. "Do not move!" yelled Quill. Clay and Arthur froze immediately.

Fuming, Quill examined the row of pale captives. His lips quivered in budding anger. "Where is the fat one?"

Arthur looked among them. Marco was missing.

Royal, Clay, Penny, and John Dunney also glanced around. In the chaos of being aroused from their sleep and bustled to the High Chamber, they hadn't realized that Marco wasn't with them.

"I don't know," Royal answered. "What's this about? Why did—"

His single good eye landed on the lifeless shape on the stone. The blood drained from his face. "Neera!" he whispered.

"Do not speak her name!" roared Quill. "You did this, Royal! You brought death to Dragonrook! We rescued you! We gave you a home! We trusted you despite my better judgement! And this is the reward we receive!"

Royal's face was frozen in shock. "I didn't...I never..." Words failed him. "I didn't want this. I was trying to prevent it. I never thought Marco would do this."

Quill lowered his giant fangs within an inch of Royal's nose. The other dragons in the chamber watched silently, waiting for the Arch-Dragon to rip into the pale pirate. "I can only kill you once, Archibald Royal. Therefore, I have no choice but to savor your end by making it as slow and agonizing as possible."

Suddenly, with violent speed and force, Quill lifted his leathery claw and smashed Royal to the floor, pinning him beneath the clutching talons. The polished stone splintered in a spiderweb of cracks beneath the pressing claw.

"No!" cried Arthur in horror. But as he rushed forward, the guards immediately held him fast.

Quill arched his spiny head over the trapped captain. "First, I will tear your sorry corpse into pieces and then I will do the same for your companions!"

Royal struggled powerlessly beneath the unyielding claws. "Wait, Quill! Wait!" he shouted. "We need to think this through! Marco must have the lance! We can help you get Askelon back!"

"Murderous traitor!" spat Quill. "The lance is not Askelon. Marco has nothing! This is just more of your tricks!"

Confused, Royal stopped struggling. His mind raced for answers.

"You tried to hide Askelon from us!" Quill continued. "You think us fools to fall for your stupid scheme? I have had it with your poor deceptions! I should have struck you down the moment you entered this chamber, but Neera would not allow it!"

Royal's jaw dropped in astonishment as the truth formed in his mind. His eye widened with surprise. "Of course!" he whispered. "It wasn't the lance!" He felt Quill's crushing claws press even harder upon his chest. "Arthur!" Royal strained for breath. "The knife!"

Arthur's horror was replaced with befuddlement. "What are you talking about?!"

"The knife in your boot!" Royal coughed. "Show them the knife! The knife is Askelon!"

Arthur scrambled in his boot and produced the small, black blade. He held it high. "This is Askelon?" Arthur asked.

At the appearance of the knife, a collective gasp washed through the chamber. Royal felt the pressure of Quill's claws lessen.

"The blade is Askelon!" Royal repeated, more strongly as his breathing became easier. "The blade was the treasure they were after. Not the lance."

Arthur studied the small knife. "This is what St. George used to slay the dragon?" He reached out and offered it to Quill. "Then take it."

"No!" shouted Royal in desperation. "Tell him to let me go!"

The boy's face was awash in puzzlement. Quill, still growling, turned a frustrated stare toward Arthur. The boy backed away from Quill. "Let him go?" Arthur asked.

Quill's lips twitched and quivered and the dragon turned his fangs once more to Royal.

"Order him!" shouted Royal.

Arthur steeled himself. With a clenched jaw, he raised the blade above his head and with renewed force, shouted the command. "Let Royal go!"

A frustrated roar rumbled from Quill's throat before he pulled back. Abruptly, he lifted his claw from the ground and Royal scrambled to his feet. The captain doubled over, clutching his chest as he gasped and coughed for breath. Quill glared at both Arthur and Royal in bristling anger and irritation.

"What do we do now?" Arthur asked.

"You tell us," Royal wheezed. His eye fixed onto the boy. "The High Dragon is dead. You are now the Holder of the High-Thrall."

"What?" exclaimed Arthur. He gave a frightened look at the dagger and then stretched his arm out to Royal. "I don't want it. Take it!"

The captain immediately held up his hands. "I'm not the one fer it."

"It belongs to the dragons," Arthur said. He extended it to Quill once again. "You can have it."

But Quill answered with another frustrated roar.

"He can't take it, either," Royal coughed. "Only a dragon scion dare wields the High-Thrall." He gestured to the many dragons circling them, waiting and watching.

"Arthur, I suggest your first order of business be to dismiss these spectators. We need to have a talk with Quill. Alone."

Arthur gazed about the room. Hesitantly, he lifted the small dagger. "All of you can leave now."

To the boy's amazement, the many dragons obediently filed from the throne room. A few curiously glanced back at the unusual sight of the small boy and even smaller blade. The towering doors swung shut. The chamber filled with a sonorous, fading echo at their closing.

Clay, Penny, and even the bleary John Dunney gaped in awe at Arthur and the knife. "Arthur!" Clay exclaimed. "You had Askelon all this time!"

A deep rumble rattled in Quill's throat. "And now you tend to slay me with it? Is that why you wished for me to remain?"

Royal shook his head. "Not at all. This chamber is too small for them and your grief, Quill. I'm sorry about Neera."

The lone dragon swung his head away from them. Heedless of their presence, he stepped to the silent form of the High Dragon draped powerlessly upon the flat stone. Quill's numb eyes traced the form of her head, her long, graceful neck, and the sweep of her now motionless tail. "I never imagined this day would be possible. This was not how it was to be for her."

Royal and the others simply watched silently, unable to provide any manner of solace.

"She had been growing increasingly sad these past many days," Quill continued. He seemed to be speaking more to himself than to the others. "She longed to return to the sea and to trade her burdens of rule for the weightlessness of the waves. That was her dream for when the new scion was ready."

Arthur slowly approached the rough stone. He had never really witnessed death before. With his eyes level with the boulder's flat surface, he could see closely the face of Neera in still repose. The rainbow light still faintly shimmered along her brow in the torch light. It was odd, Arthur thought. To every appearance, it was if she was only sleeping. But an uncomfortable stillness belied the truth. The light that once was the life of the High Dragon was slipping further and further into the past with each passing second. "I'm sorry, Quill."

"Where is the scion?" asked Royal. "Who will take her place?"

Quill's head drooped even further. "Only Neera knew the nest of the scion. As with all scions, the egg was laid in secret and is left alone until the time of hatching. Its location could not be entrusted with me. It was given only to her *locket*."

"Her *locket*?" Penny asked.

Royal explained. "The smaller dragons you have seen are *locket* dragons. Messengers of information and bearers of secrets. They're bound and entrusted by their masters." He turned back to Quill. "Where is Neera's *locket*?"

"Pinn vanished some time ago. No one knows what happened to him. Without Neera or Pinn, the next High Dragon is lost to us. Until the scion is found, the presence of the High-Thrall rests only within Askelon."

"Then why can't you take Askelon and lead Dragonrook until then?" Arthur asked.

Quill shook his head. "For me—or any dragon—to wield Askelon would be to court the dangers of *rogueskein*."

Royal nodded. "It would mean exalting oneself as equal to the High Dragon. It would be akin to mutiny." A realization dawned upon the captain. "So, that was why you needed Arthur to stay behind, isn't it? You knew he had Askelon but couldn't physically take it from him yourself."

"That is correct," Quill answered. "The boy would need to surrender Askelon to Neera only."

"Why didn't you just ask?" Arthur said. "I would have given it to her."

"We did not know what your intentions were," Quill countered. "When asked to surrender your weapons, you kept Askelon for yourself. We did not know whether to suspect ignorance or treachery. You gave us no choice but to make you all our prisoners until we determined your motives. We dared not reveal the truth of the blade for fear you would use it against us."

"Then I'm the one to blame," Royal admitted. "I instructed Arthur to keep the blade a secret. It had helped us out of one pickle, already. Not knowing what was happening, I thought it might be useful once again. I never realized I was using Askelon as a lockpick."

Clay's face reddened from embarrassment. "And I used it to clean fish."

Quill curled a lip in quiet disgust. Before the dragon could respond further, however, the massive doors of the throne room flew open. The wingless Cog, his magnifying monocle steaming with perspiration, came bounding into the chamber. When he saw Royal and the others watching him, he skidded to a halt along the polished floor. "Royal!" Cog exclaimed in surprise. "You're still here!"

"Of course I'm still here. Why wouldn't I be?"

Cog shook his head. "I awoke. The *Ivory Zephyr* was gone. I assumed—"

"Gone?" Immediately, Royal turned to the others. "Marco must have fled the island."

"We haven't loaded our treasure yet," Penny commented. "He would never leave without that!"

Royal scratched his chin. "True. Unless..." His voice trailed off in thought.

"Do you think he's still on the island?" Clay asked.

"Not at all," Royal replied. "He doesn't know."

"Doesn't know what?"

"He doesn't know that the lance is not Askelon."

"Well," Clay answered, "that means he's sailed away with a worthless stick. His loss."

With a grimace, Royal shook his head. "He's about to lose his life. He snuck in here, snatched the lance, struck Neera down in her sleep, and then fled Dragonrook. If he left here thinking that he truly had Askelon, then there's only one place he could possibly be headed with it."

"Where's that?" asked Arthur.

"Fangshard."

"Why would he go there?" Clay asked.

"For centuries," Quill explained, "Arcrellis has tempted men to find Askelon, luring them with unfathomable riches for any who finds it. He believes that Askelon is his key to claiming the High Seat of Dragonrook. The fables suggest that if one were to devour the bones of the High Dragon, that dragon would become a scion of the High-Thrall."

"Is that true?" Royal asked.

Quill shrugged. "It is only a whispered fable because time has never seen it come to pass. But Arcrellis is a desperate, unbound thinker and will cling to any possibility for a chance to rule." Quill bared his razor-sharp teeth in a wide grin. "But since the weapon Marco carries to Fangshard is not Askelon, he's sailing to his doom. Arcrellis will chew him into pulp. My only regret is that I will miss it."

"We need to stop him," Royal replied.

Quill growled. "Never! I have no reason to protect him!"

"You don't see the whole picture, do you?" Royal warned. "What happens if Marco reaches Fangshard and boasts to Arcrellis that the High Dragon is slain?"

The dragon's grin fled from his snout. His yellow eyes widened with alarm as his mind found the truth. "He will know that Dragonrook is leaderless. The day he has always dreamed of will be handed to him by the hands of that treacherous human! Arcrellis will seize the opportunity to attack and claim the High Seat as his own."

"Marco may play the greedy fool, but he's cleverer than he lets on. He's not stupid enough to take command of Dragonrook and become the enemy of Fangshard. He wants to play both ends against the middle. We need to stop him. Not to save Marco's life," Royal admitted, "but to prevent a war that would mean the utter destruction of Dragonrook."

The *Ivory Zephyr* was indeed a swift vessel. The narrow keel sliced through the waves like a sharp knife. Taut with wind, the triangular sails lifted the ship high in the water and Marco happily breathed in the rush of fresh morning air across his face. At last, he thought, I'm free. Free from the onerous burdens of Archibald Royal. Free from the dangerous circumstances that pulled him from his home. And most importantly, he was free from that wretched dragon-infested rock.

Standing tall at the wheel of the ship, he looked down at the long lance lying at his feet. The deadly barbed tip still glistened with the stain of blood. Or did it? Marco had never actually seen dragon's blood before. He squinted at it in the dim dawn gloom. It was as if the dark, congealed mess held flecks of silver or iron that winked faintly in the nascent light. Odd but inconsequential, he concluded. He awarded himself a grim smile of triumph as he remembered how he had wielded Askelon.

From the moment he had silently lifted it from the stone dais, he could feel the power surging through it. No wonder St. George was so indomitable! No wonder Royal sought it so desperately! But unlike Royal, Marco Mishmal Mossarian was not a fool. With a single thrust, he restored the ancient lance's purpose when he plunged the terrible weapon into the breast of the sleeping dragon. He had returned Askelon to its destiny just as a master swordsman returns a sword to its scabbard! Marco relished the thrill of his victory. His chest puffed with the inhalation of conquest and he let the words break the silent morning as he expelled his breath. "Marco the dragonslayer!"

He grinned with the truth of those words. But quickly the smirk faltered as the memory continued. He remembered the woeful eye of the dragon that had suddenly opened as he raised the lance. How it stared at him and watched him dispassionately. The unfeeling gaze, void of panic or alarm, gutted Marco's moment of triumph, transforming his victory into a hollow, worthless act. Marco hadn't slain the dragon. The dragon had let itself be slaughtered.

In the gloom of the dawn, his face fell. The ebullience of success vanished under the reality of hard truth. He shook his head.

"No matter," he muttered aloud, even though no one was around to hear. The sound of his own voice encouraged him. "Soon, they'll all be destroyed anyway. And all their treasures will be mine."

His plan was simple. Now that he had wrested Askelon from the reaches of Royal and his misguided helpers, he stood at the cusp of ruling all of dragonkind.

He'd start with Fangshard.

Fangshard was an island he knew well. He was the one who had charted its location for Riga and Schark. It was there that he had his first terrible encounter with dragons. And it was there he knew a massive hoard of treasure lay within its caverns. A treasure as great—if not greater— than the one he had seen at Dragonrook.

"And soon it will all be mine!" Marco smiled. "The dragons at Fangshard are stupid. They crave only one thing... the rule and ruin of Dragonrook." With Askelon, Marco could give it to them in exchange for their trove of riches. "And while the self-absorbed dragons chew each other to pulp," he mused, "I will be the wealthiest man on land and sea!" He scoffed when he remembered fretting about the lost bag of jewels on Rogue's Island. "Scraps," he laughed. "Scraps!" He laughed louder and longer.

The *Ivory Zephyr* breezed on its course and Marco soaked in the promising seascape that was slowly unveiling in the sunrise. By the end of the day, he would arrive at Fangshard. And then, the filthy, chaotic Arcrellis and his legions of dragons will do his bidding, treasures will be his, Dragonrook will crumble under their onslaught, and maybe—just maybe—the irksome Captain Archibald Royal will be vanquished under the claws of a hundred gnashing beasts.

Royal studied the odd contraption in his hands. He couldn't tell if it was a pistol or a cannon. It was heavy, that much was certain. He flipped it over to examine the opposite side and then, hefting one end upward, he cautiously peered at the bore. "What kind of shot does it fire?"

Cog shook his head. "Not a blunt instrument for pummeling." The dragon revealed a stout metal rod that fashioned to a sharp, barbed point at the tip. "For sharpness and purpose."

Royal's eye twinkled. "Ah!" he nodded. "A harpoon! But why is it so fat?"

Cog smiled. "No powder in the bore. Powder in the harpoon!"

"You clever dragon!" Royal smiled.

"Place the harpoon in the bore. Pull the cascabel. Then release with the trigger. I call it Talonshot."

Royal inwardly smiled at Cog's penchant for naming his inventions. "How far does it fire?" he asked. "How accurate is it?"

"I also call it Untested."

Royal grimaced. The heavy cannon-like weapon had a leather belt attached to it. He slung it over his back. "And I'll call it Deadweight if it doesn't work. How many harpoons do you have for it?"

"Three."

"Only three?"

Cog lifted his scaly shoulders in a shrug. "Making exploding harpoons is not as easy as making complaints."

Royal got the message. "My apologies. I'll take what I can get."

"And you will need it."

The mission to find Marco before he reached Fangshard was a risky venture and the chances of encountering one of the island's dangerous denizens was almost a surety. "I appreciate the help," Royal said as he shifted the wirght of the monstrous Talonshot and its three deadly over his shoulder.

Before Cog could reply, Quill entered the dim cavern. The Arch-Dragon never had a reason to visit Cog's odd domain. His curious glance at the cavern's unusual collection of half-built gadgets and contraptions seemed to be one of disdain but also held a small hint of impressed surprise. Wresting his eyes from the assortment of clutter, he leveled his attention at Royal. "Emberwing is ready," he stated.

"Here we go," Royal quipped to Cog. "I'm grateful for everything!" He waved goodbye to the wingless *duskar* and followed Quill out of the cavern.

Royal could sense the tension within the Arch-Dragon as they walked. "Something has your tail in a twist," he commented.

Quill didn't bother looking at the captain. "I think this plan is a big mistake. Marco has too much of a lead. He'll reach Fangshard before you can stop him."

"We have to try, though."

"If the mapmaker successfully reaches Fangshard, is it not better that we wait in readiness?"

"I can't just let that fool Marco march to his doom."

Quill's eyes sparked with checked rage. "Marco is not who I am concerned about."

Royal halted. "Enough of this pussyfooting around, Quill. What are you not telling me?"

Quill cast a cautious eye up and down the passage. He evidently did not want his words to be overheard. "There is great peril if you and Emberwing leave Dragonrook."

"You think I don't know that?" Royal hefted the bulky Talonshot weapon on his shoulder. "I'm prepared for a fight against any critter on Fangshard."

"But are you prepared to fight Emberwing?"

"Emberwing? What are you saying?"

Again, Quill glanced over his shoulder before continuing. "Royal," he whispered, "the High Dragon is dead, and now the High-Thrall dwindles."

"But you have Arthur and Askelon—"

Quill shook his head. "Askelon carries the High-Thrall, but it is not nearly as powerful as a living, breathing High Dragon. Here on Dragonrook, we feel its pulse...but the further Emberwing flies from these shores, I cannot say what will happen to her. Farther from Dragoonrook, closer to *rogueskein*."

Royal stiffened. "Does she know this?"

Quill nodded. "She has accepted the risk. And you must also, because as you approach Fangshard, you may find yourself on the back of a wild, uncontrollable beast."

Royal drew a quick breath as he processed the possibility. He then shook his head. "It can't be helped. If Emberwing is willing to risk it, then so will I."

"As you wish." Quill wheeled around and continued up the passage, his conscience mollified. He had given the captain fair warning. If he chose to fly to his doom, that was now his choice. As Royal followed after him, he sensed that Quill's true concern was only for Emberwing.

When they emerged from the cavern and into the deep canyon, the waiting Emberwing was crouched on the broad platform, ready for flight. She was a bright red *flamespire*, and probably the sleekest looking dragon Royal had ever seen. Here golden wings stretched in preparation and glowed beneath the sunlight beaming amid the cliffs. A sturdy saddle had been secured across her shoulders and when she noticed Royal, she gave him a nod of assurance. If she had any fear of approaching Fangshard, she hid it masterfully.

Once again, the captain shifted the heavy cannon-like weapon upon his back. He checked to make certain his flintlocks were secure and tested the cutlass in the scabbard at his hip.

"Captain Royal!"

Royal turned to see Arthur watching him from a distance. He smiled and gave him a wave. And then his smile faltered. Pausing his straddling of the *flamespire*, he changed tack and strode to the boy.

"Arthur," he beckoned. "Come here. I need to tell you something."

The boy dashed to him and Royal hunkered down to the ground so he could look at him face to face. Arthur watched him expectantly. "Arthur," he repeated. "I know there's a lot going on but..." He couldn't bring himself to tell the full truth. The idea that he may not return was the last thing the small boy needed to deal with. He quickly changed the topic. "...but you'll be okay. Your brother is here to take care of you. And if you need anything, talk to my friend Cog. Got it?"

"How long until you get back?"

Blast, Royal muttered inwardly. "Marco has a day's jump on us. Give me a day to catch him and a day to return." He pointed a thumb toward the dragon behind them. "This Emberwing looks like a pretty swift beast. She'll have me back in no time. But that's not what I wanted to tell you." He lowered his voice. "If I can't stop Marco in time, then we can't ignore the possibility that he'll return with a bunch of dragons at his back. You need to be safe."

Arthur's face screwed into a question mark. "How can he do that without Askelon?"

"It's not just Marco that we're dealing with. These dragons have Thaddeus Schark on their side, and Marco will use Schark's greed to his advantage. Marco will discover that the treasure here on Dragonrook is his only bargaining chip."

"Why are you telling me this?"

Royal stood up to his full height. "Like it or not, Arthur, Dragonrook is now under your rule. I thought you ought to know what might be coming."

"What do I do?"

Royal smiled. "You're a clever lad. I'm sure you'll think of something. Remember what I said before about the difference between crew and cargo? Same thing. Except this ain't a ship. It's an island. Keep everyone pullin' on the same line, and you'll be okay." With that, Royal stepped back to the waiting Emberwing. Expertly, he swung himself into the saddle. Pounding the air with golden wings, dragon and rider lifted gracefully into the sky.

Archie Royal waved once more to the receding boy below, trying his best to ignore the hard reality that this might be the last time they would ever see one another.

+ + +

The stone door with the odd etchings was just as Marco remembered it. He gazed upward at their foreboding height and stifled the nervous tightening in his throat. Mustering his courage, he gripped the shaft of the lance and with all the force he could manage, he struck the lance's iron tip against the rough portal. The solid shaft of wood vibrated in his fist, and he heard the sharp report of its echo ring distantly behind the door.

The melon-sized spyhole opened with a grating rattle far above Marco's head. The mapmaker gritted his teeth, determined to hold back any cry of terror as the large red eye examined him curiously. It simply stared in silence for an uncomfortably long time.

"I have—" Marco's voice could barely rise above a whisper. He cleared his throat and then took a deep, long breath. I had better do this right, Marco said to himself. "In the name of Askelon, I command you to take me to Arcrellis."

The giant red eye simply continued to study the small mapmaker.

"Take me to him," Marco repeated as he lifted the lance above his head, "or I will slay you!" It immediately occurred to him that, with the massive doors shut, all he could do was perhaps poke the dragon in the eye. "Open these doors!" he ordered.

The red eye narrowed. After a pause, the eye vanished and soon the gargantuan doors swung open to reveal the full, dark form of a black dragon attached to the red eyeball. Without a word, the creature turned and retreated into the dark passage.

Marco swallowed the lump in his throat and wiped the drops of perspiration from his bald. With a firm grip on the lance, he stepped within the giant entry.

The cavernous corridor contained none of the polished refinement that Marco had seen in Dragonrook. Instead, the rocky floor was strewn with loose gravel and sharp stones. It was all he could do to keep from stumbling within the dim light. At one point, his toe struck a hollow piece of debris that rolled awkwardly upon the stone. It wobbled to a stop in a patch of firelight. Marco shuddered as it revealed itself to be a cracked, yellowing skull. He chose to not wonder who the poor, hapless soul was who had spent his last living breath within this terrible pit.

The dragon lumbered ahead and disappeared into darkness. A loud snort erupted. A fireball bellowed from the dragon's nostrils and a dark, oily pile of debris burst into flame. The cavern filled with harsh red light. Black shadows of stalactites and stalagmites flickered violently against the stone, looking for all the world like a thousand snapping teeth.

The foul air reverberated with shrieks and yowls that gradually grew louder. Under the flickering glow of crimson flame, through a jagged fissure and alongside a leering chasm, the passage finally emerged into a sprawling cavern. The sound of growls and roars bounced among the walls and Marco shuddered when his eyes discovered the source.

Dragons of all sorts roiled and bit at each other. Fierce eyes of red and yellow flashed in the dim light. The fluttering of mighty wings whipped the air as beasts took flight over the writhing horde of bodies, their spiny tails lashing back and forth and their mighty talons dangling above a sea of gnashing teeth. The stench of sulfur and smoke was unbearable, and Marco clutched his nose in futility.

High above, a sharp ridge of rock protruded over the chaotic scene. Perched upon it, surveying the mass of crawling creatures, was the mighty Arcrellis.

Marco's heart froze at the sight of the dragon who ruled within the depths of Fangshard. As a *duskar*, he was not the largest of the beasts within the churning crowd. But his eyes were wide and alert. He was not hideous or repulsive like some of the others. The lithe black body glistened like polished onyx. The spurs and horns that ridged his frame were perfectly symmetrical. The tail was well-balanced and the mighty wings that arched from his back stretched and folded with grace and mastery. Even with Marco's distaste for dragons, he could not deny that it was the most amazing creature he had ever laid eyes on.

His awe was broken, however, as a rhythmic chant pulsed from amidst the unruly mob.

"Now! Now! Now!"

Another dragon burst from among the mass of monsters beneath the cliff—a *flamespire*, Marco believed—and it shot like an arrow toward the perched Arcrellis. From its jaws, a jet of flame stretched forward and engulfed the perched ruler. But the duskar was unperturbed. Instead, with lightning reflexes, Arcrellis's graceful neck coiled like a snake and then struck. His wide mouth stretched open, and his perfect, razor-sharp fangs snapped shut on the flamespire's tail. With mighty arcs, he swung the attacking beast in furious circles. Abruptly, the tail ripped loose from the snared fire-breathing dragon. The tailless beast spun across the sea of jeering denizens with relentless momentum before colliding into the cavern wall.

The churning audience burst into a chorus of ear-splitting screeches that passed for mocking laughter. Arcrellis spat the remnant of tail from his mouth and let it land on the rocky floor, where it wriggled and twisted with a life of its own. Two nearby dragons pounced upon it, snatching it mercilessly into their fangs and struggled in a grotesque game of tug-of-war.

Marco turned away in disgust from the revolting scene, but when Arcrellis began to speak, he couldn't help but cast his gaze upon the stunning dragon once more. "Away with you, Sparkbone!" Arcrellis howled. "And do not show us your worthless carcass until your tail is re-grown!"

Again, the chamber filled with haughty sneers at the disgraced beast.

Arcrellis halted and swung his attention in the direction of Marco.

"Silence!"

The jeers quieted but did not dissipate completely. The dragon's burning gaze fell upon the beast that guided Marco into the cavern. "Skorch! Why are you not at your post?"

Skorch huffed. "I bring a visitor."

The scowling Arcrellis's eyes flicked up and down as he studied the tiny mapmaker. "Who is this?" his voice rumbled.

Skorch hefted his shoulders in a dragon-like shrug. "Some wandering fool," he answered. And without another word, Skorch pivoted and returned down the passage in which they had come.

"I have suffered a bounty of fools lately," Arcrellis growled. "How is it this particular one dares to enter my den?"

Marco straightened and allowed a slight thrill to course through his spine. His lips contorted into a sneer of contempt and he lifted the long, pointed lance over his head. "I come with Askelon! By its might and power, I claim my rule over Fangshard and all of its inhabitants!"

Whatever lingering murmurings that bubbled in the cavern vanished at the sound of these words. A sea of glaring eyes watched the small man addressing Arcrellis with curiosity and confusion.

Arcrellis simply waited in silence.

A new level of anxiety crept into Marco when he realized he had the rapt attention of every dragon in the room. "But," he continued, desperately trying to disguise the cracking in his voice, "I will be a fair and just ruler if my conditions are met. I demand that you bring me your treasure. The riches of Fangshard now belong to me!"

Arcrellis lifted a leathery eyebrow. "Really?" he responded calmly. "That seems like a very gracious and reasonable request from one who wields Askelon. But perhaps there is room for negotiation? Pince! Nettle! Thorn!"

From out of the darkness, three small dragons arched

into the air above Arcrellis and swooped toward Marco. Before he realized what was happening, bat-like wings flapped about him and he felt a swarm of sharp pain as tiny talons and fangs scraped at his face and scalp. In defense, he raised his arms to shield himself from the onslaught. Blinded by the sudden assault, he could not see the unknown force that wrenched the lance from his hands. He screamed and swatted furiously at the attacking beasts while attempting to protect himself as best he could from the bites and gouges that plagued him from every direction. He sprawled onto the ground and kicked at the diving dragons.

The stinging attacks ceased. Marco looked up in shock to see that the three *locket* dragons had already returned to the top of the jagged ledge while Arcrellis loomed high above him. One of the small creatures hovered in the air, clutching the lance in its claws.

A pleased grin stretched across Arcrellis's face. "Now we shall discuss a new arrangement. What you proposed would have been completely acceptable if you actually possessed Askelon. But, alas and alack, it appears you have made a very big mistake."

All Marco's could do was stammer in disbelief. "But—but—"

Arcrellis gazed down at the torn and bleeding, beaten mapmaker. One would almost perceive a sense of pity in his eyes. With an impressive stretch of his wings, the black beast lifted effortlessly into the air and floated downward from the ledge. Silently, his talons touched the stony surface next to the trembling Marco.

The dragon studied the cowering form with small amusement, much like a cat observing a canary with a broken wing. "Stupid creature," he leered. "I don't even know your name. Do you know why that is? It's not because we've never met. It's because I don't care. You see, we dragons live for hundreds and hundreds of years upon this earth. Humans, on the other hand, are here but for a moment. You are morsels of time. You are born and then you quickly die. There is as much reason to give a human a name as there is to name each breath that I expel from my lungs. I both laugh at and despise the arrogance of your kind. Why do you not realize that you are merely playthings for us?"

Arcrellis straightened. "But I am not without understanding. I think we both agree that your life is meaningless. Therefore, in my magnanimity, I will give you a gift. I will kill you with the very lance with which you sought to slay me, and with your final breath, you can relish the truth that your meaningless life at least concluded with an ironic death." Arcrellis beckoned with a single claw. "Thorn!"

The small dragon who was clutching the long lance flitted above Arcrellis and opened its talons. With ease, Arcrellis caught the falling lance and raised it over his head, the dark, ominous point aimed at the chest of the helpless and doomed Marco Mishmal Mossarian. The mapmaker squeezed his eyes shut waiting for the sharp, swift blow.

But Arcrellis froze. His yellow eyes widened. His nostrils flared as they sniffed the air.

In amazement, his stare locked upon the tip of the lance. "I smell thrall blood on this weapon."

He sniffed again. "Yes!" His voice was a hissing rumble. "Where does this lance come from?"

Marco gingerly opened one eye. "I—I used it to slay the High Dragon of Dragonrook. I thought it was Askelon."

A unified gasp rippled across the watching dragons.

"Is this true?" Arcrellis whispered. "Neera is dead?"

"Yes!" Marco replied, omitting the fact that he slew her while she slept. No need for them to know that, he thought.

The mouth of Arcrellis split into a broad grin of ivory knives. "You may not have brought Askelon, human," he said, "but you do indeed bring us a gift! Without the High Dragon, her followers will now be lost. Without the High-Thrall, all on Dragonrook will be powerless against me! I revise my statement, human! Your death will have more significance than you ever could have dreamed. It will hearken the fall of Dragonrook, and then, once I am upon the High Seat, the inevitable doom of your own kind who have plagued this earth for far too long!" Again, in triumphant glee, Arcrellis lifted the bloody lance.

"Wait!" Marco cried. "I can help you! I'll do whatever you want!"

"There is nothing you have to offer me!" Arcrellis laughed.

Suddenly another voice broke from the shadows. "But there's something he can offer me!"

From the recesses of the dark cavern, a lone, bristle-bearded figure on a wooden leg hobbled into the firelight.

"Captain Schark," Arcrellis growled. "You have returned."

20

The Pits of Fangshard

Thaddeus Schark had not been in a good mood for quite some time.

He and his crew had spent a full day and night picking apart the rubble of Marco's demolished house, vainly trying to recover the lost Coin of Cordura and, for fun, perhaps the flattened body of Archibald Royal. It wasn't until well into dark that one weary crew member suggested they look for the *Ivory Typhoon* which they had pursued all the way to the mapmaker's island. When it was discovered that the ship, and the crew with it, were nowhere in sight, Schark's tanned features became several shades of angry red. And when they realized they had no clue as to where it had sailed, Schark's crew turned white as ghosts. Not only would they now have to set sail under the rage of a fuming captain, but also decide if they should dare return empty-handed to Fangshard and face the wrath of Arcrellis.

"We still got a bargaining chip," Schark had growled. "They may have the coin, but we have the map!" Perhaps it was ignorance or perhaps wishful thinking, but he had no reason to believe the map was fake. It was the same faulty logic that he had used when he lowered his grandmother down a well with a fraying rope, convinced that there was a chest of gold coins at the bottom. That error had been conveniently forgotten long ago. "For now, we'll hide the map in a secret place. Arcrellis will have no choice but to keep us around until we find that pest Royal and that stupid coin!"

Once at Fangshard, they discovered Arcrellis's duplicity. Unbeknownst to everyone aboard the *Sea Scar*, they were being followed by the *browgie*, Balfour, for the entire voyage. How could they have imagined that Arcrellis had grown weary of the unpredictability and treachery of pirates? The dimwitted Captain Riga had tried—and failed—to fool him. And now there was no telling what new levels of deception Captain Schark would sink to. Would he fail in his quest? Or worse, would he attempt to seize Askelon for himself? Arcrellis dared not risk it.

When they returned to Fangshard, Thaddeus Schark bristled at the black dragon's command that he and the crew of the *Sea Scar* remain at Fangshard until Balfour's return. "Balfour will wrest the coin from Royal and bring it here. Then I will decide what to do with you and your men," Arcrellis had threatened.

But neither Arcrellis or Schark had expected the massive *browgie* to come straggling through the air empty-handed with a shredded wing and fang marks in his hide from another dragon.

"What do you mean you lost them!?" both Arcrellis and Schark had bellowed at the wounded *browgie*. When Balfour explained how Royal and the others had successfully unearthed Askelon and escaped to sea, and how he himself had narrowly escaped with his shattered wing from Rogue's Island, Arcrellis was left with little choice but to dispatch Schark once again.

While crisscrossing the ocean in search of Balfour's mysterious island amidst a disgruntled crew that had clearly had their fill of dragons, and with a dwindling coffer of supplies, money, patience, and favor, Schark was seriously beginning to question if there was any remaining value in this mad quest. Once they finally found the chunk of rock where the *browgie* had dropped the *Ivory Typhoon* and its irksome passengers, his hopes had begun to lift. But to his ever-increasing dismay, all Schark found was a splintered shipwreck on a mountain and a marooned band of Penny Gayle's worthless, wailing numbskulls.

Thaddeus Scharck was quivering with rage, frustration, and dented hubris. Royal had thwarted him once again! His grubby, blunt hands wanted to strangle the life out of something or someone. And when he had returned to Fangshard to report his findings and discovered the worthless mapmaker cowering beneath the dreaded Arcrellis, fate had finally given him a chance to sate his anger.

"Aye!" Schark answered. "I have indeed returned!"

With simmering ire, he thrust his wooden leg on the throat of the fallen Marco. Marco's eyes widened and he gasped for breath.

"Where is Royal?" Schark growled, as he pressed down with his wooden stump.

"Dra-Dra-Dragonrook!" he croaked. "They're all on Dragonrook!"

Arcrellis huffed. "Royal is of no importance! And neither are you!"

Schark turned his bristling glare to the dragon. "Ha! I'm not leaving here until I have the treasure I was promised!"

Arcrellis coiled his thick neck, preparing to strike. "You think you have earned treasure? You have failed in your task, inconvenienced me repeatedly, and now dare to claim a reward? I'm finished dealing with filthy humans!"

Schark pointed a stubby finger. "You're not done yet! You need me!"

"I have no need of you," Arcrellis retorted. "Askelon has been found and is now in the hands of my enemy. Your secret map has been rendered worthless, just like your hairy head!"

"It's not my map you need, Arcrellis," snapped Schark. "It's my guns!"

Arcrellis paused. Even Marco, wrestling under the weight of the pirate's peg leg, froze to listen.

"I heard what you're planning to do," Schark continued. "Your plotting to attack Dragonrook? They have you outnumbered two to one and you know it. You're going to need firepower. And I have it."

A snort escaped Arcrellis's nose. "You have one pathetic, inconsequential vessel."

"I can get more. We have this jackal's lugger—" Schark gave a quick jab of his stump into Marco's throat, "—and there are three ships with crew waiting in Stinky Cove. All we need to do is go get them."

The pinned Marco struggled for breath, seeing opportunity. "He's right!" he choked. "*The Lock*, *The Stock*, and *The Feral*! Gayle's fleet!"

The dark dragon paused, calculating the options. "And your price?"

"Double what I was to receive for Askelon," grunted the pirate. "And Royal's skin to use as a table cloth and his bones for utensils," he added.

Arcrellis silently considered the offer.

Marco could see the beast was uncertain. Dragons, after all, have always had a very hard time parting with treasure. "I can help!" the mapmaker grunted.

"What did you say?" Schark grumbled.

"Get this lousy piece of firewood off my throat so I can talk!" he croaked.

Schark lifted his peg leg and Marco gasped for welcome breath. "I said I can help! There's a trove of treasure at Dragonrook. I've seen it, but it's well hidden. I can lead you to it. Part of it is mine, though. It was promised to me!"

"You lousy cur!" Schark gave him a swift kick. "I'll promise you a good keel-haulin'! You're a mapmaker, ain't ye? You'll make us a map pointin' the way and then wait here until we get back! I don't trust your fat hide any further than I can throw it." He delivered another jab with his wooden stump and turned to Arcrellis. "Is it a deal?"

Still, Arcrellis was silent.

"Or," the pirate continued, as he motioned to the crowd of dragons who had been watching the exchange with fascination, "are you going to tell everyone here to follow you into a losing battle knowing that you chose to make it harder for them? They strike me as a bit of a mutinous bunch."

The dragon stiffened. After another moment of hesitation, he spoke. "Very well. Your reward for your firepower will be all the treasure of Dragonrook." He looked down at the beaten Marco. "Give this human some ink and parchment and lock him away. And you," he commanded Schark, "assemble your fleet. We will gather at the Sore. From there, we will launch our attack."

+ + +

Royal pointed the spyglass at the ocean below, scrutinizing every wave through the scratched lens. Neither Marco nor the *Ivory Zephyr* could be seen anywhere. Collapsing the scope, he tucked it securely into his belt and renewed his grip on Emberwing's lash.

"You are indeed fast," he said to the dragon. "Probably the swiftest I've ever seen."

Emberwing smiled at the compliment. "Thank you," she said, "but *articas* could easily outpace us in the water. If you chose to travel with them, you might have arrived at Fangshard already...provided you'd be able to hold your breath for that many leagues."

"I'll take the high road, then," Royal laughed. "How much further to Fangshard, do you reckon?"

"Not far."

"You've been there before?"

"No. But we all know where it is. We avoid it since we are not welcome there."

"Well," Royal mused as he squinted through the wind at the speeding waves below, "it was my hope that we could reach Marco before he made landfall, but it appears he's had too much of a head start. We'll have no choice but to travel all the way to the island."

Emberwing didn't respond. For several minutes, they soared through the wisping clouds in silence and Royal kept his watch upon the sealine. A sudden twitch in Emberwing's neck stole his attention.

"What was that?" he asked.

"Nothing," the dragon answered.

Royal studied her curiously as her dart-shaped head and long neck bobbed in time with the beat of her wings. He decided to ask the question he had been avoiding the entire time. "Why are you doing this?"

Emberwing looked back at him. "Why am I doing what?"

"Why are you risking yourself by taking me to Fangshard?"

"I was told to," she answered.

Royal shook his head. "I know dragon creed. And I know Quill. He would never command another to take such a risk. You were asked and you agreed. Why?"

The speeding dragon hesitated before answering. "It was the right thing to do."

"How do you come by that conclusion?"

"There was a time," she said, "when dragons served mankind. Perhaps that part still lies within us. You yourself have served us, Captain Royal. I would think that you would not find it such an unusual thing."

"Perhaps," mused Royal. "But for Marco? He slew your High Dragon. You'd risk your life for your enemy?"

Again, Emberwing was silent for a few seconds as they continued to slice through the air. "I suppose if there is any greatness within us, it is found in how we treat our enemies rather than how we treat our friends."

Royal pondered this thought. "Then that makes you greater than me."

Emberwing's neck suddenly twitched again. And then again.

"What is it?" Royal asked in alarm.

But the dragon didn't answer. Instead, she began to buck and writhe beneath him. Royal had to use every ounce of effort to keep from tumbling from the saddle.

"What's wrong?" But he already suspected the truth...they had reached the limits of Askelon's thrall. Something deep inside Emberwing was breaking apart.

"Royal!" she finally cried. "I can't—my heart feels as if—"

Her words cut short and her limbs and sinews rippled with convulsions, battling against some inner impulse that Royal could only imagine. He tightened his grip on the leather rein and cast about for a way to help the frustrated dragon.

Then he spied the approaching isle. "There's Fangshard!" he cried. "We're almost there, Emberwing! Bring me to ground and then you can return to Dragonrook!"

Emberwing didn't respond. Her body twisted and she began to spiral and tumble through the air. Royal felt her back arch beneath the saddle and he realized that she was trying to throw him off. "Calm down! Be strong!"

The dragon refused to listen. Instead, she tumbled even more violently and a horrific screech ripped from her jaws. Coiling her long neck around, she snapped ferociously at the unwanted rider. Royal pulled back, narrowly escaping the gnashing teeth, but in doing so, he lost his balance and slipped from the saddle.

His hand clutched tight on the dangling rein, and he whipped through the air beneath the dragon like a flag on a mast. "Emberwing! Put me down!"

The enraged beast futilely craned her neck to reach the unwanted passenger. Together, they pinwheeled through the air with dizzying force. In a fit of frustration, Emberwing snorted and a fireball of heat and flame burst from her nose. Royal winced as the spout of fire brushed past him. He looked down to see the toes of his dangling boots burning with tendrils of flame.

But he also saw the rushing green of trees. They were getting closer to the safety of land.

Emberwing spat another blast of fire. Again, the flames narrowly missed him and instead ignited an unfortunate treetop below. The two traced a sporadic course above the jungle as the crazed flamespire haplessly spewed stream after stream of scorching fire in his direction.

Smoldering patches of leaves and limbs rushed past. "Blast!" Royal muttered as he felt the leather strap slip in his hand. Then, the rein slid from his grip completely. The flailing captain tumbled through the air, crashing through a mass of branches, sparks, smoke and burning fronds.

Branch after branch pummeled his chest as he dropped through the trees. The snapping of splintering wood enveloped his head. He cartwheeled awkwardly from the treetop and then smacked onto the firm earth, followed by a shower of smoldering twigs and leaves.

A groan of pain crawled from his lips. He took a moment to savor the stillness of the jungle floor. Above him, he could see a patch of sky through the burning breach in the trees. The sleek silhouette of Emberwing rushed past. "Good. Go home," he coughed feebly.

But she didn't. Instead, he watched her circle back. His breath stopped as she struck a path straight toward him. For a brief moment, he could see the vacant glare in her eyes before her jaws opened wide and spat another torrent of deadly, raging flame.

Any pain Royal felt was completely forgotten. He rolled to his side and was on his feet, sprinting for safety. If there was any kindness that had resided within Emberwing, it had now utterly vanished. The thrice-beating heart that pulsed for the missing High-Thrall was replaced with pure, animalistic fervor, just as Quill had forewarned. As he scrambled among the trees, he felt the sting of heat ripping through the foliage above him. He needed to find a place to hide.

Breaking through the tall bushes, he stumbled to a clumsy stop. A yawning cliff gaped before him. Far below, the churning ocean clawed at the island's rocky shore.

Royal spun around as the crash of shattered timber erupted behind him and the rippling form of Emberwing descended through the trees. Her claws thudded into the hardened earth. She said no words. She only stared with carnivorous malice and prowled toward the trapped captain.

"Emberwing!" he called. "Fly from here! Go back to Dragonrook!"

The dragon gave no indication that the words had any meaning. Royal searched for some hope of escape. He felt the weight of Cog's small cannon on his back but immediately banished the thought of using it against the crazed Emberwing.

But suddenly another cacophony of cracking trees tore through the air. A massive dragon—a *browgie*—burst through the jungle. A monstrous denizen of Fangshard, its fervor awakened by the scent of the intruding *flamespire*, barreled into Emberwing. Entwined and entangled, the two dragons locked into a vicious ball and rolled toward the cliff's edge.

Royal leapt out of the way.

"Emberwing!" he shouted helplessly. But the embattled beasts were oblivious to both him and the precipitous drop to the rocks below. As they teetered over the edge, Emberwing clambered for purchase. Her claws gouged massive trenches in the dirt. The *browgie*, clinging to its prey, raised its giant head and clamped its deadly fangs into Emberwing's back.

The pain elicited a hideous cry from the *flamespire*.

And something else.

For a moment, Emberwing's vacant eyes glistened with life once again. She saw Royal sprawled in the brush. Recognition and realization swept over her.

Royal called out to her again but his words were useless as he watched her scrabble against the weight of the clinging *browgie*. "Emberwing!"

"Royal!" she cried. Her talons dragged across the hard earth. She locked her eyes upon the captain and uttered what she knew would be her final words. "Save your friend! Save Dragonrook!"

The words spoken, she relinquished her grip, and the dragons vanished from sight.

The roars of the battling beasts faded away, the clattering of falling rocks ceased, and the only sound remaining was the distant crashing of waves upon the cliff. Royal carefully crawled to the edge of the precipice and cast a reluctant look below. The two dragons lay broken on the rocks. The only movement was the relentless shoving of the tide against the lifeless limbs and tails. Royal shut his eyes and offered a silent requiem for the brave Emberwing.

Slowly and achingly, he climbed to his feet and gathered his bearings. By the lowering sun, he knew he was on the west, leeward side of the island. His doomed flight with Emberwing had ended not far from where he needed to be. With battered body and heavy heart, he trudged from the devastated cliffside jungle.

After an hour's trek, Royal had found his way to a forgotten ravine where springs and rainwater gurgled to the sea.

The rocks within were dank and slippery and completely unchanged from when Royal had last seen them so many years ago. And behind what appeared to be an innocuous rift and a trickling stream of murky water, a precious secret was hiding. A secret that even the occupants of Fangshard did not know about...a hidden entrance into the interior of their subterranean lair.

But Royal knew it well. It was through this very crack that he had escaped from the interior many moons past. It seemed like a lifetime ago. Hmmph, he scoffed inwardly as he peered into the dark, narrow slit. When he had squeezed himself out of that rift, he was a pirate...a life he had since tried to leave behind. In many ways, it seemed wrong to be going back inside. Almost as if he were pulling a corpse from a grave.

He pulled the bulky cannon-gun from his back to let it hang in his hand, and he sidled into the wet, jagged opening.

There was hardly enough room for a full-grown man, much less a dragon, in the tight, angled rocks, which is why no one within Fangshard knew of it. As Royal forced his way through, every decent intuition within his body urged him to turn back. His nature had no desire to be there. The thick darkness pressed against his eyes and the silence quickly swallowed the scraping of his boots against the earth. But the darkness and quiet could not stop the wretched stench that seemed to bubble from the disturbed, slick mud beneath him. Every sensation within his body reminded him that he didn't belong in this place.

With his free hand, Royal scrabbled within the pocket of his cloak and found his tinderbox. Producing the wick and flint, he set a spark to the small scrap of linen. The slanted, coarse rocks splayed with yellow light. Royal crawled forward. The narrow passage opened into a larger chamber and he gratefully stretched himself to full height.

"Not far," he whispered and continued along the tunnel. Soon, the echoes of strange, growling voices bounced among the rocks and Royal knew he was reaching the occupied expanses within Fangshard. The sounds and rumblings were indistinct at first, but then he heard the words "I can help!"

Red, glowing light betrayed the existence of another cavern. Royal approached and he found himself high above a vast chamber. Dragons of every sort crowded far below him, their attention riveted to a small, strange scene in their midst.

Royal recognized one of the figures below. "Schark," he muttered under his breath. He extinguished the burning wick in his hand and crouched into the shadows. Pulling the spyglass from his belt, he peered at the gruesome scene. "And Marco." He watched as the bedraggled mapmaker negotiated for his life, but most of the words were far away and indistinguishable. Soon, the looming Arcrellis, the crowding dragons, and the menacing Schark backed away from the tortured form of Marco. A loping dragon grasped him by one leg and dragged him into the darkness.

This was not at all going the way he wanted, Royal thought as he collapsed the spyglass. He had hoped to prevent Marco from reaching the island of Fangshard completely. But he was clearly too late for that. Now,

Marco was a prisoner, the precarious circumstance of Dragonrook was revealed, and the dangerous threat of Thaddeus Schark lurked upon the seas.

He needed a new plan. With Emberwing gone, his only chance of escaping the island and warning Quill and Arthur would be to reclaim the *Ivory Zephyr* and, with the wind hopefully at his back, reach Dragonrook before Arcrellis and the minions of Fangshard did.

As much as Royal had his differences with Marco, the last words of Emberwing drifted into his mind. *Save your friend.* "A nice enough thought," muttered Royal, "but why bother?" Marco had set a terrible course of events into action. Saving him couldn't change that and would only put Royal at further risk. But Emberwing's words still spoke. *How we treat our enemies....*

"I can't leave here without Marco," Royal admitted. He knew exactly where they were taking him...he himself had been there before. The Pits of Fangshard were no place for a human being. In truth, a human didn't belong anywhere in Fangshard. He was not prepared to abandon the irascible mapmaker to such misery and despair.

Royal gave one last glance at the crowd of dragons below. Arcrellis had departed the cavern, but many of the restless dragons writhed and meandered aimlessly. Some fell to slumber in the middle of the floor, forcing others to scurry over or around them. As a whole, they seemed rudderless and lost, exhibiting none of the purpose or organization Royal was accustomed to witnessing on Dragonrook.

He'd have to find another way around. He scurried back into the shadows, seeking a way to reach Marco's prison without being observed.

The path into Fangshard's dungeons was slow and winding. Royal proceeded cautiously, halting frequently to conceal himself behind crumbling boulders, within darkened cracks, and once underneath an abandoned skull of a dragon. The crawling beasts that wandered among the passages displayed no sign of awareness. In fact, the eyes of the creatures often appeared glazed and myopic, and only partly cognizant of their surroundings. Despite that, Royal's circumspect route deeper into Fangshard still cost him a full two hours of stealth and hiding. Finally, he successfully slipped into the dark cavern that he recognized as the Pits of Fangshard.

The gaping chamber stretched into the black depths. The floor was honeycombed with shadowy holes, some covered with massive boulders, others latticed with rough iron bars. The width of the holes varied as did, Royal surmised, the depths. Two ragged *locket* dragons hunkered upon black bars of iron that spanned one of the pits, their attention riveted on some poor captive deep within.

Royal knew the *lockets* were not guards or sentries. Merely scavengers, waiting to pick at helpless prey. The pits within Fangshard never bothered with keepers. Fangshard prisoners—typically rebellious or troublesome dragons—were simply thrust into a hole and sealed beneath a monstrous stone. These prisoners were the fortunate ones. It was second nature for dragons to hibernate within the depths of a mountain. Being buried and forgotten was nothing terrifying to such a beast. The starkest offenders suffered a harsher sentence. Left abandoned beneath prison bars, weighted with stone, they remained exposed to any wandering presence seeking to sate compulsions of cruelty or, in some cases, a bit of hunger. Mostly, these were the smaller *lockets* who could dive and dart between the bars with impunity and, with a bit of luck, snag a piece of chewy hide before flitting back to safety.

Royal watched the two small dragons peering into the caged pit. Was that where poor Marco had been thrown? He looked about for a stone to throw as a distraction, but his search was halted by the sound of a soft wailing. A wail no dragon would make. The cry rose from a hole to his starboard.

Hunching over, Royal dashed between the scattered pits and hunkered behind a large stone. For a fleeting moment he considered what unruly dragon slept beneath it, but the thought vanished when the muffled wail grabbed his attention again.

Royal peeked within the nearest pit, straining to see into the darkness below. His eye discerned the faint outline of a forgotten dragon's skeleton. The moan rose again. This time Royal could tell where it came from. He stepped to the next hole and squinted through the rough bars. Deep within, he saw Marco's pathetic form, curled helplessly on the slimy floor of the pit. Another wail poured from his lips and his body shook as he wept.

"Marco!" Royal whispered as loudly as he dared.

Marco didn't respond.

Royal called again. "Marco! It's Royal!"

The mapmaker froze. He gazed up at the bars of the pit with reddened eyes. "Royal? Is that really you?"

"Yes!"

"What are you doing here?"

"I've come to save your rotten carcass, you dunderhead!"

Marco's response surprised Royal. "Why?" he asked.

It was a fair question, Royal thought. Lifting him from this pit wasn't going to undo the damage he had done. And was there any promise that he wouldn't cause further grief or put Royal and his friends in more danger? Royal shook the worries from his head. "You don't belong in this place, Marco. These cages are meant for *rogueskein*. Not you. Can you walk?"

Marco nodded.

"Give me a moment to move these bars."

Royal grunted against one of the heavy boulders that pinned the grate of iron. At least, he thought, it wasn't locked. Dragons like Arcrellis never bothered with the finesse of locks and keys. But maybe picking a lock would have been easier, he huffed. Slowly and grudgingly, the stone slid with a growl from off the grate. Royal turned his attention to the one remaining stone.

Marco's voice lifted up to Royal from the pit. "I told them everything," he said. "They are going to invade Dragonrook."

Royal heaved against the boulder. "Yeah, I heard."

"You were there?" he replied sheepishly. Despite the confession, Marco felt his shame magnified, realizing that it really wasn't a secret. "But you're saving me anyway?"

The last boulder rolled away. With it out of the way, Royal was able to slide the iron grate aside, just enough for him to reach his hand down to Marco. "Come out of there. Leave your remorse, though. We don't have need for that right now."

Gratefully, Marco clasped the extended hand and with a firm pull, the battered and torn mapmaker emerged from the shadowy hole. For a moment, the two lay upon the edge of the pit, catching their breath and enjoying their small moment of victory.

Finally, Marco spoke. "How do we get out of here?"

"Same way I got in. Follow me," Royal said.

Cautiously, they crept amidst the cavern of pits and boulders, careful to remain out of sight of the two vagrant *lockets* that haunted the vast chamber.

"Royal!"

Royal turned to Marco. "What?"

Marco responded with a blank stare. "I didn't say anything."

"Royal!"

Confused, Royal searched the area. A fluttering sound beat the air beneath him. "Captain Archibald Royal!" the voice said again.

Royal stepped back from a tightly-woven iron grate at his feet. He fell to his knees and peered into the depths. A nebulous form suddenly appeared from the shadows and smacked roughly against the metal. Tiny claws clutched through the grate. "Archibald Royal!"

The captain's eye narrowed. And then it widened in recognition.

"Pinn?" he whispered. "Is that you?"

A small *locket's* face appeared in the dim light. "I told them nothing! Help me!" The diminutive dragon's talons clutched the bars with a feverish grip and rattled against it helplessly. "I told them nothing!"

"Quiet!" Royal cast an alarmed look toward the distant roaming scavengers. Thankfully, the random cries of a trapped dragon were not uncommon within the Pits. "What are you doing here?"

"I was captured! Arcrellis sought me!" the small dragon cried. "I told him nothing!" Again, the *locket* shook furiously against the imprisoning bars. Royal noticed the crazed look simmering in the creature's eyes. The same madness that he witnessed within Emberwing's stare.

"Who is this?" Marco asked.

"It's Pinn! Quill said he's been missing for some time now. Quick! Help me open this!"

Royal and Marco slid the iron grate aside with a rasping heave. The imprisoned locket crawled from the pit. "I told him nothing! Skorch comes!"

"Shush!" Royal warned again. "Enough of that! We need to leave here quickly!"

Together, the three of them wound their way through the maze of passages. The occasional roar or growl reverberated from the caverns, but no dragons crossed their paths. The small *locket* dragon continued to shake nervously. "I told them nothing! Skorch comes!" he muttered.

"Be quiet!" Marco barked. "What's wrong with this dragon?" he asked Royal.

Royal realized Marco had no idea of the chaos he had unwittingly unleashed when he slew Neera. "He's out of sorts from being too far from Dragonrook. We need to get him back home."

"I told him nothing!" Pinn repeated. "Quill is afraid of rats!"

"Put a cork in it!" Royal said. "We're almost to the exit. It's strange," he said, "that we haven't encountered more dragons. They must be busy with something else."

"I'm not complaining!" Marco said as they crouched and shuffled into the narrow cleft of the wall. "But how are we going to get off this island?"

"You harbored the *Ivory Zephyr* on the lee side of the island, right? We'll take her. With a bit of good fortune, we should all be back on Dragonrook by sundown tomorrow."

"Thank goodness!" Marco breathed.

The passages and cavern began to narrow with familiarity, and Royal knew they were approaching the hidden exit. "Look!" As they crawled between the tight rocks, Royal pointed. Faint fingers of daylight crept within the space. After only a few moments, the three emerged from the cramped rift in the mountainside.

The skies were gray with thick clouds. Even though no bright sunlight pierced the sky, it made no difference to Royal and Marco. They breathed in the freshness and let the shaded daytime wash over their faces. Pinn launched into the air and did cartwheels and swoops above them, savoring the sensation of stretching his wings after his wretched imprisonment.

The coolness of the moving air filled their spirits with fresh hope. Royal began clambering up the hillside. "Over this height, down to the coast, and we'll be on our way!"

They wasted no time. Marco displayed surprising agility as he ascended the steep, grassy side. Pinn, soaring through the sky, was way ahead of them. The small dragon glided over the summit but then shuddered. For a moment, his wings faltered like a collapsed kite, and he spiraled toward the ground. Just before he hit the ground, he regained control and curved upward. With a tight, sweeping arc, he returned to the chasing Royal and Marco. The *locket* fluttered to a stop and perched on Royal's shoulder. "Trouble! I told him nothing! Neera snores! Skorch comes!" he squawked.

Royal examined the trembling *locket*. Pinn's eyes darted nervously back and forth. The cloying madness of *rogueskein* was clearly ebbing and flowing inside the dragon's inner workings. "We need to get you back to Dragonrook."

Marco was running ahead. He had reached the crest of the hill and froze. "Royal! We have a problem!" he called.

The captain rushed to the top of the rise. From the summit, they could see the stretch of rocky beach and the rough harbor beyond. Further, where the ocean faded into gray under the overcast sky, a small speck of sail dotted the flat line of water. Royal recognized it immediately. The *Ivory Zephyr*.

"We're too late!" Marco exclaimed. "Schark has taken our ship!" He watched the small vessel swiftly disappear toward the west.

"Look over there!" Royal pointed.

Further along the rocky shore, dragons emerged from the dark foliage to step into the crashing surf. They lumbered through the water before submerging completely. Wave after wave of dragons of all shapes and sizes vanished beneath the surface of the sea. Their course was clear.

"They're headed for Dragonrook!"

The three watched helplessly as the legions of dragons rambled from the trembling treeline and dove beneath the rough water.

"Skorch is coming again! I told him nothing! Skorch is coming!" Pinn cried.

Royal studied the trembling *locket*. "Pinn, can you fly? I mean, can you fly straight as an arrow?"

The wild-eyed locket simply stared. "I told him nothing!"

"I need you to focus, Pinn!" Royal snapped. "You have

to fly to Dragonrook. Stay strong! Tell Quill that Arcrellis and his followers are headed their way. They're approaching under sea, likely so they can stay hidden. But that will slow them down. If you fly straight and fast, you'll be able to warn them. Can you do that?"

Pinn's eyes were beginning to glaze over. His beak-shaped mouth hung open.

"Blast it!" Royal grabbed the dragon and with a mighty swing of his arm, he launched the *locket* upward. "To Dragonrook, you sorry excuse for a homing pigeon!"

Pinn tumbled through the air. Small wings stretched out and cupped the wind. He careened madly through the sky and Royal held his breath as he watched in dire hope. Did Pinn understand? Or was he too far gone?

The *locket* traced awkward zig-zags high above them. Then, after what seemed like an eternity, the small form sped with determination into the western sky. Royal and Marco kept their gaze upon the clouds long after the tiny speck that was Pinn faded from view.

The island was now eerily quiet as they surveyed the sea-scape around them. Pinn was gone. Their ship was gone. The dragons were gone. The two of them simply stared at the empty horizon as they succumbed to a hopeless realization. They were now marooned on the abandoned island of Fangshard.

21

Funeral for a Dragon

"I'm sorry."

Marco's apology did little to fill the silence that had settled on the island. Far below, the waves could be seen rolling onto the shore, but the sound of their breaking failed to make its way up the cliffside where Royal and Marco sat.

"I don't know what I was thinking," Marco continued. The harsh reality that hundreds of seething dragons were on their way to invade Dragonrook was beginning to penetrate his stubborn mind. As he rubbed the many scratches and cuts on his arms, he tried not to imagine Arthur, Clay, Penny, and the quiet John Dunney cowering under the clutching talons of the same ravenous, enraged creatures. He had suffered only the slightest abuse of their claws and his heart sank when he considered what worse assaults they were capable of.

Royal maintained his quiet vigil of staring across the water. His face was cold. His thoughts were indecipherable. His feelings, if he had any, seemed as distant as the setting sun.

"Aren't you going to say something?" Marco asked.

"You weren't thinking," Royal finally answered. "You were being driven by greed. Or anger, maybe. Or fear.

Whatever it was, it wasn't thinking. Just feelings. That's the problem with being a person, I guess. We've got lots of powerful emotions and lots of powerful ways to act on 'em. And when we do...well, it never turns out for the best. When a storm is blowing, you've got to trim your sails. If you don't, the storm's going to take you under. Every good sailor knows that."

"I guess I'm not a good sailor, then."

Royal plucked a tall blade of grass and began to chew on it contemplatively. "Bah! No one's a good sailor, really. We're just men in a boat thinking we're in control when we're actually just at the mercy of the waves and wind."

Marco peered across the distance, too, trying vainly to see what Royal saw. "Why aren't you angry at me? I've put you and your friends in danger, I've treated you like garbage, and yet you came all this way to save me, and now you're stranded on this awful island. It doesn't make any sense! Why did you do it?"

Again, Royal pondered in silence before he spoke. "I won't deny that a part of me wanted to let you fester in that hole. But then," he mused, "I'd be the one acting on my emotions. Like I said, none of us is a good sailor, but when I'm in a boat getting tossed about, I find there's no point in blaming the wind on the witless."

Marco felt the sting of an insult inside the comment. But he knew the hurt was bundled with truth so he didn't attempt to deflect it. He hung his head and he felt as if his neck would snap under the weight of humility. "Thank you for coming after me. I know I don't deserve it."

"You're welcome," Royal replied matter-of-factly.

Glancing around, Marco examined the stillness of the empty island. The wind rustled the dark trees, but unlike other tropical islands, the air was absent from the call or whistle of birds among the branches. Life had left this island long ago. "So, what do we do now?"

Royal surveyed the island also. "I haven't a clue."

"Do you think someone from Dragonrook will come for us?"

"You mean survivors from Dragonrook?" Royal mused. "I don't see how. With the High Dragon gone, it looks like they're all marooned like us. Fangshard seems situated just beyond the High-Thrall's reach. That's probably one reason Arcrellis chose this rock to live under. Dragonrook has got no ships to sail with, either. No," he sighed, "I don't see any help coming in that regard. And the others that know about Fangshard aren't particularly interested in helping us out. In fact, whenever Arcrellis and Schark return, I don't reckon they'll be too loving if they find us here."

Marco paled. "We can't just sit here and do nothing!"

"We're making a mighty fine go of it so far," Royal replied. With that, he pulled his hat over his eyes and laid back onto the tall grass. "It's been a long time since I've had an island to myself. Might as well enjoy it."

Marco sighed. He too settled back and stared at the gray sky. Before he could let his thoughts drift away, a tremor vibrated beneath him. In the distance, the sharp cracking sound echoed behind them. "Did you hear that? Is there a storm coming?" he asked.

Royal already had his eye open as he listened carefully. Another quake pulsed beneath them. Royal hopped to his feet. "This island isn't as abandoned as we thought." He crested the rise and Marco followed. When they saw the cause of the disruptions, they both instantly crouched in the bushes.

"Balfour!"

The monstrous *browgie* plodded across the open field, hefting boulders and falling broken trees, dipping his snout and sniffing attentively. One of his wings was completely missing, a victim of Royal's cannon shot as they soared over Rogue's Island.

"Looks like he's been left behind," Royal mused. "With only one wing, he's next to useless to Arcrellis. He'd have a devil of a time keeping up with their attack. Looks like he's foraging for something to eat."

"Wonderful!" Marco muttered. "We're trapped on an island with a dragon that hates our guts and also happens to be hungry. I don't like how this is adding up." Marco eyed the hefty cannon-like weapon slung over Royal's shoulder. "What is this thing? A harpoon gun? Can we use it?"

Turning the large device in his hands, Royal examined it carefully. "It may be our only choice. It's just a matter of time before Balfour catches our scent. Cog only gave me three bolts, though." He slid one of the harpoon-like bolts into the bore. It fit snugly and slid partly down the barrel. As Cog instructed, Royal grasped the cascabel on the end. With a ratcheting sound, he pulled it back from its slot.

Balfour continued to lumber obliviously across the field. Royal shifted the heavy gun against his shoulder as he peered along its muzzle. Recalculating, he repositioned the weapon and adjusted his aim.

"What are you waiting for?" Marco urged. "Fire it off while he's still out in the open!"

"It's not that easy!" Royal snapped. "I've never fired this thing before. I haven't got any inkling as to this thing's range or accuracy. We should wait until he gets closer."

"You're joking? Maybe I better do it, then. With that eye-

274

patch you have the depth perception of a toad in glass jar."
He reached for the weapon but Royal pulled it away.

"Balderdash! I can shoot the whiskers off a bilge rat and
you know it!"

"This isn't a time to take chances! Let me have it!" Again,
Marco snatched at the monstrous gun and pulled. A feverish, whispered tug-of-war ensured.

"Leave off!" Royal barked. But Marco wrestled harder. The iron weapon slipped from his grasp and struck
the ground with a sonorous dong. And with a crack, the
cocked cascabel snapped back into the housing. A fiery hiss
belched from the bore and the bolt burst forth, shedding
sparks and smoke as it tore along the ground. Marco and
Royal could only watch in stunned dismay as the piece of
iron bounced in the general direction of Balfour. Its chaotic, careening flight quickly ended when the barbed tip
lodged into the dirt, spraying a fountain of red-hot embers
from its casing.

Balfour lifted his gigantic head at the commotion. Spying the sizzling object, he pivoted and made his way toward it. And then it exploded. The sound of breaking metal, sizzling flame, and billowing ash pummeled the air.
The smoke cleared. Balfour shook his stunned head and
saw the two tiny faces of Royal and Marco poking from the
brush. With rage and recognition, the monstrous dragon
let loose with an ear-splitting roar.

"Run for it!" Royal yelled.

But Marco was already dashing down the slope. Royal
pulled the heavy gun from the ground and followed. He
could feel the thunderous pounding of the Balfour's paws
closing the distance behind them.

"What do we do?" cried Marco.

"Run for the trees and think small!" Royal urged. "All we can hope for is to slow him down!"

The rotting trees did little to slow the barreling *browgie*, though. The reports of cracking timber and collapsing branches filled the air behind them as they scurried among the trunks. But the trees did provide several opportunities to break Balfour's line of sight and occasionally he would stop to search out his scurrying quarry.

"We have to go to ground!" Royal called. "Head for the cave!"

Marco's mapmaking brain came alive. He immediately turned right, remembering exactly where they had emerged from beneath the caverns of Fangshard. The small rift in the rock was not far, thankfully. With surprising alacrity, Marco slid his bulky form into the dark crevasse.

Royal crammed in behind him. "Hurry!" he urged. He twisted his head around to see Balfour pounce into view. The narrow crack of daylight darkened as the dragon pressed his massive eyeball against the opening. With another mighty roar, he pulled away and thrust his ragged talons into the crack. Royal squeezed further in, narrowly avoiding the clutching claw.

Balfour's furious talons scrabbled at the rock. Chunks of stone broke from the entrance as he ferociously tore at the crack. Rubble dropped from above and showered their heads.

"He's not letting up! Keep going!" Royal shoved at Marco, huffing and puffing between the tight rocks.

The cave walls shuddered around them as Balfour hammered outside. The rocks continued to split as they emerged in the larger chamber. With every pounding blow from Balfour, stones plummeted from the cavern ceiling. One stalactite cracked and shattered on the floor beneath.

"This dragon really hates you!" Marco gasped, collecting his breath.

Before Royal could retort, an explosion of earth and rock burst across the room. For a brief moment, daylight shot into the cavern before being eclipsed by Balfour's massive, scarred head. His jaws snapped dangerously close to Marco's feet as they dove behind the nearest chunk of fallen boulders.

"I don't think hate adequately describes it," Royal muttered.

The dragon strained at the constricted entrance. With a tremendous shove of his shoulders, the entire subterranean room quaked. Dirt and skree pelted Royal and Marco from above. Royal brushed pebbles from his hat and Marco spat gravel from his mouth. "Now's our chance," Royal stated. "We'll make our way deeper into the caverns while he's stuck!" But before Royal could clamber over the fallen debris, another cataclysmic blow from the dragon rocked the cave. A cascade of stalactites, boulders, and shards of stone crashed to the ground. The air was enveloped in billows of choking dust. Waving the clouds from his face, Royal frowned in dismay as their vision cleared. Their escape route was buried under a collapsed wall of stone.

Balfour bellowed again and continued to press ferociously into the slowly widening breach.

"Now what?" Marco asked.

"It can't be helped," Royal answered, loading a second bolt into Cog's Talonshot. "There's only one way out of here now and it's through our angry friend." He could see

Balfour's head had squeezed its way further into the cavern.

Marco hunkered behind the boulder and covered his ears. "Don't miss this time."

Royal decided to let the comment go unchallenged. He pulled back the ramrod cascabel and tightened his grip on the gun. "Cover your ears and curl your toes!" he called. He popped up from behind the fallen rock and with speedy aim, fired the weapon. A spray of sparks burst toward the trapped Balfour. Immediately, Royal dropped back to the ground, shielding his head. The sound of sizzling and roars filled the cavern and with a final *clang*, silence settled in the chamber. *Clang*?

Royal lifted his head in confusion when the anticipated explosion never came. "Did I miss?"

"Maybe it was a dud," Marco suggested.

Royal peered over the boulder.

Balfour's eyes were wide with confusion. The dragon shook his head in discomfort. Slowly, the beast's leathery maw rippled as he bared his protruding fangs.

Royal saw the cause of Balfour's irritation. "Don't you hate that feeling when you got something stuck in your teeth?" he asked Marco.

Balfour shook his head again. The sputtering bolt was firmly lodged in between two ragged fangs, still shooting a stream of red sparks. A forked tongue curled and twisted from within his mouth, feeling about for the jammed object. Slowly, the spitting sparks began to lessen.

"Uh oh!" Royal crouched for cover once again. "Better brace yourself!"

The cavern erupted in a blast of stone, fire, smoke, and dust. Marco felt all manner of shrapnel pelt his huddled back. The harsh ringing in their ears began to soften and they could discern the quiet clatter of rolling rocks coming to rest. Drifting smoke was replaced with the acrid scent of burnt gunpowder and roasting meat. Daylight streamed through the crooked split in the rock and filled the cloudy interior of the cave.

Beyond the opening, laying on its side, was the grim, headless body of the massive Balfour.

+ + +

"The death of a dragon is a solemn thing. And very rare."

Quill stood mournfully over the still form of Neera, curled in quiet repose upon the palanquin. Her elegant neck turned inward so that her head lie nestled at her claws, turned in such a way to hide the hideous puncture where her life had left her. Her graceful tail was swept around, draped tenderly over her nose, to cover her closed eyes forever from all things. Eyes that would no longer gaze upon the world and, therefore, none should gaze upon hers. Flowers, ivy, and seashells carefully and modestly adorned the palanquin.

At a distance, Arthur listened respectfully while the Arch-Dragon gifted himself these final moments. "It is such an uncommon thing that there are not many traditions to honor a dragon in death," Quill said quietly, presumably to Arthur, since no one else was present. "For a High Dragon, even less so. This time is like none before it. Though we are in it, we know nothing of it, and the past is only a meager proctor."

The arrangements had been made. A funerary procession would occur. Two mighty *browgies* would bear the somber form of Neera upon her bier. Quill would follow along with the High Dragon's attending *lockets*. The procession would take Neera across the land of Dragonrook, through the deep canyon thoroughfare, along the highest ridge, and ultimately down to the seashore where *articas* were to carry her beneath the waves. A secret grotto had been prepared somewhere in the depths, they had told Arthur. An undersea grove where sea lilies and banners of kelp danced languidly with the movement of the water. Sea beams twinkled yellow in the morning and orange with the setting sun, they said. And when the rains brushed the surface of the ocean, it would sound like the whispers of the warm wind from the west. At last, the High Dragon Neera would rest forever in the embrace of the sea that she loved.

"Normally, when the end is to come," Quill continued, "the High Dragon would leave Dragonrook to the birthplace of the scion and pass the thrall of leadership. When the scion is hatched, all who inhabit Dragonrook feel the passing of the High-Thrall to the new High Dragon and wait with earnest hope for the coming of our new leader. But now," Quill whispered, "the Thrall has passed but hope does not follow."

Arthur shifted uneasily. Without a scion, he knew that the burden of leadership had fallen unexpectedly upon him. He kept his silence, suspecting that any words would only remind Quill of the hard truth during an already unhappy time.

Abruptly, Quill turned from the palanquin. "Come," he said. "We have many things we must attend to. We will leave the High Dragon to her throne."

Obediently, Arthur followed, and the tall doors shut behind them with a sonorous thud.

As the echoes of the closing door faded, a dark form emerged from the shadows. The wingless dragon paused, listening carefully to the retreating footfalls of Quill and Arthur as they continued down the passage. Assured that he was finally alone, the dragon approached the palanquin.

Cog lifted his monocle from his eye as he gazed upon the still body of Neera. "The perfect rest. The barter's rest. The rest that gives release but yet takes all in return." His eyes scrutinized the carefully posed form of the High Dragon. Finally, his attention fell upon her delicate folded wing. Gently, his talon caressed the long delicate length of the wing, until it came to the small pin-like protrusion upon the joint. "The pollex. Yes," Cog said. "That will suffice."

With deft skill and a tiny, honed blade, he made a small incision beneath the scales of the lifeless body. In only a matter of moments, his work was complete, and the wingless Cog slipped back into the shadowy corner from which he came.

✢   ✢   ✢

All those who dwelt on Dragonrook congregated at the chosen time. The sun stood at its zenith, casting shadowless rays into the slot of the narrow canyon while dragons emerged from the honeycombed cliffs. From the dark opening, the first *browgie* moved into the light, leading the regal form of Neera upon the heavy palanquin from its shady repose. Behind it, the second *browgie* followed, head hung under the mournful burden. Grief cast its grip on the watching dragons as the body of the High Dragon moved past.

From the passage stepped Quill, and with him Arthur, feeling conspicuously out of place. As the wielder of Askelon, he inwardly knew that he was expected to be a part of the procession. Clay, Penny, and John Dunney, on the other hand, found themselves a discreet place near the shore where they could observe Neera's final moments. Together, Quill and Arthur moved slowly and solemnly, struggling to keep their eyes guarded against thought or emotion. A quintet of *lockets* followed. Neera's attendants and keepers of her deepest secrets and knowledge. The small procession moved steadily forward and the sea of waiting dragons parted as they gazed upon their leader one last time.

It was not the plan for any to follow as the procession began its lengthy journey around Dragonrook, but as the palanquin moved forward, every dragon fell in somber step behind, forming a wake of dragons, treading the land that would no longer witness the careful rule of Neera, the High Dragon. Scion of Lockswift. Holder of the High-Thrall. Keeper of Dragonrook.

Like an undulating serpent, the line of dragons stretched behind the palanquin. Through the cliffs. Among the rocks. Between the quiet trees. The winding procession continued in heavy silence as it peaked along the curving mountain ridge. From here, Arthur could see the circle of the flat ocean and the unbroken sky. The green slopes of the forests ended and the sandy coasts began, etched with the white traces of pulsing waves.

Arthur surveyed the land and sea and his eyes fell on a distant object protruding from the water. He had forgotten about the pallid-eyed Hogarth that had brought them to these shores. He was still there, inert, unmoving. Did he know of Neera's passing? Did he feel any connection at all to the lost High Dragon? He forced the thoughts from his mind and pulled his attention back to the palanquin in front of him. His legs were growing weary but he was determined to keep pace with the others.

The slow march wound its way down the hillside where a quiet bay awaited their arrival. To Arthur's surprise, the parade of dragons began to break from the procession. Under the call of some unspoken inner sway, the dragons gathered in kind. The large *browgies*. The graceful *articas*. The sleek *flamespires*, The intelligent *hyrexes*. The diminutive *lockets*. They all formed perfect ranks, turning their stoic faces to the western sea where the sun was now sliding into its last fading course.

Arthur studied the pageant of dragons curiously. Together, there were hundreds. All invisibly bound in lock and step to honor the last rites of their departing leader. One dragon, however, sat by himself. The wingless Cog also gazed toward the west but apart, isolated. Surveying the legions of dragons, Arthur realized a curious fact. There were no other *duskars*. Was Cog the only one? If this truth affected the solitary dragon, it didn't show in any way. Cog simply sat and watched with the others as the two pallbearing *browgies* hunkered to the ground and removed the palanquin from their shoulders.

Four *articas* appeared from the ranks of the sea dragons. Each moved to a different corner of Neera's palanquin and in effortless unison, lifted it toward the lapping water. Slowly and reverently, they moved toward the sea. Or did the sea move toward them? So elegant and graceful were their motions that, to Arthur, it seemed as if they were not moving at all. But gradually, their lithe forms were in the glistening water, carrying with them their kindred leader beyond the froth.

And then the song filled the air.

Arthur's head turned as he heard the trill emanate from the other *articas*. It was not a song, in truth, he realized, but simply a pleasant reverberating hum. Then the *lockets* sang, adding a high note to the sound. The *flamespires* joined with a solid, baritone hum of their own. And, with heavy resonating vibration, the *browgies* added a rumbling note that seemed so low it was more of a feeling than a sound. The notes from the dragons blended into a perfect chord that was like nothing Arthur had ever heard. He closed his eyes and let himself be lost in the sweeping sound.

Then the *hyrexes* joined in, supplying a compelling melody that crowned the chord. Arthur's eyes opened as the rising and falling notes pulled at the stubborn sadness that simmered in his breast, somehow finding order and purpose within the sounds. And with soft release, the sadness magically transfigured into a comforting wave of acceptance and peace.

He cast his eyes to the distant, solitary Cog. He, too, was singing with the massive dragon choir, but Arthur could hear nothing. Either the *duskar's* voice was either too far or too small to reach the boy's ears.

The palanquin was now far into the sea, and with one silent and final movement, it vanished beneath the undisturbed surface of the ocean. The *articas* were bearing it to the secret grotto that had been carefully prepared. Arthur wished that he could see it. To him, it sounded peaceful and serene. He resigned himself to the truth that it would have to be a place he could only imagine, knowing that even his most daring efforts to conjure it within his mind would never capture it fully.

Soon, the song that filled the air faded away. The golden sun touched the line of sea far away. And with that, Neera, the High Dragon of Dragonrook and of dragonkind, was gone. The many dragons began to slip away, awaiting the night and the new day behind it.

"She is now where her heart desired," Quill said as he watched the silent vista, "while we who remain are left to wander. Are we lost? We have not been given a word to describe such a time as this."

"We have one where we come from," Arthur said. "Orphans."

"Orphans." Quill quietly pondered the sound of the word.

Arthur vainly tried to discern the point on the waves where the *articas* had lowered Neera, but the ocean remained immutable despite its constantly undulating face. Squinting into the sunlight, Arthur noticed something.

"What is that?" he asked.

Quill followed his gaze. Silhouetted against the orange disc of the sun was a small shadow. Arthur would have mistaken it for a bird if it weren't for the lengthy, barbed tail waving behind it. Its wings flapped fervently but then halted as it plummeted precariously toward the water. Catching itself, its wings struggled once more to climb upward and maintain its course.

"It's a dragon!" Arthur exclaimed.

Quill's eyes narrowed. "It's a *locket*."

The small dragon beat the air, exhausted from its long flight. Its small size had deceived Arthur into thinking it was farther than it really was. But quickly it reached the shore.

With an outstretched hand, Quill caught the exhausted *locket* as it dropped from the sky. Shock and surprise filled his normally stoic face. "It's Pinn! He has returned!"

The small *locket*, bedraggled and winded, seemed lifeless in Quill's open talon. "Pinn!" Quill whispered. "Where have you been?"

Pinn's peered through heavy lids at the *hyrex*. "Fa-Fangshard," he croaked.

"Fangshard?" Arthur cried. "Did you see Royal? Did he make it?"

"Royal," Pinn coughed, "saved me."

"What of Emberwing?" Quill asked. "Is she returning?"

But Pinn didn't answer. He weakly shook his head. "Ar-Ar-crellis is coming. Skorch is coming. They're all coming."

And with that feeble warning, Pinn closed his eyes, his small chest rising and falling as he slipped into weary, long-awaited sleep.

22

Councils

Pinn was left to his much-needed rest while Quill urgently called for a session among his lead counsels. Arthur, Clay, and Penny were present and together they carefully delved into the meaning of Pinn's warning deep into the night. Pinn's declaration that Royal had saved him clearly implied that Royal had reached Fangshard. But the fact that only Pinn had returned and not Emberwing could only mean Royal's endeavor came at great cost.

"We need to rescue Royal," Arthur said. "He can help us."

The idea seemed to irritate Quill. "We have lost Emberwing already. She crossed the boundaries of the High-Thrall and is now likely *rogueskein*. I will not risk another. A dragon here on Dragonrook is of greater value than a pirate like Royal. He has chosen his path and left us to ours. Now is the time to prepare for war."

"If Arcrellis is indeed moving to attack," said one worried *hyrex*, "then there is little we can do."

"We can abandon Dragonrook," suggested an *artica*.

Quill shook his head. "There is not enough time to scout for a suitable haven."

"Then we go underground. Deep underground, as in times of olde," a *browgie* said.

Quill contemplated this. "Arcrellis will find us still."

Arthur lifted his hands in frustration. "I don't understand. Why don't we just fight? From what I've been told, your numbers are greater. There's no way Arcrellis and his army can outmatch you."

"It is not that simple. It is forbidden for us to take the life of another dragon. We may defend our lives or lay our lives down for the High Dragon, but that is all we may do."

"It would seem that Arcrellis has no compunctions of killing any of you," Clay chimed in.

Quill growled. "Arcrellis is *rogueskein*. We are not. We hold fast to the High-Thrall and dare not abandon it."

Arthur felt the small blade pressing against his side. He mustered the courage to speak. "But I am the wielder of the High-Thrall now. I grant you permission to fight Arcrellis and his army."

At the sound of these words, it was as if the temperature within the High Seat plunged. The eyes of the dragons stared coldly at Arthur and the boy realized immediately that something was wrong.

After a moment of icy silence, Quill answered. "You dare to blaspheme the way of the High-Thrall? Because you wield Askelon, you believe you have the authority to overrule the very law that is written in the thrice-beat of our hearts? The blade you carry may resonate with the power of the High-Thrall but it does not have the ability to corrupt itself! You speak as a child who knows nothing of dragonkind or what it means to lead us! The ways of humans have brought us to this precipice of destruction and now your words bear more of the same terrible consequence. I grow weary of this foolishness!" With that, Quill spun and lumbered toward the doors. "Come with me, dragons. We must prepare the citizens of Dragonrook with the awful truth of what is to come."

The dragons obediently filed after Quill. A few gave Arthur disparaging looks as they exited the High Seat, leaving only the three small humans in the large empty space.

"That probably could have gone better," Penny commented unhelpfully.

+ + +

Sleep didn't come to Arthur. Despite being bone-weary from the long funeral procession around the island, and the emotional burden that had accompanied it, his eyes refused to close. Alone in the dark, he watched the distant stars beyond the chamber opening. It was not the dread of a looming attack that plagued his thoughts. Nor was it the idea of Royal trapped—or maybe even killed—on the island of Fangshard. Rather, it was what Quill had said to him in the High Seat. Every word the Arch-Dragon had spoken was true. Arthur was only a child. He had no business—or ability—to lead Dragonrook. And now, at the time of their greatest need, he was failing them.

"What do I do?" Arthur said aloud to the empty room.

The last words that Archibald Royal had spoken to him floated to the surface of his memory.

He climbed out of his bed, donned his boots, and hurried out of the chamber.

+ + +

"If you need anything, talk to my friend Cog."
As Arthur descended the long corridor to Cog's cavern,

he wondered what he was even hoping to learn. But he reminded himself that it was the only option he had. At the end of the passage, he could see the play of firelight upon the stony walls. The soft tinkle of tools could be heard but then were silenced. "Behold, Arthur comes!" he heard Cog's voice call.

Arthur stepped into the chamber and saw the large wingless dragon squatting at his work bench. He lifted the magnifying monocle from his eye and draped a piece of cloth over an item he had been attending to, obscuring it from view.

"How did you know it was me?" Arthur asked.

Cog smiled. "Askelon precedes you. It announces itself."

The boy looked down at the knife in his belt. "Yeah. I keep forgetting."

"And what brings the Bearer of the High-Thrall to my shop?"

"Well," Arthur said, finding a perch upon a small boulder, "I think I need your help. Captain Royal said you're someone who can help me."

Cog shrugged, neither confirming nor denying the statement.

"You and Royal seem to get along pretty well," Arthur continued.

"Yes. For a man with only one eye, he sees much more than most," Cog mused. "Friends like him are rare."

Arthur remembered how Cog stood alone at the funeral. "Are you the only *duskar* on Dragonrook?"

"Yes. We are not common."

"Hogarth is a *duskar*, too, isn't he?"

Cog nodded. "Yes."

"Grindash didn't seem to care for him very much. Quill doesn't seem to hold you or Hogarth in high regard, either."

"Hogarth is *rogueskein.*" Cog gave Arthur a stern look. "Arcrellis is *rogueskein.* And *duskar.*"

Arthur stiffened. "Are—are all *duskars...*" he let the question trail off.

Cog completed the thought for him. "*Rogueskein?* No. But it's understandable why Quill gets confused. Quill is *hyrex.* It is his nature to seek order. Structure. *Hyrex* calculate outcomes based on the things they control. The things they cannot control, they distrust because they do not understand them. Such things challenge their perception of the truth."

"Their perception of the truth?" Arthur asked. "What truth is that?"

Cog smirked. "The truth that it's never promised that all things can be understood or controlled. Order and structure require boundaries, but boundaries imply the end of structure and the beginning of something else. *Duskars,* on the other hand, are drawn to exploring the unexplored." The wingless dragon shrugged. "For some, like Arcrellis, that nature manifests itself in lack of control. Rebellion. *Rogueskein.*"

"But not you?"

"No. I desire to be temperate. Growth requires reaching beyond oneself, but not to one's own detriment. I explore, but not for selfish purpose or desire. Like the dragons here that fly but never too far from Dragonrook, I, too, stretch my mental wings, but never beyond my conscience. To do so would break my fellowship with dragonkind and be like *rogueskein.*"

Arthur nodded. Cog's words of fellowship made him think about how the dragons had coalesced into collective song during Neera's procession. "Dragonkind truly is connected, isn't it? I saw you singing earlier today, but I couldn't hear your notes."

The memory of the music brought a smile to Cog's face. "Dragon Song is rare. Perhaps as rare as *duskars*. But *duskars* do not bring notes to the music. Harmony is for the *lockets, articas, flamespires*, and *browgies*. Melody is for the *hyrex*. *Duskars* bring words."

"You were the only one singing words? What were they?"

The dragon tilted his head in thought. "I cannot say. Not because they are secret, but because words are phantoms."

Arthur was puzzled. "What do you mean?"

Cog reached for a small candle that flickered on the workbench and slid it toward himself. He played his large claw around the flame and gestured to the cavern wall. "Tell me what you see on the wall."

"I see your claw."

"No. Try again."

Arthur nodded. "I guess I see the shadow of your claw."

"Correct. You see the idea of my claw. Its shape. You even see its movement. But what you see is only an effect brought about by my true claw and the light of the flame. Take away either of those and the shadow ceases to exist. Words on paper and shadows on a wall are one and the same. Merely shallow representations of something more real. That is why I can't tell you the words. Because the things that formed it—the light and substance—are no longer here. Dragon Song is but for a moment. That is why it is so special when it happens."

Arthur's brow furrowed in frustrated confusion. "I guess there's a lot I need to learn about dragons, and so much I don't understand. That's the reason I came to you. As long as I possess Askelon, I'm expected to lead but I haven't any idea what I'm supposed to do." Arthur sighed. "If you were to ask Quill, I'm not a leader at all."

"He's right."

Arthur's head lifted in slight offense. "What is that supposed to mean?"

"You lack the one thing that a leader must have."

Thinking back to his first day with Quill, Arthur remembered the challenging questions he was asked about what he thought makes a leader. Every answer he had given, though, was wrong. The boy shrugged. "So what is it? What do I not have?"

Cog's eyes twinkled. "Followers, of course."

Arthur scratched his head. "Followers?"

"Yes. A leader with no followers is not leading anything."

"But why would someone follow me? When I tried to tell Quill what I wanted to do, he was angry about it and stormed off!"

"No," Cog shook his head. "Followers do not simply do what you want. You give them what they need. A leader and a follower have a mutual relationship. Each requires something from the other."

"But what is that?" Arthur asked.

Cog shrugged. "You'll have to ask your follower. Everyone requires something different." Cog crossed his arms and studied the small boy. "My counsel for you is to think about what you are trying to achieve, then think about who you wish to have follow you. And then find out what that follower needs. Before you know it," he smiled, "you will have an army behind you."

✢   ✢   ✢

As the light of dawn greeted Dragonrook, Quill was stealing a much-needed moment of rest within his chamber. A small *locket* swooped in from the open entry that overlooked the eastern bay. It was Kitt, the personal *locket* assigned to Arthur.

"Quill! Quill!" she said. "Wake up!"

The *hyrex's* head lifted in alert. "What is it?"

"Arthur requests your presence at the High Seat."

"Is that so?" A part of Quill was irked at having to be at the small human's beck and call. The other part, however, was relieved that Kitt was not bringing news of Arcrellis's arrival. "Very well. I am on my way."

When Quill arrived at the High Seat, he found Arthur sitting on the edge of the large flat stone, his feet dangling casually in front of him. Clay, Penny, and John Dunney were also there, waiting with curious looks of satisfaction on their faces. He suppressed his ire at seeing the humans making themselves at such ease in the chamber and attempted to lace his voice with a semblance of politeness.

"Did you have need of me?" he asked.

"Yes, I do need you. All of Dragonrook needs you," Arthur replied. "Clay, Penny, and I have been discussing the situation. We have a plan to protect the island, but it will require your help and cooperation."

"I've already told you," Quill simmered, "that we will not blaspheme the High-Thrall and kill at your request."

"And you won't have to," Arthur said.

"And how can this be?"

Arthur slid from the flat stone. "You may be prevented from slaying *rogueskein*," he said, "but we are not. Clay, Penny, Mr. Dunney, and I are prepared to battle for you."

"Hmmph," Quill snorted. "And what is it you think you can achieve."

Penny chimed in. "Not much at the moment. That's why we need your help. I have three ships waiting at Stinky Cove with men and weapons. If you are willing to give us transportation, we can retrieve my ships and fly the banner of Dragonrook. Our cause will be yours."

"I know of Stinky Cove," Quill said. "It is aptly named. But it's dangerously close to testing the limits of the High-Thrall."

"Which is why we are asking you," Arthur said. "There is risk. But there is also reward. And I think Dragonrook is worth it. Will you agree to help us?"

Quill silent calculated the situation. While there was the danger that whichever dragons journeyed from the island would fall to the *rogueskein*, there was also the unpleasant reality that those same dragons would fall in battle on the shores of Dragonrook. The decision was an easy one. "And you believe these men will fight for us?"

Penny nodded. "I believe I can convince them."

"Then it is agreed."

"Also," Arthur said, "I heard Royal mention that he has an armory here. Is that true?"

"Yes. He kept stores and rations for provisioning the *Ivory Typhoon*. Much of it is loot from his pirating days."

"And it has weapons?"

"Yes, it does. Quite a few cannons, if I remember correctly," Quill answered. Hope was beginning to creep into his voice.

"Perfect!" Arthur smiled. "We're told that Mr. Dunney here is an excellent gunner. We have plans that just might give your dragons an edge over Arcrellis! Send someone to show Clay and Mr. Dunney the armory. I have some other arrangements for it, also. Royal warned us that should Marco return, he'll likely be after Dragonrook's trove, so we'll need to make some changes. Clay will tell you what those are."

Arthur began to stroll past the confused Quill and through the tall doors. "Where are you going?" Quill asked.

"There's something else that I need to take care of personally."

+ + +

The waves softly lapped upon the sand as Arthur observed the quiet hulk of Hogarth. The giant *rogueskein* remained an unmoving monument within the shallow water, neither on land nor in the depths of the sea. The *flamespire* sentries continued their distant vigil, watching for any attempt from the unwanted dragon to encroach upon the shore. But, as always, Hogarth remained stoic and still, crouched in the waving water, his pallid gray eyes staring blankly toward land.

Slowly, and with not a little trepidation, Arthur waded into the water toward him. The cool ocean reached his waist as he drew closer. The half-submerged Hogarth stirred. "Askelon," he rumbled.

Arthur paused, wondering what sensations lurked in the clouded mind of the *rogueskein*.

"Have you come to slay me, Askelon?" the dragon's gravelly voice uttered.

The boy shook his head. "My name is Arthur."

Hogarth disregarded the information. "Have you come to slay me?"

Wondering if the dim eyes of the *duskar* could see him, Arthur spoke clearly. "No."

The dragon stood still, waiting for more words.

Any uncertainty that Arthur held began to fade as he recognized the passive nature of the *rogueskein*. He looked over his shoulder. The distant *flamespires* upon the shore were watching the exchange with curiosity. Arthur knew they were out of earshot, but he spoke softly anyway. "Why are you here, Hogarth? You have been given the freedom to depart, yet you remain."

Still, the dragon didn't respond, so Arthur continued. "I think I know why you're here," he said. "You're here for the same reason you were on Rogue's Island. You're here for the same reason you aren't with Arcrellis or the others on Fangshard."

At this, Hogarth stirred amid the lapping waves. "I am *rogueskein*," the dragon answered. "Has Askelon come to take my life?"

Arthur realized that the dragon still did not distinguish him from the small blade that he carried in his belt. "No," he answered again. "Askelon has the power to take your life. But it also has the power to give."

"What command does Askelon give?" Hogarth asked.

"Askelon does not give a command. I have come to give you what you need."

The dragon heaved a mighty sigh. "Has Askelon come to slay me?"

A wave of sadness welled up within Arthur. He pondered the weary, half-blind dragon laying collapsed in the water. For how many centuries had despair weighed upon its back? How many nights ended in anguish when a new morning greeted it, bringing with it another day of pain and grief and utter worthlessness? Had misery driven this dragon to the point that it now felt death was the only remedy? Was that why it clung to the shores of Dragonrook? Hoping that someone one would bring a final release to the centuries of bitterness and lost meaning?

"I don't come to give you death, Hogarth," Arthur said. "I've come to give you what is truly needed."

Hogarth's heavy breathing paused. He twisted his head slightly.

"I've come to give you forgiveness, Hogarth. If you want it."

The *duskar* was frozen in confusion. "I am *rogueskein*."

Arthur shook his head. "You don't seek *rogueskein*. You seek escape from it. I believe that's why you dwelled alone on Rogue's Island instead of with the others on Fangshard. The same *duskar* nature that led you to rebel is now seeking more. Within you, your heart still desires to pulse with the thrice-beat."

The thrice-beat. The thought stirred something long forgotten within the dragon. "Once for life," Hogarth whispered. "Once for passion..."

"...and once for the High-Thrall," finished Arthur. "Askelon has the power to forgive you, Hogarth. You just have to let the heart within you beat for a passion greater than your own."

Hogarth's body trembled. His body shuddered as if new life was pulsing through him. "What is this? Does Askelon forgive me?"

"Yes," Arthur said. "Yes, I do."

A guttural growl budded deep inside the dragon's throat. A quiver rippled from shoulder to tail. The growl within him grew and soon blossomed into a mighty roar.

The bulk of Hogarth's body rose from the water as his giant legs lifted in a sturdy crouch. In alarm, the four *flamespires* on the shore braced in shock and wariness at the sudden burst of energy from the normally placid beast.

Arthur stepped back. In awe, he watched the mighty wings of the duskar stretch to full length. The pale gray of Hogarth's eyes began to glow with fresh light, and the rough lifeless scales flowed with green as new vitality seemed to course throughout the dragon's body. His massive sinews rippled with waves of budding, potent strength. Another sonorous roar rolled from Hogarth's massive jaws. "What is this? Am I...am I no longer *rogueskein*?"

"You are not *rogueskein*," said Arthur. "Askelon has forgiven you."

"Not *rogueskein*," Hogarth repeated. "Then what?"

"Something new."

Hogarth looked down in amazement at the small boy standing in the waves, his glistening eyes seeing more clearly than they had in centuries. "Then I may come to land? I may enter Dragonrook?"

Arthur smiled. "Not yet. there is something else I have for you to do."

23

The Battle of Stinky Cove

Stinky Cove was everything Clay expected it to be and then some. The bay not only welcomed ships into its deep, protected harbor but also any flotsam and jetsam the water had to offer. The ocean happily shoved every piece of seafaring detritus into the narrow opening of the cove before going on its merry way. Adding to the pungent odors were the random pieces of effluvium that plopped from the ramshackle village hoisted on wooden stilts above the slapping water. The air was so noxious that most travelers upon the sea avoided it as if it were the very plague itself. This fact happened to make it a perfect stop for the less desirable ships and crew who found the atmosphere of Stinky Cove not much different than their own cluttered, dank cabins.

Clay held his nose in disgust. "This must be the armpit of the sea!"

He and Penny sat in the small dinghy as it glided upon the surface of the murky cove. "Agreed," Penny said. "I wish Dozer and the men hadn't brought my ships here. It's gonna take weeks to get the smell out of the sails!"

"Are those the ships you were talking about?" Clay pointed to three small vessels moored along the rickety jetties.

Penny's eyes lit up. "They sure are! *The Lock*, *The Stock*, and *The Feral*! All still ship-shape, it looks like!"

"What's that fourth ship?" Clay asked, regarding another larger vessel that was also waiting in the cove.

Penny squinted at the faded lettering over the transom and her face fell. "Uh oh," she muttered. "That's the *Sea Scar*! Thaddeus Schark's ship!"

"What's he doing here?" Clay wondered in dismay.

"Bringing down the ambiance, I'd say."

"Ahoy!" a voice called. "Who goes there?" Penny and Clay turned to see a blobby excuse for a sailor standing on the wooden dock pointing at them.

"Gargleby!" Penny tried not to look irritated as she called back. "It's your captain, returning for her ships!"

The sailor looked confused. "Dozer said yer dead. How is it you're bobbin' in the water like a coconut?"

"That's right. I'm supposed to be dead. Fortunately for me, you rudderless gang of swabbies can't do anything right without a decent captain. Where's Dozer?"

"He's inside the tavern. Nee-gotchee...Ne-goat-tating." The sailor gave up trying to say the word. "Something to do with goats."

"Negotiating?"

"Nah, I don't think that's it."

"Well," Penny said, "tell him I've come to see him. No, wait," she stopped. "I'll tell him myself. I want to watch the swill he calls blood drain from his face when he sees me. Stand back. We're disembarking."

The confused sailor scratched his head as the little dinghy inexplicably moved sideways to the crude jetty. Clay hefted a small chest from the bottom of the boat and they stepped onto the creaking dock. Penny pointed to a somewhat lopsided shack. "That's the tavern. Whatever you do, don't order the fish."

When they swung the shack door open, the raucous commotion that filled the tiny space immediately silenced. Several grateful flies zipped out into the open air. The crowd of disheveled crewmates stared with mouths agape. Plopped in a broad wooden chair at a crooked table sat Thaddeus Schark alongside the bald and aghast pirate that Clay assumed was Dozer.

"Well!" Thaddeus laughed, "tie a hanky to my leg and call it a mast! If it isn't the scrappy Penniless Gayle!"

Dozer stood to his feet in worrisome surprise. "How did you get off that island?"

"Wouldn't you like to know, you rotten mistake of a first mate!"

Thaddeus pulled the bald sailor back to his chair. "It seems the two of you have a quarrel. And you are welcome to settle it after we've finished our bit of business here."

"I don't care about your business," Penny replied. "I'll take my ships and be on my way."

Thaddeus laughed. "I'm afraid that's not going to happen. You see, these men are in the process of signing on as my crew. *The Lock*, *The Stock*, and *The Feral* are now a part of my fleet."

Penny scowled. "I don't own the men. But *The Lock*, *The Stock*, and *The Feral* are mine and, as such, they have no right to sign them away."

Dozer chimed in. "We claim those vessels as prizes! The way we all see it, you owe us wages, and until you settle up, we'll exercise our rights to sell 'em."

"That's right!" echoed Schark. "And since we all know Penniless Gayle ain't got a single farthing to her name, there's not a man-jack in here who's going to take your side!"

"We're tired of being paid in parasols and pomegranates!" growled Dozer. "We want gold! So, we're signing up with Schark! He's got a plan to raid an island that's swimming with loot!"

Penny feigned disappointment. "Oh. That's too bad. Since I don't have any crew, then I guess I'll just have to keep this payment for myself."

Thaddeus shot her a suspicious glare. "What are ye blathering about?"

"Show him, Clay," she said.

Clay obediently opened the lid of the small chest. Within it, jewels and golden coins sparkled with fresh luster, filling the dim tavern with splendid reflections of light. The sailors of *The Lock*, *The Stock*, and *The Feral* all gazed in captivated astonishment as Penny continued. "I know what my crew want. They want pay and I have it to give them. What did you bring, Schark? Promises and possibilities?"

The one-legged pirate fumed. "Parasols and pomegranates! Promises and possibilities!" he spat, much to the dismay of the pirates in range of his spittle. "You think you can waltz in here and take my ships out from beneath my foot?"

"I'll tell you what I think!" Penny retorted. "I think you're a liar and scum-barrel who doesn't care a lick for these men. You're promising to lead them into a fight and maybe find some treasure you don't even have! Well, I have it!" She turned to the brigands still gaping at the box of glistening riches. "This is for my crew. They earned it, but the only way to get it is to serve aboard *The Lock*, *The Stock*, and *The Feral*. What do you say, men? Who wants to sail with me out of this stink-pit?"

Before anyone could answer, Thaddeus rose quicky upon his wooden peg, a primed and vicious-looking flintlock jutting from his fist. "Hold fast, boys!" He leered at Penny. "The way I see it, I can make this easier for all of us. I shoot you, take the gold, the men, and the ships. I got a bloodthirsty crew aboard the *Sea Scar*, twenty-six guns primed and pointed at this shack, and a real itch to be done with the both of you. So I ask you...what have you got?"

Penny smirked. "I have a dragon."

Suddenly the tavern shuddered and the creaking planks of the floor burst asunder. In a spray of splinters and blackened water, the spiny head of a giant *artica* exploded through the wood. The pointed jaws let out a heart-stopping roar and bared a fierce display of row after row of triangular fangs. The long, coiling neck snaked into the trembling tavern as terrified sailors screamed in horror.

The winding sea dragon clawed its way through the shattered floor, the small dinghy that Penny and Clay rode in still lashed to its back. A few unlucky men tumbled through the collapsing planks into the filthy water beneath.

"Quick!" Penny yelled to Clay. "To the ships!"

They dashed through the lopsided doorway and onto the shuddering docks. Thaddeus uselessly fired his flintlock over his shoulder as he hobbled after them. The tavern's wide-eyed patrons stumbled over one other and attempted to squeeze through the small entrance in a single mad press. The door jamb cracked but stubbornly refused to give under the onslaught. Instead, the entire front wall of the shack collapsed and grubby sailors poured forth like rats out of a drainpipe, fleeing the snapping jaws of the dragon.

Penny cheered the sea serpent. "Nice work, Arwiss!" Then she pointed to one of the ships. "*The Feral* is mine!" She and Clay bolted up the gangplank and beckoned to the escaping sailors. "Now's your chance to sail with me, boys!"

Several panicked and eager men dashed up the bouncing gangplank. The bald Dozer blindly followed the line of fleeing sailors.

"Except for you!" Penny said. Her small hand balled into a perfect fist and landed it square on Dozer's nose. The bald sailor reeled from the surprise blow and cartwheeled down the plank while uncaring crewman trod over him. Dozer quickly gained his feet, however, and made his way to the next ship at the dock. Penny frowned in dismay. "He's taking *The Stock*!" She grabbed one of the dashing men. "Mr. Rodney! Take *The Lock* before one of Schark's poltroons seize it!"

The blunt-faced sailor didn't bat an eyelash. "Aye aye, Cap'n!"

Penny smiled. The crew, she realized, wasn't resisting. When she, Clay, and Arthur contrived their plan back on Dragonrook, the simple suggestion that Arthur had made was working. "The men will follow you if you give them what they need." And right now, she thought to herself, they just need to escape!

The writhing *artica* continued to snap at the retreating men as it broke free from the collapsing tavern. Penny saw Thaddeus Schark limping along the length of dock to the waiting *Sea Scar*. She called to the dragon. "Arwiss!"

The sea dragon turned his attention to Penny. She pointed to the largest of the ships. "Can you take down the *Sea Scar*?"

Before the dragon could answer, the air shook with tremendous explosions. A barrage of cannon fire ripped across the dock. Penny watched as roundshot pummeled the shoulder of the coiling *artica*. Arwiss roared in pain and anger.

Penny searched for the source of the attack. Smoking cannons protruding from the sides of *The Stock*. "Dozer isn't wasting any time!" she shouted. "He's firing broadsides." She turned her attention to the men crowding on the deck. "What are you standing around for? Weigh anchor and get this tub to sea. Pinky, give me some sail! Mr. Pew, take some men and prime the cannons!"

As *The Feral* swung toward the open ocean, Clay noticed that Mr. Rodney was doing the same thing with *The Lock*. We've managed to reclaim two of the ships, Clay thought. *The Stock*, on the other hand, had invoked the wrath of the furious, bleeding *artica*. In one graceful movement, the sea dragon dove beneath the waters and re-emerged from beneath the vessel. The entire ship teetered to one side and all the men on the deck spilled over the rails. Soon, *The Stock* was completely on its side, surrounding by splashing, flailing seamen. With clutching talons, Arwiss climbed onto the bobbing side of the floundering craft and proceeded to dunk it repeatedly beneath the waves. He let out an enraged roar over the heads of the paddling pirates. *The Feral's* crew erupted in cheers and Clay joined in. Arwiss, their secret weapon and brave *artica* that brought them so swiftly to Stinky Cove, was on the cusp of securing an easy victory.

"Arwiss! Watch out!" Penny suddenly shouted in alarm. She pointed to the *Sea Scar* which was now also slipping toward the opening of the cove. The twelve guns on the port side of the ship rolled forward on their caissons and pointed directly at the perched dragon.

The dragon's reaction was too slow. A dozen cannon-balls hammered into his side. He stumbled from his perch upon the capsized *Stock* and collapsed into the murky water with a thunderous splash.

"Mr. Rodney!" Penny shouted over the rail. "Bear all guns on the *Sea Scar* and fire at will!"

"Aye aye!" he called back.

The cove gave little room for three vessels to maneuver, and even less for the bulky *Sea Scar*. With its port guns spent and no place to hide, Schark was now at the mercy of *The Feral's* broadside. With a ferocious cry, Penny Gayle gave the order to fire. The six guns on The Feral's star-board roared with smoke and flame as iron balls rattled from their bores and savagely raked the fleeing *Sea Scar*. The upper decks cracked and splintered and Penny could tell that at least two of the *Sea Scar's* port side guns were destroyed by the pounding.

Before anyone aboard Schark's ship could respond, *The Lock* sent its own barrage of fire at the departing stern. At first, the damage seemed light, but a sudden report of splitting wood could be heard. The *Sea Scar's* mizzen mast slowly toppled over the side in a tangle of sail and rigging.

A unified cry of victory rose from the decks of *The Feral* and *The Lock*. Oddly, none of the sailors seemed to re-member that only moments ago they were ready to sign aboard as crew for Thaddeus Schark. The opportunity to wreak carnage on another ship seemed to overrule any lin-gering loyalties.

The *Sea Scar* crawled out to sea. Schark bitterly recog-nized his predicament. Without a mizzen mast, his speed and maneuverability were sorely diminished. He still had a fair number of guns that could match those of Penniless Gayle's smaller craft but he didn't relish the idea of two ships hounding him like jackals on a wounded elephant. To say nothing about his chances against a monstrous sea dragon.

"We should follow him!" Clay shouted. "This is our chance!"

Penny woefully watched the departing ship. Part of her wanted to, but instead she grimaced. "We need to check on Arwiss." Clay's exuberance dimmed. He looked over and saw the ragged form of the dragon. The bleeding Arwiss clung to the floating wreck of *The Stock*, green eyes half-closed.

The Feral slowly came alongside. "Arwiss!" Penny shouted. "Are you okay?"

A faint smile played across his torn lips. "I'll be better once I'm out of this nasty cove," he coughed.

"Can you swim? How badly are you hurt?"

Arwiss laughed. "Can an *artica* swim? Humans are always asking such strange questions."

"We did it, Arwiss!" Clay said. "Thanks to you, we have ships to defend Dragonrook. We couldn't have done it without you!"

The sea dragon's eyes began to slowly shut. "Yes," he said. "We shall return to Dragonrook. There is still much to do." Arwiss laid his head on the crushed hull. "But first..." His raspy voice trailed off.

More words never came. Slowly, the dragon's grip lessened. Penny's cheeks were wet with tears as she and Clay watched the limp form of Arwiss slide from the splintered wood and disappear beneath the black water.

Much of the return journey to Dragonrook was filled with tense silence.

A few brave crewmen, eager to smooth over any lingering bad feelings about marooning their Captain on Rogue's Island, tried to curry favor by giving pointless reports or performing random tasks. Their efforts were repaid with bursts of rage and stinging rebukes. Even Clay was careful to avoid the abnormally cantankerous attitude that had descended upon Penny Gayle. All they could do was to nervously watch her stiff form as she gripped the helm and stared ahead at the open sea.

Just as the men had accepted and grown accustomed to the wordless voyage, Penny abruptly let loose with an explosive outburst. "Would someone at least say they're sorry?!"

Every man froze in place.

"You!" She pointed to a bearded sailor, who halted in the act of coiling a line of rope. "Say you're sorry for leaving your captain and shipmates to die on that horrid island!"

"I'm-I'm sorry, Cap'n," he stammered.

"And you!" Penny singled out a skinny crewman who was trying to discreetly hide behind the mast. "Tell me you're sorry that *The Stock* sank in Stinky Cove!"

The crewman straightened immediately. "I'm sorry, Captain Gayle!" he gulped.

Penny leveled her finger at another older pirate standing rigidly at attention. "And you! Say you're sorry for having such a tremendously large nose!"

The man nodded. "Aye, Cap'n! My apologies! It won't happen again!"

Penny stamped her foot. "You're all sorry! Every one of you!"

The crew shouted out in unified confusion. "We're sorry, Cap'n!"

Penny released her grip on the wheel and plunked down on the deck. To everyone's surprise and confusion, she buried her face in her hands and began to cry.

The crew awkwardly traded blank looks and puzzled shrugs, seeking someone who knew what they were supposed to do.

Quietly and slowly, Clay settled down beside her. As he slipped his arms around her, she didn't resist. She nestled deeper into Clay's embrace and he felt the violent sobs rack her body. "I'm sorry Arwiss is gone," he whispered.

Penny brushed the tears from her face. "Captains aren't supposed to cry."

"Well," Clay replied, "you don't have to be a captain right now."

The sun sank beneath the sealine and the two of them simply sat together and let the wind carry *The Feral* and *The Lock* across the waves.

The battered *Sea Scar* slowly crept toward the Sore.

The Sore was a small blight of craggy rock that gracelessly rose above the waves. Somewhere far beneath it, a ragged cleft gurgled and gasped, sometimes spewing a torrent of subterranean gas before choking on the seawater that flooded into it. The result was that on any given day, the rocks would be surrounded by a bubbling, churning tide or a swirling maelstrom of froth that drained into the hole beneath it. But mostly it was a thorn in the sides of passing ships that, if not paying attention, would find their hulls ripped asunder by the sharp, hidden rocks that lurked around it, leaving them to rot with the rest of the trapped wreckage and debris.

Today, however, the sporadic field of rocks were covered with the creeping forms of dragons. Attempting to find some measure of rest after the long swim beneath the water, the dragons of Fangshard snapped and snarled at one another, fighting for a place to bask in the sun. Many, not finding a place to stretch, huddled in the shallows, the tops of their horned heads poking up amid the waves like the many boulders around them. The stolen *Ivory Zephyr* bobbed nearby. With no guns, it was of little value for now. Schark had given command of the lugger to the round first mate, Arbo, who was choosing to keep the unarmed vessel at a safe distance from the treacherous rocks and an even safer distance from the swarm of swimming dragons.

As day turned to dusk, Skorch studied the horizon. "A ship approaches," the dark *flamespire* growled.

"Finally!" Arcrellis crawled to the center of the Sore, treading over the lazing, squirming bodies of the other dragons to follow Skorch's gaze. "I see only one, though."

Soon, the *Sea Scar* furled its sails and came to a standstill.

"Captain Schark," Arcrellis growled loudly. "I see you have disappointed me again. You promised me a fleet of armed ships and instead you return in this oversized piece of driftwood. Do you care to explain what happened?"

"I'll tell you what happened!" Schark fumed over the rail. "Somehow, they caught word that I was coming and put up a fight! I think one of you festering pocks betrayed me!"

"Impossible!" Arcrellis snapped. "Don't blame your continuing incompetence on us! Your propensity for failure is becoming legendary!"

Skorch leaned over and whispered. "Let me turn him to ashes." Arcrellis ignored the request.

Schark's bristled beard shook with barely suppressed rage. Every dram of boiling blood in his body wanted to rain cannonballs on this pile of dragons. But he also knew it would be a losing battle. And, besides, these nasty beasts were his only chance to get his hands on the trove deep within Dragonrook. He took a deep breath and spit over the rail—that always seem to help him calm down—and tried to salvage the situation. "It don't matter!" he grumbled, as spittle dripped from his beard. "Those ships at Stinky Cove were small potatoes anyway. I still have two dozen guns and forty armed men. That's all I need!"

"That's all you have to offer, is what you mean to say," the dragon retorted. "Tonight, we gather our strength. In the morning, we move. And by this time tomorrow, Dragonrook will be ours."

24

Assault on Dragonrook

The golden rays of dawn fell upon the still cliffs and trees of Dragonrook. Slowly, the sun rose above the water, its full attention seemingly only upon the lonely secret island in the sea. The sun lifted higher, curious and pensive, waiting and watching for the day to bring its fate to the small isle.

The yellow eyes of Arcrellis also rose from the water as he scrutinized the rocks and shore. After several contemplative minutes, he rose from the lapping waves. The salt water rolled from his scales as he breathed in the smell of land and dirt. Closing his eyes, he savored not only the warmth of the morning sun but the sweet moment of victory.

He took another step and his talons clutched at the wet sand beneath. A snorting chuckle broke from his snout. At last. The day had come when Dragonrook was under his feet. The last bastion of the High-Thrall would now be crushed under the inevitable power of Rogueskein.

Arcrellis examined the island. It was quiet. Had they all fled in fear? Did they abandon their precious cliffs and towers? Did they finally recognize their hopelessness? He sniffed the air. No. They were here. Watching.

"Quill!" he shouted.

No answer came. He was tempted to take flight over the island. That would certainly stoke their fears, wouldn't it? To see their enemy's wings stretched over their home, blocking the sun, and owning the very air they breathe. Yes, that would be a pleasure, he thought. But caution held him back. The inhabitants of Dragonrook surely knew he had arrived. The stillness reeked with intention. Better to not separate himself too far from the legions at his back.

"Quill!" he called again. "I know you can hear me. You do not have to show yourself. I give you the gift of hiding in fear while your followers watch. All you need to do is listen!" He studied the motionless trees beyond the sandy beach. "I know your High Dragon is dead. I have seen her blood with my own eyes and tasted it with my own tongue. We both know what that means. The line of the scions is broken. You have no leader. You have no hope."

The forest continued its silent vigil. Arcrellis searched the high cliffs beyond, seeking any sign of response. Finding nothing, he continued. "Do not blame yourself, my friend! The rule of High-Thrall was always destined to succumb to the power of Rogueskein. We both know it. You have clung to your noble experiment and pointless belief that your righteous goodness will always reign. But now you finally see that there are forces greater than your pathetic *hyrex* mind could ever fathom. The cry of *rogueskein* will always be louder than the pulse of the thrice-beat. Behind me, my army waits for me to give the word and claim our right to Dragonrook. You are powerless to stop us—your precious High-Thrall forbids you to take the life of another dragon—so for that reason I offer you a rare opportunity. You may come forward and relinquish the High Seat of Dragonrook freely. In doing so, you will spare the lives of many dragons. And then, at last, we can all be unified under the bond of Rogueskein. Doesn't that sound like an equitable arrangement?"

At first, it seemed that the words of Arcrellis would go unanswered. But then Quill appeared, high and distant upon the cliff.

"*Rogueskein* can never reign, Arcrellis," Quill called back. "You think you can rule by giving others what they want, instead of what they need. Without the needs, the fruits of want soon become tasteless and empty. And dragons need order and peace. This is why you have failed in the past, and why you will fail today. Dragonrook is not yours to claim."

Arcrellis bristled. "The High-Thrall is broken. Dragonrook belongs to whomever is strongest."

"Dragonrook belongs to whomever is wisest. The High-Thrall still remains. Just as you remain a fool."

The rage in Arcrellis flamed but was tempered with a twinge of carnal satisfaction. "Your choice is made then! By the time the sun has set, we will know who the fool is!" Arcrellis pounded the waves with his writhing tail. "Armies of Fangshard! You are unleashed!"

The water churned and broiled. From the chaotic waves, the heads of dragons rose. Massive *browgies*, fierce *flamespires*, coiling *articas*, razor-headed *hyrexes*, and darting *lockets* charged upon the shore in a mad rush.

"Find them!" Arcrellis shouted. "Find them and kill them all! Dragonrook is ours!"

The army of dragons flooded past Arcrellis as he laughed in scorn and wicked pleasure. His glee quickly vanished, however, when the air suddenly burst with explosions. Billows of black smoke roared from the line of trees. Cannonballs ripped through the air in a deadly chorus of whistles, and tore into the first wave of charging beasts. Many dragons collapsed heavily into the sand. Others, wounded or frightened, scattered and took to the air, circling away to safety.

Mr. Pew, the lead gunner from Penny Gayle's crew, stood tall from his position and gave the signal to his men. "Re-load, and fire at will, all of ye! Don't let Captain Gayle down again, boys!"

But the command wasn't needed. The expert cannoneers were already sponging and priming the concealed guns for the next volley.

+ + +

Schark stood upon the aft deck of the *Sea Scar* and studied the carnage through his scope.

"It's begun!" he muttered.

Gunther, his newly-assigned first mate, was perplexed. "That's cannon fire! I thought they was supposed to be fighting dragons."

"Not our concern. We'll do our part of the bargain and give them some return fire. Level the guns at that shore and lay into that defensive line." He pocketed his spyglass and strolled from the deck.

"But what about the dragons, Cap'n? We'd be endangering our own side."

"The only good dragon is a dead dragon!" Schark barked back. "I don't give a roach's hindleg who gets hit. We said we'd give 'em guns, so that's what we're doing. If they don't have the sense to stay out of the way, that's their problem." He snapped at a waiting brigand. "Barfby, ready my launch to go ashore!"

Schark unrolled a piece of parchment from his pocket. On it was a rough but detailed map, scrawled in the nervous, shaking hand of Marco Mossarian. The pirate grinned. "Soon, lads, the greatest treasure of the ages will be ours!"

Quill observed carefully as the clouds of spent gunpowder wafted across the beach. The first volley of cannon fire was effective in disrupting the Fangshard charge but did little to thin their ranks...as was expected.

The nervous Pinn, still only slightly recovered from his lengthy imprisonment, also watched the attack unfold beneath them. "The sailors are in danger, now that their positions are revealed. Perhaps this is the time for our dragons to emerge and provide a distraction."

"No. We must stay concealed and let Arcrellis come to us. He is a blunt, emotional force. He came with no plan. Only rage and desire. We will use that against him."

From the water, a boom sounded. Quill and Pinn saw the puffs of smoke drift from the *Sea Scar* floating off shore. The falling cannonballs fell short of the trees and instead pounded the surf and sand and any random Fangshard dragons unluckily caught in between. One soaring round-shot struck a fleeing *flamespire* as it flapped through the air, causing it to pinwheel into the water below.

+ + +

Emerging from the northern side of the island, *The Feral* and *The Lock* took full advantage of the prevailing winds and sped into view. Penny Gayle's eyes lit up with determined and unconcealed delight. *The Feral* was poised to neatly slide itself in between the *Sea Scar* and the shore.

"Okay, boys! It's our turn to surprise them!" she shouted. "Broadsides for both!"

Six blazing cannons on *The Feral's* starboard side peppered the decks of the *Sea Scar* with grapeshot. *The Feral's* port guns bellowed with smoke as they levied more cannonballs into the scrambling dragons at the rear of the Fangshard charge.

The Lock eased up behind them. "Mr. Rodney!" Penny shouted across the water. "We've got their attention! Keep those guns high and expect visitors! We'll take care of the *Sea Scar!*"

"Aye aye!" the crewman shouted back. "Ready the port guns!" he ordered. "Don't let those beasties get too close, men!"

Penny smiled as she watched the pirates aboard Schark's ship scrambling in panic. Still hobbled without a mizzen mast, and with guns elevated for firing across the bay, *The Feral* easily slipped beneath the threat of their weapons. With perfect precision, Penny's quick schooner trimmed sail and curled around the *Sea Scar's* bow. She grinned wickedly when she saw Schark's flummoxed first mate Gunther watch in dismay. The crew of the *Scar* was not expecting an attack from the sea. Their starboard cannons, never primed for battle, sat quiet. By this time, *The Feral's* guns were already reloaded and run out for another volley.

"This is for Arwiss, you lousy pieces of filth!"

The Feral's cannons roared again. At close range, the low balls hammered the hull mercilessly below the waterline.

Arcrellis bellowed in rage as he watched the cannon balls flying onto shore from front and back. His dragons were scattering in confusion. A few of them had broken through to the trees, but the dragons of Dragonrook were still nowhere to be seen, and his followers were flustered by the completely unexpected defense.

"Skorch!" Arcrellis called as the giant *flamespire* ran past. "Strafe those cannons in the trees! We'll burn that forest to the ground and dance on its ashes!"

Skorch grinned wickedly. "My pleasure!" With that, he stretched his long, black wings and lifted into the air, expertly dodging a whistling cannon ball.

Arcrellis spun to an enormous *browgie* that was lumbering to the shore. "Argle! Those ships are getting on my nerves! And Schark's men are not helping, either. Get rid of them!"

Without a word, the bulky dragon changed direction and lifted from the water with his widespread wings, pushing towards the three battling vessels.

Another barrage of cannon fire ravaged the air and a pummeled *hyrex* was flung backwards into the surf. Arcrellis watched with satisfaction as the mighty Skorch shot across the line of cannons hidden in the trees, spewing a torrent of fire upon the irritating defenders. The cannoneers screamed in panic, leaping from the storm of flame. A waiting store of gunpowder erupted under the conflagration, sending one of the cannons and its caisson spinning into the burning trees.

Arcrellis laughed. But the glee of the moment quickly

fled as he spied the watching Quill atop the cliff. With a snarl, he launched himself into the air. The pompous *hyrex* would be the first of Dragonrook to fall under his talons.

In only a matter of moments, the raging *duskar* was upon Quill. His claws pierced into Quill's throat and the two tumbled one over another along the high cliff. Pinn scurried for safety as they spat and gnashed in vehement wrath.

"Where are they?" Arcrellis fumed. "Where are all the dragons?"

"Safe!" Quill retorted. "Do you think we're foolish enough to engage on a battlefield of cannon fire like you?"

Arcrellis pinned the struggling Quill to the ground. Blood seeped slowly up his claws as they sank deeper into the *hyrex's* scales. "Your stupid cannons only delayed the inevitable!" Arcrellis spat. "But now they are useless! I gave you a chance to surrender, yet you refused. So now we'll prowl every crag on this island and rend every last one of you to pieces...starting with you!" Arcrellis raised his razor-sharp talons, arching for a final, slicing blow. And then he stopped.

The soft sound of flapping wings beat above him.

The rhythmic shadows played hypnotically on the ground around them as a silhouetted form of a *flamespire* hovered in the sunlight. Arcrellis squinted upward.

"So," he murmured. "It's true. Askelon is here."

Astride the hovering Tindlass, Arthur gazed down at the crouching, black *duskar*. "Yes," he said.

Quill grinned. "The High-Thrall is not broken. It rules still."

Arcrellis sneered at Arthur. "You're no dragon. You are no ruler of Dragonrook. I'll crush you like the others and Askelon will be mine."

"You'll have to catch me first," Arthur teased.

Before Arcrellis realized what was happening, Arthur and the flapping *flamespire* shot like lightning from view.

"Arrrgh!" Arcrellis bellowed in anger. With a mighty burst of his wings, he lifted upward in pursuit. But Arcrellis soon balked in amazement at the *flamespire's* speed. Drawing every available ounce of strength, Arcrellis forced his wings to move with desperation to catch his prey.

Arthur leaned forward. "Nicely done, Tindlass! You really are the fastest dragon alive!"

Tindlass smiled. "Emberwing was faster. But," he added with a twinkle in his golden eye, "not by much!"

"You know where to go! For Emberwing!" Arthur cried.

"For Emberwing!" Tindlass echoed.

The distance between them and the chasing Arcrellis grew. In frustration, the angry Arcrellis shouted to his army of dragons still tormenting the fleeing cannoneers. "Leave them! Catch the boy!"

The dragons looked upward in confusion. Seeing Arthur and the escaping *flamespire*, they mounted the air and gave chase. Arthur stole a quick glance behind them. A swarm of dragons streamed in the wake of Tindlass, furiously stretching forward to match the speed of the incredibly swift dragon.

The pursuers whipped and wound behind the darting dragon like a scaly, prickly tail of a kite. Clutching tight to his lash, Arthur crouched close to the *flamespire's* sleek neck, hiding as best he could from the rushing wind. Tindlass veered in a wide, sweeping arc. Arthur glanced back once again. It seemed as if every dragon from Fangshard was snapping at their heels.

Arcrellis, however, began to lessen speed. Something wasn't right. *The boy is leading us somewhere,* he thought. *He's choosing the battlefield.* Immediately, he dropped back. As he did so, two gigantic *browgies* lifted above a nearby ridge. He tried to peer past their beating wings but he still could not discern what was perched upon their backs.

+   +   +

"Fire!" Clay yelled.

The heavy cannon belched smoke and flame. The twelve pound iron ball rattled down the bore and smashed into one of the pursuing dragons. Clay's companion, Hadley, laughed as they watched the crumpled beast plummet to the ground.

The platform secured to the *browgie's* back had just enough room for the two men, a cannon, and a stockpile of shot and powder. The giant *browgie* didn't even flinch under the recoil of the heavy cannon. Instead, he looked back at his passengers and smiled. "Your plan is working, human! The High-Thrall forbids us from slaying dragons, but I am happy to get your cannon as close as possible!"

"Much obliged, Gared! Now it's Dunney's turn!"

Dunney and his fellow cannoneer atop the second *browgie* approached with another cannon. Their dragon swerved and lined up the cannon with a flapping *flamespire*. Clay watched as Dunney touched the fuse and the cannon roared with dead-center aim. The fiery dragon dropped like a rag from the sky.

"This is like shooting fish in a barrel!" Clay said as they primed their cannon.

Arthur and Tindlass wound in a tighter circle, closing the gaps between the pursuing dragons. Another blast from the gun was rewarded with another falling dragon.

"Break off!" Arcrellis shouted. "It's a trap!"

But the dragons persisted, spinning and twisting after the fleeing boy, oblivious to the crashing comrades around them. Arcrellis fumed, angry for allowing himself to be caught up in the ruse. He was stupid to think that a *hyrex* like Quill wouldn't have a plan. But, he grinned, *hyrexes* don't react well to change. All I have to do is disrupt his scheme.

"Skorch! To me!" he shouted.

With a slight show of frustration, the black *flamespire* broke from his fruitless pursuit of Arthur and the fleeing dragon. He hovered in the air alongside Arcrellis. "What is it?" he huffed.

"These stupid dragons are crazed by the scent of Askelon, but they'll never catch it. This *flamespire* is too quick."

"I can catch him!"

"No, you can't!" growled Arcrellis. "Not unless he stops." He studied the swerving swarm of dragons below them. "What's that dragon's name? The one in front. What's its name?"

"That's Coldash."

"Kill him," Arcrellis said bluntly.

Skorch didn't hide his look of surprise. "But he's one of ours."

"Don't argue with me!" Arcrellis hissed. "Just do as your told!"

Puzzled, the mighty *flamespire* dove towards the twisting swarm. With expert precision, he threaded through the speeding cloud of dragons. Seeing the waving tail of

Coldash ahead, he afforded himself a quick burst of acceleration and in a lightning-fast second, he sank his black talons into the haunches of the unsuspecting dragon.

Coldash's wings halted in surprise. With a sturdy yank, Skorch pulled the dragon closer and sank his fangs into the spine of the trapped beast. Coldash's screech of pain and anger split the air. With a twist of his snout, he sprayed the air with fire but was unable to singe his attacker. Skorch tore a mound of flesh from his victim's back and then clutched the faltering beast's wings in either hand. With his back talons still embedded in his victim, Skorch ripped Coldash's wings from his bleeding back in one savage pull.

The killer *flamespire* laughed in unexpected delight as it watched the shredded body of Coldash plummet to the ground far below.

In terror and shock, the chasing dragons broke from their pursuit and scattered in confusion. A few took enraged swipes and dives at the bloodthirsty Skorch, who responded with a belching inferno of flame and fire. A burning *locket* spiraled from the blast and fell to earth with the descending Coldash.

The sudden attack gave the precise effect Arcrellis wanted. The streaming swarm of dragons became a disparate, chaotic mass of frenzied killers. The idea of catching Askelon and the escaping *flamespire* was now the furthest thing from their minds.

+ + +

Arthur looked behind him and his face fell. "Tindlass! You went too fast! We lost everyone."

Tindlass shook his horned head. "I'm fast, but not that fast." He craned his neck to steal a glance. "They stopped pursuing us."

Tindlass folded his wings to lessen speed. With a graceful twist, the dragon came to a stop mid-air to hover and observe the cloud of maddened dragons. "I don't understand," Tindlass said. "Why are they attacking each other?"

"I don't get it, either," Arthur replied. "But we can use this to our advantage!" He waved to get the attention of Clay and John Dunney atop the two monstrous *browgies* who had been following after him. "Keep firing!" Arthur said. "They're distracted!"

He saw Clay give a quick salute and the armed *browgies* swerved to return to the fray.

Arthur leaned forward, waiting to watch his brother and Dunney send another volley of cannons into the mass of beasts. But he never had the chance to witness it.

A solid mass of dark scales and claws rammed into them. The sky spun in circles and the ear-shattering laugh of Arcrellis filled the air. Arthur desperately clutched the leather straps, but it was not needed. He was pinned tight between Tindlass and the merciless grip of Arcrellis. Tindlass rolled helplessly, unable to stretch his crumpled, trapped wings. Together, Arthur and the clawing dragons tumbled toward the ground.

+ + +

When Penny Gayle saw the enormous dragon crash angrily onto the deck of *The Lock*, she abandoned any thoughts about sinking the *Sea Scar*. "Take us around!"

she shouted to the crewman at the helm. "We need to help *The Lock*!" *The Feral* continued to move effortlessly in the water, but not fast enough to avoid the musket balls of the *Sea Scar* brigands as they fired from their deck.

Penny's crew crouched and answered with a volley of their own. Soon, *The Feral* swung around the bow of the large ship. Once in view, they could see the huge dragon ripping mast and men from the deck of *The Lock*. "Ready the guns!" she ordered. "Knock that giant beastie off that ship!"

The cannons rolled out. But the blast of the six cannons simply bounced off the iron-like hide of the rampaging *browgie*.

Another blast of cannon fire shook the air. The deck of the *The Feral* trembled under an onslaught of vicious roundshot. Penny realized her horrible mistake. In her desperate attempt to return to *The Lock* and save its crew, she had put herself at the mercy of the *Sea Scar's* guns pointed at the island. But this time, they were ready for her. She and *The Feral* were now trapped between *browgie* and broadside.

25

New Creature

Once they safely made it inland, Schark carefully studied the unrolled map, ignoring the echoing booms of cannons and explosions in the distance. With any luck, he thought, all these dragons would kill each other and he could carry away his trove of riches in peace.

Arbo anchored the *Ivory Zephyr* not far from a stretch of ignored beach but refused to come ashore. Instead, he elected to wait and help ferry the discovered loot to the *Zephyr's* hold on Schark's return. The *Zephyr* was a small ship—and odd—but it was Schark's only remaining option for hauling his waiting booty since his original plan to use *The Lock*, *The Stock*, and *The Feral* fell apart.

The burly pirate examined the map closely and then looked at the large cave entrance. "This is the way in alright," Schark smiled. "So far, that weasel Marco's not pulling our chain with this map."

Torches aloft and pistols at the ready, Schark and the three deckhands strolled into the mountainside.

The passages were oddly quiet. Any sound of the conflict above ground was completely hidden. "You don't suppose there are any of those filthy dragons in here?" asked one of the pirates.

"Dubious," Schark answered. "They'd all be up top, defendin' the fort."

The men breathed a small sigh of relief, even though they weren't thrilled with Schark's choice of the word *dubious*. With each passing step, Marco's map indicated they were growing closer to Dragonrook's hidden treasury and Schark's exuberance began to show. "A little something you should know about me, lads," he said jovially, "is that I can smell gold. I can smell it just like it was cheese in my moustache! And I smell it now. Hordes of it!"

"Gold smells like cheese?" one crewman asked.

Another sneered in contempt. "Shut up! It was a metaphor!"

"No! It was a simile," the third answered. "You see, when you use the words 'like' or 'as' to express commonality—"

"Put a cork in it!" Schark snapped. He pointed to the end of the dark corridor and waved his torch to illuminate the wall above the entry. In the rock was etched a diamond shape surrounded by three circles. "This is the place! Just like Marco drew on the map!"

The four of them hurried through the entrance and raised their torches high.

But their faces fell in disappointment. Stretching into the darkness of the large chamber was not gold or jewels. It was filled with numerous stacks of innocuous crates and barrels.

"Well," Schark said hopefully, "if these are full of loot, then it'll be that much easier to cart off."

One of the men lifted a lid from the crate. "This isn't gold. You've got a good nose, though, Cap'n! It really was cheese you smelled." He pulled a block of yellow muenster from the crate and nibbled at it.

Another of the other men pried open a barrel. "This one is gunpowder." He studied the long rows and stacks of barrels behind it. "These are all gunpowder. This isn't a treasure trove. It's a storehouse and armory."

Schark's body slowly began to quiver with rage which then blossomed into uncontrollable vehemence. "Marco!" he bellowed. "He tricked us! That nasty, fork-tongued, double-crossing, worthless snake!"

A deckhand snapped his finger and nodded. "That," he said unhelpfully, "is a metaphor!"

"Shut yer gob!" the fuming pirate barked. "I didn't come all this way for grammar lessons from the lot of ye. Keep looking!"

The three deckhands began to search the room, happily putting distance between themselves and the irate captain. "There's got to be treasure in here somewhere," they heard him mutter.

"Dubious," whispered one crewman to the others.

+ + +

Arthur struggled to work himself free from between the pressing bulk of Arcrellis and Tindlass. The blood-curdling shrieks that tore from the gnashing maws of the dragons stung his ears, and between the clawing, writhing blows of the talons, he caught glimpses of the ground rushing towards them.

He felt something hard dig into his side as he was squeezed between the two battling beasts. His heart skipped a beat when he realized what it was. Snaking his hand to his belt, his fingers curled around the solid hilt of Askelon. "It worked against Balfour," he thought.

Without a moment's hesitation, he pulled the knife free and plunged it into the belly of Arcrellis.

If Arthur thought the shrieks were deafening before, the screech that ripped from Arcrellis was even more so. Immediately, the raging dragon tore away from them. Arthur, caught by surprise, tumbled from the back of Tindlass. His fleeting moment of panic was cut short as he found himself rolling upon hard, polished stone.

Askelon skittered from his hand as he came to a bruised and disorienting stop. In the corner of his vision, he saw Tindlass tumble lifelessly in the opposite direction.

He rubbed his head as his senses slowly righted themselves. He looked up. His heart sank when he realized where they were...they had come to ground in the narrow, hidden canyon.

Arcrellis, too, had crashed ungracefully to the hard floor. His dark, horned head lifted in stunned amazement. Reaching down, his claw traced the small, bleeding puncture on his underside. "You cut me!" he roared. The words boiled with fury yet were tinged with shock and worry. Slowly, the black *duskar* crawled from the ground.

Arthur scrambled for the spinning Askelon. Clasping it tight, he clambered to his feet.

But Arcrellis paid him little attention. Instead, he examined the long, narrow canyon. Crowded around them, watching in awe and trepidation were the many dragons of Dragonrook.

"So," Arcrellis leered. "This is where you have all been hiding. Your precious High-Thrall morality has turned you into worthless cowards! Rather than making you noble fighters, it has abandoned you. Now, rather than taking death to your enemies, you wait here for death to come to you."

"Only the High Dragon has the right to bring the judgment of death."

Arthur turned at the familiar voice. Cog bravely stepped from among the press of dragons.

Arcrellis lifted a brow in surprise. "So! A fellow *duskar*. I would have expected greater wisdom from you. But," he added as he examined Cog's wingless form, "I see you were spawned with a host of deficiencies."

Arcrellis raised his voice so all could hear. "Your High Dragon is dead! There is none here who can bring death to me." His burning eyes locked onto the small form of Arthur, wielding the tiny blade. "Not even the wielder of Askelon!"

The dark dragon reared back his glistening head and with a bone-crumbling roar, he cast his voice beyond the canyon. "Dragons of Fangshard! Come and feast upon your enemies! Today, Dragonrook falls!"

For a moment, there was silence. But soon the distant shrieks of the attackers could be heard. The shadowy, winging forms appeared in the thin crack of sky, tails twitching, claws outstretched, and teeth bared. Arthur stood transfixed in horror as the murderous swarm descended into the canyon in one mighty wave.

"And now," Arcrellis said, turning his fuming eyes onto the small boy, "I will devour Askelon and you with it!"

Rigid with fear, Arthur could only watch as Arcrellis stepped toward him. Then his senses returned and he did the only thing he could think of.

He ran.

+   +   +

Penny Gayle gave another desperate command to fire, but the six cannons on *The Feral's* port were doing little to sway the creature pummeling *The Lock*. The helpless crew were abandoning ship, fleeing the ravaging dragon by leaping into the ocean. Penny glanced behind her and could see the *Sea Scar's* guns being primed for another merciless barrage upon *The Feral*. She needed to find a new course of action. Indecision would spell their defeat.

Against every inclination of pride, she had to accept that *The Lock* was lost, and *The Feral* would be the next to fall. If not by the pounding of the mighty *browgie*, then from the blows of Schark's menacing cannons.

Lifting her cutlass, she rallied *The Feral's* crew. "Let's take this fight to the *Sea Scar*, men! All hands, ready your grapples!"

With rapid skill, the grappling hooks from *The Feral* flew into the air and found purchase among the *Sea Scar's* yardarms and rigging. In only a matter of seconds, Penny and the crew were swinging across the span of water between the two ships.

"For *The Lock*! For Arwiss and Dragonrook!" Penny's grip tightened around her cutlass as her press of marauders flooded the deck and they fell upon the surprised brigands of the *Sea Scar*. The cannons were abandoned as defenders swarmed from the deck below. The din of clashing blades rang from every side, the reports of gunfire burst the air, and the maddened roar of fighting seaman poured across the smoke-filled, splintered ship.

Penny was no match in strength against the pirates of the *Sea Scar*, but she frustrated her attackers with her surprising speed and ferocious agility. Every swing of her opponent's sword landed on empty air and was answered with two stinging cuts from her blade from another direction. Her swift movements and unflagging grit made short work of two falling brigands, and she turned to find a third.

The deck was awash with smoky haze and confusion. The crew of *The Feral* and the curs of the *Sea Scar* seemed evenly matched. With perseverance, she thought, the battle just might be theirs.

A shadow flitted across the planks. Penny glanced upward and immediately her heart sank.

A massive dragon was descending toward them. "Oh, great! Another one!" Her hopes of victory were quickly sinking.

The dragon descended with incredible speed, aiming straight for the battered stern. Penny dashed forward. "Brace yourselves, men!"

The impact of the beast hammered the *Sea Scar* like a hundred cannonballs. The bow of the ship jerked from the water as the stern plunged into the waves. Every person aboard lifted four feet into the air and tumbled in stunned confusion upon the fractured deck.

Stretching its leathery wings wide, the dragon let loose with an ear-splitting bellow that rattled every plank and pirate.

Penny squinted through the smoke and falling wood and her eyes widened in surprise.

"Hogarth?"

The giant *duskar* crouched to the deck as two riders dropped from his back.

"Royal? Marco?" Penny smiled in shocked delight.

"Aye!" Royal cried, pulling his cutlass from his belt. "But no time for pleasantries. Looks like you're causing trouble!"

She didn't waste a second. "Hogarth! Do something about that dragon!" She pointed to the *browgie* that had demolished *The Lock* and was now tearing into *The Feral*.

Hogarth obeyed instantly. His massive arms reached for the main mast of the *Sea Scar* and snapped it like a twig. With jaw-dropping force, he swung it across the water with yardarms, sails, and a few clinging pirates attached. The thick beam bashed brutally across the *browgie's* skull. Stunned, the dragon crumpled under the blow and crashed into the ocean in a towering spray of saltwater. With one quick leap, Hogarth boarded *The Feral*. Before the floundering *browgie* could even think of pulling itself from the water, Hogarth raised the splintered mast like a harpoon. And with a single, deadly thrust, the beaten *browgie* and broken mast disappeared beneath the waves.

"Well, that was easy!" Penny grinned.

"Hogarth!" Royal shouted to the *duskar*. "Get to land and help the others! Marco, let's finish up here!"

Marco pulled two flintlocks from a collapsed *Sea Scar* pirate. "Aye aye, Captain!"

The canyon was a churning sea of carnage. The dragons of Dragonrook and Fangshard clashed in desperate conflict, fending off tooth and claw in a desperate contest of strength and survival. Arthur forced the horrid sounds of the dragon fury from his mind as he bolted down the nearest cliffside passage. He had no conscious plan or awareness of where he was. He simply knew he needed to escape.

The sound of Arcrellis's pounding talons echoed behind

him as he navigated the maze of corridors and lofty halls. Arthur scurried around a corner and flattened against the wall, affording himself a precious moment to catch his breath.

The growling voice of Arcrellis rumbled down the passages. "Do you think you can hide from me?" the dragon taunted. "You can flee, but you cannot escape. Wherever you go, Askelon betrays you. It bleats like a wounded animal, letting all dragons know it is near."

Arthur plucked the knife from his belt and stared at it in dismay. Where it went, Arcrellis would follow. Should he throw it away? He could hide it and escape the hunting dragon. Arthur could be far away before horrible Arcrellis realized the deception. But then what? Arcrellis would have Askelon. And Dragonrook with it. But what else could he do?

In a silent plea, Arthur squeezed his eyes shut, searching his mind for a solution. Who would have an answer? "Cog? Quill?" he thought to himself, "What should I do? Help me!"

No answer came. The floor began to shake and the footfalls of Arcrellis grew louder.

Arthur sprinted from his hiding spot and continued his quest for safety.

+ + +

Quill watched in despair as the dragons of Fangshard swarmed into the canyon. This was the final battle. Now, the struggle for Dragonrook would ultimately be determined by the sheer strength between dragon and dragon. Were the delaying tactics enough to diminish the army of

Arcrellis and give Dragonrook hope? The time had arrived for Quill to stand within the battle and witness the conclusion of this long-awaited conflict.

He turned to the small *locket* at his side. "Come, Pinn. The hour has come for us to join the others."

As Quill stretched his wings to take flight, a movement caught the corner of his eye. A lone dragon soared from the sky. With precision, it traced a perfect arc that came to rest on the wooden ship off the coast. Quill focused his eagle-like vision on the newcomer.

"The *rogueskein* Hogarth," he growled. "So, he has decided to join his dark brethren in battle!"

But then his eyes flooded with rage when he saw the passengers that jumped from the *duskar's* back. "Royal and the mapmaker!"

Without another word, he launched into the air and raced toward the battered, listing vessel. "Today I will die," he whispered to himself, "but first I will gift myself the revenge of my beloved Neera and High Dragon of Dragonrook!"

Confused and forgotten, Pinn watched as Quill whipped toward the distant sea battle. Should he follow to die alongside the Arch-Dragon? Or fly to the canyon in the last stand against Fangshard? Before Pinn could decide, a brush of wind told him something approached from behind.

"So, we meet again, little *locket*!"

Pinn spun to find the hideous, black Skorch arching over him.

"Finally," he grinned maliciously, "we can finish what we started. Except this time, I have no orders to keep you alive!"

In terror, Pin whisked into the sky. The evil Skorch gave chase.

✦ ✦ ✦

"We almost have them!" Marco cheered. He had tossed his spent pistols and snatched a fallen cutlass from the deck.

"Aye!" Royal shouted. He parried an attacker's swing and, with a sturdy shove of his boot, sent the sword-wielding *Sea Scar* pirate tumbling into the water.

Together, Royal, Penny, and Marco twisted to face the last of the *Sea Scar* crewmen. Three pirates remained and they raised their battered cutlasses in readiness, each with glowering looks of determination on their faces.

Their expressions quickly turned to fright, however, and their jaws dropped. To Penny's surprise, they threw their cutlasses to the ground and hurriedly sprang over the rail and into the sea.

"Ha!" she laughed. "They know better than to cross swords with us!"

A raging voice announced itself behind them. "Marco!"

They turned and discovered what had spurred the pirates' sudden fright. Quill lunged forward and with blinding speed, snatched the unsuspecting mapmaker into his talons. The dragon lifted his poor victim high above his head. His feet kicked helplessly at nothing.

Penny screamed in shock. "Quill! What are you doing?!"

Royal joined in. "Put him down, Quill!"

The enraged dragon glared at the horrified pair. "I thought you were dead, Royal!" he said. "And every time I believed you had finally outlived your usefulness, you surprise me again. Now, you return and grant me my final wish! To see the death of the one who killed my mate!"

Royal and Penny pulled futilely at Quill's sturdy, tightening arm. "Let him go!" Royal shouted. "He's with us! He knows he did wrong and apologized to me for it!"

"He apologized to you?" Quill retorted. "This has nothing to do with you! He owes you no apology! But he owes me everything!"

"No!" Penny screamed again as Quill's talons squeezed around Marco's throat. The mapmaker continued to flail, prying uselessly at the clutching claw. Penny and Royal wrestled with all the weight and strength they could muster to break the dragon's grip, but their efforts were powerless. In desperation, Royal snatched his cutlass and landed a hard blow on Quill's arm. The blade simply vibrated under the strike -- not nearly strong enough to damage the dragon's armor-like scales.

It was enough to irritate Quill, however, and with a tremendous sweep of his tail, he sent Penny and Royal flying across the ravaged deck. They crashed against the rail, stunned and bruised.

Quill lifted the choking Marco higher. He laughed with grim satisfaction as he watched the mapmaker's eyes roll back into his skull.

"Let him go!" Penny begged.

Royal reached over his shoulder and hefted the bulky Talonshot cannon. He rapidly loaded the last explosive bolt.

"Quill!" he shouted. "Don't make me do this!"

But the enraged dragon didn't care. His talon continued to tighten around the throat of the now limp Marco Mossarian.

Royal leveled the deadly cannon and squeezed the trigger.

+   +   +

Perhaps his feet were simply following habit or memory. Or perhaps somewhere deep in his mind, Arthur hoped Quill would be there and he was subconsciously running for help. Whatever the reason, Arthur found himself approaching the High Seat chamber. But as he sprinted through the massive, towering doors, he realized his mind had played a cruel, terrible joke on him.

There was nothing waiting for him within. The vast chamber was empty – barren except for the large, rough, silent stone. And no escape. Arthur's panicked brain had unwittingly steered him into a dead end.

The rumble of Arcrellis's approach grew louder.

He twisted around to find the dark *duskar* marching steadfastly toward him.

"Ah!" Arcrellis grinned. "Here you are!" He examined the spacious hall. "So, this is where the High Dragon met her end!" With a snarl, he snaked his head toward the retreating Arthur. "I should thank you for leading me here."

The dragon took another step forward.

"It didn't have to be this way, boy. You ran away before I could let you beg for mercy and plead that I spare your life in return for Askelon. I probably would have granted it, too. After all, it would have been a nice display for the others to see. They would marvel at my generosity and scorn you for your cowardice. What a gift that would have been!"

He took another ominous step forward.

Trembling, Arthur continued his retreat. But he was

halted by the cold surface of the High Seat pressing against his back.

"Sadly, we are now here all by ourselves," Arcrellis sighed. He clucked his tongue in mock sadness. "With no one to witness my incredible grace. And you? You'll have to die all alone. You're quite inconsequential to me. Just some small pathetic thing that happens to stand in the way of what I want. Under other circumstances, I wouldn't even bother with the effort to kill you, since your life is as meaningless as your death, but—" the dragon fingered the small, dripping cut on his breast "—but what of this? Someone must pay for this."

Arthur whipped Askelon from his belt and wielded it as menacingly as he could. "You'll get a lot worse if you take another step!"

Arcrellis lifted his back foot. "Oh my! You mean another step like this?" The dragon laughed and with a dramatic effort, he slapped his clawed foot harshly upon the polished floor. Suddenly, Arcrellis sprang toward him.

Suddenly, the walls reverberated with a resounding roar. Arthur dove to the ground in surprise as the dark dragon spun over his head like a limp rag and careened across the flat stone with uncontrolled momentum.

Lifting his eyes, Arthur saw the mighty Hogarth crouched atop the stunned Arcrellis, pinned against the rough stone. Arcrellis' eyes were wide with confusion and surprise. He wrestled to remove the massive claws from his neck. "Who – who are you?"

"I am Hogarth the *duskar*!"

Arcrellis's face glinted with faint recognition. "You're *rogueskein*! I am your leader!"

Hogarth sank his talons deeper into Arcrellis's neck.

"I am no longer *rogueskein!*"

"The—then—" Arcrellis struggled for breath "—you cannot slay me or else you blaspheme the High-Thrall!"

Hogarth bared his deadly fangs. "I am neither of the Rogueskein nor of the High-Thrall. I am a new creature. I have come to protect Askelon!"

Arthur watched as the look of confusion in Arcrellis's eyes melted into fear.

+ + +

Pinn dodged and swerved. The face of the speeding Skorch stretched into a malicious smile as it pursued the terrified *locket.*

"You're mine, little morsel!" he mocked. He spewed a torrent of fire that barely missed the small, agile dragon.

Pinn had tried every maneuver he could think of. He zipped through the trees, dove amid the rocks, and looped in every direction to evade the horrid *flamespire.* Although he was nimble and adroit, he still could not outpace the swiftness of the fire-spitting dragon. He feverishly sought out any small space that would offer escape but nothing provided a way to elude or shield him from the blasts of flame.

"I see that you're tiring, *locket!*" Skorch laughed. "It's just a matter of time before I run you to ground!"

Ground! Pinn's mind raced. Skorch might have rule over the skies, but the *locket* knew every corner of Dragonrook. He veered upward and circled toward the canyon.

Far below, the mass of battling dragons grappled in deadly struggle. Pinn's heart flooded with pain at the sight of the strewn, lifeless bodies of those who had fallen under the claws of Fangshard. Quill's last words whispered in his mind...*the hour has come for us to join the others*.

Pinn's small jaw tightened in a determined scowl. "I did not choose the time of my end," he growled, "but I can choose the place."

He dove into the deep canyon and with a tight bend, disappeared within a cliffside passage.

Skorch followed doggedly into the corridor. "You still can't hide, you brat!" He punctuated his insult with another burst of fire. But then Skorch faltered in hesitation. The twisting corridors and hallways were not as forgiving as the open sky. The *flamespire* found himself lessening his speed to negotiate the tighter turns. His eyes latched onto the tiny, flapping dragon and summoned every bit of speed he could. "I'll be picking my teeth with your little bones soon enough!"

Schark slammed the crate of the last lid in disgust and frustration. "Nothing!" he roared. "Not even a gold tooth!"

The three crewmen from the *Sea Scar* had rolled out every barrel, box, and crate and inspected its contents. They even dug beneath the packages and straw to make sure nothing had been hidden at the bottom. "It's all stores and provisions," the brigand said. "We've got ropes and rigging. Biscuits and lemons."

"I found some hats!" another exclaimed. He placed a feathered tricorn on his head and smiled at its good fit.

Schark pointed to the wall of stacked barrels. "Did you check all of those? Maybe some of them are ale!" It was a wishful attempt to salvage hope from this haul of disappointment.

The crewman shook his head. "Sorry, Cap'n. They're all black powder."

"Bah!" In a fit of ire, Schark gave one of the barrels a sturdy kick with his hard wooden leg. The knobby end of his peg stoved in the side of the keg. A cascade of coarse gunpowder streamed from the broken crack. "That lousy Marco! I'll have his head on a mast when we get out of here! Let's go, boys!"

One of the pirates pocketed a piece of cheese and ran after his departing companions.

"What's that noise?"

A feverish, flapping sound whispered in the air. It quickly grew louder before a small shape emerged from the dark entrance. It whisked over their heads and upward to the high ceiling of the cavern.

"It's a bat!" a deckhand cried.

"That's not a bat!" Schark retorted. "It's one of them runt-sized dragons! *Lockets*, I think they call 'em." The pirate picked up a rock-hard biscuit from one of the crates and threw it in the air. "Get lost, you filthy lizard!"

The *locket* easily dodged the small projectile. The small dragon circled once around the ceiling before finding a perch on the stack of barrels. Another pirate picked up a hard biscuit also and with a laugh tried to pelt the creature himself. The petrified piece of bread fell short and bounced off the powder keg with a thud. The dragon was unperturbed, paying no attention to the ruffians. Instead, its gaze remained fixed on the entrance to the cavern.

Schark huffed and turned away. "Stupid beast. Leave him be."

The four men froze. An odd yellow light glowed from the passageway, followed by a reverberating shriek like a cut-

lass scraping on iron. The large, beating wings of a dragon appeared, speeding down the corridor toward them.
Flames flickered between the beast's charred fangs.

Schark's face fell in horror. "It's Skorch!"

They waved their arms in panic, desperately urging the
maddened dragon to turn away.

Resting on Royal's store of gunpowder, Pinn smiled
smugly as the breast of the pursuing *flamespire* expanded
like a massive blacksmith's bellows and then let loose with
a raging stream of fire.

+ + +

Hogarth's claw tightened mercilessly under the jaw of
Arcrellis. Grinding his hind foot into the dark dragon's
chest, the gray and green *duskar* stretched his victim's
long neck taut. Arcrellis's eyes bugged in terror. Arthur
could see Arcrellis desperately trying to form words, but
his lips only sputtered in lack of breath.

"You deceived me!" Hogarth growled angrily.

"I...gave...you...freedom!" Arcrellis choked.

"You robbed me of freedom!" Hogarth roared. With
those words, he lifted the ragged, struggling Arcrellis and
turned to Arthur. "Give me the word, Askelon."

Arthur paused when he realized what Hogarth was asking. To his surprise, he couldn't bring himself to utter the
command the *duskar* was seeking.

"I don't want you to be a killer, Hogarth. And you don't
wish it, either. If you had, you wouldn't have asked."

Hogarth silently studied the trapped, terrified face of Arcrellis. And with a sudden swing of his arm, he whipped
the body of the dark dragon overhead and slammed it

mercilessly upon the polished floor. Not releasing his relentless grip, he dragged the battered yet struggling form from the chamber.

Arthur followed Hogarth down the long corridor and into the harsh daylight of the canyon. Still, the raging, embattled dragons gnashed and roiled in a sea of fang and lashing tails, shredding the very air with vicious cries of terror and violence.

"Denizens of Fangshard!" Hogarth roared. He raised the trapped, dangling Arcrellis as high as he could. "Behold your leader!"

And with that, he catapulted the reeling body of Arcrellis into the sky. Every dragon in the canyon watched in awe and disbelief as the dark silhouette spun through the air, scrambling for control. Soon, the black wings stretched and found purchase and began to beat madly...and the wounded and broken Arcrellis fled in fear and confusion.

Suddenly, a rolling rumble shook the island. Arthur felt the ground beneath his feet shudder and vibrate. Rocks and dust spilled from the canyon walls. And just as suddenly, the tremendous quaking subsided, and the stunned dragons returned to their senses. With overwhelming dread, the dragons of Fangshard launched themselves skyward to follow after their escaping leader.

+ + +

The acrid smoke from the exploding Talonshot drifted from the *Sea Scar's* deck. The collapsed Marco coughed as his lungs gasped for welcome air. Royal and Penny stumbled to the fallen form of Quill. The dragon rolled powerlessly to one side and his lidded eyes took in the carnage of the sudden explosion and the pounding pain of his now missing leg.

"What have you done to me, Royal?" he croaked.

A tear formed in Royal's good eye as he examined the maimed dragon. Above his black eye patch, his brows furrowed in unfeigned sorrow. "You'll be okay, Quill."

The air shook with a sudden boom.

Penny and Quill looked up. A massive cloud of rock and smoke rose from the side of Dragonrook, showering the trees and bay with pelting stone and debris.

And then, a stream of shadowing shapes shot upward from the midst of the island. A weaving and tangled swarm of dragons soared into the blue sky and twisted away toward the horizon.

"Fangshard!" cried Penny. "They're fleeing!"

Royal watched in disbelief at the dark mass of dragons fleeing above them. And then he let loose with a hearty cheer. Pulling his hat from his gray head, he swung it as if he was chasing the dragons from the air with it. "Arthur did it!" He turned to the wounded Quill and laid a consoling hand on the dragon's shoulder. "Dragonrook is safe!" he smiled.

Quill didn't respond. His eyes closed in exhaustion and the injured *hyrex* slid into blackness.

26

The Bone Compass

Arthur penned the last words on the parchment and gave the ink a moment to dry. Carefully rolling the paper into a scroll, he fastened it with a short length of rough, brown twine. As he did so, Kitt fluttered through the open window. The *locket* settled on his nearby roost and waited as Arthur gently placed the scroll into a wooden box.

"Give this box to Hogarth when we return," Arthur said. "He knows what to do with it."

"Understood. The others are ready for you," the small dragon said.

"Thank you, Kitt. Tell them I'm on my way."

Kitt whisked through the window as Arthur climbed from his seat.

The walk to the bay was a long one, but Arthur appreciated the time to himself. The past few days had been busy, but it had been a busyness borne with sadness. Which are always the worst, in Arthur's opinion. While mind and body dealt with the tyranny of duties, the heart wrestled with the tyranny of emotions and, by the end of the day, making a person doubly weary. The lengthy walk at least gave his mind a moment to stop and not think about numerous repairs to the halls in Dragonrook, the reorganization of duties among the dragons...and the most heart wrenching task which was the arrangements of funeral pyres for the many who had fallen in the attack. His mind unwillingly conjured up the thought of Tindlass and his heart ached as his brain added one more heavy memory to it.

When he stepped onto the sandy beach, Royal, Marco, Clay, Penny and the mighty Hogarth were waiting. He waved to them half-heartedly. In the distance, the *Ivory Zephyr* floated patiently in the bay.

"So," Royal greeted warmly, "the mighty Askelon has arrived."

Arthur tried to not let a grimace etch his face. He hadn't quite accepted or enjoyed the appellation that the inhabitants of Dragonrook had bestowed upon him.

Royal realized his greeting fell flat so he quickly moved on. "Thank you for seeing us off. It would be a hard journey without saying goodbye. And besides, I never had a chance to thank you for rescuing me and Marco from Fangshard. If you hadn't sent Hogarth to get us, who knows what would have happened."

"You don't have to leave," Arthur replied.

"We've had this discussion already. After what Marco and I have done, our presence here would be unfair to both you and all of Dragonrook. Even if you commanded it, the sight of us would always be a thorn in everyone's side."

"I wish I could go with you," the boy muttered. But he knew that wasn't possible. He was now Askelon, the Keeper of the High-Thrall, and until the day the new scion arrived—whenever that could possibly be—Dragonrook would have to be his home. He cast his eyes to the rough sand. "I wish I never picked up that stupid knife."

Royal scowled. "Avast there, boy. None of that. If you start counting miseries, you'll be no good to anyone."

"What are you going to do?"

"Not entirely sure," Royal answered. "I still have a bounty on my head from my pirating days, so roaming about the open sea isn't a safe bet. Maybe we'll find an island somewhere and grow radishes."

Penny raised an eyebrow. "Radish farming? I find that hard to swallow."

"Well, maybe not," Royal admitted. "However, it probably wouldn't hurt to find out what happened to the *Sea Scar*. Arbo will help us out with that."

Arthur nodded. Although crippled in the battle, the vessel and its remnants of crew had managed to make it out to sea in the dark of night. Arbo, who had remained on the *Zephyr*, explained that Schark never returned from their raid into the treasury.

"It's not good to have a few bitter pirates sailing around knowing where Dragonrook is," Royal continued. "Schark was likely sent to Davy Jones' locker in that explosion, but if his men latch on to a new captain, they might be itching for revenge." He gave Arthur a shrewd stare. "That was mighty clever of you to have all the treasure moved. What made you think of that?"

"You did," Arthur replied. "You said that Marco would probably be coming back with Arcrellis to raid the trove, so I swapped it. I didn't realize it would be Schark that would be trying to steal it, though. And were still not sure why the weapons exploded."

"Ah, well," the captain shrugged. "The treasure's safe anyway. And we know how fond dragons are of their treasure."

Arthur turned to Marco. "Part of it belongs to you. The

dragons agreed to uphold their bargain for returning Askelon. You're allowed to take your share."

"I don't want it." Marco avoided the boy's eyes, and Arthur understood. The poor mapmaker was still wrestling with his shame. He had already taken something much more precious than jewels from Dragonrook.

"Very well," Royal said. "We best be off. If for some reason you have need of us, send Hogarth to find us." He eyed the giant, silent *duskar* with curiosity. "I don't know what you did to him, lad, but he's a different beast. I'd barely recognize him."

And with that, Royal and Marco gave their friends a final hug and clambered into the small dinghy. As they watched them row toward the waiting *Ivory Zephyr*, Arthur heard Marco say, "You know, Royal...there's still a lot of treasure left in that tomb of St. George."

Awkward silence filled the High Seat chamber. No one wanted to draw attention to Quill's huge wooden stump of a leg that replaced the one lost to Royal's explosive Talonshot. It was murmured that the dragon's new appendage had been crafted from the fallen mainmast of the *Sea Scar*, but no one was brave enough to inquire. The wounded *hyrex's* mood had been understandably dour. Some suspected that it was spurred by pain and discomfort from his injury. But Arthur felt there was something much deeper burning in Quill's heart.

For now, Arthur, Clay, and Penny waited in the High Seat while Quill glowered in silence. Finally, Quill spoke. "What are we waiting for?"

Arthur shrugged. "I received word that Cog had something he wanted to show us."

"What is it?"

"He didn't say, but he requested that the four of us be here for it. We'll find out when he gets here."

Quill made a small roll of his eyes and muttered something about *duskars* and their lack of punctuality. But his irritation was quickly mollified when the wingless dragon loped into the chamber. He held a small object in his hands covered with a cloth.

"Ah, good!" Cog declared, as he looked at the group. "Everyone is present!"

"Yes," Arthur replied. "Just as you asked. What is this all about?"

Cog nodded. "I believe I have something that will help us with our problem."

"Our problem? What do you mean?"

"For the first time, Dragonrook is without a High Dragon. Ever since our beloved Neera was taken from us before the new scion could come. And now Arthur—er, Askelon—as Dragon Steward must hold the sway of the High-Thrall until the line is restored. Unfortunately, Askelon's hold is only an echo of the true High-Thrall. We are in a precarious state, unable to completely come and go from Dragonrook or to wield the full power and order of the Thrall."

Quill grumbled. "We are aware of the situation, Cog. What is this solution you propose?"

"Even though the scion has not yet arrived, the High-Thrall still resides within its egg at its nesting place. We can restore the rule of High-Thrall by bringing the scion here to Dragonrook. Even in its egg form."

Arthur looked confused. "But I thought the nesting place for the scion was a secret that only the High Dragon knows."

Cog nodded. "Yes, that is the result of an instinct within dragonkind to protect the scion from *rogueskein*—or others—who wish to interfere with the lineage of the High-Thrall."

"Since Neera is gone, how could we possibly find this scion egg?" Clay asked.

Cog's eyes began to shine. "With this!" He pulled the cloth from the object in his hands to reveal a large disk made of crystal and brass. He laid the disk on the rough surface of the High Seat.

"It looks like a compass." Penny craned her neck to get a better look.

"Exactly!" Cog said. "But not any normal compass. This should point us to the nesting place of the scion egg."

Quill awkwardly limped over to peer over the humans' heads at the strange device. "How is this possible?"

Cog shifted nervously. "To explain, I must first plead for forgiveness. The only way to construct such a device was to use the bones of the High-Thrall itself."

Arthur examined the large compass more closely. "This needle is bone!"

"Yes," Cog nodded. "It is a bone from Neera. Like the blade of Askelon, it holds the sway of the High-Thrall and is closely connected to the scion itself."

Quill could not contain his rage. His wings stretched wide and he leveled a maddened roar at Cog. The *hyrex's* fangs came uncomfortably close to Cog's head. "You dared to desecrate the body of the High Dragon? You stand here and confess that you stole from the body of my mate for your...for your...MACHINE! You fiddle with experiments and dabble with ideas that stink of *rogueskein*! You are a traitor to Dragonrook!"

"Enough!" Arthur shouted at Quill. "If you had stayed with Pinn and protected him during the attack as we had planned, it would never have come to this! Because of you, we have no idea what happened to Pinn. He might have been taken back to Fangshard for all we know. If that's the case, then Cog's solution may be the only chance we have to bring the scion to Dragonrook before anyone else!"

Quill's rage tempered only slightly under Arthur's scolding. "I don't like this," Quill growled. "And I want nothing to do with it." The Arch-Dragon turned his back to them and with the pounding of his heavy wooden stump, he hobbled from the High Seat.

Arthur stared at the empty door, wondering if he should call the angered dragon back. He decided against it. When he turned back from the door, he saw the concerned faces of the others. "He'll be alright," he said. "He just needs some rest." He gestured to the compass. "So does it work?"

"I don't think so," Clay said, watching it closely. "The needle just keeps spinning."

"Perhaps," Cog answered. "Or perhaps we are too distant from the scion for it to feel the Thrall."

With hope and curiosity, the four of them watched, transfixed upon the chaotic turning of the gray needle within. It spun furiously and restlessly. And for the slightest of moments, the needle hesitated, quivering and fluttering in a single direction.

+ + +

The partial moon blanketed the buildings and cobbled streets with its pale light. The night was quiet and calm and no one was awake to see the large wing-shaped shadow that flitted across the rooftops and upon the curtained windows.

The shadow shrank as the dragon descended. And soon the shadow connected to its form and Hogarth's mighty talons came silently to rest upon the bricks of the crumbling building. He paused for a moment to gaze upon the sprawl of crooked roofs and smoking chimneys that slumbered under the moon and sea of stars above. With one last look around, he crawled silently down into the shadows of Twofarthing Lane.

✦ ✦ ✦

"Mr. Dempster!" Nora ran into the parlor, excitedly carrying a small wooden box. "Someone left us a package!"

"Really?" Duncan Dempster stepped down the stairs in his customary nightcap and mismatched slippers, tying his robe tightly. "From whom?"

"I don't know. It was just sitting on the steps."

"I say! It's rather heavy." He sat down in his tattered armchair as the many orphans of Dempster House crowded around.

"Open it!" they all shouted.

Mr. Dempster unlatched the wooden box. Within it rested a bulky leather bag and a small, rolled piece of parchment. Curiously, he lifted the bag and in doing so, it spilled open. Dozens of rubies, emeralds, sapphires, pearls, and golden coins poured into the wooden box. The children's eyes glowed with amazement over the glistening and sparkling treasure.

"My word!" he exclaimed.

"It's a fortune!" cried Elliot, his eyes wide. "Where did it come from?"

Mr. Dempster untied the rough twine from the roll of paper and studied it. "It's from Arthur and Clay!"

Nora's heart leapt with unexpected joy. "Arthur! Then he's okay! What does the letter say?"

Duncan Dempster began to read...

Dearest Mr. Dempster,

I hope this message finds you well. I have finally been given an opportunity to write to you and let you know that Clay and I are safe. We have been in the care of our daring friend (who must remain nameless for certain reasons) that you met on that dreadful night when unpleasant pirates invaded Dempster House. We have had many adventures since then...too many to really write about and you probably wouldn't believe them, anyway. But all has ended reasonably well and now we find ourselves overseeing a very peculiar orphanage of our own on an island far, far away. I think of you and the others at Dempster House often and wanted to let you know how much I have come to appreciate the tremendous care you always gave to us. You never failed to meet our needs, which is one of the most precious things one can give another should they have the ability to do so. Through a very complicated set of circumstances which I, again, cannot share, I now have the opportunity to give something back in return. Enclosed is a gift from me and Clay for you and the others. Please consider it an award for a life well-lived. Give our love to Nora, Lizzie, Marjorie, Dot, Aria, Elliot, Miles, Percy, Carlton, Jeremy, Phillip, Nigel, and Crispin. And Warty, too, I guess. We miss you all and will ever remain...

Your Loving and Grateful Wards,
Arthur and Clay Cross

P.S. There's a lot more where this came from.

THE END

of

DRAGONROOK
BOOK 1

About the Author

Daren Hatfield is a writer, illustrator, and graphic designer who delights in bringing new adventure stories for young and young-at-heart readers. His novel "Nothing Ever Happens on Main Street" has merited 5-Star reviews and has been a receipient of both a Literary Titan Gold Book Award and a Reader's Favorite Silver Medal. He currently resides in Tucson, Arizona with his wife and daughter.

For more information or to contact him, you are invited to visit www.darenhatfield.com

or connect with him on Facebook, X, Instagram, or Goodreads.

If you enjoyed this book, please consider letting other readers know by rating and reviewing it on Amazon or Goodreads! Your thoughts make a big impact in the reading community who are looking for fresh, new adventures!

www.ingramcontent.com/pod-product-compliance
Lightning Source LLC
Chambersburg PA
CBHW021435240626
47153CB00001B/159